BLACK LIGHT DEATH

A beam of twisting black light erupted from Smiler's hand. The dark luminous beam streaked in a circle around Bob Max's prone form. Smiler snapped his wrist. The light stopped circling and plunged downward, burying itself in Max's spine. He jerked once and then lay still.

Paula clutched her son—a grip of maternal protectiveness mixed with sheer terror. She knew Max was dead and she knew what had killed him.

The two attackers: Sad-eyes and Smiler. Contrasting speech styles—a voice too inflective and a voice without emotion. Oddly coordinated movements. AV scramblers. And the final clue—the black light of the Cohe wand, a hand weapon so deadly that its mere possession would subject the owner to E-Tech's harshest penalties.

The two men who were not really two men would have little concern over such laws. They were not human. They were a creature born out of the dark years before the Apocalypse, over two hundred years ago.

A Paratwa.

"ENTERTAINING THRILLER . . . A sweeping future panorama." —*Publishers Weekly*

"The characters are finely crafted. You'll find yourself melding into their world, laughing and crying with them. HINZ HAS A WINNER HERE, AND I FOR ONE AM LOOKING FORWARD TO HIS NEXT BOOK."
—St. Louis *West County Journal*

LIEGE-KILLER

CHRISTOPHER HINZ

ST. MARTIN'S PRESS/NEW YORK

Grateful acknowledgment is made for permission to reprint "Sappho of Mytilene" from *Greek Poetry for Everyman* by F. L. Lucas, J. M. Dent & Sons Ltd., London, England.

LIEGE-KILLER

Library of Congress Catalog Card Number: 86-27723

ISBN: 0-312-90056-2   Can. ISBN: 0-312-90434-7

Printed in the United States of America

First St. Martin's Press mass market edition/January 1988

10 9 8 7 6 5 4 3 2 1

For my parents

Helpless halts my tongue; a devouring fever
Runs in flame through every vein within me;
Darkness veils my vision; my ears are deafened,
        Beating like hammers;

Cold the sweat runs down me; a sudden trembling
Sets my limbs a-quiver; my face grows paler
Than the grass in summer; I see before me
        Death stand, and madness.

—"Sappho of Mytilene"
6th Century B.C.

Prologue

The shuttle crouched between skyscrapers, in the center of the desolate street, dwarfing rusted cars. Gouged and dirty wings—arched slivers of white metal—swept upward from the squat body of the craft like floppy ears from a fat rabbit. The underbelly quivered, radiating heat. Gray smoke drifted out from beneath the craft, swirling into oblivion as it met the perpetual Philadelphia gusts.

"What's the level?" asked Bronavitch, younger of the two crew members. He stood beside the monster engines, oblivious to the waves of heat pouring from the vertical landing jets. Their spacesuits were designed to protect them from far worse perils.

Kelly grinned. Parched walnut skin crinkled across his cheeks, made him look older than his forty-six years. "Nothing to worry about within five miles of here." Kelly twisted his neck forward, peeked out through the top of his helmet visor, and checked the readout counter mounted to his thick utility belt. "The scan reads less than point-oh-seven—we're in a fairly safe area. We could probably even take our suits off for a minute or so."

"Yeah," Bronavitch grumbled, "and we could gulp some air and say good-bye to the Colonies." Bronavitch did not need Kelly or a poison-counter to tell him that there was enough organic death in the smog to keep a cleanup crew busy for years.

Kelly's grin expanded. "The air does seem a bit thick."

Bronavitch shook his head. He was not in the mood for Kelly's humor. "I'm telling you, I've had it. I'm sick of the whole damn planet. My contract is up in two months and I'm not signing on for another tour. I've had it."

His partner rumbled with laughter. "You told me that last year. Hell, admit it. You like it down here. You told me that you thought it was very serene."

1

"It pays good."

Skyscrapers—metal and concrete shells—lined the boulevard. A few smaller structures were nestled in their midst like scared children clutching at their mother's skirts. Chunks of unidentifiable debris lay everywhere.

To the west, a mountain of trash poked up through the lower smog cover, interrupting the flow of the street. Bronavitch thought he detected form in the junk pile. It seemed to resemble a giant frog. He suspected some mad humans had been responsible for its creation during the final days. His theory seemed reasonable. Dying of radiation and a host of other ecospheric poisons would have justified the creation of such a weird monument.

"Do you know what they used to call this place?" asked Kelly.

Bronavitch shook his head.

"The City of Brotherly Love." Thankfully, the black face had lost its smile.

Bronavitch booted a crusted brick. "Let's get on with it. I want to get the hell out of here."

They marched down the street. Open doors and glassless windows seemed to stare at them; dark eyes, full of death, contemptuous of the living. Bronavitch felt a familiar twinge of fear tighten his stomach. He hated these dead cities. It always seemed as if someone were watching, like they were intruding upon some private domain.

Kelly broke into a fresh grin. He appeared to be enjoying himself.

"All right, we know the pirates landed where we touched down. They must have been close to whatever they were looking for."

"How do you know they were looking for anything?" Bronavitch argued. "Maybe the bastards just dropped in at random, hoping to pick up a few artifacts. Or maybe they had shuttle problems and were forced to land for repairs."

"I don't think so. First of all, they couldn't have been here for more than two or three hours—in and out real quick, not nearly enough time for a profitable artifact hunt. And when did you ever hear of a shuttle dropping into a supercontaminated zone like this for repairs? Even if they lost their main engines, the vertical landing jets were still functioning—had to be in order to touch down safely in the middle of this mess." Kelly shook his head. "No, if it had been an emergency landing, they would have coasted down toward the Virginia area. The contamination's not as bad."

Bronavitch sighed. "These are Costeaus you're talking about. They're not always that rational."

Kelly laughed. "Maybe not, but most of the bastards got better ships than we do. Don't believe all that Guardian crap about stupid pirates and their rundown equipment."

It was no sense arguing. "All right, which direction? This is a goddamn big city."

Kelly pointed toward the frog-shaped mountain. "That trash pile' could have been their landing mark—there's nothing else down here that's so easily recognizable from the air. And if I were a Costeau captain, I wouldn't have touched down any closer to it than this."

"Landslides?" Bronavitch asked uneasily.

"Right. That mess doesn't look too stable. At this distance, at least the shuttle would be safe even if the whole damn mountain came tumbling down."

Bronavitch nodded. "That still leaves a big area to search. Why don't we call base and request help?"

"No way," growled his partner. "I'm not gonna get chewed out by some commander for tying up a whole unit just to find out what some pirates were looking for."

Bronavitch clamped his mouth shut.

They had come from E-Tech—from the Berks Valley base, about sixty miles to the northwest. Berks was one of E-Tech's major experimental arenas where scientists and engineers sought methods for removing the contamination from the environment. Ecospheric Turnaround was the long-term goal of the huge organization, a goal in which Bronavitch no longer had much faith.

Working down here as a shuttle pilot for the past two years had slowly eroded his belief.

Too much of the Earth was dead. There were still insects and a few of the hardier forms of plant life, and there was man, in his protective garments. Most of the evolutionary links in between had perished; the complex chain of life had been broken by the madness of two centuries ago. Bronavitch believed that the Earth would never again be a hospitable place for humanity.

He and Kelly were assigned to perimeter duty. They checked on the status of various bioprojects that Berks initiated, searched for signs of natural life, ferried scientists to and from other bases, and policed the zone surrounding the Berks Valley. Today's duty fell into the last category.

Early this morning, Berks radar had picked up an unauthorized ship heading toward the Philadelphia area. Although the fix had been lost before the ship landed, computer projection had indicated several likely touchdown locations. Naturally, the pirates had already departed by the time he and Kelly located this landing spot. Costeaus generally knew just how long they could remain in an area before E-Tech tracked them. Heavily smogged cities like Philadelphia made visual detection nearly impossible, and sensor analysis took time. Pirates were rarely caught on the surface.

The best that could be hoped for now was that he and Kelly might locate some evidence identifying the pirate clan. Then E-Tech or the Intercolonial Guardians would launch an official investigation up in the Colonies. With exceptional luck, the trespassing pirates might be arrested.

Unofficially, though, Bronavitch knew that this Costeau incident would be treated like most of the others—largely ignored. The Costeaus' antique-hunting expeditions to the surface were tolerated as long as they did not directly interfere with any of E-Tech's projects. Today's hunt, and the subsequent official report, would be made primarily to assuage the Irryan Council, which, in its wisdom, was demanding a final solution to the pirate problem.

Kelly halted and directed a gloved finger toward a large hole in the side of a small, brick-faced building. "That looks new."

Bronavitch nodded. This could be easier than he had thought. The five-story structure appeared a bit better preserved than the surrounding skyscrapers. The building had probably been shielded from the higher-elevation nuclear shock waves that had mutilated Philadelphia back in the twenty-first century.

The hole was rectangular and larger than a man in a spacesuit. It was also newly formed. One learned to easily recognize such anomalies after a few trips through any of Earth's decimated urban areas.

Kelly stepped carefully over the lip of the opening and turned on his helmet spotlight. "Looks like some kind of an old food store."

Bronavitch followed his partner into the darkened interior, panned his helmet light across the rows of dusty shelving.

Crushed cans and smashed plastic jars littered the racks. Ceiling rubble, foodpaks, and shattered fragments of glass covered the floor. Kelly's spotlight froze momentarily on a human skeleton slumped over a low counter. Bronavitch looked away.

"This is it." Kelly shined his spotlight down the center aisle, traced the trail of overlapping bootprints that led toward the back of the store. In a few spots, the centuries-old layer of deep dust had been disturbed enough to reveal the original tiled floor.

"Looks like there were at least four or five of them," Bronavitch observed.

"Either that or they made several trips through. C'mon."

He followed Kelly down the aisle, keeping his attention along the upper edge of the surrounding shelves. It felt as if they were walking through a dark canyon. The only sounds were their footsteps, picked up by external suit mikes and amplified into their helmets. He shivered. Outside, at least there was the wind and the smog-filtered sunshine. In here, silence and darkness created an entirely different mood. Bronavitch imagined that something was waiting to leap down on him from the top shelves.

Kelly halted when they reached the back of the store. Bronavitch followed his partner's downward gaze.

The hole in the floor was roughly the same diameter as the one the Costeaus had cut into the outer wall, although more circular in shape. They knelt carefully at the edge and shined their spots into the opening. About ten feet below was a cellar floor of pale concrete. That floor also had been cut through. Their spotlights reflected off a dark pool of water well below the basement level.

"Oh, shit," Bronavitch muttered. He did not relish the idea of climbing down into some sewer beneath this dead city.

"Must be at least fifty feet to the water level," Kelly said quietly. "I wonder why they made such big holes? They must have used at least two beam cutters to be in and out of here so quick. Hell of a lot of work."

The question had a simple answer. Bronavitch said, "They hauled something up from down there that was bigger than a man in a spacesuit."

Kelly nodded. "They probably used a portable winch. Want to run back to the shuttle and get ours?"

"A ladder will do," Bronavitch said reluctantly. They might as well get this over with as quickly as possible.

The portable ladder was in Kelly's backpack. In a few minutes, they had unrolled it and fastened one end to a sturdy pillar some ten feet from the edge of the hole. There was no question as to who was going down first. Kelly eased himself over the lip and began the descent.

"What if this place caves in?" Bronavitch asked nervously.

"If it didn't cave in on the pirates, then it probably won't fall on us."

Somehow, that did not sound very reassuring.

Kelly quickly passed the cellar mark and rapidly approached the pool of dark water. Bronavitch could hear the end of the ladder flapping against the surface of the liquid.

"What if the water's too deep to stand in?" he called down. "It might be a couple hundred feet to the bottom."

Kelly laughed. "Don't be ridiculous. We're almost at sea level."

Maybe it was the ocean.

His fears were eased by a loud splash as Kelly hit the water. "It's up to my waist and everything feels solid underneath. It's way too big to be a sewer—must have been one of those old subway transport tunnels. C'mon down."

Bronavitch took a deep breath and climbed over the lip. In a minute he was standing beside Kelly in three feet of water.

They stood silently for a moment, playing their lights over the dank and slimy walls. The water had a slight flow to it and the gentle current licked at their waists. They could not see the bottom—the water was almost black. Bronavitch took a step toward the left wall, tripped on something solid, and almost fell.

"Shit!"

"Old railway tracks," Kelly said calmly. "This tunnel looks wide enough for two sets of them."

"Yeah, right," he muttered. "So which way do we go?"

"I'll go upstream and you go downstream."

Bronavitch thought his partner was joking until he flashed his spotlight into the solemn black face. "Look, Kelly, this is weird enough down here without us separating. . . ."

"Relax. The Costeaus obviously had a map of some sort. They knew just where to cut that hole in the food store and just where to make their descent. I'll bet they knew exactly what they were looking for and exactly where it was located. It's got to be real close by." Kelly turned and began a slow march against the current.

Bronavitch repressed a shudder. *Two more months.* Just two more months and then his contract was up and he could be off this damn planet forever. He thought briefly of home; the orbiting Colony of Kiev Beta—even in perigee, more than a hundred thousand miles away.

Kelly vanished from sight as the subway tunnel curved gently to the right. Bronavitch sighed and began moving in the opposite direction, splashing his gloves against the dark liquid to create as much noise as possible. He hoped he would not trip over anything. There were probably rotting corpses in this foul water just waiting to snag his ankles.

After two hundred years, there couldn't be anything left but bones, he reminded himself. *Rotting corpses,* insisted his imagination.

"This tunnel has a grade to it," said Kelly. "Water's getting a bit deeper down my way."

Bronavitch stopped, stared at his waistline. The water was a couple of inches below where it had been. Good. Maybe the tunnel would lead up to the surface.

"Dead-end," Kelly said a moment later. "There must have been a cave-in. There's rubble all over the place down here and the water's up to my chest. The pirates couldn't have come this way."

"Care to join me?" Bronavitch cracked. He was feeling better each step of the way, mainly because of the decreasing depth of the water. He figured that by the time he rounded the next bend, the level should be down to his knees.

"I wonder what the hell they could have been searching for?" Kelly asked. "Do you think maybe someone hid a treasure down here two hundred years ago?"

Bronavitch heard the guarded excitement in his partner's voice. He sighed. "I know what you're thinking, Kelly, and you may as well forget it. The pirates were already here and if there was a treasure . . ." He stopped, stared at the huge form that was coming into view around the bend. "I've found it," he said simply.

The last car of the old subway train appeared heavily rusted but otherwise in good shape. All the windows were intact, although layered over by grime. The wheel trucks were underwater, giving the illusion that the transit cars were floating on the surface of the opaque liquid. He moved alongside the train and examined the now-familiar hole cut through the age-scarred metal. His light reflected off something shiny inside.

He waited until Kelly came splashing around the bend before grasping the edge of the hole and hoisting himself up into the train.

His spot illuminated a glittering white cavern. Ice. The whole interior of the car was covered with it. He checked the temperature readout on the panel within his helmet.

"Jesus, it's almost ninety below in here!"

A huge silent generator took up the rear half of the eighty-foot car. An open airlock led toward the front of the train. Icicle-coated conduits trailed along the ceiling, connecting the generator to a rack of glazed monitors beside the airlock. Kelly hopped in behind him and whistled softly.

"A stasis operation."

Bronavitch nodded. He felt relieved now that they knew what they were dealing with, although he still wanted to be away from this place as quickly as possible.

They pushed on through to the next car—the stasis chamber itself. The room was even colder than the generator car, although the Costeaus must have shut off the power hours ago. Thin milky stalactites hung from the ceiling. Hard icy patches obscured portions of the metallic floor. Until today, this chamber had probably been a sealed freezer for over two hundred years. Now the inexorable process of temperature equalization had begun. The ice was melting. If any stasis-frozen humans had remained, they would be well on their way to a more permanent sleep.

The occupants of this freezer were gone, however. The pirates had found what they were looking for.

"There were two of them," Kelly said quietly. The pair of large plastic cradles in the center of the car were empty, the pale ivory cocoons missing. The genetically manufactured tissues that surrounded the sleepers would keep their metabolisms stable for at least thirty hours—long enough for the Costeaus to get them to a Wake-up facility up in the Colonies.

Bronavitch felt even more disturbed than he had earlier. There were two of them. Jesus! Why couldn't there have been one . . . or three . . . or twenty-six?

Kelly walked past the cradles to the other end of the stasis chamber. He used his glove to wipe the frost from a pair of glass gauges.

"The other cars in the train must be tankers. This meter says there's enough fuel left to run the generators for another fifty years or so."

Bronavitch grimaced. "And why were there only two capsules? This car's big enough to hold a dozen and it wouldn't have taken much more fuel. Yet there were only two capsules."

Kelly turned from the gauges and looked straight at him. "There's probably a simple explanation. The capsules contain a husband and wife, I'll bet—somebody's great, great—whatever—grandparents." Kelly smiled like a three-year-old with a new toy. "Now, recently, some rich young kid up in the Colonies finds a family heirloom that tells how his wealthy ancestors put themselves into stasis during the final days. The heirloom explains where and how they were frozen and the kid thinks it would be just great if he could bring them out of hibernation. To do it legally, of course, you've got to get E-Tech's permission, and that means going through all sorts of official channels and maybe getting turned down after a year of fighting the red tape. So the rich kid figures he'll avoid all that hassle. He hires himself some Costeaus, gives them the map, and tells them they'll get a nice fat bonus if they succeed in waking up his ancestors."

"That doesn't answer my question, Kelly. If this was some rich husband and wife, why didn't they buy their way up to the Colonies? Or if they couldn't do that, then why not have ten other people frozen in here with them? They must have had some friends."

His partner smiled annoyingly. "Maybe they were a couple of greedy industrialists. You've read how crazy things were in the final days. People got selfish. They did just about anything to survive.''

''Yeah, and it wasn't just people who did anything to survive.''

Anger broke across Kelly's face. ''Now I don't want to hear what you're thinking! They were wiped out—nobody's seen one in two centuries. They're gone—long dead. Now if you go spouting your thoughts back at base, E-Tech's gonna go into a mild panic—all for nothing, I might add. And you and I are gonna spend the next two weeks down in this tunnel, searching for clues so that some E-Tech exec can get his official report made up and shoved into the archives. All for nothing, dammit!''

Bronavitch shook his head. ''How can you be so certain? Jesus, what if you're wrong? What if one of those bastards gets awakened up in the Colonies? Things could get real messy and you and I could get in a hell of a lot of trouble for not reporting this.''

Kelly stared up at the ice-crusted ceiling. ''Maybe,'' he said softly, ''there could be a cave-in down here. We could report that the Costeaus were probably artifact hunting . . .''

''That's irresponsible! I'm not going to have this on my conscience, Kelly! This could be the beginning of a bad situation and we're duty bound to report it.''

Kelly's jaw tightened. ''All right, dammit! We'll report. But no speculation. We tell E-Tech exactly what we've found and let them come to conclusions. I don't want any extra trouble from this.''

''Agreed.''

Kelly brushed past him and stomped back toward the generator car. Bronavitch paused to stare at the two empty stasis cradles. *Two of them.* He could not shake the fear. Stories that he had learned as a schoolboy came back to him; stories made even more terrifying by two hundred years of legend.

He shuddered. It was neither the time nor place to dwell on such things. He turned and quickly followed Kelly back out into the tunnel.

Her son, Jerem, spotted the strange men first. His twelve-year-old face expanded into a grin as he pointed across the grassy lot that separated their home from Bob Max's antique-cluttered yard.

Such a mess, Paula wailed privately, wishing once again that Max would be miraculously struck by an urge to scour, arrange, and clean his two-story tiled house, or else sell his land to someone with a better sense of propriety. He was hardly ever home, anyway.

Jerem tugged her sleeve, forced her to acknowledge the two figures wandering among the old cars, fridge units, freefall worksuits, hydrospheres, and general debris that forested the dealer's yard. She glanced at the two men, then instinctively turned her attention to a particularly obtrusive piece of twenty-first-century Earth furniture—a home accelerator couch—that Max had mounted along the edge of his front porch. Paula could have accepted the couch by itself, but Max had chosen to adorn it with the lifelike model of a nude, spread-legged woman, thus cueing visitors to the couch's original function as a sexual toy. She certainly did not consider herself a prude, but these days she worried for Jerem. Lately, he seemed to spend a lot of time looking at that model.

"Mom!" This time he tugged the sleeve of her old blouse so forcefully that she almost lost her balance. She gave him a scolding glare, but he just grinned and wagged his finger excitedly toward the two men.

The grassy lot that separated their yards was about a hundred feet wide. A narrow road bisected the lot, twisting its way through a forest of oaks and pines to the north and south. Eastward, beyond Max's home, the twin forests came together and rose upward, vanishing into a thick layer of white cumulus. The clouds darkened as she raised her gaze; precursors of tonight's special occasion—a thunderstorm.

"They're weird," Jerem exclaimed. "Do you think they're freefallers?"

Freefallers? Paula craned her neck to stare almost straight up through a break in the cloud cover. She glimpsed a portion of their cylindrical world's major city, New Armstrong, four miles and nearly a hundred and fifty degrees away. "Freefallers would have trouble standing up without adjustor suits," she explained. "When they visit the Colonies, they usually have to stay at the north or south pole hotels."

"I know. Or they can stay two miles up—at the center—where there's no gravity!"

She nodded, brought her attention back to Max's yard. The two men stood back to back in front of one of Max's most prized possessions—a nine-foot-high ceramic/steel statue of an Apollo astronaut. As she watched, the two men separated, circled the relic, and met again on the other side. Jerem was right. There was something very odd about them.

The boy cracked a laugh. "I know—they're clactors!"

"Col-lec-tors," she corrected.

"No, clactors! Clown actors," he said proudly. "It's a Quikie word."

She smiled. Quikie was her son's latest preoccupation. Over the last few weeks, she had been bombarded with his semisecret school language. Quikie apparently was the current rage throughout the Lamalan educational system.

Last month it was fantasies of cave exploring and next month . . . She thought again of the nude figure on the accelerator couch and wished, not for the first time, that there was some way of making him grow up a bit slower.

A series of rhythmic booms sounded from the sky—windholes being formed in preparation for tonight's thunderstorm.

For the past several weeks, all of the local channels had been proclaiming the artificially created gale. It would be the first one in Lamalan in almost two years and would affect the entire twenty-three-mile length of the floating cylinder that was their home. Naturally, Jerem was desperately excited.

She glanced from her son back to the men in Max's yard. They were frozen in catlike poses, back to back, faces searching the sky. Paula followed their gaze and saw only pale clouds, chunks of the faraway New Armstrong, and sporadic patches of sunlight gleaming from the mirrored reflectors that striped their world.

Lamalan followed the basic design of most of the other Colonies. The northern end of the cylinder faced the sun in order to harvest the solar energy necessary for their electrical needs. The original architects had divided the inner surface of the cylinder into six strips, each twenty-three miles long. Alpha, Gamma, and Epsilon were land areas, and the other two-mile-wide arcs—Beta, Delta, and Zeta—were composed of thick slabs of cosmishield glass. Outside the glass, in the vacuum of space, rows of mirrors caught the northern sunlight and directed it through the transparent shields. The mirrors were programmed to rotate through a twenty-four-hour cycle, providing Lamalan with standard day and night. Paula had lived in the Colonies all her life, yet she still felt awed by the technological geniuses who had designed these space islands over two hundred years ago.

Jerem leaned over their porch railing until she feared he would somersault into the flower bed, three feet below. "The windhole startled them," he proclaimed.

He was probably right, but who in the Colonies would be startled by windholes? Small children, perhaps, but certainly no one who had been brought up in one of the slowly rotating cylinders.

"Mom, aren't there Colonies that never have thunderstorms?"

She nodded. That could be the answer. A few of the cylinders were dedicated strictly to agricultural purposes. Profarmers certainly would not allow thunderstorms or wind turbulence to interfere with their crop raising. If these two men had spent their lives within agricultural cylinders, many aspects of an urban colony like Lamalan might appear strange to them.

"What do you think they're looking for?" Jerem asked, leaning out another precarious inch over the railing.

Paula decided the men had occupied enough of their time. "It's none of our business." She gripped the nape of his collar and gently pulled him back onto the porch. "Come on, we've got some work to do. I want you to help me clean up that dutytrunk we picked up at the auction last week."

"Awww, Mom! It's Saturday morning!"

"I know. Help me clean the dutytrunk and then haul a load of junk down to Turman's port for recycling. After that, you can take off."

"I'm not a slave," he argued. "All my friends get to do whatever they want on weekends!"

"And so can you, as soon as you finish your chores."

"That's cruel!"

"Yes, I know. A few hours of work each week is pretty harsh."

"Yeah, right." He tried to make the words sound indignant, could not.

She smiled with affection into the lively blue eyes. He was a good-looking young man, still boyishly thin, but growing at a rate that sometimes startled her. Heightwise, he was almost up to her shoulders. And the mop of tangled brown hair added an extra couple of inches.

"Ya know," he began, in a subdued tone she recognized as being fraught with trickery, "I could probably take that junk down to Turman's on the way to school Monday morning. It's almost in the same direction."

"No."

"But it would make more sense to do it all in one trip! I could bike there in less than a half hour and then cut straight over to Alpha sector and catch the rail to school."

Paula slipped into one of her mildly disapproving frowns. "No.

You're enough trouble waking up at the normal hour on school-days. I don't intend spooning you no-grog before we face sun.''

He gave an exaggerated sigh and hopped onto the railing. "Ma, ease-lee-me, lo-life, high-no!''

It was Quikie and she still had not figured out the basis of the language. It did not sound obscene, though. She would let it pass.

"Come on, let's get to work. The faster we get moving, the more time you'll have for yourself.'' She slid open the screened front door and stepped into the house.

"Hey, they're coming over here!''

Paula turned around in the doorway. The two men had hopped Max's low decorative fence and were making their way across the grassy lot. Jerem giggled.

It was the odd way they walked that amused him. Long, rhythmless strides seemed to degenerate every few steps, became mincing shuffles, as if their feet were about to buckle out from under them. Both men kept their left hands tucked into the side pockets of long gray jackets.

"C-ray ignors,'' Jerem whispered.

"I've never seen ignors act like that,'' Paula said. Mental retardation had been a serious problem among the descendants of the early spacefarers. Asteroid and Lunar miners in particular had often risked too much time away from the shielded Colonies and had suffered chromosomal damage, which they had passed on to their children. But cosmic-ray ignors were usually too mentally deficient to even dress or bathe themselves. Most of them still alive in this day and age were institutionalized; those who remained free usually gravitated to one of the slum Colonies.

The men crossed the road. Loose trousers blossomed from well-worn boots. The gray jackets were winter issue, certainly too warm for Lamalan, even in its coldest season. Pocono Colony boasted year-round snow weather, and a few of the other leisure cylinders offered perennial cold climates. Yet she sensed that these two had come from none of those places.

They hopped the small fence that defined her property.

Both looked to be about Paula's age, perhaps a bit older—closer to forty. The shorter one stood about five foot seven. A bang of frizzled gray hair drooped across the left side of his forehead, almost touching the eyebrow. The mouth was narrow, downturned, and delicately flaccid. Sad brown eyes avoided Paula's gaze.

The other man had a carefully groomed blanket of coal-black hair topping his six-foot frame. A tiny mustache accented a handsome and more open face. He halted a few feet from the porch and produced a salesman's smile. His sad-eyed companion stopped two paces behind and to the left of him.

The smiling man withdrew his hand from the jacket. He coughed delicately into his fist. "Excuse me, please, but would you perhaps know the whereabouts of the gentleman who owns that house?"

His voice emerged deep and bountiful, like a professional announcer's. As he spoke, the shorter man pointed toward Max's home.

Paula came back out onto the porch. She closed the screen door behind her. "Bob Max is probably away on one of his buying trips. We haven't seen him for several days."

The smile lost none of its luster. "Did he perhaps leave word with you regarding his return? You see, we had an appointment with him this morning . . . to purchase some antiquities. We do not know him very well, but his reputation suggests that he is a most prompt and gracious host. Today's tardiness is most upsetting."

Jerem leaned over the porch railing. "We sell antiques! Super-quality stuff . . . and we're bonded by the Antiquer's Guild."

"How fascinating! Perhaps I could spend some time browsing through your merchandise while we await our host. I'm sure he won't be much longer . . . likely there's been some scheduling mix-up with his shuttle. My friend could wait outside and watch for his arrival."

Paula laid her arm across Jerem's shoulders. It was the signal that he was to be silent and allow her to handle this exchange.

"Where are you from?" she asked pleasantly.

The smile brightened. "We come from the Colony of Velvet-on-the-Green. Have you heard of it?"

She had. "A hedonist island, as I recall." That was about the nicest thing she could think of to say about the place. Velvet-on-the-Green was a leisure Colony, catering mainly to rich perverts.

His fingers groomed the contoured mustache. "It is difficult being away from home. . . . As you may know, our Colony has seven-eighths normal gravity." The smile expanded until Paula thought it would explode from his face. "We do not leave home very often. These G forces are simply punishing. Why, it makes one self-conscious merely walking!"

She smiled back. "I'm sure it's hard on you." She had never been to Velvet-on-the-Green, had no intention of ever going there. But it did have subnormal gravity and that could explain the odd gait of these two. Then again, there was something strangely disquieting about them—some hidden facet that ran counter to the smiling man's words. And those heavy jackets . . .

"You two must be sweating in those things."

He tried for a dismal nod but the smile burned through. "Yes, we are quite uncomfortable. However, we dare not remove our garments, for the attire bespeaks our current status. We are being disciplined by our owner because of some recent errant behavior. Our sentence will not end until we return to Velvet—only then may we remove these cold-weather jackets."

"Are you slaves?" Jerem asked, with a touch of awe.

The man grinned momentarily at Paula, then turned to her son.

"We're not real slaves—not the kind you've probably read about in school. We're sort of . . . pretend slaves. It's like a game. When you're older, I'm sure you'll understand it much better."

She hoped Jerem would never understand it.

"Is your owner here?" the boy asked.

Jerem's wide-eyed expression warned Paula that a barrage of questions were forthcoming. She debated trying to silence him before the conversation became too embarrassing, decided against it. She wanted to learn more about these two before she allowed Smiler into her gallery.

He answered calmly. "Our owner has remained in Velvet-on-the-Green. After all, why should he have to suffer through this terrible gravity when he has slaves to do his bidding?"

"But if he's not here," Jerem argued, "then why don't you take off your jackets?"

"Ahhh, but the pleasure of the game would be destroyed. You see, in order for us to feel like slaves, we must act like slaves. We must do exactly as we are commanded or else risk marring our integrity."

"But why would you want to be slaves when you could be free?"

Smiler put his hand to his mouth, pivoted, and sneezed. Sad-eyes grinned mirthlessly and, in a voice that seemed totally devoid of emotion, said: "We like being slaves. It's exciting."

Paula stared at the shorter man. She repressed a shudder when his tongue slithered between his lips and licked at the air.

Smiler delicately wiped his nose and turned back to Paula. "And wearing cold-weather jackets is mild punishment. Whippings are much worse."

Jerem's curiosity climbed to a new level. "You mean you get beaten? For real!"

Smiler laughed. "Oh yes. A very special excitement flows to your soul when you learn you are to be beaten. Hasn't your mother ever spanked you?"

Jerem shook his head vehemently, more to hide embarrassment than to contradict the man. Occasionally, Paula bent him over and smacked him good.

"A beating," Smiler continued, "can become a special pleasure."

"But if you . . ."

Paula interrupted. "Jerem, that's enough. These two men are probably weary of being questioned." Her son was already well on his way to learning about the bizarre world of adults. She did not intend for these perverts to advance his education.

"Such questions are rather tiring." The smile degenerated into another sneeze. He produced a kerchief, blew his nose. "Excuse me, please, but these trees . . ." He waved his arms at the surrounding forests. "I believe I've developed an allergic reaction."

"Don't they have trees in your cylinder?" Jerem began.

"Yes," Paula answered, "they probably have trees, but of a different variety."

She faced Smiler. "Our gallery uses a filtered air system. You would probably be more comfortable inside." She did not want to let him in, but she could not think of a polite way to refuse. Best to get it over with.

"Jerem," she continued, "I want you to go upstairs and get the key to the gallery."

He nodded and dashed into the house. "Get the key" was their signal that the security system monitoring the gallery was to be turned on. The control panel and recorder were located upstairs in a hall closet. A pair of microcams, hidden in the gallery walls, fed audio/video to the master unit.

Antique robberies seldom occurred on Lamalan and a surveillance system would certainly not prevent one from happening. However, the police could later use the recording to ID suspects.

Many galleries employed a permanent on-line security system. Paula dealt with clients who requested anonymity and she honored such requests. She used the security system only in unfamiliar situations.

She nodded to Smiler. "Follow me, please."

They don't look like robbers, she thought. *Then again, they don't look like anyone else I've ever met.*

She led him down the entrance hall, past their living and dining rooms to the imposing wooden door near the back of the house. *I should be thankful for small favors,* thought Paula. Sad-eyes had elected to remain outside.

"Marth Antiques," read Smiler. "A most phonetically pleasing name."

The sign was mounted on the thin strip of wall beside the gallery door; gold letters etched onto a flat-black rectangular plate. The door itself was solid oak, grown on Earth and chiseled into diamond patterns by a woodcarver some two hundred years ago. Inset emerald bands glittered under the hallway's soft golden light.

"A most beautiful portal!"

"Thank you."

Jerem bounded down the stairway and, with a breathless nod, handed her the old-fashioned twistkey. She felt a bit safer knowing that the security system was activated, though a faint chill swept up her spine as Smiler followed her into the gallery.

He appraised the room carefully. The chamber was a twenty-five-foot square with rounded corners. Lush ivory carpeting covered the floor and rose up the walls to blend into vertical slabs of white pine, which were hesitantly streaked with rainbow gloss. The pine studs tongue-and-grooved into the slightly darker ceiling timbers. Brass lanterns hung from the rafters, spotlighting the various daises under diffused yellow light. The lanterns were computer-controlled and randomly programmed to vary the intensity of illumination so that different exhibits were periodically accented by stronger light.

Paula cleared her throat, caught Smiler's attention. "We specialize in twenty-first-century microprocessor tools. I believe you'll find that we have one of the finest small collections outside of the museums. Naturally, we have a full E-Tech license for the vending and purchasing of machine antiques. And we are always interested in new acquisitions, provided they are at least one hundred and seventy-five years old."

Smiler nodded. His eyes calmly panned the gallery.

So much for her standard speech. As always, she had intimated that Marth Antiques dealt strictly over the counter, which was not really true. Occasionally, she came across black-market items, and although she never purchased them herself, there were trader shops over in New Armstrong that would. If one of Paula's referrals resulted in a sale, the trader shop would kick back a small percentage. It was a fairly safe way of making a little extra money. The Guardians had their hands full just trying to keep tabs on the major black marketeers; people who made referrals were almost completely ignored. And Paula had her principals—she refused to consider dangerous or degrading items. Weapons and genetic toys were the province of the more covert dealers. Like Bob Max.

Smiler hesitated for a moment in the doorway, then walked to the nearest dais. He examined the steel-gray rectangular box with a critical eye.

"It's a mid–twenty-first century. Pre-Apocalyptic," she added needlessly. "It's a programmable tablesaw with an enclosed beam sander. Cuts and polishes all woods and most plastics and metals."

"Made on Earth?" he asked.

"Yes. And it still functions. We sell only fully operable antiques. Would you like to see a demonstration?"

"Indeed, yes!"

Paula flipped open the recessed control panel beside the doorway and activated the switch for that exhibit.

The tablesaw's plastic casing jerked upward, split in half, and unfolded rapidly to expose the inner working surface. Paula was always prepared for demonstrations—a piece of sheet aluminum had already been placed within the chucks.

She hit the second switch and a soft hum filled the gallery as microlasers ignited and carved a preset pattern in the aluminum sheet. In less than ten seconds the work was done. The tablesaw shut itself down.

Paula walked to the dais and withrew the aluminum doily that had been carved out of the sheet. She handed it to Smiler.

He held it up to the light, examined the finely laced edges. "My. Such a pretty example. Why, with such a machine, one could quickly become an artist!"

"Yes, they could." Paula had been in the business long enough to know that the machine was of no real interest to him.

She decided to probe. "What sort of antiques are you here to see Max about?"

Smiler moved to the next dais—a modular ice cutter—and ran his fingers in a circular pattern on the side of the casing. "We seek the esoteric."

He pivoted to face her. "That is not to say that you do not possess a most beautiful collection, Ms. Marth. At my owner's bidding, I have traveled extensively. Rarely have I come across a more beautiful selection. I am surprised that you do not advertise yourself—a small sign outside this building would doubtlessly attract more attention."

"This is also my home," said Paula. "Besides, we are a little off the main urban routes. And I do advertise in the Antiquer's Guild bulletins and on several of the major trade channels."

"Of course."

Jerem coughed loudly from the doorway. "Mom, can I go now? To do my chores," he added wistfully.

Paula nodded and he was out of the gallery in a flash. Being around a pair of self-professed slaves obviously did not compare to the prospect of a free Saturday.

Smiler wandered through the room, carefully examining each item. Paula patiently responded to his simple questions, knowing all the while that he had no interest in her answers. It was all a polite game.

She came to the tentative conclusion that he was a black marketeer. Bob Max certainly operated on the fringes—her trader friends in New Armstrong claimed that Max had even been to the surface on illegal prospecting expeditions. That was very risky business. Lately, the Irryan Council seemed to be making a more concerted effort to crack down on the pirates. Costeaus, however, did not scare easily. They would take their shuttles anywhere for the right price.

Paula did not think that Smiler was a Costeau, but he could be an illegal dealer. There was a quality of toughness beneath his manners that reminded her of some of the hardcore traders she had come across.

He finally ran out of questions. "A most blessed collection, Ms. Marth. You may be assured that my owner will be apprised of what I have seen. Perhaps he will someday have me return here . . . to make purchases. Exquisite!"

Paula forced a smile, ushered him toward the door. "Come back anytime," she said tightly.

Outside, the sky had darkened considerably. Black storm clouds masked the Colony's three alternate sun sectors, and only the east-ward forest, gently curving up the cylinder, still received a measure of reflected light. To the north, visibility had been reduced to less than a mile. The usually comforting view of the south pole circle, six miles distant, was hidden beyond thick clouds.

Sad-eyes stood like a sentinel at the corner of the porch. "No sign of Max," he said without turning. Paula repressed another shudder at the sound of that bleak voice.

Smiler shook his head. "This is most disappointing. We have come a great distance and unfortunately cannot linger any longer. Other appointments await us."

Paula shrugged. "Would you like me to give Max a message?"

He seemed to consider her question for a moment. Then the smile brightened. "Yes, please do. Tell him that his Philadelphia friends were here. Perhaps you could even gently chastise him for being tardy."

"Of course."

Without another word, Smiler turned and ambled away from the porch. Sad-eyes fell into step beside him. In that same awkward mincing shuffle as before, they stepped over Paula's small fence, marched to the road, and headed north. Jerem appeared around the corner of the house.

Her son carried a bulky white plastic case. It was an authentic dutytrunk used by spacemen over two hundred years ago.

"Mom, I still don't understand why they'd want to be slaves."

Paula shrugged and watched the pair vanish as the road curved into thick woodlands. "It's sort of an illness . . . they probably can't help it."

"Will they always be like that? Can't they get into a psychplan?"

She smoothed the front of her culotte. "I don't know." Answers would be complicated enough if the men were really slaves, but she doubted there was much truth in anything Smiler had said.

Jerem produced a serious frown. "Maybe they were real slaves and they were too embarrassed about it, so they pretended to be pretend slaves."

Tension broke and she exploded with laughter. "Come on, I'll help you get to work on that trunk." She gave him a quick hug as he set the case on the porch. He grimaced.

"Mom, I'm too big for that!"

Paula matched his somber tone. "Of course. Now why don't you run upstairs and get a sprayer. The inside of this trunk is filthy."

He nodded, ran through the doorway.

"Oh, and turn off the security system!" she yelled. "And code the last segment for filing."

Normally, the system erased its data after twenty-four hours. But Smiler . . . he was going into her permanent files.

She scratched a fingernail across the compartmented interior of the dutytrunk, searched for a nametag or corporate logo beneath the layers of encrusted grime. The Antiquer's Guild possessed a master list on the millions of workers who had constructed the Colonies. Dating the relic would be simple if the original owner had indeed marked his property.

Jerem dashed from the house. The security recorder was clutched in his arms.

"Mom, look at this!"

He thrust the square plate in front of her face and tripped a sensor on its beveled edge.

An image appeared on the surface of the plate—the gallery as seen from high up on the southern wall. The door opened and she watched herself enter the room. But behind her, where Smiler should have been, came a twisting blur of multicolored motion.

The blur moved through the gallery. Paula stared in disbelief, heard herself explain the buying policies of Marth Antiques and the operational capabilities of the tablesaw.

She shook her head. "There must have been a malfunction in the recorder . . ."

"Shhh!" Jerem hissed. "Listen!"

A weird undulating sound came from the screen. It reminded her of a crowd of whispering people.

The noise stopped and she heard herself ask what sort of antiques Smiler was interested in. There was a pause; again, haunting whispers sounded. Jerem clutched her arm.

"That noise comes whenever he talks!"

She nodded thoughtfully, switched off the device.

"Maybe he wasn't human! Maybe he was an alien! Maybe the starships have come back!"

She gripped his shoulder. "Calm down. He was a man. And he was wearing a device called an AV scrambler. It distorts security systems, even passive ones like ours."

"I never heard of that!"

"They're very rare," she explained, trying to keep the fear out of her voice. *Rare, hell!* On the black market, such a device would cost a fortune. AV scramblers were part of E-Tech's outlawed technology.

"Do you think they were Costeaus?" A bit of eagerness was gone from Jerem's voice, but real live pirates would still be considered an event.

Paula nodded calmly. "Yes, they were probably Costeaus." She did not believe it.

"I want to see where they're going!" He dashed across the yard but careened to a halt at the sound of Paula's words.

"Jerem Marth, get back here!"

"I just wanna see . . ."

"Jerem!" She used her sternest voice.

"Awww, Mom!" He kicked at the grass and reluctantly trudged back to her side. "I wasn't going to do anything dumb!"

She looked him straight in the eye. "Those men could be dangerous. If they saw you following them, they might get angry."

"I'll bet I could run faster than they could," he whined.

She nipped the argument by pointing at the dutytrunk. "Where's that sprayer?"

His reply was sullen. "I left it upstairs."

"Go get it."

He booted the grass. "Even if they were slaves, I'll bet they got more freedom than I do!"

The storm grew steadily throughout the afternoon. By five o'clock, the air had become sticky and humid. Sporadic thunderclaps could be heard in the distance. Sunlight disappeared altogether. Black and gray clouds rolled across the sky, dissolving into one another and reemerging in new formations. The first lightning flashed just before six. There was no longer any evidence to indicate that they were living inside a huge cylinder. Jerem was ecstatic.

Paula came to the porch with his jacket, ignoring, as usual, protests that he did not need to cover up. He squirmed into the nylon garment just as a thunderbolt cracked directly overhead, shaking the air. In a matter of minutes, the temperature plummeted at least twenty degrees and cold mist began to dampen their faces. A huge fissure blossomed in the western clouds. Scarlet-yellow lightning strobed the heavens.

"Did ya see that!" Jerem whispered. "That was chroma-controlled! You wouldn't believe how hard that is to phase into the storm! Our science teacher says that they gotta generate millions of volts and then they put petro dust into the atmosphere and they trip the banks and inject feeder currents and they can make it any color they want by changing the chemicals in the dust!"

Paula faked a fascinated nod and tightened the velcro tab on the collar of her own jacket. Despite the claims of safety, these immense storms unsettled her. There was something inherently disturbing about megavoltage forces ripping apart the sky, sucking at the very air: ecospheric temper tantrums.

Throughout the day, local news channels had been proclaiming the storm. Psychologists gave testimony to the benefits of allowing regulated loss of control. Lamalan social planners congratulated themselves for creating an evening of mass entertainment. People tended to buy excessive amounts of food and supplies prior to a storm, a curious phenomenon that inspired grocers and the Intercolonial Profarmers Union to roundly endorse thunderstorms.

Others objected to the raging spectacles. The Anti–T-storm League fought for the abolition of thunderstorms throughout the Colonies, and they had been vocally demonstrating their cause on Lamalan during the past week. Paula suspected that there were a great many adults like herself who tread the middle ground—disliking thunderstorms but tolerating them. Jerem's obvious joy had a lot to do with her own acceptance.

Green lightning spiraled lengthwise through the cylinder. The accompanying roar shook their porch. Jerem's excited words were lost beneath crackling aftershocks.

One thing was for certain—the controversy over thunderstorms was growing. Lamalan's last storm, two years ago, had sparked only a handful of protests. Today's event ignited official statements, both pro and con, from numerous organizations.

Even major Intercolonial groups had been drawn into the fray. E-Tech's archnemesis, La Gloria de la Ciencia, had come out strongly in favor of the storms, praising Lamalan's "courage in the face of a vocal minority." E-Tech had issued a statement denouncing the excessive technology inherent in T-storm creation, although their protest had been carefully worded to assure everyone that they no intention of calling for the outlawing of such events.

The heavens burst apart into a spiderweb of fierce golden light. Paula covered her ears as thunder rocked the house.

"Jerem, why don't we go inside and watch the rest of it from the window? You can see just as well."

He shook his head and wiped the rain from his face.

"Okay, so why don't we at least move back from the edge of the porch. There's no sense in getting completely soaked."

A trio of loud booms drowned out his reply.

"Jerem?"

"What'd ya say, Mom?"

"Why don't we . . ."

Blue-white explosions blistered the sky. Paula gave up. She *had* promised that he could watch this storm outside, a privilege that she had denied him two years ago—much to his chagrin and to her later regret. Arguments that had nothing to do with thunderstorms inevitably ended with: "Yeah, and you wouldn't let me watch the storm like everyone else, either!" Another two years of that was not worth it. She had, however, put her foot down when he suggested observing tonight's aerial calamity from atop their gently slanted roof. There would be a different sort of lightning right across his backside if he dared set foot off the porch.

"They say it's gonna end with red bolts!" he shouted above another wave of thunder. "They're the wickedest and loudest of all!"

Wonderful. It was going to get worse.

A light came on in Bob Max's house and Paula saw the old man's scrawny form briefly silhouetted through the large front porch window. He must have just gotten home—there had been no sign of activity throughout the day.

She felt that it was important to tell Max about the two men as soon as possible. She debated a wet dash across the now-muddy lot. It was a short debate. Max did not even have a public phone— doubtlessly, only smugglers and Costeaus had access to his private line. And Jerem would become impossible if Paula left the porch while he was not permitted to.

Lightning flashed and another movement caught her eye. A gray shadow danced through the dealer's yard, froze momentarily against a large fridge unit, then disappeared. She squinted, searching the clutter of antiques for the source of the shadow.

The rain picked up, became a wind-whipped downpour, cascading in torrents across the porch. Their jackets were waterproof but Paula's thin summer slacks were not—they now clung to her like a second skin. She shivered. Jerem looked completely drenched, oblivious to all but the ravished sky.

And then they appeared—two men, dressed in dark clothing. They came out of Max's yard and crept along the edge of the old man's front porch. Dull red lightning sparkled in the air immediately surrounding their bodies—they were wearing active crescent webs. The defensive energy shields were usually invisible, but the rain was playing tricks, outlining the protective barriers.

Even though the men had their backs to her, Paula knew she was looking at the same pair who had come to her gallery this morning. Smiler and Sad-eyes. It was not just a logical guess. There was something instantly identifiable about them—a quality in their movements, as if they had been born in tandem.

She had no time to consider the ramifications of her thoughts. The two men stood up. The taller one—Smiler—leaped catlike over the porch railing. Sad-eyes slithered between the legs of the obscene model propped on Max's accelerator couch. In one swift motion, he lashed out and tore the head from the nude torso. It sailed over the railing and splattered into the mud.

Paula dropped to her knees beside Jerem. "Come on," she hissed, "I want you to move!" She clamped a hand across his shoulder and dragged him behind the railing.

"Mom!"

"Hush! There's something going on over at Max's. I want us to be absolutely quiet and still. We can watch through the slits in the railing."

Her urgency got through to him. They crouched behind the railing like scared rabbits. For a while, nothing happened. The men had become statues on Max's porch—bold outlines, shimmering with each new stroke of lightning, but as still as if they had been de-energized by a switch. Paula began to feel silly.

And then with a swiftness that took her breath away, the two men leaped into the air and crashed through Max's plate-glass front window.

"Wow! Did ya see that!"

Paula nodded. For another eternity, there was no movement from inside the dealer's home. The light remained on, illuminating Max's living room. A table and some cushioned chairs were visible through the shattered window. Purple lightning splashed across the sky, casting a brief eerie glow across the landscape behind his house.

I should call the police. Her hair whipped across her face. She tucked it behind her ears and reached a decision.

"Jerem, I want you to stay right here. I don't want you to move. I'm going to run in the house and call—"

Bob Max jumped—or was pushed—through his broken window. He landed feet first on his porch, stumbling forward. He slammed into the railing and flipped over into the mud. He struggled to his knees and tried to stand up.

Thunder blasted. Smiler appeared suddenly on Max's porch. Sad-eyes came around the side of the house—he must have exited through the dealer's back door.

Paula dared not risk calling the police—not now. Smiler was looking in their direction. He would certainly spot her if she stood up.

Max made it to his feet just as Sad-eyes came up behind him. Max must have sensed the man's presence. He started to turn around. Sad-eyes kicked Max's legs out from under him. Max hit the mud like a felled tree.

A beam of twisting black light erupted from Smiler's hand. The dark luminous beam streaked in a circle around Max's prone form. Smiler snapped his wrist. The light stopped circling and plunged downward, burying itself in the dealer's spine. Max jerked once and then lay still.

Paula clutched her son—a grip of maternal protectiveness mixed with sheer terror. She knew Max was dead and she knew what had killed him.

Data streamed through awareness—facts about the two men that had nagged at her since this morning. Sad-eyes and Smiler. Contrasting speech styles—a voice too inflective and a voice without emotion. Oddly coordinated movements. AV scramblers. And the final clue—the black light of the Cohe wand, a hand weapon so deadly that its mere possession would subject the owner to E-Tech's harshest penalties.

The two men who were not really two men would have little concern over such laws. They were not human. They were a creature born out of the dark years before the Apocalypse, over two hundred years ago.

A Paratwa.

She clutched Jerem even tighter. Smiler seemed to be staring straight at them. *It saw us earlier. It knows we're hiding here. It's going to kill us.*

"Mom," Jerem began anxiously.

"Shhh!" *We could make a run for the front door, lock it—no, it would come through the windows! The woods! We'll make a run for the woods, keep running until we find help! We might make it . . .*

"Mom, they're leaving."

Smiler and Sad-eyes stepped past Max's body and headed for the road. Moments later, they disappeared behind the swaying trees.

Irrya's morning sunlight, tinted ocher by a spectral shift within the cylinder's outside mirrors, stained the office walls, discoloring the pale ivory and, in some spots, transforming it to rust. Potted juniper shrubs cast slim shadows, their upswept branches forming pencils of darkness against the bright light. The massive uncluttered desk was authentic oak and easily dominated the room's sparse furniture—three stout chairs, a corner table, a small glass-enclosed shelf maintaining four books in a sealed environment. A darkened comconsole rose from the back edge of the desk like a miniature mountain. A portly man occupied the leather chair opposite the console.

Despite his two decades as master of this office, the man still considered himself a temporary fixture. It was a proper enough attitude for the Director of E-Tech.

Does consistency have a source?

Rome Franco searched his feelings for the origin of that particular musing.

Minor spat with Angela this morning. He had worn his dreamtube to bed last night. In her sleep, she had rolled over and knocked the headboard sensor out of alignment. A good dream interrupted. He had awakened, thoughtlessly yelled at her.

No, that was not the source. The emotion was strong enough to be the first recalled—only natural, since Angela had been his wife for thirty-nine years. It was a full sharecare relationship; in tandem most of the time, at worst, communicating. Any pulsations within such a marriage demanded preeminence.

The children? Lydia and Antony lived in the distant L4 Colonies and each managed to open a channel several times a month. Lydia was pregnant again—grandchild three would be a boy. Antony's engineering group had offered him a surface assignment and he was still debating the merits of acceptance. His salary would almost double but the jobrisk factor would climb into a higher percentile as well. He was wise to ponder such a choice.

Rome shook his head. Not the children and not Angela. What then? Today's upcoming Council meeting?

His stomach tightened—he had pinpointed the turmoil. *Does consistency have a source?* Perhaps the Council of Irrya, governing body of the Colonies, was that source. The Council had certainly always been a wellspring of consistency.

It had ruled, uninterrupted, for over two hundred years, ever since those dark days following Earth's abandonment. Today, five people sat on the Council and it was their collective wisdom that determined the progress and direction of the Colonies. Rome and four others represented the hopes and fears of over a billion people. The five of them supplied the orbiting cylinders with a gestalt leadership that in two centuries had never floundered.

Yes, consistency appeared to have a source. But some of the current Councillors sought to disrupt that harmony of understanding that had guided the survivors of Earth to a new beginning. Those Councillors seemed to have lost the great considerations of the past.

The globe of the Earth spins below us and it is dead. Rome wanted to shake those Councillors and point to the homeworld and say: *Look at it! See what was done to it! The same madness that destroyed the world is festering again within this Council! Can't you see it?*

They could not. All that they seemed capable of perceiving was E-Tech, omnipotently powerful for two centuries. And Rome Franco, Director of the organization, was seen as their enemy.

He sighed. If consistency had a source, it also had a terminus. And when that point was reached, the cycle could begin again. History would be free to repeat itself.

I am afraid.

The underlying feeling was clear. *I, Rome Franco, fear that the past will repeat itself.*

The Irryan Council was slowly eroding the power of E-Tech. The march toward madness was beginning all over again. Limits were being ignored. Science and technology were poised to run rampant throughout the Colonies. People again seemed willing to denigrate themselves before the machines. The twin gods of profit and progress had risen and the voices of reason and balance were about to be drowned beneath the apocalyptic waves.

It must not be.

He recognized the crisis just as his forefathers had recognized it over two hundred years ago. Only their conception had come too late to save the Earth. E-Tech had sprouted from the madness of those final days; a diverse band of politicians, scientists, industrialists, engineers, and scholars who had united in order to limit the unchecked growth of technological advancement.

The Ecostatic Technospheric Alliance had struggled for acceptance in those early years; its goal of limiting humanity's knowledge ran counter to a long tradition of science without boundaries. Not until the genetic and nuclear horrors had fully manifested themselves had E-Tech grown to its full stature.

We must remain powerful.

Today, more than ever, E-Tech's guidance was needed. Voices of unreason seemed to be everywhere—their cries had infested the Irryan Senate and lately, the Irryan Council itself. Rome had been E-Tech's representative to the Council for close to twenty years and until recently, his organization could count on strong support. But the tide had changed.

A steel guitar twanged softly. He suppressed his worries and leaned back in the soft leather of the chair. A brush across the light sensor of the intercom opened a channel to his execsec, whose office was two stories below.

"Yes?"

His secretary's formal baritone filled the room. "Sir, Pasha Haddad is calling. He requests an immediate secure conversation. Should I seal the lines?"

Rome sighed. E-Tech's Chief of Security would request a sealed line to discuss rose gardening. "Put him through when you're ready."

It took only a few seconds for Rome's deskscreen to coalesce into the familiar lean dark face and shaved skull.

Pasha Haddad wasted no time. "We have a problem." His voice was deep, poised. "A murder took place in the Colony of Lamalan early last night. A smuggler—a man named Bob Max— was killed by Cohe wand. Two neighbors witnessed the execution. They claim that the killers visited their antique gallery earlier in the day, inquiring about the victim. The witnesses are convinced—and so am I—that the killer was a Paratwa assassin."

If Haddad's hand had reached from the screen and slapped him, Rome could not have felt more stunned. "A Paratwa . . . in the Colonies?" He found himself gripping the leather armrests.

Haddad's face wrinkled, betraying his age. The Pasha, too, had spent a good deal of his life in the service of E-Tech.

"The witnesses are a woman and her twelve-year-old son. Fortunately, the woman had the good sense to call E-Tech rather than the local police or the Guardians. Mother and son are now in our protective custody and the entire incident is still under wraps."

Rome found himself unwilling to believe. "A Paratwa? Are you certain?"

The Pasha gave a curt nod. "I've not spoken personally to the witnesses as yet, but my people are convinced of their sincerity. The woman was terrified. If the killers were not a Paratwa, they were certainly trying to imitate one. And there is no doubt about the murder weapon—it was a Cohe wand."

That in itself should be proof of identity. In his sixty-two years, Rome had only once seen the weapon. E-Tech had confiscated a wand from a private collector during a high-tech raid some twenty-five years ago. The collector had traced the weapon's ancestry clear back to his great-great-grandparents, who had retrieved it from a dead Paratwa outside their urban Texas home. The outlawed wand had been smuggled to the Colonies and treasured for two centuries as a family heirloom.

Rome recalled an E-Tech specialist demonstrating the captured weapon down in the Irryan vaults. Such a tiny device, the size and shape of an egg—a pale sliver of metal projecting from one end. How could such a simple-looking thing possess such a perilous reputation?

In his naivete, Rome had assumed that the weapon's association with the Paratwa killers had exaggerated its deadliness. The E-Tech specialist, naturally inexperienced with such a device, had gently squeezed its smooth surface. The twisting black light had lanced across the vault, slicing through the torsos of four practice dummies like a fin through water. Rome remembered being astonished at the speed of the incinerating beam and the way it seemed to whip from the specialist's hand as if it were some unbound power from within his very body. At that moment, Rome understood why the people of pre-Apocalyptic Earth had feared such weapons and why E-Tech had totally outlawed them.

Paratwa assassins had spent their entire lives training with the wands. It was said that the deadlier assassins became so skilled that they could whip a beam up a spiral staircase and still pierce or slice their target.

A Paratwa in the Colonies. He did not want to accept it.

Pasha Haddad seemed to read Rome's feelings. "It was a shock. We've always known that many of the assassins were unaccounted for at the time of the Apocalypse. There was always the possibility that some of them went into stasis during the final days, hoping to be awakened into some future era. But after two centuries . . . I truly believed that we had seen the last of them."

Rome nodded, found that his thoughts were suddenly on Angela and the children. Irrational worries. There were more than a billion people in the Colonies—his own family was certainly statistically safe.

"We suspect," Haddad continued, "that Costeaus were involved in this creature's revival. Four days ago, an illegal shuttle expedition retrieved a pair of stasis capsules from a sealed subway tunnel in the Philadelphia area. There was some concern that it could be a Paratwa, although that information did not reach my desk until a few hours ago." Haddad looked angry over that fact. "Last night's victim—Bob Max—was known to have Costeau contacts. And the witnesses claim that one of the killers specifically mentioned Philadelphia."

Rome twisted uncomfortably in his chair. The leather seemed to be resisting his movement, preventing an easy uncrossing of his legs. "What about the Wake-up facility?"

The Pasha shrugged. "Naturally, we'll check all the registered stasis centers, but I am not optimistic. The Costeaus are known to have their own Wake-ups—illegal, of course. I doubt if we'll have much luck learning where this creature was revived."

Rome stared past the viewscreen to the velvet leaves of a potted calimer plant in the far corner. *A Paratwa assassin.* Of all the technological excesses of the twenty-first century, none had inspired the growth of E-Tech more than the Paratwa. The interlink killers had ravaged the world for some thirty years before the Apocalypse, carving a niche in the history texts that surpassed even the Nazi monstrosities of the previous century.

If a Paratwa assassin had indeed arisen, the political ramifications could be extraordinary. Rome felt a touch of guilt, but he was far too experienced to ignore the possible advantages for E-Tech. A Paratwa, threatening the Colonies, could provide certain gains to his organization. Within the Council, the erosion of E-Tech's power base might be halted, at least temporarily. No Councillor would dare weaken E-Tech's scientific and social controls with an assassin on the loose. In the public mind, the eradication of the Paratwa was still linked with the rise of E-Tech. Even La Gloria de la Ciencia could not fail to recognize that fact.

Rome smiled to himself. Dear Angela often said that he could never become a great Councillor, since he cared too much about other people. Then the sweet brown eyes would sparkle and she would crush him under a proper Sicilian hug.

In a way, though, she was right. There were Councillors who, if they were in Rome's position, would secretly impede the assassin's capture in order to strengthen their political base.

He faced the screen again. "You say that the Guardians have not yet been notified. I believe that places E-Tech in the position of violating the Irryan charter."

It was rare to see Haddad smiling. "I took the liberty of withholding the incident from you until this morning. This is a proper—and legal—position for an underling to take. Since you, as Director of E-Tech, are officially responsible for informing the Guardians, no laws have yet been broken."

Rome nodded wryly. Haddad's rationale was open to debate. "I gather that you've used the extra time to work on leads."

The Pasha gave a slow nod. "Unfortunately, we haven't learned too much. It's mostly speculation at this point. Bob Max could have been the one who organized the Costeau expedition that retrieved the stasis capsules from Philadelphia. He definitely had pirate contacts and we know he had been to the surface—illegally—at least three times. No one could ever prove it in court, but my people are certain of their information."

"Why do you think he was killed?"

The Pasha shook his head. "Perhaps he tried to double-cross the Costeaus. Or maybe he didn't realize what they were waking up. Bob Max may have panicked, threatened to report that they had brought a Paratwa out of stasis. The pirates could have sent the assassin to kill him. It's also possible that both Max and the Costeaus were being used by some third party. Max may have been the middleman who hired the pirate crew to go to Philadelphia."

"And this third party could have had Max killed in order to prevent him from talking."

Haddad nodded. "It's possible. But right now, everything's guesswork. We do have some deepthroaters with the smugglers and I've already authorized that they be contacted. They may be able to learn more about that shuttle expedition to Philadelphia and about Bob Max's pirate friends. We'll need time, though. If word of this goes public, the Costeaus will clam up for certain. Artwhiler's people will come blundering in, demanding answers, and the pirates will react by shutting all the doors."

Rome winced. Councillor Augustus J. Artwhiler was the Supreme Commander of the Intercolonial Guardians. Not only would the Guardians stamp out any possible leads but Artwhiler himself would turn the whole incident into a political fireball. The man approached problems with the subtlety of a battering ram.

"How long do you think we can keep word of this killing under wraps?"

Haddad stared. "There are about twenty of our people who

know about it thus far, plus the two witnesses. Everyone has been made aware of the security issues involved. I don't think there will be any immediate leaks, although eventually word could get out."

Rome made a decision. He did not like the idea of bending the law, but they needed time to check on leads before word of the killing spread through the Colonies. "All right. We'll keep the incident restricted." *And to hell with Artwhiler.*

"These Paratwa—I assume you've had our historical section dredging up data about them."

The Pasha gave a vigorous nod. "Yes, mainly to see if we can identify the breed. There was quite a variety of Paratwa assassins, originating from many different labs. Each breed had its own peculiar characteristics—fighting strengths and weaknesses, methods of operation, contractual reliability, end-user techniques for subjugation and manipulation . . ."

Rome held up his hand. It was disconcerting to realize that he knew very little about these creatures. Never in his career with E-Tech had it seemed important to learn about them. "Give it to me simply."

"Most of them were mercenaries," Haddad explained, "but their user loyalties varied considerably. Some could be hired to perform a kill for cash and others demanded payment in the form of reciprocal loyalty. Some assassins spent their entire lives as bodyguards for wealthy industrialists and others drifted from user to user—true soldiers of fortune, seeking out the most profitable enterprises. Some specialized in political assassination while others hired out to do battle with police or army units. Still others took anything that came along. And in the later years, many of them fell under the dominion of the Ash Ock—the Paratwa leaders."

The royal Caste. Rome remembered reading about them as a youngster. "The Ash Ock—their breed was wiped out, wasn't it?"

"Yes. There were only five of them and our records show that the last three were destroyed shortly before the Apocalypse. Besides, they were not really assassins. Those of the royal Caste were created in order to unite the others—bring into being a society of Paratwa.''

And replace humans, Rome recalled. He suppressed a shudder.

"Of the pure assassins," Haddad continued, "the worst appear to have been the Voshkof Rabbits and the Jeek Elementals. It is not likely that we are dealing with a member of one of those breeds.''

"Why not?''

"According to our history files, they never left witnesses.''

Rome shook his head. He did not believe in supermen. No matter how awful the Paratwa were, they were fallible. They could be defeated. An assassin in the Colonies was a problem that could be solved.

Another thought occurred to him. "These witnesses . . . do you think they're safe? They obviously got a good look at this creature.''

The Pasha wagged his head. "Even the lesser Paratwa breeds were thoroughly trained in the art of disguise. Many of them were reportedly so good that witnesses were later not even certain of their gender.'' Haddad paused. "I do not believe that the woman and her son are in any danger. To be on the safe side, though, we're going to keep them in our custody for as long as possible.''

Rome nodded. "Do we have a chance of capturing this creature before it kills again?''

"I tend to doubt it. To begin with, we should get our terminology straight. No one has ever *captured* a Paratwa assassin. When cornered, they fought to the death. Always.''

Rome took that in stride. "Do you think there will be any sort of panic when word of this assassin finally goes public?''

Haddad spoke slowly. "I believe . . . that there will be a certain degree of alarm within the more educated realms of our society—the people who are most aware of historical parameters and who might see themselves as possible targets for a Paratwa. I do not think there will be any panic among the general populace, at least at first.''

"You don't believe we can easily . . . stop this creature." It was more a statement than a question.

"It will be difficult."

"Recommendations?"

Haddad drew a deep breath. "We've got to learn more about the behavior of these creatures. There's a wealth of data in our historical archives, but there's no one alive today who has the background knowledge to formulate a specific plan of action. We should assign a priority crew to the historical section."

"How about Begelman?" E-Tech's archives were the finest and most complete in the Colonies and it was not difficult to access general data from the computers. But relevant information was sometimes hidden, improperly filed or lost amid gigabytes of similar data. Occasionally, E-Tech's original programmers of two centuries ago had deliberately camouflaged data within unrelated programs. There was an art to retrieving such information. Begelman was one of their finest computer hawks.

The Pasha typed something into his own console and waited a moment for the computer to respond. "Begelman is available. I'll have him assigned."

"Good." Rome felt like they were getting somewhere. It was a start, at any rate.

Another fear took shape. "What about La Gloria de la Ciencia?"

Haddad's eyes widened. "You think that they could have had something to do with bringing this assassin out of stasis?"

Rome knew he was being irrational. There was no logical reason why E-Tech's perpetual foes would risk their expanding power base by awakening a Paratwa. La Gloria de la Ciencia had existed for almost as long as E-Tech, but it was not until recently that the proscience fanatics had developed into full-fledged opponents. Their ultimate goal—never publicly stated, since it violated the Irryan constitution—was to eliminate Rome's organization and remove all limits and checks on science and technology. Just the thought of it made him wince.

Madmen—blind to history, blind to the horrors of pre-Apocalyptic Earth.

And I am afraid. Until this morning, he had not consciously recognized the fear. It had been like the steady hum of a generator—a background noise present for so long that it had come to seem natural.

Does consistency have a source? He had known for a long time that E-Tech was losing its hold throughout the Colonies. Five years ago, La Gloria de la Ciencia had gathered enough support to form a powerful voting bloc within the Senate. That had been a notable turning point—the recognition of a changing society. Rome had been aware of the altered parameters but he had never acknowledged the fear as a gut sensation. He had not truly felt afraid until this morning.

Is this what it was like for the humans of the pre-Apocalypse? he wondered. Had they lived with the horror of nuclear weapons, biological poisons, and genetic perversities for so long that they lost all touch with the corresponding fears?

Whatever the answer, living with such anxiety, acknowledged or otherwise, could not be good for the soul. And suffering souls created dangerous civilizations.

E-Tech must remain powerful.

Haddad waited patiently until Rome returned his attention to the screen.

"Although it's not likely to occur," the Pasha said, "we must give our Security people special orders in the event they come into contact with this assassin. They must ignore standard policy. They must attempt to kill the creature."

"Attempt" was the right word. Rome recalled disturbing tales of the Paratwa from his own childhood; of how some of them were able to wipe out scores, even hundreds of armed soldiers in open combat. They were bred to be fanatics—and trained for combat at an age when most human children were still in the throes of childhood.

The intercom twanged. The sharp features of his execsec dis-

44

solved onto the lower left corner of the screen. "Excuse me, sir, but your aides have all arrived. They have urged me to tell you that there is much information to go over before today's Council meeting."

"Send them to the upper conclave. I'll be there shortly."

"Very good, sir." The execsec's image disappeared.

Rome faced Haddad. "Keep me informed. If anything breaks, interrupt me at Council."

The Pasha nodded solemnly, vanished as Rome broke the contact.

He sat for a long moment staring at the darkened screen. *A Paratwa assassin.* An episode from childhood came to mind—a game that he and his friends used to play, a savage parody where two boys pretended to be a Paratwa, hunting down the others in the wild woodlands of Canopus Colony.

So long ago. The memory was still crisp, unimpeded by more than a half century. *And now I am the master of E-Tech and the game has become real.*

Another memory—a primary class in his ninth year; a rare non-Socratic seminar conducted by a shabbily dressed substitute teacher: ". . . and as countless miniwars raged across the Earth, E-Tech rose up and became a power, waging open battle with the inhuman Paratwa until the final days were upon them all . . ."

Abruptly, Rome stood up. His hands were shaking and he could feel beads of perspiration across his forehead. *We must remain powerful.* He sensed the hollowness of the thought—a mockery of strength to hide his feeling of weakness.

For I am afraid.

Bishop Vokir knew that his pleasures were changing. He did not know why. These days, he could stand here in his office for hours at a time, staring out the huge one-way picture window and absorbing the magnificent landscape that funneled away from him. The huge cylinder shrank in perspective as it retreated from vision, the sun and land sectors coming together miles away into a point that was the Colony's huge north polar plate. Thirty years ago, the vista had meant nothing to him. Thirty years ago he had felt no appreciation for the purity of magnitude.

Irrya was the capital of the two hundred and fourteen Colonies—the heart of civilization. The seventy-mile-long cylinder boasted a resident population of over twelve million and at any one time, another three to five million visitors breathed its air. Irrya defined urbanity. Had not half the land mass of the Colony been utilized for sunstrips, Irrya would have grown into one gigantic city. Even so, six hundred-foot stilted skyscrapers crept right up to the edge of the sun sectors, looking like giant beasts about to step off the edge of the world.

Everything points toward the center, the Bishop observed. It was an interesting, if not novel, thought. Other than a lack of gravity, there was nothing at the hub of any consequence. Some freefall swim circles and a few nontoxic industries, whose officials had probably bribed local politicians in order to secure zoning permits, accounted for centersky. Today, all were hidden behind a plodding apron of high cumulus clouds.

Bishop Vokir backed away from his picture window and depressed a wall switch, closing the curtain. Illumination came on automatically, bathing his small private office in golden light.

On Earth, humanity lived on the outside and looked up to gaze upon other possibilities. In the Colonies, humanity lives on the inside and looks up to gaze upon itself. Bishop Vokir could appreciate the difference, having lived within both realities. But he knew he lacked the ability of his monarch to distill the fine social relevancies from such a dialectic.

With a flurry of robes, he crossed the room and opened one of the telescoping peepholes disguised in the metafab tapestry of the wall. The huge chapel filled his sight.

It was an imposing theater, capable of seating two thousand worshipers when the motorized balconies were trolleyed into position. All the velvet-cushioned chairs faced the altar. Chrome pipes backdropped the chancel and flowed upward and outward to form the chapel ceiling. The shiny pipes were more than ornamental. Hidden behind the altar was the main pumping system that maintained a steady flow of organic fluid—blessed misk—through the pipes. Misk temperature was variable and served to keep the chapel at seventy degrees Fahrenheit, no matter how many warm bodies filled the arena.

Directly behind the steel lectern, a series of feeder tubes branched off the main pipes. They narrowed to form thin hoses, which hung like a veiled curtain across the front of the altar. Blue and green jewel lights were embedded in the hoses. From the Bishop's position off to the left side, no pattern was discernible. But to any of the three dozen worshipers currently meditating in the chapel, Church of the Trust would be spelled out by the symbolic colors of the Earth.

In turn, he zoomed the peephole toward each of the meditators who were scattered like ants across the main floor. A smile crinkled the Bishop's ancient eyes. The tways were well disguised indeed if he could not pick them out.

Caressing a hidden control dot on the tapestry, he tripped open the chapel's AV sensor system. Concealed cameras automatically focused on each meditator. A woman in the front row and a man kneeling along the furthest aisle did not register. Where faces should have been appeared only multicolored blurs.

I must warn him about using the scramblers. It occurred to the Bishop that the Jeek would already be aware of the risks. Reemul possessed many strange characteristics, but stupidity was not among them.

The woman moved first. She stood up and shuffled out a side door that led to the Bishop's chamber. He switched to his hallway peephole, watched her duck into his outer office. The other tway waited in the chapel for several minutes before repeating the woman's maneuver.

Bishop Vokir had already placed two chairs back to back. One faced him and the other faced the entrance. He sat down behind his laminated mahogany desk, touched the door control, and took a deep breath, preparing himself. A meeting with Reemul could easily mutate into an ordeal.

The Jeek entered his chamber. The woman came first, hands folded daintily in front of her blue cotton skirt. She halted just inside the office, allowed her eyes to appraise—the Bishop at his desk, the chairs, metafab wall, curtained window, wood-framed paintings, a central chandelier with pseudocandles flickering at odds with the golden light from the ceiling panels. She produced a sad-eyed grin and gracefully seated herself in the chair facing the Bishop. Legs crossed demurely; the skirt was tugged over her knees in a careful display of modesty.

"Such a pretty place, Bishop!" The voice was high and sweet, a good imitation of a real female's. "I do love the way you decorate—those gauze curtains, for instance—quite exquisite. My. Does your wife help with the decor?"

The man entered with a laugh, closing the door behind him. He was taller than she and neatly dressed in a high-collared brown jacket with matching pants. His face was shaven and the blond hair was bundled into a stylish ponytail that fell over his right shoulder.

"Such a wonderful Colony!" the woman exclaimed. Delicately, she ran a hand through her short brown hair. "Irrya is seventy miles long, I'm told! My. So big that it simply takes my breath away! And all those people, moving constantly, always busy, going from there to here and here to there and . . . oh, my. They seem so very . . . so very . . . ." She frowned. "Goodness! I can't think of the word."

"Helpless?" offered the man. He folded his arms and leaned against the wall next to the door.

The woman smiled brightly. "Yes! Just the word I was looking for!"

They both laughed.

The Bishop pretended to observe one of his desktop monitors. *Patience*. Serious conversation with Reemul had always been a problem; only a threat was guaranteed to push the Jeek into a more level mode.

The woman stood up and gazed at a framed still life on the wall behind the Bishop. "What an adorable painting!"

The man sat down with his back to them.

"May I have it?" the woman asked.

The Bishop shook his head.

"Pretty please?" asked the man.

"Pretty pretty please?" begged the woman.

"I can give you something better," offered the Bishop. "But first we must discuss your initial assignment."

Both heads nodded in unison.

"Bob Max is no longer among the living," said the woman. She winked at the Bishop.

"Complications?"

The woman stuck her tongue out and licked at the air. It was an obscene gesture.

So everything went as planned, the Bishop thought. It was best to make sure, though.

"What was the nature of your imitation?"

The woman crossed behind the Bishop and stopped in front of the painting.

"Cezanne?" asked the man.

"Yes," replied the Bishop. And he thought: *I sit between a Jeek and both tways have their backs to me.* "You're very trusting this morning," he said drily.

"Not really," replied the woman. Her voice was just a shade lower than before.

The man turned slowly. He spoke calmly. "Should you have attempted something rash, like reaching under your robes for a weapon, I would have heard you."

"You would have died before you had a chance to fire," said the woman.

The Bishop relaxed. This was the Reemul of two centuries ago—shrewd, distrustful, supremely confident. And the confidence was based on the purity of experience. Reemul did not brag. *He is the liege-killer. That is what the humans of two hundred years ago had called him.* It had been a name spoken in fear.

The man grinned. "Back in our time, Bishop, I would never have worried about turning my backs to you."

The Bishop projected astonishment. "You truly suspect treachery—from me?"

The woman laughed. "I've been asleep for hundreds of years, whereas you, Bishop; you and the mighty Codrus . . ."

"Don't ever voice that thought!" the Bishop snapped. "Not even here, within such privacy."

The man shrugged. "As you wish. It's just that there has been time, these past few days, to consider my awakening."

"Could it be," the woman continued, "that I am to be permanently put to sleep once this affair is over?"

The Bishop sighed. The Jeek merely needed soothing. "That Cezanne you admire—do you know why it is valuable?"

"It is ancient," said the man.

"Quite true. But what really makes it priceless is the fact that there are only four paintings by that artist still known to exist. It is almost unique . . . and by that virtue, irreplaceable."

The man stood up and turned to face him. "There were many Paratwa hidden before the Apocalypse. You said so yourself."

"And most of them perished," replied the Bishop. The thought illuminated an edge of genuine sadness. "Some capsules were damaged by poisons or plague—others were found and destroyed by the doomed humans remaining on Earth after the Apocalypse. E-Tech claimed their share." The Bishop paused. "I should have hidden all of them with the care I lavished on your entombment."

The woman's reply was brittle. "I will say this but once, Bishop. Don't ever cross me."

The Bishop nodded slowly. *Shrewd and distrustful.* Reemul could not help it—the qualities were part of his makeup. Such attributes elevated the Jeek Elementals above the other breeds, placed them among the deadliest of the assassins.

"As long as there are humans, you remain valuable," he concluded. "Now, let us return to my earlier question. What was the nature of your imitation?"

The woman moved to his side and hopped onto his desk. Sad eyes stared down at the Bishop.

The man spoke. "I portrayed the characteristics of one of those sloppy Terminus assassins. During the first contact with the witnesses, I gave the impression that I was having trouble walking— this called attention to me. I told outrageous lies that the woman did not believe, thereby further heightening her suspicions. I made one tway appear emotionally dead and the other gloriously alive!"

The woman chuckled.

"The witness had her gallery covered by a security system, so I had to use my AV scrambler in order to plant the bugs without being seen."

The Bishop frowned. "You are aware that few people utilize AV scramblers within the Colonies. Use them frequently and you will call attention to yourself whenever you pass under surveillance cameras."

With a sharp laugh, the man turned away. "My, but you do worry so!"

"If it will satisfy you," said the woman, "I won't use them again."

The Bishop drove home his point. "Hardly anyone in the Colonies has even heard of auto-targeting weapons. You have nothing to fear."

AV scramblers had originally been designed to foil the tracking systems contained in the sophisticated attack robots of the mid-twenty-first century. No such robots existed today—they had been successfully outlawed and contained by E-Tech.

The man continued. "When I returned to perform the kill, I made sure the witnesses were positioned to observe. They thought that I did not notice them hiding on their porch."

Again, the woman laughed.

"Naturally, I used a wand to destroy the target."

The Bishop allowed a smile. "Good. And the witness notified the authorities?"

"She only called E-Tech."

"Excellent." In the long run, it would not have made much difference who the witness contacted first. But the Bishop knew that Codrus preferred this variation. The plan would be well served when Rome Franco attended today's Council meeting, believing that only E-Tech was aware of the Paratwa.

The man grinned. "This could develop into an interesting game. I wonder how long it will take these E-Tech fools to come after me?"

"Don't underestimate them," the Bishop warned. "E-Tech is a far more complex organization than it was in our century."

The woman, seated on his desk, rubbed her bare leg against the Bishop's arm. "One of our monarchs taught me that complexity is a cavern for the blind."

Where did Reemul hear that? the Bishop wondered. *Sappho?*

"Anyway," the man continued, "E-Tech does not frighten me."

"Then again," added the woman, "nothing does."

The Bishop raised his hand in a futile effort to stop the Jeek's stereo laugh. There was no use trying to counter such an ego. He quickly changed the subject. "Where are you staying?"

"Sirak-Brath," the tways said in unison.

The Bishop shook his head. "That's an uncivilized place, Reemul. Pirates, smugglers—half the misfits in the Colonies wind up in that cylinder."

The woman smiled. "But Sirak-Brath has such interesting diversions . . ."

". . . special treats that make a Jeek's heart flutter," the man finished. He clapped his hands and laughed.

The Bishop had a fair idea what those diversions were. "Just be aware that E-Tech can track you by your vices."

The man spoke calmly. "I am aware. I shall be very selective in choosing my treats." He could not hold back a grin.

"Very selective, indeed," said the woman. "My. She will have to be quite young—between one and two would be ideal!"

Again, they both laughed.

The Bishop waited until Reemul calmed down. "Enjoy your games, but remain alert. E-Tech and the Guardians will soon be tearing apart the Colonies to find you."

"Let them tear," said the man. His expression denoted complete disinterest.

"But let me tear first," said the woman.

An intense look suddenly exploded across both of Reemul's faces; a hunger that widened the eyes and tensed the muscles.

The Bishop responded quickly. "You used to have better self-control."

The twin gazes fluttered momentarily, then broke into identical smiles. They spoke in unison. "The mighty Codrus knows that the sword must be used lest the swordsman grow dull."

Reemul became motion. The woman leaped—the man lunged. A tablet of hand-scrolled documents was knocked from the Bishop's desk. By the time the tablet hit the floor, the black light of a Cohe wand wavered inches away from the Bishop's neck.

The woman stood off to his side, the weapon clutched in her fist. He could feel the heat of its unbound energy. A slight twist of the wrist and Reemul could decapitate him.

The man leaned across the desk until their faces were only inches apart. The Bishop smelled orange cologne. He saw the hunger in Reemul's eyes.

The Bishop felt no fear. "I told you there would be more . . . many more."

The man hissed. "I cannot wait."

"You must."

"I cannot."

The man backed away. The black light of the Cohe vanished. The Bishop turned and watched the woman replace the wand in a slip-wrist holster beneath her sleeve.

"I cannot wait," the man repeated. He was calm again, but a hint of wildcat remained in his eyes.

The Bishop folded his hands on his lap. *Reemul must be allowed to flex. I've got to turn him loose ahead of the plan.*

His monarch, Codrus, had intended using the Jeek slowly and with discretion—the murder of Irryan diplomats on their way to a bioconference in Jordanian Paris next week, the destruction of an E-Tech warehouse on Oslo a few days later. But Reemul's needs would have to take precedence.

Flexing—the mental orgasm of being totally out of control. No one—not even Sappho—had ever fully understood the deep-seated urges afflicting all Paratwa. One theory suggested that flexing was a way for pain to be released from the system, for the interlace to keep itself healthy. Many Paratwa had been raised under rigorously imposed discipline and had learned to equate suppression of feeling with virtue. Such training produced a burden of internalized pain. That pain needed to be periodically expunged.

Whatever the theory, Reemul's flexing urge would have to be relieved. The Jeek had to go mad—kill without restraint.

Codrus had allowed for this eventuality. Reemul could not yet be permitted to carve an open path of destruction through the Colonies. But there were other ways for an assassin to flex.

"Come, Reemul. I have decided to give you an assignment that will allow your spirit to excel." The Bishop keyed his desk terminal and a multicolored geomap of the Colony of Northern California appeared on the screen. The woman circled the desk and peered over his shoulder.

"Right here," the Bishop pointed. A cursor flew across the screen to stab into a heavily wooded area in the center portion of the sixteen mile-long Colony. He sensed, rather than saw, the double smile alighting on Reemul's faces. "Here is a place where you may have your way."

* * *

Reemul exited, one tway at a time so as not to arouse any suspicions. The Bishop watched his surveillance monitors and was pleased by the way the Jeek blended into the crowded Irryan thorofare outside the Church. At the end of the block, the woman crossed the street and stopped to help a very old man who was weighted down with packages and who was having trouble getting over the curb. A few moments later, Reemul, the good Samaritan, vanished into the masses.

The Bishop dimmed his office lighting until only a dull glow surrounded the desk. From the top drawer, he withdrew a small mounted photograph depicting the original Church of the Trust. The squat rectangular building had stood at the corner of a narrow London street over two hundred years ago.

At the time of the photograph, the Church had just begun to attract millions into its fold, becoming a powerful symbol of the planet's hope—an icon for human salvation from the madness of a doomed world. The Bishop remembered well those early days. He had gone by another name, of course, but his sermons had been as powerful as they were today and he had drawn crowds from all over the planet. Back then, the Church had even attracted worshipers from the new orbiting Colonies; converts inspired by one of his frequent satellite transmissions. In an era of massive human misery, a Church that responded to the antithesis of that misery could not help but succeed.

Inscribed at the bottom of the photograph was the phrase *Spirit of Gaia*. The Bishop touched the letters in the proper sequence and the image of the Church dissolved into speckles of silver. In a moment, the transformation was complete. His own reflected face appeared in the frame.

He threw his thoughts into the mirror, knowing that his tway was doing the same. The Bishop was powerful and so was the one he was interlacing with, but neither of them could hope to match the intense mind of Codrus, their monarch. And Codrus had to learn of the Bishop's decision regarding the flexing of Reemul. Only an Ash Ock Paratwa could hope to grasp all the ramifications.

He spoke clearly. "I am Councillor Rome Franco."

The imposing black door silently activated its scanners and made hundreds of instantaneous comparisons between the squat curly-haired man standing before it and the ROME FRANCO contained in its data banks. The door was intelligent enough to ignore some slight discrepancies, concluding rightly that the Councillor had expanded his caloric intake in the four days since the last Council meeting without a corresponding increase in physical exercise. The door was not programmed to chide him about such things.

The door opened and Rome entered the inner chamber of the Council of Irrya, paramount governing body of the Colonies. A polished round table, ringed by ten evenly spaced chairs, dominated the twenty-sided room. Data terminals rose from the armrests of the five plushest seats—the other chairs were reserved for Council guests. A huge prism chandelier, supported by wire mesh that disappeared into the darkness of the arched ceiling, hung to within six feet of the table. Wood-framed paintings stared out from leather-veneered walls; oil originals, mostly, dating from before the Apocalypse. Each painting was sealed behind a glareless humidity partition.

Rome felt a familiar twinge of guilt at the sight of those paintings. *Enough wealth to build a Colony*, he thought.

Many years ago, as a freshman Councillor, he had proposed that they sell the artwork and reinvest the money in the general fund. His suggestion had been politely declined. It had been one of his first real lessons in high-level politics. One does not sell the symbols of one's power.

And in the ensuing years, Rome had come to greatly admire one of the masterpieces: a savagely brushstroked cornfield; yellows and browns on an ancient canvas. He deliberately refrained from learning more about the artist through E-Tech's vast historical archives. Somehow, he felt that such knowledge would destroy, or at least reduce, his appreciation of the painting.

Angela felt his self-control was paradoxical. When he mentioned the canvas to her from time to time, she urged him to learn all he could about the artist, to enhance his passion. *It is not necessary,* he would reply stoically. The painting existed as a whole complete thing; its life grew from the colors. Vincent Van Gogh would remain a mystery.

"Greet-ings, Fran-co." The artificially generated voice came from a pair of tiny wafer speakers implanted in the lower cheeks of a regal, black-haired woman. Nu-Lin, Councillor of Intercolonial Affairs and head of the Commerce League, looked stunning, as usual. A sleeveless blue gown swirled from her shoulders, fell across her breasts, and exploded into a waffled pattern as it reached her ankles. The narrow face betrayed few signs of age, though Rome knew she was at least sixty. Thick hair was pulled back into reverse bangs, allowing the gleaming blue eyes to dominate.

Her mouth remained closed as she spoke. "Re-fresh-ment, per-haps? Drake and I have or-dered."

Rome crossed the chamber to stand beside her. "I'm afraid Angela and I had a rather large breakfast this morning." He patted his bulging stomach.

Nu-Lin smiled. "A pi-ty. Drake has had his chef pre-pare fi-let jas-ka à la misk. I un-der-stand that on-ly in the fi-nest res-taur-ants of Vel-vet on the Green can such a del-i-ca-cy be found." The gold-shadowed eyes widened—a gesture intimating Drake's passion for expensive dining.

She had lost her speech center in a childhood accident. A person of lesser character would have suffered from such a disability, but Nu-Lin had an innate dignity that overwhelmed her robotic articulation. More lifelike vocal generators were available too, but

Rome felt she had made the right decision in having a primitive model implanted. She distinguished her infirmity rather than trying to hide it.

"Where is Drake?" Rome asked.

"In his cham-bers . . . a pri-vate call."

"You've seen today's agenda."

"A full pro-gram." She stroked the fur bracelet below her el-bow. "Those two new Sen-ate bills a-lone mer-it hours of dis-cus-sion. And our es-teemed Coun-cil-lor Art-whil-er has made a late ad-di-tion."

Late, indeed! Rome had just come from the briefing with his aides and no last-minute programming had come into their termi-nals.

"Art-whil-er wishes to bol-ster our per-i-me-ter warn-ing sys-tem. He claims that we are gross-ly un-pre-pared for the pos-si-bi-li-ty of in-va-sion." Her eyes danced.

Rome would have laughed had it not been for the fact that too many of Artwhiler's ideas were being endorsed by the Council these days. "What is it this time—the return of the starships?"

Nu-Lin nodded.

Five years ago, Artwhiler had begun a lengthy campaign to gain support for a series of deep-space probes. The unmanned ships would have been sent out in the direction of the original starships, which had been launched from orbit during the final days.

The two great hopes for humanity: the Colonies and the star-ships. The Colonies had proven themselves, had enabled millions of people to escape the dying Earth. Hundreds of thousands of others had opted for a more distant and precarious future. The Star-Edge project had constructed huge vessels in Earth orbit and had launched them from the solar system in an effort to reach other colonizable worlds.

Something had gone wrong, though. One hundred and seventy years ago, the regular transmissions had begun hinting of trouble. There was dissension aboard the starships—people had been brought out of stasis ahead of schedule; fighting had erupted. Some of the crew had wanted to turn back; others had insisted on pushing on. The conflict had expanded into armed combat. The last message told of nuclear detonations destroying several of the vessels. No further transmissions were ever received.

Artwhiler had publicly expressed concern that some of the star voyagers might have survived and could someday return as enemies of the Colonies. Deep-space probes would give humanity advance warning, allow time for Colonial defenses to be expanded to meet any threats.

Artwhiler had garnered a disturbingly large amount of support for his theory, though not enough to sway the Council into diverting funds to his Office of Intercolonial Guardians. He had apparently given up the campaign three years ago.

"My sources in-form me that Coun-cil-lor Art-whil-er has had a fall-ing out with his lat-est mis-tress." Her face took on an expression of mock sympathy. "He is feel-ing in-se-cure a-gain."

Rome could not help it—he had to laugh. "Do you think this will blow over?"

"Per-haps. If not, we shall have to come up with a way to de-fuse him."

The door opened. Elliot Drake strode into the chamber. He was a six-foot-six, black-skinned giant—a ghost of one of those ancient football linebackers who used to brutalize each other in an effort to move a small object from one end of a field to the other. Rome had seen the videos.

Angela was somewhat in awe of Drake. She claimed that he possessed *elan vital*, which was her way of saying that Drake could walk into a room and command attention without having to utter a word. Rome had pointed out to his wife that Drake was usually *bigger* than everyone else in the room and would naturally command immediate attention. Angela rejected the argument as spurious. Rome found Angela's awe of Drake more mystifying than the man himself.

"Battle strategies?" The voice matched Drake's size—a deep bass that seemed only a few decibels beneath a shout.

"Na-tur-al-ly. The be-sieged must re-main a-lert."

Drake grunted out a laugh. "I've word that Artwhiler is going to force a vote today to create his Research Applications Institute."

"We've been through this before," Rome said calmly. "Artwhiler has no legal base to stand on. His proposal violates the Irryan constitution."

"It did. But he's engineered a new variation. The Institute he now envisions will become a precursor to E-Tech, will deal strictly in feasibility studies, and will pass along all recommendations to your people." Drake paused. "He has strong Senate support. And Lady Bonneville is favoring the plan."

Another thorn in E-Tech's side, Rome thought. It was obvious, though, that Drake was going to propose some sort of a deal. With Rome and Nu-Lin firmly on one side of the fence, and Artwhiler and Lady Bonneville generally on the other, Drake, as the fifth Councillor, could swing the vote either way.

Drake lowered his voice. "I've got word that the two of you intend cosponsoring a special subsidy fund to renovate Sirak-Brath."

So that's it, Rome thought. "To begin to renovate," he corrected.

Drake shook his massive head. "It's an unwise project."

Nu-Lin narrowed her eyes. "A worth-y cause, Coun-cil-lor."

"Yes, it is. And I do not dispute your motives, merely your business sense. There is a long history of money being spent to rejuvenate that Colony and an equally long history of failure. My people compute that less than fifteen percent of the funds targeted for rebuilding are actually spent there for that purpose. Sirak-Brath must be politically cleansed before any real change can occur."

"How do you pro-pose to ac-com-plish such change with-out at least some fi-nan-cial in-vest-ment?"

Drake shrugged. "I believe that we're on the right track in cracking down on the pirates. Sirak-Brath is a hotbed of Costeau trouble. If we can remove their influence, some real change might be initiated."

Nu-Lin nodded. Although she favored renovation, she basically agreed with Drake's opinions regarding the Costeaus.

Rome argued, "The pirates have been with us for two hundred years and no one has yet found a way to get rid of them. It's folly to hinge Sirak-Brath's restoration on a solution to the Costeau problem."

Drake stared down at Rome. His face looked like it had been abruptly turned into black marble. "The ICN does not share your view."

ICN—the Intercolonial Credit Net—the banking and finance consortium that was the key to Elliot Drake's strength. The ICN controlled the monetary-exchange system throughout the Colonies and Drake steered its course within this chamber. In purely financial terms, Drake was one of the most powerful men in the cylinders.

Rome played out the game. "In the matter of Sirak-Brath, Artwhiler and Lady Bonneville support us."

"Yes, it's a popular cause." Drake scratched his chin and smiled. "But perhaps the two of you could postpone this subsidy fund idea for a few years."

Rome glanced at Nu-Lin, caught her nod. "Perhaps we could hold off on the proposal for six months."

"The ICN would not like to have to address this matter for at least another year."

Again, Rome exchanged looks with Nu-Lin. "Agreed. One year."

The black giant smiled. "I no longer believe that I can openly support Artwhiler's Research Institute . . . not this year."

"An ab-sten-tion will not suf-fice," Nu-Lin warned.

"Absolutely not," Rome added. If Drake abstained, forcing a tie vote, the matter would be decided by the Irryan Senate. There was little love for E-Tech among the 642 Senators. These days, many of them would vote against Rome's position on principle.

Drake shrugged his huge shoulders. "Artwhiler's proposal will be defeated three to two."

Another trade-off, Rome thought. From a political standpoint, such deals made sense. But he remembered a time when E-Tech had dictated the terms of such arrangements.

A beeper sounded beneath Drake's coat. The Councillor excused himself and marched to the door. He ordered it to open. Two young chef-servants entered the chamber, carrying steaming white platters. Drake told them where to place the luncheons.

Nu-Lin sat down and began to gently pick at her filet. Rome regretted not ordering. The beef derivative smelled good.

He took his seat and activated his typer-console, automatically opening communication lines to a dozen E-Tech departments. Scrambled teletext appeared on the screen, changing to English as he typed in the current security codes. There were no messages but all departments signaled they were ready for access.

The fourth Councillor strode into the chamber with his head raised and his chin thrust forward. Augustus J. Artwhiler gave the room a regal scan, fastened his gaze on Rome for a long moment, then took his place at the table. His black and gold uniform was adorned with medals, including three white cylinders on each collar denoting his rank as Supreme Commander of the Intercolonial Guardians. The blocky face bore the faint trace of a smile. Angela claimed that she had never seen Artwhiler without that expression, whether on television or in person at one of the many banquets or public functions that she and Rome attended. She said that Artwhiler reminded her of a schoolboy who had just gotten away with cheating on a test. Rome wished things were that simple.

Drake's voice boomed. "Irryan Council will come to order. Let it be shown that a quorum is present and that Lady Bonneville will not attend today's meeting. I believe she has contacted us concerning individual proxy votes."

Artwhiler smiled.

"Old business first," Drake intoned. "We'll maintain regular order and begin with Nu-Lin."

Artwhiler interrupted. "With the Council's permission, I request that we postpone old business and move right along to new matters.''

What's he up to this time? Rome wondered.

"Objections?" Drake asked, forking a mouthful of filet jaska. The black face panned the table, searching for dissent. No one spoke.

"That puts E-Tech first, Franco."

Rome stood up slowly, gathering his thoughts. There were several new issues he wished to raise, but they all hinged on the conclusion of various pieces of old business. The subsidy proposal for Sirak-Brath would have been the only unfettered item on his agenda.

"E-Tech has no new business at this time."

Artwhiler broke into a wide grin and threw a sharp glance at Drake. The black Councillor frowned.

Rome sat down quickly. *Something's wrong.* Artwhiler looked like he had just scored perfect grades on an exam.

The Guardian Commander rose to his feet. His tone was triumphant.

"Fellow Councillors," he began with a sweep of his arms. "It is no great secret that each of us maintains our own little pockets of information, our own sources of data, and that we keep these things hidden from the Council." He paused. "We are, after all, political animals." His smile vanished as quickly as it had appeared. "But to deliberately hide a matter from this Council that could affect the future welfare of some of our citizenry indicates a selfishness that I did not believe Councillor Franco was capable of!"

He knows about the Paratwa! It was the only possible explanation. Rome typed rapidly, opened a line to Security.

HADDAD READY, appeared on the screen.

Artwhiler leaned back in his seat and smiled. "I suppose that Councillor Franco concluded that the mighty E-Tech could deal with a Paratwa assassin without our help. Pride is a strange vice.''

Rome typed: ARTWHILER AND DRAKE KNOW ABOUT PARATWA. Then he half rose, attempting to interject.

Drake stopped him cold. "Councillor Artwhiler has the floor."

The Guardian Commander could barely contain himself; the words came out in a rapid jumble. He described last night's murder of Bob Max and how two witnesses were taken into custody after they contacted E-Tech. Rome listened with amazement, transcribing Artwhiler's words into the keyboard while keeping an eye on the screen for Haddad's response.

Nu-Lin turned to him. "Is this true?"

Rome nodded. He could offer that he had intended to bring the Paratwa matter to their attention later in the meeting, but no one would believe such a lie. E-Tech's credibility had just taken a swift kick. Soon, the bruises would start appearing.

The screen printed. HADDAD. NOT LIKELY THAT LEAKS CAME FROM OUR OWN PEOPLE. SUSPECT THE TWO WITNESSES OF INFORMING ARTWHILER.

Artwhiler pointed his finger at Rome. "Security matters of this magnitude are to be brought immediately before this Council."

"Agreed," said Drake. "E-Tech has no right to preclude us."

"I be-lieve Rome should be al-lowed to of-fer an ex-plan-a-tion."

Artwhiler gave Nu-Lin a gracious smile. "I relinquish the floor."

Rome remained seated. He spoke with as much calm as he could muster, recounting the chronology of Paratwa events and adding a few facts that the Guardian Commander had not touched upon. He addressed the three Councillors in turn, but made sure that he was facing Artwhiler whenever he mentioned something new.

Augustus J. Artwhiler was a shrewd man, but Rome had learned long ago that he did not possess a subtle face. Artwhiler could be read; a flicker of eyebrows, the quiver of jaw muscles—or the lack of such—served to reveal his thoughts.

Artwhiler's expressions seemed to bear out Haddad's theory.

The Guardian Commander did not know that Bob Max had Costeau contacts, nor did he know about the stasis capsules stolen from Philadelphia several days ago. It was unlikely that the woman and her son knew of those things either. The witnesses could be lying. They might indeed have told someone else about the killing.

Rome finished his explanation. "E-Tech did not want word of this assassin to spread. Full public disclosure at this time could greatly hinder any efforts to track down the creature."

Artwhiler twisted his lips. "You are suggesting that informing this Council is the same as public disclosure?"

Rome regarded him wryly. "It's been known to happen that way."

"A flimsy excuse, Franco," said Drake, wolfing down his last strip of beef. "It was your duty, as an Irryan Councillor, to inform us without delay."

Arthwiler quoted: "Irryan charter, chapter one, paragraph seven—'Knowledge of living binary interlinks shall be made available to the council.'"

"I'm aware of the law," Rome said coldly. "I'm also aware, as a sovereign of E-Tech, that a Paratwa assassin in the Colonies constitutes a grave and unique threat."

Artwhiler barked laughter. "Let us not lose our sense of proportion. A solitary Paratwa amid a billion people is certainly no cause for serious alarm."

"I must differ with you. A Paratwa in the Colonies could prove to be a severe problem."

Artwhiler sneered. "The severe problem, as you say, is the manner in which E-Tech has tried to hide this incident. Perhaps you wanted the capture of the Paratwa to be reserved for your own organization. Perhaps you wish to return E-Tech to its former glory."

Rome felt his guts tighten. He had let Artwhiler's previous remark pass. But not this time. "Pride is a weakness usually reserved for the hopelessly vain, Councillor."

Artwhiler started to rise in anger. Drake intervened. "Enough.

We'll get nowhere hurling insults. As I see it, there are two matters to be dealt with. One—E-Tech's breach of an Irryan law. And two—the possible threat of the Paratwa itself.''

"Ag-reed," said Nu-Lin, chewing on a morsel of filet. Her ability to eat and talk simultaneously, without violating any rules of etiquette, seemed perfectly natural. "I sug-gest that a-ny dis-ci-pli-nar-y ac-tion a-gainst E-Tech be post-poned un-til La-dy Bonn-e-ville is pre-sent.''

"I favor that," said Drake. "Is a vote necessary?"

Artwhiler scowled. "I believe that E-Tech's failure to inform is the major issue here. But in the interest of fairness, I'll agree to a postponement.''

Drake nodded. "Good. Then we'll discuss how to handle this Paratwa problem. Franco has the floor.''

"Thank you." Rome typed rapidly, opened a line to E-Tech's historical section. "May I begin, Councillors, with some basic background information on these creatures?"

Artwhiler broke into a tight smile. "We do not need a history lesson.''

"Franco has the floor," Drake repeated.

Artwhiler crossed his arms and leaned back with a grim smile. Rome began reading from the screen.

"The first Paratwa was created in the mid-twenty-first century. Scottish scientists injected a pair of lab-bred human fetuses with cells from another artificially grown lifeform, called a McQuade Unity. The McQuade Unity had rocked the scientific establishment several years earlier when it was discovered that two samples from one of these primitive cellular masses were capable of remaining in telepathic contact with each other, even when separated by thousands of miles.

"Segments of this McQuade Unity were injected into these fetuses in the hope that the two genetically different humans would develop a permanent telepathic link. But what actually occurred was far more significant.

"The two fetuses metamorphosed into a single consciousness.

The McQuade Unity enabled their brain patterns to interlace—to develop as one entity. The result was a creature with one discrete awareness—one mental/emotional consciousness—yet inhabiting two randomly selected physical bodies. The first Paratwa had been born—a creature with four arms, four legs, two sets of eyes and ears, and the incredible ability to exist simultaneously in two separate locations."

Rome paused, accessed another page on the screen. "In 2058, the New Jersey division of Intellitech Hydrocomco released the first brood of combat Paratwa onto the world armaments market. From a military standpoint, these combat models were an immediate success. By the year 2070, with the world coming apart at the seams and over a hundred miniwars being fought on any given day, the demand for these Paratwa increased to almost astronomical proportions. By the year 2080, there were over thirty different breeds available from the genetic labs of two dozen countries.

"Warriors, bodyguards, assassins . . . the genetic labs created them and sold them to the highest bidders.

"Accelerated developmental programs were used to train the Paratwa. The breeding labs utilized drug and neuromuscular enhancers—anything that might give their Paratwa an edge over the competition.

"By the time a binary interlink reached the age of five, it had already learned to hunt and kill its own food. They were trained in all methods of hand combat and were given state-of-the-art weaponry. By 2090, there were two breeds—namely the Russian Voshkof Rabbits and the North American Jeek Elementals—that were considered undefeatable in normal combat situations."

Artwhiler shook his head and smiled. "Councillors, I must interrupt. Our E-Tech colleague is quite probably correct in his history of these creatures. But undefeatable? Perhaps two hundred years ago that was true, with thousands of them on the loose. There was corporate and national disintegration everywhere and there was biological and nuclear terrorism rampant across the globe. It is only natural that the citizenry of that awful era perceived these Paratwa in the darkest light.''

He opened his arms expansively. "Fortunately, we are not living under pre-Apocalyptic conditions. We have over a billion citizens spread across two hundred and fourteen Colonies and we have *one* possible Paratwa. Let us not overlook simple arithmetic. I do not believe that any single creature is too awesome for my Guardians to contain.''

Rome wanted to argue that the Colonies were indeed heading toward a new set of pre-Apocalyptic conditions. It would have been a waste of breath.

Drake spoke quietly. "Perhaps E-Tech has overreacted. This is quite understandable. After all, Rome, your organization was primarily responsible for containing the original Paratwa threat and you naturally feel duty-bound to handle the current situation. But one wild assassin amid a billion people does not seem particularly frightening.''

Rome continued reading. "The Paratwa threat was stopped not so much by human intervention, but by the Apocalypse of 2099. The obliteration of our homeworld succeeded in destroying the assassins, along with most of humanity." He paused. "Yet during the final days—that thirty-year period preceding the Apocalypse— some seven thousand Paratwa assassins were believed to have been directly responsible for the deaths of over one hundred and fifty million human beings.''

Artwhiler released a deliberately loud sigh. "Yes, we're impressed by your figures. It was a terrible time for humanity. But as you said, Rome, the Paratwa were seven thousand strong. And they were organized.''

"Precisely," said Drake. "They were under the spell of those mad leaders.''

"The Ash Ock," Artwhiler clarified. "And your own records show that those of the royal Caste were destroyed.''

Artwhiler turned to Drake. "I propose that the Council officially relegate this problem to my Guardians. I truly believe we can deal with this anachronism in short order.''

Rome clenched his fists. ''E-Tech must handle this investigation. We have the most extensive records on these assassins and we are most equipped to deal with them. Past experience . . .''

''This is not a twenty-first-century problem,'' Drake pointed out. ''I see no advantage in having an E-Tech–controlled investigation.''

''I must raise another objection, then. Councillor Artwhiler's frequent public support of La Gloria de la Ciencia should preclude the Guardians from this investigation.''

Nu-Lin frowned. ''Do you have rea-son to sus-pect that La Glo-ri-a de la Ci-en-ci-a is in-volved with this crea-ture?''

Rome hesitated. There was no sense in lying. ''We have no evidence indicating that. I wish to point out, however, that on several recent occasions, La Gloria de la Ciencia has suggested that Paratwa research be reinstituted.''

Artwhiler reddened. ''Come now, Franco! They were speaking only of a general research project that would examine the binary interlink phenomenon in a more positive light. They were certainly not advocating the awakening of a Paratwa assassin from two centuries ago!''

''You're reaching,'' Drake said quietly.

Rome looked at Nu-Lin for support. There was something akin to sympathy in her deep blue eyes, but she remained silent. She did not join lost causes.

Drake called for a vote. It was a quick show of hands—two to one, with Nu-Lin abstaining. Artwhiler was placed in charge of the Paratwa investigation.

Rome swallowed his bitterness. ''Should the Guardians desire any assistance, E-Tech will naturally make every effort.''

Artwhiler basked in his victory. ''Very generous, Rome, very generous. I'll have a liaison sent to your headquarters.''

Rome knew that the Guardian Commander would fulfill that promise. He also knew that the effort would be a token one. He doubted if Artwhiler's people would even be interested in accessing the Paratwa archives.

"The matter is closed," announced Drake. "Councillor Artwhiler, do you have any other new business?"

"Indeed I do. Some information has just fallen into Guardian hands that suggests that we should begin a concerted effort to bolster our perimeter warning system. An independent study has recently been completed and the results strongly indicate that the Colonies are grossly unprepared for the possibility of invasion. I have keyed this study into your monitors. Please refer to item fourteen on the agenda."

Rome sighed and caught Nu-Lin's subtle frown. She had obviously not come up with a way to defuse Artwhiler on this issue.

It was going to be a long meeting.

Paula and Jerem were detained at E-Tech's Lamalan headquarters, in New Armstrong, for nearly eighteen hours. They were questioned, probed, and badgered to exhaustion by an endless parade of solemn men and women who trickled through the utilitarian room where they were being held. Most of the inquisitors seemed to be professional bureaucrats. They were impossible to communicate with.

"Are we prisoners?" Paula had asked several times. Words varied slightly but the response was inevitably the same. "Of course not, Ms. Marth. We are merely trying to assure a condition of safety prior to your release from our protective custody." Then they would smile and offer her and her son something to eat. Jerem ordered boysenberry pancakes three times in the space of five hours. He threw up at eleven o'clock Sunday morning.

They only managed six hours sleep, side by side on a small

sofabed in the corner of the room. On Saturday night, with the killing still fresh in her mind, Paula was too tired to be angry about the way they were being treated. But by morning she was ready for a fight.

She accused E-Tech of harassment and threatened to expose their actions to the freelancers. These unofficial news reporters had their own Intercolonial channels and were always eager for stories hinting at official incompetence. The freelancers provided an alternative to the organizational channels—the huge networks run by E-Tech, the Guardians, the Profarmers, the Commerce League, and whoever else had enough money to sponsor their own telecasts. It was frequently suggested that the freelancers disliked all organizations equally and thereby managed to paint a fairer picture of Colonial life.

Paula demanded that she and Jerem be freed, promising the most dire consequences if they were not. At one point she threatened to kick a grinning little bureaucrat in the crotch after he slyly suggested that they were perhaps in league with the Paratwa killer. He had backed away from her, smirking: "Now, now, Ms. Marth. We mustn't get excited."

At two o'clock Sunday afternoon, a bald man with a lean dark face entered the room. Paula recognized him from E-Tech telecasts.

"I'm Pasha Haddad. I am prepared to give the order for your release. All I require from you is one small bit of information."

"What do you want?"

He sat down facing them. "I must learn who it is you contacted prior to calling us last night."

She shook her head wearily. "No one."

"Come now, Ms. Marth. We know you called someone. Was it the Guardians? Or perhaps the local police?"

What was left of her calm veneer began to splinter. "Listen, I don't care who the hell you are, but I'm sick and tired of this room and these damned questions. I've tried to help you and all I get is a runaround and more questions."

Cold eyes appraised her. "Maybe you would like to talk with me alone. We can take your son to another room . . ."

She threw her arm around Jerem and clutched him. "He stays here." She was prepared to physically fight if they attempted to touch her son. Haddad had no trouble reading her intentions.

He spoke calmly. "We do not want to harm you, Ms. Marth. Believe me, I truly understand your anger. But you must be aware that you have involved yourself in a very grave situation. If necessary, we must err on the side of caution."

"I've told you everything."

"Maybe you've overlooked some minor detail. Another phone call, perhaps?"

Paula sighed. "After the killing, I made one call—to your people, here in New Armstrong. And I'm beginning to think that that call was a mistake."

Haddad gave her a tight smile, then turned to Jerem. "Son, your mother is telling the truth, isn't she?"

Jerem nodded vigorously.

"And if she was lying, you'd tell me the truth, wouldn't you?"

"She never lies!" he said indignantly.

Haddad reached over and patted Jerem on the shoulder. "Of course she doesn't."

Paula gripped her son's hand. "We've told you everything."

"Of course you have. But in going through our records, Ms. Marth, it turns out that we have a bit of a file on you. You are known to have had dealings with some major black marketeers here in New Armstrong."

"Prove it." If they had evidence implicating her in black-market referrals, they would not have waited this long to threaten her with it.

Haddad smiled grimly. "It is doubtful that we can prove your involvement. You know that. But perhaps now, Ms. Marth, you can begin to see our dilemma. On the one hand, you claim to be telling us the truth about this incident. Yet we know that Marth Antiques has done illegal trading and we know that your neighbor,

Bob Max, was a major conduit to the black market and that he dealt directly with Costeaus. Which truth would you have us believe, Ms. Marth?''

Paula seethed. "Bob Max was a neighbor—nothing more. He was hardly ever at home and when he was, we didn't associate with him. If he knew Costeaus, that was his business."

"Then you did not know any of Max's Costeau friends?"

"No."

Haddad pretended to look puzzled. "But you do know some Costeaus?"

She hesitated. "Yes, I've met a few. That's not illegal, nor unusual for someone in the antique business."

"No, it is not. But, Ms. Marth, judging by this file, I would say that you've done a bit more than simply *meet* a few Costeaus."

Paula felt herself tense. "This has absolutely nothing to do with Bob Max's murder. You should be out hunting for this creature rather than persecuting me and my son!"

Haddad smiled. "E-Tech is a large organization. We are not all in this room . . . persecuting you."

"For the last time, we've told you the truth."

"Have you?" Haddad gazed at Jerem. "Son, did you know your father?"

"His father," Paula snapped, "died ten years ago, when Jerem was only two years old. Jerem never knew his father, nor anything about him, other than what I've told him." *And I wish to keep it that way!*

Paula caught Jerem staring at her. She avoided his eyes.

Haddad nodded with understanding. "All right, Ms. Marth, we will not go into certain matters. Not now, at any rate. But if we discover that you've been lying to us, I'm afraid we'll have to openly discuss some of your . . . Costeau relationships. Understood?"

She nodded. "You've made yourself very clear." A feeling of relief washed over her.

Jerem's vision of his father was a fabrication. Over the years,

Paula had carefully cultivated an image of a strong working man whose life had been cut short by a freak accident. Jerem was better off with the lie, although Paula knew someday he would have to learn the truth.

"All we need, Ms. Marth, is the name of the person or organization that you contacted last night. We are not interested in any other aspects of your personal dealings."

She shook her head wearily. "For the last time, I called no one."

A woman stepped into the room. "Sir, there's a call for you."

"Not now."

"Sir, it's Director Franco. The Council meeting is over and he wishes to speak with you immediately."

Haddad stood up and stared down at them. He spoke like a stern father, addressing errant children. "When I return, I expect some straight answers. The seriousness of this situation demands it." He marched out, leaving them alone in the room.

Jerem scratched at his cheek. "Mom, I don't think he believes us."

"He doesn't."

"How come he's asking all that stuff about Costeaus? Do you really know Costeaus?"

Paula glanced at the far corner, where earlier she had spotted one of the hidden microcams. "In the past, I knew some Costeaus. Not anymore." No doubt their words were also being recorded.

Jerem folded his hands tightly across his chest. "Do ya think they're going to let us go soon?"

She rumpled his hair. "I don't know. I hope so."

He frowned. "Do ya think maybe they're making us stay here 'cause they don't want us to get hurt?"

"What do you mean?"

"You know—like the kind of stuff we learned about at school. Like the Paratwa."

She put her arm around him. He did not resist her affection. "Oh, Jerem! No one's going to hurt us! And that Paratwa is probably in another Colony by now.'' She squeezed him tighter. "Hey, Mom says it'll be all right! I guess that's 'Ma sa fine' in Quikie, huh?''

He pouted. "That's not Quikie.''

She smiled. "You could teach me?''

"It's private. Do ya think that the Paratwa saw us last night on the porch and is just waiting for us to be released?''

There was no use in trying to deter him from his line of questioning. "Jerem, we're going to be okay. I promise. Even if that creature did see us, I really don't think it cared one way or another. They're supposed to be able to disguise themselves so well that we probably wouldn't even recognize it if we saw it again. We couldn't identify it so we're no threat to it.''

"I'd recognize it.''

Maybe he would. Paula certainly felt that way in the back of her own mind. Smiler and Sad-eyes were imprinted onto her consciousness.

Haddad returned, wearing an angry expression. "You are to be released. I'll have one of my people drive you to wherever you desire.''

She raised an eyebrow. "Why the sudden change of heart?''

"This investigation has been officially turned over to the Intercolonial Guardians.''

Paula felt no sympathy for him, but she did feel obligated that he know the truth. "I want to say this one more time. Neither my son nor I contacted anyone but E-Tech last night. I have no reason to lie about this.''

Haddad looked thoughtful. "Perhaps you are being honest.'' He hesitated. "I must warn you . . . I would not return to your home just yet.''

"Why not?'' Jerem asked abruptly.

The answer was not the one they expected to hear.

"The Guardians will probably take you into custody. I can assure you that no matter how badly you feel you've been treated by us, it will go worse for you with them.''

She stared into the dark eyes. "Thank you."

They were escorted from the building and driven by ground car to Paula's chosen destination—the New Armstrong West shuttle port. She wished that they could have gone home first, at least to pack some clothes, but Haddad's warning sounded sincere. There was no way Paula was going to spend another day locked up and grilled by the authorities.

Her first thought was to get a shuttle ride to the Slavik Colony of Kikinda. She had friends living there and it would be no problem to drop in on them unexpectedly and sleep over for a few days, until things calmed down.

She abandoned that idea when they reached the elevator terminal leading to the docks. Her experience with Costeaus was indeed limited, but she had learned enough from them to know when she was being followed. The short brunette standing two pillars away was an obvious tail—the woman watched too closely, turned away too quickly when Paula glanced in her direction.

Spotting a tail was not the only skill Paula had learned from the Costeaus. They had also taught her how to lose one.

Jerem complained when she took him by the hand and marched across the crowded terminal.

"Mom!"

"Now listen carefully. Do you see those patrollers?" She pointed to the pair of large and somber police officers who were leaning against a railing next to the departure/arrival grids.

He nodded, tried to break her grip. "I see 'em," he whined.

"We're going to play a little game. Now I believe that E-Tech has sent someone to follow us. I'm going to try and shake them but I need your help."

"Can you let go of my hand?" he pleaded.

"Just listen. I'm going to speak to those patrollers and I want you to agree with everything I say. Okay?"

"Okay, but can you . . ."

"It'll look more real if I'm holding onto you. Please?"

He gave a loud sigh. "All right."

They walked quickly over to where the two officers stood. Paula kept her voice low and full of fear.

"Sir," she whispered, "please listen carefully. Pretend that you don't see me."

The patrollers grimaced, probably assuming that she was just another crazy who loitered in terminals.

"Sir, my boy and I saw it! There's a woman by a pillar behind us and she has a thruster gun in her handbag! And she threatened my son!"

Jerem nodded vehemently. The patrollers were suddenly interested.

"A short brunette," Paula continued. "Can you see her?"

One of the patrollers glanced over Jerem's head and nodded.

Paula feigned terror. "We were just walking past her and she pulled out this thruster gun and grabbed my boy's arm . . ."

". . . and she stuck the gun right in my face!" Jerem added with a low shout.

That did it. The patrollers headed toward the brunette. When they were far enough away, Paula whispered to Jerem: "Run!"

They dashed for one of the street exits. Behind them, a commotion erupted. Paula glanced over her shoulder.

The brunette could not have acted more suspiciously if she had tried. When Paula and Jerem began to run, the woman reached into her purse, probably to send a com signal asking for backup. Then she began to jog in Paula's direction.

The two officers yanked thrusters from their belts. "Freeze!" they shouted in unison.

A trio of arriving passengers dove to the floor. Screams filled the terminal. Paula caught a final view of the brunette, desperately arguing with the patrollers. Then she and Jerem were out of the terminal and racing onto a crowded boulevard. She flagged down a taxi and did not breathe easily until they were a half a mile away.

"Where to now, Mom?"

"You're on-line, woman," the taxi driver added. "I need a destination."

Paula stared at him through the mirror. "Take us to the trader district."

Artwhiler was screaming. "This is outrageous, Franco! You promised that E-Tech would cooperate fully. Yet your first action was to order the murder witnesses released! And then you *claim* that your people lost them!"

The standard video conference setup for a two-person interact featured a head-and-shoulders shot of the other participant. Artwhiler had zoomed his own camera into a tight close-up; his blocky face looked ready to leap out of Rome's office monitor. And the color appeared to be misaligned. No one's face could be that red.

"A mistake was made," Rome said calmly. "My people suspected that the woman might have known more about the murder than she was letting on, so they released her and had her followed. Unfortunately, she gave us the slip."

There was venom in Artwhiler's words. "And you tell me that your security people did not even bother to plant surveillance transmitters on the woman? I find that difficult to believe! Perhaps you know where this woman and her son are hiding and have decided to violate the edict of the Council!"

Rome shook his head wearily. "Believe me, we do not know where they are. And E-Tech is not in the habit of planting bugs on every witness who comes through our doors."

The conversation was leading nowhere. Rome was tempted to simply break the link. He was tired. It was almost 9:00 P.M and he wanted only to go home and lie down and persuade Angela to rub his back until he fell asleep.

"You are trying to use this entire incident for your own political advantage, Franco! You do not fool me!'' Artwhiler wagged his finger. With the short distance between camera and subject, the finger resembled a tree trunk.

Rome forced patience. ''I'm sure the woman's disappearance will only create a temporary setback. Your Guardians are bound to locate her.''

''We had better,'' Artwhiler warned. ''Or Wednesday's Council meeting will be your personal hell!''

It seemed a good time to end the conversation. Rome switched off his monitor and leaned back in the soft leather of the desk chair. He imagined Angela's strong fingers kneading his spine.

The intercom twanged.

''Yes?''

''Sir, the Pasha is on the line. He says it's urgent.''

''Put him through.'' There was no need for anyone to mention securing the line. After today's mess, Rome had ordered that all channels be scrambled.

Haddad took shape on the screen. ''I'm in the archives. The main data-retrieval section. We've found something.''

''Can it wait till morning?'' He could feel Angela's fingers slipping away.

The Pasha shook his head. ''You'd better come down right now. It's important and it's too complicated to explain over the intercom.''

Rome sighed. ''I'll be right there.'' He had no idea what Haddad could have found, but he was certain that it had cost him a backrub.

The vaults took up almost the entire first floor of E-Tech's Irryan headquarters—nearly two million square feet of floor space.

Rome passed through the outer security checkpoints with ease. Guards and electronic monitors recognized him; doors opened quietly, detection portals flashed SAFE TO PROCEED. Although the walk down these long corridors seemed simple, he knew he was passing through a series of sophisticated tracking/ID systems. He would have been stopped at the first indication that he was not who he claimed to be.

Beyond these walls lay the heart of E-Tech's power: the great data archives. Information about thousands of technological disciplines was encoded into the computers; a wealth of data taken from the days of the pre-Apocalypse, when science had overreached its human masters. Here in these archives, and in duplicate facilities on another dozen Colonies, resided knowledge of many of the technologies that had contributed to the decimation of the Earth two centuries before. This was the goal of La Gloria de la Ciencia: E-Tech's warehouse of riches—knowledge being held in trust for a time when humanity might use it without self-destructing.

In the years since the Apocalypse, much data had been declassified and reintegrated into society. Along with Ecospheric Turnaround—the combination of experimental bioprojects that were attempting to restore habitable conditions on the surface of the Earth—the reintegration of information was E-Tech's most important function. A long-term plan existed. Before any scientific facts were declassified, the effects of the "lost" technology on the holistic quality of Intercolonial life were carefully studied by E-Tech scholars and scientists.

E-Tech never initiated this process. The request for reintegration of a restricted technology had to come from an outside agency. Rome and his predecessors were all painfully aware of the potential for fascism engendered by an organization with such power. The Council of Irrya had been created two centuries ago, primarily at the request of E-Tech's founders, who realized that their own organization had to be tempered by a system of checks and balances.

Under E-Tech's grand scheme, it would take hundreds of years before the bulk of the information was reintegrated. La Gloria de la Ciencia, if given their way, would undam the archives and flood society overnight. There was no accounting for such madness.

Rome passed through a door into the deepest sector of the vaults, a stretch of corridor studded by large metal airlocks.

Beyond each portal lay hundreds of sleeping humans, in stasis since the time of the Apocalypse. The tombs of Irrya were a depository for scientists and welders, mechanics and secretaries, the skilled and the unskilled; all those who had opted for a frozen future rather than take their chances on a dying planet.

During the final days, E-Tech had been unable to guarantee living space in the Colonies for all of its supporters. The organization had chosen the next best option. Millions of people had been frozen and transported in bulk up to the Colonies, and were now stored in over a hundred E-Tech facilities throughout the cylinders.

Currently, the Irryan Council set a quota for Wake-ups. Every month, a few hundred more humans were unthawed and introduced to the world of the cylinders. Someday the stasis tombs, like the data vaults, would be emptied.

"Identify," demanded the door at the end of the hall.

Rome gave the current password and stuck his hands against the door's body-sensor.

"Proceed," said the door, in the same angry tone. It slid open on invisible hinges.

He entered the prime data-retrieval section, a cramped circular room filled with instrumentation. Pasha Haddad stood at the main terminal. A stringbean of a man fluttered beside him.

Begelman had a first name, but no one ever used it. Like Haddad, and most of the other senior E-Tech officials, he preferred as much anonymity as possible. His time within the organization rivaled Rome's and it was sobering to realize that among the three of them, they accounted for more than a century of experience.

Haddad began. "Begelman started accessing Paratwa info this morning. He believes that he has tentatively identified the breed of assassin that we're dealing with."

"Terminus," said Begelman, in a quick high voice that sounded more like a chirp. "Terminus labs, circa 2075. Money-motivated. Not the worst of the assassins. On a scale from one to ten, about a four."

"What else?" Haddad would not have called Rome down here just to tell him that.

Begelman's scrawny fingers abruptly attacked the nearest keyboard. Rome wondered how the programmer avoided getting blisters.

"Ran into angels," Begelman whined. "Called Haddad. Strange stuff. Soft-perimeter and sticky. Real sticky. Like zero-G glue." He grinned as if he had just told a joke.

Rome gazed at Haddad, waiting for a translation.

Begelman batted away at the keys while the Pasha explained. "It seems that he came across two secret programs concerning the Paratwa. Now, we find hidden programs down here almost every day, but most of them can be accessed by password—hard-perimeter programs, one way in and one way out. What Begelman found is much more complex. These two programs have soft perimeters. That means in order to gain access to them, you have to share your own knowledge with the programs—feed them data every step of the way. And if you don't feed the right data, your entrance is rejected."

Rome nodded with understanding. "You can't guess your way in."

"Right," squawked Begelman. "Designer was no dummy."

Haddad continued. "He believes the programs are pre-Apocalyptic."

Begelman wagged his head. "Vittelli or Quincy Gorman or Martin Riley—maybe even the Asaki brothers."

"Those were cutting-edge programmers who worked for E-Tech during the final days."

"Genius," spouted Begelman. "Pure genius!"

Rome nodded. "So what did you find?" He tried to keep the impatience out of his voice.

Begelman ignored him. His attention was suddenly focused on a monitor screen.

Haddad explained. "We think these two programs were put into the files for just such a situation as we're faced with today—a

Paratwa on the loose. Begelman believes that the programs might be keyed to you—not personally, of course, but because of your position as Director of E-Tech. Is there anything that you're aware of that no one else in the organization would have access to?''

Rome smiled. "I'm sorry to disappoint you, but there are no secret keys passed from one E-Tech Director to the next. I have access to the same information as the two of you."

"Thought I had it," Begelman chirped while scanning the screen. "Another dead end."

"How did you find out about these programs?" Rome asked. This felt like a waste of time, but he might as well cover all the bases while he was here.

Begelman appeared to stare at a spot on the ceiling. "I asked for a rundown of Paratwa unaccounted for following the Apocalypse. Got a couple thousand names. Nothing unusual there—Research has confirmed the figures in the past. But! An x-line showed up at the end of the list!"

An x-line meant that there was related information stored somewhere else within the network. "Go on."

"First thing I did was check Research. Assassin rundowns have been requested many times in the past . . ."

"For doctoral theses and such," Haddad added.

"But! Not once in all those years did an x-line show up."

The Pasha nodded. "All the previous requests were from Research. Ours was the first in two centuries to have a Security code tagged onto it."

Rome was beginning to feel some of their excitement. "You think that someone two hundred years ago foresaw the possibility that we might someday encounter a Paratwa? And that we might need help?"

"Exactly!" Begelman clapped his hands. "I asked the computer to identify the x-line and the computer asked me who I was!" The programmer's frail body shook with excitement. "I identified myself and then it asked me why I was interested in the Paratwa. I provided it with all the information we had concerning the assassin. Then it split in half!''

"Two separate programs," Haddad clarified.

"The first program started asking me all sorts of questions. Where was E-Tech located? How was it run? What were the current goals of the organization? Etcetera, etcetera . . .''

"A morality test?" Rome wondered.

"Yes, I believe so.'' Begelman looked suddenly disappointed. "But although I apparently provided the correct responses, I haven't been able to get any further. The program tells me that I have done well and then it simply stops. There is something that I'm still overlooking."

"What about the second program?" Rome asked.

Begelman's eyes lit up. "Even stranger! Again, it asks questions. Bizarre questions. How many seeds in a watermelon? Why is love of family conducive to the formation of less rigid social institutions? Do gray cats have claws? Why are there no tropical rain forests in Kansas? What are the two nicest aspects of Hawaii?''

Begelman shook his head. "It goes on and on—question after question, each apparently unrelated to any of the others. It's obviously a heavily coded program. But that's not the only mystery.

"Neither of these programs can be entered by a computer, because of the soft perimeters. A scanner simply is not designed to interpret such complexities. But I did manage to create a counter to search through the program and find out how much bulk data is contained.'' He gave a wicked grin. "This second program would require incredible patience. Allowing for an average human reaction time, and providing you had the correct response to each question at your fingertips, it would take approximately six hundred years to get through it.''

Rome frowned. "Six hundred years? Are you sure?''

Begelman waved his hands violently. He looked like a bird trying to take off. "Of course I'm sure! And I'm equally sure that I must be wrong! It's very frustrating!''

Haddad smiled grimly. "You're doing your best."

"No, no! If I was doing my best, I'd solve it!"

Rome shook his head. "You're saying that a computer cannot run this program and that it would take a human being six hundred years to complete it?"

"Very well put," said Begelman. Genuine admiration appeared on his face.

Haddad frowned. "The first program—the morality test. Could it be keyed to a conglomeration of data—a special set of facts that only a person in the position of E-Tech Director might consider important?"

Rome shrugged. "I can't think of anything. Why do you believe that these programs are tied to me?"

"Just a hunch," Begelman said. "A lot of these pre-Apocalyptic encrypters played around with sophisticated targeting techniques. It seems natural that they'd chose an E-Tech Director as their key—especially if the program contained sensitive data."

Rome shook his head.

"Knowledge of your predecessors?" Begelman prodded. "Long-term goals of E-Tech that are not necessarily officially formulated? Structural changes within the organization?"

"Honestly, I can't think of anything."

"We have passed the test," Begelman insisted. "I'm sure of it. The first program should open . . ."

"*We* have passed the test!" the Pasha snapped. "Rome Franco, E-Tech Director, has not!"

Begelman exploded. "Of course! That has to be it! How utterly simplistic. How could I have missed it?"

"We all have our bad days," Rome said drily.

Begelman did not hear him. The frail programmer dropped to his hands and knees and groped beneath the console. A moment later he popped up clutching a hand modem—a flat gray plate connected by cable to the bottom of the terminal.

"Put your hand against it," Begelman ordered. "Now, type with the other hand . . . that's it . . . tell the machine who you are."

Rome keyed in his name and waited for the invisible sensors of the modem to confirm his identity. Begelman brought the first program onto the screen.

With one hand remaining on the modem, Rome read each question and typed in his response. He answered as truthfully and as accurately as possible.

Begelman, observing his own monitors, spoke with awe. "The program is scanning our entire system—accessing whatever files it can get into! It's actually studying our records to make sure that Rome Franco is who he says he is. It's making sure that we're not trying to trick it by using a false modem. Incredible!"

The last question was the simplest of all.

HAS E-TECH REMAINED TRUE TO ITS ORIGINAL GOALS?

YES, Rome typed.

PROCEED, said the screen. Begelman leaped up and down in a fit of triumph.

"So simple," the programmer whispered. "So beautifully simple."

"What now?" Rome asked. The screen had gone blank.

Begelman fluttered his arms in exasperation. "It's an open program! Just ask it what you want to know."

He typed: WE HAVE A PARATWA ASSASSIN ON THE LOOSE. WE NEED HELP.

The program responded instantaneously. PLEASE PROVIDE ACCESS TO CURRENT STASIS FILES.

Begelman instructed him and Rome typed in the requested data. Again, the screen went blank. Then:

AWAKEN STASIS CAPSULE MH-785462. END OF PROGRAM.

"Aha!" cried Begelman. "That's it! I've got it! Whoever is in that stasis capsule will know how to enter the second program!"

Rome nodded. It seemed like a strong possibility. He looked at Haddad. The Pasha was frowning.

"If we awaken this person," Haddad began, "E-Tech will be in violation of the Council edict."

Rome shrugged. "We're already in trouble for not reporting the murder.'' He paused. ''Are you absolutely sure that the Paratwa leak did not originate with one of our own people?''

For a moment, Haddad looked glum. ''You know that I cannot say such a thing for certain. I can only reiterate what seems likely—that Paula Marth, or her son, contacted someone else before they called E-Tech last night. Such a scenario fits the known facts.''

''Perhaps,'' Rome said, ''we've got this whole thing backward. The Paratwa assassin, or whoever woke the creature, could have leaked the facts about the murder.'' He recalled the Council meeting. ''Maybe such actions were meant as an attack on E-Tech.''

''I thought of that. But how could the Paratwa know that Paula Marth would only call E-Tech? You said yourself that today's incident at Council looked like a setup, as if Artwhiler and Drake *knew* E-Tech—and no one else—had been alerted to the existence of the Paratwa.''

Rome saw his point. Yet there was still too much they were in the dark about.

''Where is this stasis capsule?'' Rome asked.

Begelman smacked the keyboard and read the screen. ''MH-785462 is in our storage facility on Shaoyang Colony. We could have the capsule here by tomorrow morning.''

''A routine transfer,'' Haddad offered. ''No one would have to know about this other than the three of us and a Wake-up team.''

It seemed a safe enough move for them to make. Rome could not bring himself to turn this program information over to Artwhiler's Guardians. No matter what the Council proclaimed, a Paratwa was a matter for E-Tech to handle.

''Let's find out who's sleeping in that capsule.''

Miles Yukura, with feet propped on the heavy console that ringed his chair, glanced sharply at viewscreen number nineteen. The flash of movement that had caught his attention was gone by the time he focused on the image—a hilly, near-barren vista in the northernmost part of the Preserve. Miles activated the joystick for infrared camera nineteen and panned and zoomed across the two dozen acres that fell within the instrument's field of vision.

He saw nothing out of the ordinary. A pair of small waddling groundbirds pecked at the dirt; a doe and buck, brave enough to have ventured from the southern forests, stood frozen at the base of a small rise. Hector, the albino wildcat and unofficial mascot of the Preserve, boldly roamed the perimeter of a small waterhole. The liquid glittered weirdly under the camera's infrared sensors.

Miles shrugged and turned back to the main terminal to resume his studies. Probably one of the deer had run in front of the camera. There were over two hundred of them within the Preserve's forty square miles and their sudden movements provided frequent distractions. Miles did not really mind. These long night shifts passed slowly enough and he was sometimes secretly glad to find excuses for playing with one of the thirty-six sets of camera controls under his command.

Miles was content being a night warden here at the Preserve; it gave him plenty of time for his schoolwork. In fact, he liked to think it was this job that had helped him mature. Northern California's wildlife Preserve was the fifth largest in the Colonies, boasting some animals that were extremely rare. One variety of jackrabbit could be found nowhere else.

Miles had seen videoclips of old Earth, and he sensed that the Preserve captured a spirit of what the planet had once been like. Often, when his studies were complete, in those early hours before the Colony mirrors rotated into dawn, he would sit quietly in this control room and listen to the world. Sensitive audio pickups captured a wealth of animal sounds. Deer crashed through the underbrush; skunks, groundhogs, and raccoons scurried madly about; birds chirped and predators growled. There were bats and wildcats and a growing family of speckled squirrels, expanding geometrically from the original four that had been purchased from Noche Brazilia three years ago.

Most of the animals were tame but a few of the predators—the wildcats in particular—bore watching. During the day, when as many as ten thousand people were hiking through the Preserve, a half-dozen controllers were on duty here. Many of the creatures had microscopic regulators implanted in their brains, and at Miles's fingertips lay the power to either summon a particular animal to the control center or to put it temporarily to sleep by inducing a narcoleptic response. Summoning was used for medical checkups or special feedings—it was easier to have the animal come here than to track it down in the forests. Narcoleptic triggers were not touched unless human life was endangered. Most of the bigger and meaner cats had been broken of their attack patterns, but there were still occasional incidents of animals threatening hikers. A controller observing a potentially dangerous situation could knock the predator unconscious with the touch of a button.

From the corner of his eye, Miles spotted another sudden movement on screen nineteen. This time he resolved to find the cause. He grabbed the joystick and panned in a wide-angled 360-degree arc until he had visually located all the animals in that sector: three deer, Hector the albino wildcat, a pair of groundbirds, and one of the Preserve's two Komono dragons—a notoriously uncooperative eight-foot hunk of lizard. He energized the sector's gridmap, located above the monitors, and watched the computer display the ID codes of the eleven animals currently in that area. The grid showed that the four animals not visible on the monitor were behind one of the gentle slopes, out of camera range. And the seven he had seen were too far from the camera to have caused the distraction.

Miles grimaced. There *was* an explanation. Someone had either gotten over the high fence that ringed the Preserve, or else had managed to remain undetected after visiting hours ended. The latter possibility was unlikely; all visitors were supplied with a pocket-sized tracking sensor that transmitted their location to the master grid system. The badges were returned before they left the Preserve. There had been no "lost" badges today—check-ins had equaled check-outs. That meant there was probably a fence hopper. The sturdy wire-meshed barrier was twelve feet high and safe-guarded by sensors that were supposed to alert Miles to breaches, but determined pranksters had gotten in before, undetected.

Most likely they were standing at the base of the tree that housed the camera—its only blind spot. *Well, they won't get away without being seen,* Miles adjusted the camera to observe the widest area and then set it rotating at top speed. Eventually the intruder, or intruders, would have to move, and when they did, he would certainly spot them. He was reaching for the key that would put sector nineteen's camera into the record mode when the screen burst with blue light and went dead.

Shitsuckers! The bastards had broken the camera. That called for an altogether different response. Youthful pranksters were one thing, but when they became destructive, he had no choice but to call the police.

He typed his request for assistance into the terminal. The black and gold seal of the Intercolonial Guardians flashed on the screen. Although the Preserve was part of Northern California, the Guardians had jurisdiction here, as they did in all wild animal domains.

A visual message from Guardian Central informed him that a patrol unit was being dispatched and that he could expect assistance within five minutes. Unless the vandals left immediately, Miles felt sure that the Guardians would arrive in time to catch them.

A warning buzzed. Miles almost jumped out of his chair. The worst possible event had just occurred—an animal, somewhere, had just died and its implanted regulator had transmitted its death-pulse to the computer. Miles located the animal an instant later on the gridmap. Hector, the albino wildcat, was dead.

There was no time to react. Miles sat in stunned silence as, one by one, the animals in sector nineteen died, registering as bright pulsing numerals on the gridmap. The buzzer howled. The groundbirds perished first, then two of the deer and the Komono dragon. Except for the animals beyond the hill, the third deer was the only survivor. He spotted it on the camera monitoring the adjacent sector. It was racing to the south.

The deer galloped into a more level area with thick underbrush and skinny trees—the outer perimeter of the central forests. Miles activated the controls on that sector's camera and aimed it toward the deer's direction of approach.

The frightened animal jumped over a narrow brook and was knocked sideways in mid-leap by some invisible force. It tumbled end over end, came down in a patch of thorny rosebushes, dead before it hit the earth.

What is happening!? With shaking hands, Miles panned the camera, searching for whatever was responsible for the killing. The deer looked like it had been hit by the blast of a powerful hand thruster—a police weapon.

Think, Miles, think! Another deer winked out of existence in sector seventeen just as the emergency drill came to him. He tore the restraining bracket from a large switch and flipped it on, instantly transmitting a summons signal to the entire population of the Preserve. In a few minutes, it would be animal chaos outside his door, but he had done the right thing. In an emergency of undetermined origin, the animals were to be brought to master control. He triggered the large gridmap to display the entire Preserve, watched nervously as the multicolored blips began to converge on his position.

A faint mechanical roar sounded in the distance, like a highly charged aircar flying by at top speed. He set all thirty-six cameras on remote panscan and searched among the blurs of animals racing by each screen for some sign of what was killing them. The screens in sectors eleven and twelve blanked out simultaneously and something exploded out in the forest. Miles froze. More lights winked out on the status board—many more. The buzzer wailed like a forsaken child. He fumbled for the manual override switch and shut off the horrendous noise.

Destiny of the Trust! Where is that patrol unit? He forced clammy fingers down on the keyboard, jabbed in the code for a priority-one emergency. Three more explosions came in rapid succession, the last one so violent and close that Miles felt the shock wave hitting the building.

Must be calm—must be calm. Whatever was happening, the Guardians would be here in minutes to take care of it.

Something came flying directly at the sector-six camera. Miles instinctively threw his arms up as a foot lashed out and slammed into the lens. The screen flickered and went dead.

A man on a skystick! The vehicle was little more than a saddled tube with propulsion and lift controls mounted on the handlebars, capable of carrying a single rider through the air at dizzying speeds. He felt abruptly calmer knowing what was causing this madness. No wonder he had been unable to spot the intruder. The maniac was riding above the Preserve, dropping or shooting explosive missiles down on the animals.

Another series of detonations sounded—more distant, yet still frightening in their intensity. A glance at the gridmap told Miles that many more animals had perished—hundreds of them. *Almighty Earth! This madman is trying to destroy the Preserve!*

Ominous quiet descended on the control room. *The recorders!* He had forgotten them. With a deft terminal command, he activated the transmission recorders for all of the remaining cameras. His action was not a moment too soon. Flying across the horizon in sector eight was a bizarre sight.

There were two of them, both saddled on skysticks. Shafts of light whipped out from their hands—dark light, with only the edges of the wavering beams illuminated and with cores that seemed even blacker than the night sky. The twin beams flogged the earth. A trio of terrified wolves were decapitated as the black light slashed through their necks.

If it were not for the skysticks, Miles would have thought the Preserve was being invaded from outer space. The two figures weaved past each other at frightening speeds, performing mid-air twists and crosses as if they had been born on the little jet scooters. *They have to crash!* No one could fly in tandem like that, not even skystick acrobatic teams from Pocono.

A bell clanged and Miles jerked away from the screens in panic. The outer door! He keyed the release mechanism and three helmeted Guardians tumbled into the room, their thrusters drawn.

"Officer Salikoff, Station Five," barked the first man. "What's your incident?"

Miles pointed breathlessly to the gridmap.

"Speak, boy, we heard the explosions! What the hell is going on out here!"

Words bubbled out. Miles watched the other two Guardians exchange wry grins when he mentioned bombers on skysticks. Salikoff listened gravely, stared at Miles for a long moment, then turned to his men. "Karousis, notify Central, tell them we need full backup out here. And break out the range thrusters."

One of the men hustled out to the car as Salikoff checked the gridmap. The third Guardian whistled softly. "Damn, I think the kid's right. There should be a lot more lights on out there. It looks like . . ."

An explosion shook the building. A new batch of trouble sirens wailed.

"Christ!" yelled Salikoff, pointing through the open door. "Our car's been hit!"

Both Guardians dashed for the entrance. Salikoff got there first. He halted in the doorway with a sharp grunt. He turned around slowly, with effort. His chest had been skewered from neck to waist—blood was spilling to the floor. He collapsed into his own puddle.

The last officer scampered backward. "Close the fuckin' door!" he hissed.

Terrified, Miles threw the latch. The portal snapped shut. There was a silence that he hoped would last forever. Salikoff lay face down at the entrance with countless rivulets of blood streaming from his body. Miles had never seen a dead person before—he could not take his eyes off the slain Guardian.

The remaining Guardian knelt beside the terminal and typed in a query for emergency assistance. "Kid, I want you to . . ."

The door blew inward with a loud crash, falling on the slain officer. The Guardian threw Miles down behind him and fired his thruster wildly into the darkness. A thin shaft of black light seemed to curl lazily around the right corner of the doorframe, spearing into the room.

For a moment, Miles thought nothing had happened. Then the Guardian leaned forward, dropping his gun. There was a sizzling hole in the back of his helmet where the beam had exited his head.

Miles pressed himself to the base of the console. A dark shadow hurtled through the doorway. The figure moved in short jerking strides—a palsied ballerina that would have brought laughter in another time and place. Miles could only shudder.

It was dressed entirely in black—a uniform of beaten leather with face masked by an opaque visor extending from the crown of the helmet. In its left hand was a thruster. The other palm clutched a small object with a tiny protruding needle.

"Recorders on?" the nightmare hissed.

The creature towered over him. Miles bobbed his head, began to cry.

"My. We can't have that, can we."

Invisible waves of energy cascaded from the creature's thruster. The huge gridmap exploded into flying shards. The gun swung down toward Miles. He shielded his head in terror. Pyrotechnics sizzled across the back of his neck as the control console above him was blasted. Hot metal touched his bare arm. He cried out in pain.

Through half-clenched eyes, Miles watched the black demon aim its thruster at him. But it did not fire. The creature stood there and let out a peal of heavy laughter. "My. Such a beautiful night in the neighborhood!"

Quickly, the creature backed out of the room, vanishing into darkness. Miles closed his eyes and wished that the loud screams coming from his own mouth would stop.

At two A.M., the Pasha disturbed Rome's dreamless sleep to inform him that the Paratwa had struck again. Rome put Haddad on hold, hoping to sneak off to the study so as not to awaken Angela. The effort was unsuccessful. His wife brewed taco tea in the kitchen while Haddad related over the phone the few details known about the tragedy in Northern California.

A dry shower, two snorts of no-grog, and a quick groundcar ride brought him to E-Tech headquarters by two forty-five. He spent the next five hours down in the archives.

Begelman was a study in motion, dashing madly from terminal to terminal, accessing data from as many as twenty historical files at the same time. Pasha Haddad was more subdued, which was to say, he exhibited the same calm energy he did in the daytime. Neither of them looked like they needed sleep, which was more than Rome could claim, despite the no-grog.

By the time Irrya faced sun, the three of them were certain they knew why the Paratwa had attacked the zoo. History texts were quite lucid on the subject of Paratwa "flexing." The creatures had no choice but to periodically erupt into violence. It seemed the only explanation for the vicious assault.

Councillor Artwhiler, however, shared his own theory as to why the Paratwa had decimated the zoo.

"As children," Artwhiler claimed, during a short early morning teleconference with Rome, "this assassin was never allowed to have pets. So the monster took out its lifelong frustrations on the helpless animals of the Preserve." Artwhiler also released an official statement implying that the Paratwa was a coward, since it had not engaged his slain Guardians in fair combat.

Artwhiler provided other frustrations. Not only did the Guardian commander refuse to divulge information to E-Tech about the tragedy, he also refused to accept any data that Rome, Haddad, and Begelman had spent half the night retrieving from the archives.

To make matters worse, the existence of the Paratwa was now public knowledge. A pair of Northern California freelancers came to the zoo and spoke with the terrified young warden before the Guardians organized themselves enough to cordon off the area. By nine o'clock Monday morning, the story was appearing on every channel in every Colony. Freelancers were proclaiming it the biggest news item to hit the cylinders since the Colony of Metro Germania had been partially destroyed by an explosion sixty-eight years ago.

Stasis capsule MH-785462 arrived at E-Tech headquarters shortly before ten A.M. Rome no longer had the slightest doubt that they were doing the right thing by awakening this sleeper without Artwhiler's knowledge.

The stasis engineer turned to Rome. "Sir, the capsule's been brought up to room temperature. We're ready to begin."

Rome and Haddad were seated behind the engineer in the main Wake-up facility. Begelman had gone back to data retrieval.

The glass-walled control room overlooked the frigid stasis chamber where the seven-foot-high pale ivory egg lay nestled in a cradle. The ice had melted and had been drained from the room. Preliminary tests had been accomplished with positive results. Although they could locate no archival history for this particular capsule—a not unusual circumstance—a data brick had been found beneath the ice of the cocoon and successfully accessed.

According to the information found in the brick, the capsule contained a man named Austin Rudolph, who had been an E-Tech financial adviser. He had been put to sleep in 2097, two years before the Apocalypse. The records indicated that he had been sixty years old at the time of his freezing.

"Financial adviser" was one of those skills that the Irryan Revival Committee considered time-decadent. Complete retraining would be necessary for Austin Rudolph to fit into the world of the twenty-fourth century, which meant that he would never be a priority revival. Rome suspected that the information contained in the brick was false, put there to prevent Austin Rudolph, or whoever was frozen down there, from being accidentally awakened.

The engineer manipulated the controls. Spinning blades descended from the ceiling of the chamber, gently touching the skin of the egg. Water jets ignited. Organic tissue shredded and splattered wildly across the room.

The membrane was carefully whittled away until the inner cocoon was reached. Then the engineer withdrew the blades and released dissolvent gas into the chamber. Thick clouds of greenish smoke hid the egg as the powerful gas reacted chemically with the inner membrane. Rome waited impatiently for the engineer to satisfy himself that all his gauges were reading positive. Blowers came on. The chamber was cleared of smoke and gases.

As they stared down at the contents of the inner cradle, Rome was reminded of an old Earth proverb—something about fighting fire with fire.

Austin Rudolph was not a man.

He was two men.

Gillian awoke, feeling cold. He could not move. He seemed to be adrift, floating within some vast inner sea.

From beyond the imaginary waves came a vision—a hot noonday sun piercing a covering of tall trees, a warm hexagonal room filled with a golden glow.

A muscle in his leg quivered violently and the dreamy image was replaced by pain.

Pain.

Awareness blossomed. Shreds of memory intertwined. Cortical and limbic systems relinked after years of dormancy. Left and right hemispheres fought a phylogenetic battle for preeminence. An immeasurable moment passed and then catharis swept through him, igniting nerves and muscles throughout his naked body. He arched backward and moaned with the agony of stasis restoration.

*   *   *

"Howdy," said the midget.

The room was barely furnished; four chairs and a table, two cots, a data console, and the medical cart that stood between the two revivees. Both men had intravenous feeding tubes stuck into their arms. The needles were merely a precaution. A med team had pronounced the midget and his full-sized companion in excellent condition, untroubled by any of the side effects occasionally encountered by Wake-ups.

Rome and the Pasha took seats on the other side of the table. Although there was no one else in the little room, microcams were observing. The Pasha was taking no chances; an armed combat team waited on the other side of the door. One of the most disturbing facets of the binary interlink phenomenon was the inability of medical science to effectively distinguish one of the creatures from two normal humans. Short of an autopsy, there was no way for Rome to know for certain whether he was sitting across the table from a Paratwa.

Stasis revivees were always naked and no clothes or artifacts had been found in this pair's capsule. The med team had dressed them in standard loose white coveralls.

The midget turned up the collar of his garment and chewed on the fabric. He winked at the Pasha, and when that brought no response, he turned to his dark-haired companion. Tiny shoulders gave a shrug. His face filled with another smile.

"Howdy," the midget said again.

Rome did not recognize the word. The tone of voice suggested that it was a greeting. He offered: "I'm Rome Franco and this is Pasha Haddad."

The standa procedure with Wake-ups was to allow them to take the initiative—say as little as possible and let them explore their new environment. Rome's first impression of these two was that revivee shock would not be a problem.

The midget ran a hand through his slick blond hair and beamed.

His face was dominated by thick lips and a wide mouth. Bright blue eyes seemed to shine with some inner pleasure.

"I'm Nick. My big friend here is named Gillian."

"Do you have last names?" asked the Pasha.

The midget grinned. "How about Smith and Jones?"

The Pasha raised his eyebrows.

Nick held up a tiny hand. "Hey—only joking! But we really don't have last names. We gave 'em up years ago. Can't even remember mine."

Rome stared across the table, tried to guess their ages. The midget was at least in his mid-forties, probably older. Gillian was younger, but Rome could not have said how much. He had one of those timeless faces, mature, yet boyish. He might be in his late twenties. He would probably look the same when he turned fifty.

Gillian stared across the table, registered the strangers. The one called Rome Franco hid behind a friendly smile. The other man— Pasha Haddad—had a face that understood violence.

"What year is this?" asked Nick.

"2307," replied Rome.

"Holy shit!" the midget exclaimed. "That was some sleep, huh, Gillian!"

The bigger man did not react. Rome studied his composed features, met sharp gray eyes. Angela would have considered him good-looking. Dark brown hair was cropped short on the sides but long in the back. He was six foot tall, a touch on the slender side, and well-muscled.

Nick rubbed his hands together. "I suppose this ain't Earth?"

That was the question that usually separated the quick adapters from the revivees who were prone to cultural shock. Rome had no qualms about giving this pair the unsweetened truth.

"Earth is uninhabitable. You're in Irrya, capital of the orbiting Colonies." Rome spoke uninterrupted for a good five minutes, providing them with a brief history of humanity since the time of the Apocalypse.

When Rome finished, the midget sighed. "It doesn't surprise

me. Earth was going down the tubes for a hell of a long time before that.''

The Pasha spoke. ''Do either of you know of an Austin Rudolph? His name was on your capsule.''

The midget shrugged. ''Never heard of him. Sounds like a bookkeeping mistake.''

Bookkeeping, Rome thought. What an odd word. ''When were you born, Nick?''

''1977.'' The midget held up his hand, countered Rome's surprise. ''I was one of the first people to go into stasis—in 2010. They revived me in 2086. Biggest goddamn mistake I ever made. Thought that things were totally crazy in 2010, but I didn't know what crazy was. 2086 was crazy.''

''I've never heard of two people sharing a capsule,'' the Pasha commented.

Nick threw up his arms in mock exasperation. ''Yeah, a hell of a thing. We went under in 2097—both of us were tired of the nutty world. They were a little short on capsules that year and since I was so small . . . well, it made sense to share a bed.'' He beamed.

''Who put you into stasis?'' Rome asked. He felt the midget was lying, or telling half truths.

''E-Tech,'' said Nick. ''We both did a little work for them now and then.''

''What kind of work?'' asked Haddad.

''Oh, different kinds of things.''

''Could you be more specific?''

''No.'' Nick amended himself hastily. ''I mean, I'm a little worried about this situation. You gotta look at things from our point of view. It's very strange being awakened and stuck into a little room and asked questions by strange people. Maybe you guys ain't human. Maybe the Earth's still inhabited and you guys are from another galaxy and you're trying to suck information from us so that you can invade the planet. Maybe you're from Los Angeles.''

Rome smiled. "I believe I understand your position. But you must understand ours." He paused. "Perhaps you are not two men at all. Perhaps you are only one."

Gillian studied their reactions. The man Franco exhibited just the barest hint of fear as he spoke. His companion, Haddad, came erect in the chair, prepared for action.

Nick chuckled. "Well, I know I'm not a Paratwa. And neither is Gillian. Now what about yourselves? Maybe we've been awakened into a galaxy full of Paratwa and you're trying to trick us!"

There was something strangely trustworthy about Nick. Rome decided to drop all pretense.

"I'm the Director of E-Tech. Pasha Haddad is the head of our Security section. We have a Paratwa assassin on the loose and our history archives suggested reviving you."

"Well, well!" chortled the midget. "That sounds a bit more like it—a job that's right up our alley. What do you say, Gillian?"

Gillian said nothing.

Nick continued. "Our fee is pretty high for such work. We'll expect to be paid at the rate of a 9-7 specialist of 2097. Naturally, all inflation and prime-rate adjustments will be adhered to. And our contract should include a danger clause based on the breed of assassin we're up against. Also, there should be a bonus option based on solving your problem ahead of an agreed-upon schedule."

"Anything else?" Rome asked drily.

"Well, I do like women . . . but we can work that out later." Nick grinned.

"Perhaps," the Pasha began, "we could simply put you back in stasis and consider this revival a mistake."

Nick shrugged. "I might decide we're not interested in your troubles and demand that you put us to sleep again."

Haddad warned, "You're not in a position to demand anything."

"True enough. But then you obviously don't know what the hell to do about this Paratwa of yours. Must be pretty bad, huh?"

Rome explained the situation. When he finished, Nick stroked his chin, looked thoughtful.

"A Termi, huh?"

"Pardon?" said Rome.

"A Termi—an assassin from Terminus labs," the midget explained. "That's what we used to call 'em. What do you think, Gillian? Think we can help these people out of their troubles?"

An emotion touched Gillian, a vague pleasure as he recalled the rhythms of earlier hunts.

"I think we can do it," the midget concluded after Gillian failed to respond.

"What exactly is it that you will do?" asked Rome softly. He was beginning to think that the man Gillian was not even paying attention. The gray eyes seemed distant. Of course, it was still possible that these two were indeed a Paratwa.

Nick drawled, "Well, shucks, guys! We'll find this here Termi and challenge him to a gunfight in the center of town. Draw, buster! Let's see how fast you really are!"

The Pasha raised an eyebrow. "You will kill this creature . . . for money."

"You catch on quick," Nick said cheerily.

"What makes you so sure you can do such a thing?" Rome asked.

"'Cause we've done it before. We'll need your cooperation, of course. A team will have to be assembled. We'll need access to tactical computers and we'll need a place to train. It goes without saying that we'll need the best weapons you've got."

"Does that include your Cohe wands?" the Pasha inquired.

Nick grinned. "Say, you're a suspicious one, aren't you? Now I'm going to say this one more time—I'm Nick and this is Gillian. Two of us. Count again to make sure. One . . . Two. Separate, but equal. Now Gillian, he's a little slow right now, but he'll come around. As to your question . . . I haven't the faintest idea how to use a Cohe wand—I'd probably squeeze the damn egg and cut my dick off. Gillian, though . . . he knows how to use a wand. He'll need one."

"They're totally outlawed," said Haddad.

"I guess you'll have to make an exception."

Rome nodded slowly. He had not really known what to expect when they had learned about this capsule, but in the back of his mind had been a suspicion. Although the archives contained no clear data on the subject, there were tales that had been passed down over the years—stories of secret teams that had been trained by E-Tech to hunt and kill Paratwa.

"There are some special conditions," Rome explained. He told them about Artwhiler's official responsibility for the investigation and about the relative peace of the Colonies compared to the Earth they had known. His own doubts surfaced even as he spoke.

I feel like some ancient "believer," considering a pact with the devil. Maybe we're overreacting to this whole situation. After all, there is just one assassin roaming the cylinders. Despite its abilities, it is a flesh and blood creation. It can be killed . . . or maybe even captured. Perhaps Artwhiler and the Council are correct in their assessment of the situation and E-Tech is in a state of needless panic.

Nick shattered his doubts. "You're going to have to be prepared for a lot more killing. On the average, it took us about a month to complete a search-and-destroy mission. And that was under more ideal conditions—we didn't have to train a team and there was a full support network already in place. Even a Termi can kill an awful lot of people in a month.

"As for secrecy, that's fine with us. Underground operations usually work best."

Rome looked at Haddad, saw displeasure on the lean face. His own doubts gnawed at him. *These men are contract killers—and I am considering hiring them.* A day ago, he would have found such actions proposterous—and deplorable. But now . . . He shook his head. *Is this how it starts? Violence against violence and to hell with the rules of civilization? Is it truly this easy to descend into pre-Apocalyptic actions?*

Does consistency have a source?

Gillian observed the doubt on Rome's face. He understood. His voice, unused for centuries, sounded strange to his own ears.

"The human who does not fear is the human who has lost his boundaries."

Rome frowned, stared into Gillian's sharp gray eyes. He had misjudged the man, equated his failure to speak with brutishness. Intelligence lay poised beneath the silence.

Nick grinned, patted Gillian affectionately on the shoulder. "Now that we're all here, how about some food. I've got two hundred and ten years of eating to catch up on!"

"Jerem, wake up."

Paula shook the small cot. Her son groaned and opened one eye. "What time is it?" he whined.

"It's almost eleven. We've slept most of the morning away." There was no denying that they had both needed the rest.

"I wanna sleep some more." He turned over on his stomach and covered his head with a pillow. She reached over and gave him a light smack on the rear.

"C'mon, we can't lie here forever."

"What about school?"

"You're taking a few days off."

"That's gonna mess up my Science schedule," he groaned, "and this is the week that my gym class gets to go freefalling!"

"Sorry." Paula recognized his mood, knew that he was eager

for an argument. She was not. "You've got five minutes. I'll be out in the front shop with Moat."

"Yeah, all right," he moaned from beneath the pillow.

The trader shop owned by Moat Piloski was on the outskirts of New Armstrong, in one of the more decrepit sections of the city. Moat feigned poverty, though Paula had seen pictures of his three homes, including the small chalet tucked under a Pocono speed slope. It was probably true that Moat earned very little money from the shop itself, at least in over-the-counter sales. His small back rooms, one of which she and Jerem had slept in, were reserved for, as Moat put it, "the more elegant transactions." Moat was one of Lamalan's primary funnels to the Intercolonial black market.

Paula had sent some good referrals to him over the years. He had always made it plain that she could call on him if she needed a favor. After yesterday's escape from the terminal, she and Jerem had come straight here. Moat had taken them in, offering them sanctuary for as long as they wished.

Paula entered the shop, squinted at the morning sun pouring through the skylights. The front wall, facing the street, had no windows; only a tiny peephole at the top of the heavy wooden door permitted a view of the boulevard.

Moat was standing behind a glass counter, bartering with an old woman. The lady wanted to sell Moat an oscillation cooker and she wanted sixty-five bytes for it. Moat told the woman, in his loud, growling voice, that the price was outrageous. She muttered a religious curse and angrily suggested that Moat had evacuated his brains into a toilet.

It took a few more minutes of nasty haggling before the woman came down to fifty-five bytes. Moat raised his offer to forty. Glaring at each other, they settled on forty-five. The woman counted the cash cards twice, gave Moat the finger, and shuffled out the door. Moat picked up the aluminum oscillation cooker and tossed it onto a junkpile in the corner.

Moat enjoyed overdressing. Today he wore blue silk trousers

and a banana-stripe shirt. Tufts of gray hair fell almost to his shaggy eyebrows. The gray beard was longer on the left side than it was on the right. He had the waist of a hippopotamus and the ankles of a gazelle.

His thick lips twisted into a grin as he spotted Paula. "I love that old woman. Reminds me of my dear departed wife, the Trust bless her poor spirit. A bitch from the heart."

"We really appreciate you letting us stay."

"Hey, forget it. You and the splinter can have the back room for as long as you like." His eyes twinkled. He rubbed his belly. "And if you ever want more space, you can sneak over into my bedroom any time!"

Paula had a good comeback for that one, but she restrained herself as Jerem shuffled in from the back. "As I recall, Moat, the last time I was here there was a young lady—and I stress the word young—flitting about these rooms."

Moat laughed, then snapped his fingers. "Bodies of the Trust! I'm forgetting—you've been asleep for half a day. You haven't heard the news!"

"What news?"

"That Paratwa friend of yours dropped in on a zoo over in Northern Cal last night. The shitsucker wiped out half the animals and then killed three Guardies who tried to stop it."

Moat filled in the details. Goosebumps raced up Paula's spine as she recalled Smiler and Sad-eyes, standing so casually in front of her home.

Jerem frowned, then brightened. "Does that mean we can go home?"

Moat chuckled. "I expect it won't be long, kid. This Northern Cal mess has Arty's Guardies in an uproar. You know the Guardians. There's about a million of 'em and they're all gonna be pissed that this Paratwa dared to strike down three of 'em. They'll be shootin' all over space till they find the bastard."

"I hope they kill it," said Jerem.

"From what I hear, that's about the only way you stop one of these bastards. Paratwa ain't exactly known for surrendering."

Jerem hopped up onto the counter. "How long do ya think it'll take for the Guardians to kill it?"

Moat rubbed his beard. "I shouldn't think it would take too long. Hell, kid, you'll probably be back in school by next week."

Paula regarded them gravely. She did not want the trader giving Jerem false hopes. Moat had not seen the creature, had not experienced the fear. There was something horribly shrewd about Smiler and Sad-eyes, as if they were so smart that the possibility of losing had never entered their minds.

Mind, she corrected herself. Smiler and Sad-eyes was singular. It was difficult not to think of them as a pair.

A buzzer sounded. The front door slid open. Two men entered the shop. Jerem's mouth dropped. Moat eased himself back behind the counter and laid a hand on the hidden shelf where he kept his thruster.

They were big men, garbed in coarse dark fabrics. Their shirts were ragged, their pants stained and dirty. Odorant bags hung from short chains fastened to their belts. The putrid smell of dead fish filled Moat's store.

Costeaus.

One had shoulder-length brown hair and piercing green eyes. Paula would have found him handsome had he not had a large scarlet penis tattooed on the left side of his face.

His black-skinned companion wore wide suspenders that looked like they were made from raw meat. The black pirate ambled to the counter and glared at Moat.

"Either use that thruster or bring your hands out where I can see 'em."

Moat regarded the pirate gravely. For an instant, Paula thought the trader was going to yank out his thruster and start shooting. Instead, Moat smiled and placed his hands on top of the counter.

"What can I help you with?"

The pirate with the penis tattoo answered. "Nothing." He turned to Paula. "You're Bob Max's neighbor?"

Paula nodded dumbly. "How did you . . . know that?" She was so stunned that she could think of nothing else to say.

"Word has it that you know most of the traders along this row. We got lucky."

She found her voice again. "What do you want?"

The black pirate approached Jerem. "You with your mom Saturday night—when Bob Max got vacuumed?"

Jerem nodded meekly.

"Let him alone!" Paula snapped. "I asked you what you want."

"It's a clan affair," said the pirate with the tattoo. "You're to come with us."

"She's not going anywhere," Moat warned. His hands were still on the counter but his fat body had tensed.

"Not your affair," said the black man. He laid a huge hand across Jerem's shoulder.

Paula grabbed the pirate's wrist and yanked it away from her son. Moat's right hand shot under the counter. He pulled out his thruster and leveled it at the black pirate.

Neither of the Costeaus appeared upset by Moat's action. The one with the tattoo smiled at the trader. The scarlet penis seemed to worm its way across his cheek.

"Recognize our smell?" he asked softly.

Moat's eyes narrowed. "Educate me."

The tattooed pirate addressed Jerem. "Know anything about clans, boy?"

"No, sir."

"We each got our own smell, boy. Some people are smart enough to know the difference between odors. Other people are dumb. They can't tell the difference between shit and mashed turkey. Smart heads, but dumb noses. People like that had better stay

108

out of the jungle, 'cause they're liable to get their smart heads
bitten off by a lion.''

''A lion?'' Moat asked quietly. The gun wavered in his hand.
''You're from the Alexanders?''

Penis tattoo nodded.

''Shit,'' Moat grumbled. He gave Paula a helpless shrug and
then laid his thruster on the counter. ''I'm sorry, Paula. You and
the splinter had better go with 'em.'' There was fear in his eyes.

''We're not going anywhere!'' Paula raged. ''Jerem, I want you
to—''

The black man grabbed Jerem by the shoulder and slapped his
hand against the boy's arm. Paula caught the flash of a small needle in the pirate's open palm. She grabbed for the arm, missed.

The pirate with the penis tattoo was suddenly behind her—the
odor of dead fish intense, almost overpowering. The pirate's hot
breath blew against the side of her face. She started to scream. A
clammy palm covered her mouth. A needle pricked the skin below
her right elbow.

Paula tried to kick him, but he wrapped his leg around her ankles, pinned her against him. She stood helplessly, her mind awash
in a melange of feelings: fear for Jerem as he fell to unconsciousness in the black pirate's arms, anger at Moat for allowing
this to happen, surprise at the utter boldness of these Costeaus.
And then the drugged needle took effect and she felt herself drift-
ing away.

—from *The Rigors*, by Meridian

*I once gave my advanced class of humans a lesson in the complex
process that the pre-Apocalyptics had dubbed sapient supersedure.*

On the day of the lesson, only one of my tways entered the classroom and took its place at the double podium. The twenty-eight humans, seated in a semicircle before me and obviously wondering where my other tway was, whispered in hushed tones. I eased their curiosity and explained jokingly that my better half had taken ill with a minor physical affliction and needed a day of bed-rest. The humans laughed. With their fears mitigated, I launched into the scheduled lesson—a discourse on the proper methods for humans to set and initiate goals within a Paratwa-dominated society.

I discussed the essence of Paratwa rule and highlighted the advantages of a totally structured society—no wars, no poverty, no sharp peaks and valleys, nothing to stand in the way of satisfying, contented lives for both Paratwa and humans. The class easily followed the logic of my argument; these were, after all, some of the brightest humans we had. Generations of breeding and training within a controlled environment had eliminated rebellious attitudes. In fact, most of these particular humans were so intensely loyal to us that they would have reported any signs of perfidy among their classmates.

That was how we learned that one of the twenty-eight had indeed been engaging in anti-Paratwa activities.

I continued my lecture, gradually shifting emphasis to some of the shortcuts that the pre-Apocalyptics, including the Paratwa, had used to attain goals.

"Sapient supersedure," I said with a smile, "was one of the fastest and most famous methods for social advancement. Before the Apocalypse, sapient supersedure almost achieved the mark of a religion. The process engendered achievement in all walks of life but it was particularly successful on the high corporate levels, where interpersonal relationships remained more data-oriented than feeling-based."

One of the students, a young male, raised his hand. "Sir, I've read Merkhoffer's standard history on the subject. But frankly, I'm still at a loss to understand how these incredible substitutions went undetected.''

Excellent, *I thought. I turned to the young man.*

"Sapient supersedure—the process of killing an individual and assuming his identity—is far easier than one might expect.

"There are three phases necessary for the fulfillment of a supersedure. First—the substitute must have access to the victim's biocharts and history files. Within the framework of an information-conscious age, like the mid to late twenty-first century, worldwide computer networks made the acquisition of such data relatively simple. With a bit of perseverance, one could easily learn all about an intended victim.

"Second—the substitute had to arrange for his own alteration. Ideally, both the victim and his substitute should be physically similar, but other than a vast difference in height, there was little that mid-twenty-first surgical techniques could not accomplish. Even if victim and substitute were of different sexes, it was possible to identically match them." *I paused.* "Of course, that required a bit of determination.''

Several students chuckled.

"Along with surgical alteration, the victim also had to arrange for the camouflaging of his own vital signs, most particularly his brainwave and biorhythmic patterns. Again, by the mid-twenty-first century, there was an entire science dedicated to the generation of false physical indexes.

"The final phase necessary for a successful supersedure was the most difficult. The substitute, who now looked like—and was capable of perfectly imitating—his victim, had to kill the prototype. The murder had to be done in such a way that no evidence of the victim would remain. An intense fire, incinerating flesh and melting bones and teeth, was the preferred method.''

I smiled and provided an example. "One day, a man leaves home and heads for his corporate headquarters. On the way, he is ambushed and assassinated and his body hidden for later disposal. The substitute arrives at corporate headquarters, greets everyone *perfunctorily as he does every day, and assumes his new social responsibilities.*

"Naturally, the substitute would have already been involved with the corporation on a lower level and if he has done his homework, he will be familiar with what is required of him in his new position. The home and social life provided greater challenges, which is why most substitutes chose childless, unmarried victims."

I shrugged at the young man who had asked the question. "Unless you committed some gross error during the three preparatory phases—unless your information about the victim was wrong, or your surgical alteration was done sloppily, or you messed up the murder and disposal of your victim—chances were that you would not be caught. And even if people grew suspicious of you, the fact that a substitution had occurred was almost impossible to prove.

"If you look and act like a person, you are that person. Sapient supersedure works because most people want to believe that simple adage."

I faced a man seated in the front row.

"Korasan, stand up please."

The man stood.

"Class, if I were to tell you that this man Korasan was actually my other tway and that the real Korasan is awaiting trial for engaging in anti-Paratwa activities, would you believe me?"

The humans murmured among themselves, staring at Korasan with incredulous looks. Most of the students shook their heads.

I laughed and spoke through Korasan's mouth. "Well, you had better believe it, because it's true!"

I moved my Korasan tway up to the podium, and for the benefit of those few students who still looked doubtful, I spoke in stereo through the mouths of both tways.

"So you see, sapient supersedure is not nearly as difficult as some of you might have believed. I have been substituting for Korasan for the past three days, trying to learn if any other humans were involved with him in his traitorous activities. As a result, several other men from his domicile have been arrested."

The class came spontaneously to their feet. I received a standing ovation.

Pasha Haddad had suggested that they split the revivees up—more information could be garnered in that way. The Pasha had taken Gillian. Rome had spent his day with the midget in tow. Rome had originally intended talking with Nick for only an hour or so and then turning him over to one of Haddad's lieutenants. But the afternoon had passed quickly.

"Runaway technology," said Rome, "was not the only factor that led to the Apocalypse."

Nick shrugged his tiny shoulders. "Of course not. It's just that runaway technology was the most apparent symptom of the problem." The midget grinned. "Ask any good doctor about treating symptoms!"

Rome laughed. Despite his best efforts to remain impartial, he found himself becoming genuinely fond of this strange little man.

Nick sat cross-legged on Rome's deskchair, his eyes fastened on the monitor screen. "La Gloria de la Ciencia," he quoted softly. "So those bastards are still around, huh?"

"And far more effective than they were in your era."

Irrya's late-afternoon light, beaming through Rome's office windows, was begining to change. Timer-controlled prism optics started refracting only certain colors; chemical dusts flowed out of huge centersky blowers above Irrya's three cosmishield strips.

A red sunset had been programmed for tonight—Rome's favorite. It was one of those peaceful beauties capable of piercing the intellect, touching that part of him where only pure sight and sound held power. He felt desperately in need of such a diversion.

Nick had been at Rome's desk monitor for the past three hours, accessing data fed up from the archives. The midget possessed the natural flair of the computer hawk, that ability to trace information through a myriad of paths and eventually arrive at its source.

Nick cleared the screen, jumped to another display. "I might be wrong, but it sure seems as if E-Tech has been losing support lately."

"That's correct," said Rome. He did not add that Nick had perceived in one afternoon what many of Rome's own staff people seemed unable to grasp.

"La Gloria de la Ciencia . . . these whackos appear to be generating a lot of support."

"They are. La Gloria de la Ciencia now has an effective voting bloc within the Irryan Senate. Many industrial conglomerates are behind them. At Council, Artwhiler and Lady Bonneville are strong supporters." He sighed. "In another three years, the Council will come up for reorganization. At that time, there's a good possibility that La Gloria de la Ciencia will be able to place an actual representative on the Council."

"Sounds pretty bad."

Rome nodded, tried to explain. "Our society has been changing. People seem to be growing more dissatisfied with the Colonial lifestyle. Many are looking for ways to return to the past. Many believe that the old technologies are the answer.

"The antique market, especially for machines and hi-tech tools, has grown by leaps and bounds over the past thirty years. There's a tremendous fascination with pre-Apocalyptic history. Religious feeling has also been on the rise. In fact, the most popular religious faction in the Colonies right now is the Church of the Trust. Their broad appeal is partly based on promising eternal salvation to any loyal follower who allows himself to be buried on Earth."

"Sounds expensive," Nick quipped.

"It is. But people seem to think it's important and are willing to pay the Church transport and service expenses just so that they can be laid to rest on the planet."

Rome shook his head. "This growing dissatisfaction with Colonial life—it's a very complex problem. E-Tech tries to address the social aspects of it. But on an individual level . . ." He shrugged.

"What makes a human being happy?" Nick said with a smile. "That's an age-old question."

"Yes it is. But what I don't understand is why our society is going in this direction. The average person here in the Colonies leads a more comfortable life than did most of his ancestors."

"They want more," Nick said. "Maybe it's the natural state of human beings to have no limits. Maybe the race is responding to inbred desires."

Rome spoke bitterly. "The last time the race responded to its inbred desires, most of the world was destroyed. There must be self-discipline, and if it can't be instilled on a personal level, then institutions such as E-Tech must be there to regulate the social consciousness."

Nick smiled. "You, Rome Franco, sound a lot like your predecessors. I think that the founders of E-Tech would be pleased."

Rome felt touched by the compliment. Outside, Irryan skyscrapers began to alight as the first hint of dusk arrived.

Nick changed the subject. "Your computer archives—the way you located Gillian and me. Was there a second program?"

Rome stared out the windows. The Pasha valued secrecy and had wanted to hold back information on the second program, at least until more was learned about Nick and Gillian. But Rome felt that he knew enough about Nick. There was a quality to the man; an inner poise reflected on the small face. Nick could be trusted.

Pasha Haddad would consider such a leap of faith reckless. But Rome was rarely mistaken with first impressions. It was a skill that had guided him well throughout his career with E-Tech. Angela understood.

Red clouds colored the air, accenting the nearest skyline.

"There is a second program," Rome said quietly. "We haven't been able to enter it as yet. Our programmer says that it would take six hundred years to run."

Nick took a long time to reply. When he did, Rome thought he detected a hint of sadness in his words.

"Please don't tell Gillian about the existence of this second program. And please don't ask me why."

Rome turned away from the dusk, caught a flash of pain across Nick's face.

The midget spoke slowly, as if the words were coming to him in a dream. "The E-Tech leaders of my era were faced with terrible problems. They knew in their hearts that no matter what they did, the Earth was doomed. The insanity surrounded us. It was a time when truly compassionate humans were forced to make the most cold-blooded decisions. They did what was necessary for the race to survive.

"The two great hopes were these Colonies and the starships. I see by your records that the voyagers of Star-Edge did not survive. That's very sad. I didn't know much about the details of Star-Edge—E-Tech was only peripherally involved in the project. But I did know people who had spent their entire adult lives designing and working on the starships. It's best that they're not alive today to know that all their efforts ended in failure.

"As for Colonial life . . . there were rigid tests given to all those who applied for emigration. E-Tech did its best to make sure that no Paratwa left the planet. There could be no guarantees, of course. Some of the assassins were shrewd—and there were the Ash Ock.

"They were the most terrible of all. Other Paratwa killed and slaughtered, but under the dominion of the Ash Ock, an apex of destruction was reached. They had a power of intellect that went beyond the pedestrian genius of mere humans. And they had the power to unlink—to function as two separate beings, to disguise themselves as normal humans, as it were. The Ash Ock, alone among the Paratwa, had the ability to live in both worlds."

Rome turned back to the window, mind's eye nailed to images he could not fully understand. The Ash Ock were shadows— words from a computer file.

Nick went on. "We did not know much about the Ash Ock. The labs that created them were destroyed, the genetic designers all perished. It was rumored that the royal Caste murdered many of their own creators, but no one was ever able to substantiate such a claim.

"Eventually, though, two of the Ash Ock were killed. Aristotle died by accident, caught in a South African firestorm while trying to bribe that nation's president. Empedocles, youngest of the five, was still undergoing training in an Ash Ock facility deep in the Brazilian rain forests. E-Tech raided that base and he, too, was destroyed.

"The other three—Sappho, Theophrastus, and Codrus—were believed to have perished during the biological plague of twenty ninety-seven. E-Tech was never certain of that, however. So rather than burden the future with such a frightening heritage, the organization chose to announce that the royal Caste had been destroyed."

Rome took a deep breath. "You're telling me that three of the Ash Ock could still be alive."

"It's possible. I tell you this because you are the leader of E-Tech. You should know such a thing."

Rome felt a swell of bitterness. "And the leaders of your era—they took it upon themselves to change the facts of history, to lie about the fate of the royal Caste. What we don't know can't hurt us."

"Yes! And they also made sure that should the time arise, you would be made aware of such knowledge. The intent of their manipulation was to give the Colonies a chance—to take away the burden of fear that our leaders lived with every day of their lives."

"The way a parent protects a child," Rome said angrily. "Only this child has grown up and the lie was still maintained."

Nick's laugh was brittle. "You are children. You are a society of children, and you should be thankful for it." He pointed to the monitor. "I see the outlines of your society and I see a world that the people of my time could only dream of. You have peace and you have a measure of security and you have accomplishment for its own sake. My era had accomplishment too, but not for the good of humanity. We had the science of greed and hatred and the technology of chaos. We had a world of the dead.''

Rome stared up at the reddening sky. *And we have a world that wants to become what you were.*

"And when do the lies stop?" Rome demanded. "You say that you don't want Gillian to learn of this second program. Fine. But what about us? Have you decided there is too much truth hidden there? Is it more than we can bear? What gives you the right to make such decisions?''

Nick stared at the blank terminal screen. "The second program—that's for Gillian, and him alone. The secrecy is for his benefit, not yours.''

Rome heard the genuine feeling in Nick's voice and some of his anger left. "He's been a good friend to you.''

"Yes. A good friend.'' The midget shut off the monitor and turned to Rome. The smile on his face seemed dreamlike, unreal.

"Let me tell you a story,'' Nick began, "about a young man whose parents were slain by a Paratwa.

"Gillian was only eleven when it happened—a small town in the Midwestern United States, decimated by an assassin on the run. The Paratwa fought its final battle on the streets of that town, but not before it had wiped out several hundred citizens, Gillian's parents included.

"Later, when the town was cleaning up, the local E-Tech officials discovered that one of the Paratwa's Cohe wands was missing.''

"Gillian took it?" questioned Rome.

"Yes. Secretly, over the next eight or nine years, he taught himself to use the weapon. Now, a Cohe wand is a strange implement—anyone can make it work, but it takes special skills to use it effectively. Some claimed it required unique motor coordination. Others said that an inner calm was neeeded, like that of a Zen Buddhist. Anyway, whatever the mysterious ability, Gillian had it.

"One day, Gillian met a young woman—love at first sight, that sort of thing. Her name was Catharine and they were together for several years. They were on their honeymoon in South America . . ." Nick stopped. The smile vanished from his face. "There was another Paratwa."

"She was killed," Rome said quietly.

"Yes. Gillian came to E-Tech a few months later. He wanted vengeance. The E-Tech people were ready to dismiss him as just another crank until he gave them a demonstration of what he could do with a Cohe wand.

"After some debate, the E-Tech leaders proposed that Gillian train and lead a secret team. That team's sole objective would be to search and destroy Paratwa assassins.

"I was an E-Tech programmer at the time and that's when I met Gillian. We hit it off. I joined the team. Gillian recruited and trained the actual combat unit: three soldiers from the old Earth Patrol Forces—mercenaries, real hardasses. I used my more humble skills to work on computer probability programs for tracking the assassins.

"If the Paratwa had one fault, it was their predictability. Many of the lesser breeds were easy to track. Most assassins were rigidly territorial, doing their killing within small geographic areas. A few even had homes in respectable suburban communities. If an assassin committed enough murders and remained within its territory, it was just a matter of time before we tracked it down.

"When we located a Paratwa, Gillian and his team were sent out. Most of the assassins were taken by surprise. The team was good. But it was Gillian's skill with the wand that made the difference."

Rome held up his hand. "You mean to tell me that Gillian and a few mercenaries were able to actually kill Paratwa assassins? I thought it took large military efforts to destroy them."

"Usually, it did. Before Gillian, there were basically two methods of stopping a Paratwa. One was saturation-bombing of the area where the assassin was believed to be located. Naturally, since most Paratwa were found in cities, the civilian death toll was quite high.''

Rome frowned.

"The second method was to send an urban combat company into the area. On a successful mission, where the assassin was killed, the company could count on fifty to a hundred casualties. If they were unlucky and happened to encounter one of the more dangerous breeds . . ." Nick shrugged. "Often, only the Paratwa survived.''

Rome nodded. It was hard to visualize such madness. But he was beginning to understand. In Northern California, the Paratwa had slaughtered close to a thousand animals.

"In the first two years, Gillian's team killed twenty-one Paratwa. We were E-Tech's secret success. They couldn't brag about us, of course. It wouldn't be proper for an organization dedicated to such noble causes to be associated with hired killers.

"At any rate, E-Tech eventually decided to send us after bigger game. A Japanese assassin from the Loshito breed had been terrorizing the south of France for seven months. I located him living in an apartment house overlooking the Mediterranean. Gillian and the team blew him away on the beach.

"Later, we learned that this Loshito had been serving the Ash Ock. The royal Caste apparently decided we were growing into a nuisance, so they sent a KGB-trained Voshkof Rabbit after us.''

Nick grinned. "Gillian and company rather unceremoniously dispatched that assassin in an alleyway behind the Push-'n'-Shove speedball arena in downtown Alberta, Canada.''

Nick's smile became distant. "At that point, I suppose the Ash Ock decided we were becoming a major threat. The last assassin they sent was better—a real nasty son-of-a-bitch, even by Paratwa standards. A Jeek Elemental named Reemul. He was known as the 'liege-killer.'

"There were many Paratwa who did not want to be united under the Ash Ock. This Jeek was sent out to show them the error of their ways." Nick paused. "In an odd way, this assassin actually helped us. Reemul hunted down and killed Paratwa who refused to serve the royal Caste.''

Rome shook his head. "This Jeek murdered your team?"

"Everyone but Gillian. It happened in a tavern in Boston. Gillian and I thought we were setting an ambush for this assassin, when, in reality, the reverse was true. The liege-killer was waiting. Gillian escaped only because he used his wand to create a wall of fire that briefly trapped Reemul on the other side of the room.

"That was in 2097. A few months later, it was publicly announced that the last of the Ash Ock had perished. E-Tech decided that Gillian and I might better serve the future." Nick's bright smile returned. "Whammo! I go to sleep and I wake up here!"

The sky was almost completely red. Irrya's skyscrapers were ablaze with light. Tonight, however, Rome felt immeasurably distant from the beauty.

He chose his words carefully. "In the event that I give you and Gillian permission to go after this Paratwa, and you do indeed eliminate him . . ." He hesitated. "Have you given any consideration to your future here?"

Nick grinned. "Do we have one?"

"Yes. Of course. It's just that if you were to become legal citizens, certain formalities would have to be observed. You would have to be endowed with useful occupations."

Nick looked mildly amused. "The E-Tech treasury will not continue to support us? Gee. I was counting on a life of luxury."

Rome turned away.

"Hey, I'm joking. All that stuff about the money. You know, I really don't give a damn about that. Neither does Gillian. Really! I mean, all the riches in the world couldn't have gotten me into this profession. Know what I mean?"

Rome nodded. "It's just that the Council of Irrya has certain regulations concerning stasis revivees. There are requirements for permanent citizenship."

Laughter flooded the office. "Do you mean to say," Nick asked mischievously, "that Paratwa-killer would not be enough?"

"You have skills as a programmer. I was thinking more of Gillian."

"Ahh, yes . . . Gillian. Well, Gillian too has other skills. I suggest, however, that we don't look that far ahead just yet."

"All right. But there's another potential problem. Under Intercolonial law, should you actually kill this assassin, there is a possibility that you could be tried for murder. Councillor Artwhiler might bring such charges against you just to hurt E-Tech."

Nick looked grave. "That may be so. But your worries are based on the tenets of a civilized society and the Paratwa is not a civil creature. Right now, this assassin is something novel in the lives of your people—a vicarious excitement, a break in their monotony. After it brutalizes your Colonies for a while, the public mood will change." He chuckled softly. "Take my word for it. If Gillian and I destroy this creature, they'll make us public heroes."

Codrus closed his four eyes and generated the internal peace necessary for holistic thought. Sounds and odors continued to bombard him from two locations almost a mile apart, yet the interference factor brought on by those senses was negligible when compared to the omnipresence of sight. Intense cerebral reflection remained easier when two visual fields did not have to be interlaced.

Reemul has flexed. It has been done in such a way that no one will suspect his identity. Any Paratwa could have attacked a zoo and slaughtered wild animals.

Two faces smiled.

The flexing, although savage, also serves to reduce the factor of terror throughout the Colonies. It is an act of violence amenable to rationalization. The Paratwa could have killed hundreds of citizens, yet the assassin—or the force guiding it—chose a zoo as the target. Therefore, the Paratwa does not wish to deliberately harm humans. After all, the Guardian patrol stumbled upon the scene— had they arrived a few minutes later, their lives would have been saved. The assassin spared the young warden, didn't he? And the first victim—well, Bob Max was a smuggler, and had probably deserved such a fate.

A billion humans will cling to such rationalizations once their thoughts are directed. (The Bishop/tway would help in that regard. His next sermon would be developed along such lines.) *A billion humans will be relaxed when the next shock occurs.*

It was the essence of terror. When Codrus was a child, he had been fascinated by old videos dealing with twentieth-century amusements. Images of roller coasters had been particularly intriguing. At the crest of the ride, faces were strained, poised for the shock of the downhill run. At the bottom of the hill, a sense of deliverance could be detected. And then, unexpectedly perhaps, the roller coaster would plummet down another mountain, and collective terror would again disfigure those countenances.

The terror would be instantly repressed, of course. Cathartic laughter and cries of relief would serve as substitutes for what few humans could face directly.

The roller coaster was a microcosm of social reaction; the same emotions could be created throughout a society when the proper techniques were applied. Unfortunately, the Ash Ock had not developed such control in the beginning. They had held humanity at the frightening crest for too long. The terror had numbed the senses, the riders of the roller coaster had been forced to repress even cathartic reactions to their fear, thus making the emotion more potent. Eventually, humanity had become oversaturated by terror and had been unable to contain it. The world had flexed. The roller coaster had collapsed.

For the second coming there would be no such mistake. The terror of Reemul would build gradually, deepening with time, yet cries of relief would be allowed. The summation of the roller-coaster crests would be directed, the proper social changes would occur, and then the final downhill run would take place and humanity would emerge from the train, shaken yet essentially unharmed. Most would never realize that they had been switched to a different track until it was too late.

By the timeframe of the Ash Ock, Reemul's reign of terror would not last very long. It was a minor correction in the social flow, inconsequential when viewed up close, yet critical when perceived on a grander scale.

Codrus chuckled. Two mouths shaped laughter. He felt childishly pleased by the flow of events. He stretched out his four arms and allowed himself to relish the experience of being whole, of simply being Codrus. Too often, these days, he was forced to function as independent tways. Such a life was acceptable, but certainly not desirable. The Ash Ock, alone among Paratwa, possessed the power to interlink and unlink at will—to be whole or to be separate—to exist as two pseudo-humans or as Paratwa. When Codrus was younger, the unlinking into two distinct entities had been a satisfying game. But nowadays he desired only to be what felt natural.

I desire unity.

He sighed, exhaling through one tway, then the other. Even the pattern of slightly out-of-step dual breathing brought exquisite pleasure.

He reined in his emotions. It was too easy to simply forget his troubles, to bathe in unity. The second coming would not be brought about by such self-indulgence.

And Codrus had already made one mistake. He had underestimated human greed. Bob Max was supposed to have had the pirates destroy that stasis tunnel in Philadelphia. But Max—or the pirates—failed to carry out that order. There was only one explanation: someone had hoped to return to the stasis tunnel, perhaps to search for hidden treasure. *Foolish humans. Couldn't they see that Reemul was the treasure?*

E-Tech had gotten a look inside that tunnel and had seen the stasis operation. Codrus knew there was little chance that the humans would learn much from their discovery; nevertheless, an error remained an error. There was nothing he could do now except phase the schema into his overall plan.

At least the Irryan Council meeting had gone well. A delicious interlacing of possibilities had spiraled into the choice pattern. Rome Franco had performed as expected. His doomed attempt to hide the existence of the Paratwa from the Council had further accentuated E-Tech's position of weakness.

As the clear underdog, Rome Franco's organization was now perfectly situated for a remarkable ascent. E-Tech would shortly be springboarded into the role of Colonial savior. Rome Franco would satisfy society's need for a hero. About one month from now, a celebration of majestic proportions would overwhelm the dedicated Councillor when it was announced that E-Tech had destroyed the Paratwa assassin.

Naturally, Reemul would not die. Codrus had still to establish the final details, but the basic plan called for Reemul to be trapped by E-Tech and to purportedly perish in a fire. The lack of identifiable bodies would leave a certain residue of suspicion within E-Tech, but the ending of the Paratwa attacks would soon convince nearly everyone that the threat had indeed been crushed.

And should Reemul actually be destroyed ahead of plan, Codrus knew of other sleeping assassins, hidden before the Apocalypse. If a second or third Paratwa had to be awakened, so be it. That correction in the social flow was the only item of importance.

Of course, the chances of Reemul failing were negligible. He was a Jeek Elemental, the deadliest of the breeds. And Reemul had an ability that went beyond the intentions of his creators.

Due to some flaw in the McQuade Unity that had been injected into his two eggs, Reemul had been born with a synchronization disturbance. The standard interlacing of his two brains had not occurred in the normal manner. Horizontal and vertical scanning patterns had been supplanted by strange diagonal flows, theretofore unknown to Jeek scientists. Reemul had been honed under the vigorous tutelage of the Jeek fighting masters; all the while, the scientists had studied his strange interlacing, never intending for him to be sold on the world armaments market. But by Reemul's teenage years, it became obvious that his inherent difference had made him even deadlier.

Unpredictability. The Paratwa assassins tended to lack that quality. They were creatures who had been specialized almost to the point of absurdity, and such specialization inevitably led to the formation of strong habits. Repeated actions were predictable actions.

Reemul was the exception to the rule. His skewed interlace patterns had made a shambles of E-Tech's computer-tracking methods. He did not quite fit the known parameters of the Jeek Elementals. Even after Reemul had entered the Ash Ock fold, his bizarre ways of carrying out assignments had left E-Tech stumped. They knew he existed—somewhere in the world was an assassin whose primary identification was his failure to fit into a probability matrix. E-Tech had gotten no further. Even their greatest weapon—that secret little band of soldier-hunters—had succumbed to Reemul in the end.

No, Reemul would not fail, but he must appear to. The Colonies had to emerge from the Paratwa onslaught with a sense of victory. The essence of Codrus's problem was that Reemul would have to be put back into stasis at the end of this affair.

Reemul would not like that. The same qualities that made the Jeek unpredictable also made him the least malleable assassin in the Ash Ock fold. Two centuries ago, when the royal Caste had deduced the inevitable coming of the Apocalypse, Reemul had balked at being frozen. Codrus knew that this time it would be even more difficult to convince the Jeek to go peacefully to sleep.

Reemul would have to be told the truth soon, however. The longer he was allowed to rampage, the harder Codrus's chore would become. Eventually, the Jeek might refuse to obey. The problems inherent in that scenario had to be avoided.

With trickery, Codrus might get a shot at killing Reemul. However, if he failed . . .

It was likely that the ultimate plan would still succeed—it was just that Codrus would not be alive on that glorious day. He held no illusions about his chances for survival against a renegade Jeek.

Timing was the critical factor. If Reemul was informed of his fate too soon, his effectiveness might be hindered. And if Codrus waited too long . . .

Someone's coming. A loud knock on the Bishop's sanctuary door broke his concentration.

"Bishop Vokir?" the voice called. "The Priests from the Chow Kwi Colony have arrived."

Codrus answered through the Bishop's mouth. "Please see that they are made comfortable. I will join them in the proctor hall in ten minutes."

"Yes, your eminence." The servant's footsteps trailed off down the corridor.

Codrus dissolved the link, sensed the interlace patterns coagulating back into two distinct entities. As usual, he felt a sadness wash over him—the loss of Codrus and the rise of his tways. Someday, the passage from unity to duality would be a memory. *Someday I will be free to exist as a whole.*

It was Codrus's final thought. The passage was completed. The Bishop arose from the bed to prepare for the day's activities: five baptisms in a vat of purified sea water brought up from the Pacific Ocean, the royal misk wedding of two wealthy lesbians from Pocono, formal talks with the heads of the Church's Missionary sector. All of that would follow a lengthy meeting with the Chow Kwi Priests.

The Bishop sighed. The Church asked much of him. In his busiest moments, he felt a profound longing for the unending comfort of unity. *Someday.*

He could still sense the presence of his tway, of course. The link was never totally broken, just weakened to the point where the two halves could operate independently. The Bishop was pleased that his tway also had a full agenda for the day. It was good that they both kept busy lest they dream too much of Codrus.

Actually, the Bishop knew that he possessed the lighter responsibilities. His tway, being an Irryan Councillor, was perpetually confronted by greater demands.

On Tuesday morning, nearly twenty-four hours after his awakening, they allowed Gillian to leave the Irryan headquarters building. Pasha Haddad had objected; he did not trust Gillian, did not want him walking without escort through the city. Nick had convinced Rome Franco that Gillian's immediate acclimation to the Colonies was vital and that a solitary venture would do him immense good. Nick had not forgotten how to stretch the truth.

It *was* important, of course. Nick could learn about the Colonies from behind a computer terminal, but Gillian needed to walk the streets. There were rhythms, accents—unprogrammable facets of a world, begging to be experienced. He had to allow his senses full rein to—collect raw data, route it through awareness, correlate it. Only then could he get a feel for this world, make unbiased judgments.

Usually.

There were things out here on the Irryan streets that reminded him of Catharine.

He had been warned about vertigo—a common problem for Earth-born revivees confronted with the reality of standing on the inside of a cylinder and not falling down. Or up.

He leaned against the side of the E-Tech headquarters building, stared past twelve stories of antique white brickface, and calmly observed another part of the city six miles above. His first thought was that the structures were upside down and that they should fall on top of him. He explored the feeling, recognized his Earth prejudices, and dealt with them on a base level. This was reality. It was that simple.

If only his feelings for Catharine could be dealt with so easily.

The thorofare was four lanes wide and stringed with slow-moving cars. The autos did not look much different from those of Earth—low-slung, four-wheeled, many of them painted with rainbow patterns. All were quieter than terrestrial cars, and many were convertibles. There was no rain scheduled for today, he had learned.

The sidewalks were wide and clean and jammed with people. There was a quality about the movement of the pedestrians that seemed foreign at first, until he recognized the distinctions. There was no street hustle here, no urban crush of humanity ramming itself along the boulevards like in the Earth cities. The Irryan pedestrians seemed polite to one another—conversations developed as people waited at street corners, pausing for the traffic monitors to alter flows. Smiles, everywhere there were smiles, and few of them looked false. People seemed genuinely contented. Even the few police officers he spotted seemed unconcerned, stopping to talk with strangers along the sidewalks.

Nick had explained that many of the Colonies seemed to be this way. Still, it was hard to accept these happy crowds until you saw them for yourself.

A Paratwa assassin in such a world would be a wolf among sheep.

Even the three E-Tech Security people who were following Gillian seemed much too placid for such a chore. He hoped that the men and the woman did not represent Haddad's best. They had been ridiculously easy to spot.

He debated losing them, more as an exercise in antishadowing than for any intrinsic reason. It would give him something to do. But he recognized that such an action would make Haddad even more suspicious than he was now. Perhaps next time the Security Chief would resort to more sophisticated methods.

Gillian halted in front of a store window and gazed at his smiling image reflected in the dark glass. *I'm not thinking,* It was suddenly obvious that Haddad must indeed be using other tracking tools. The three tails were a diversion, designed to be spotted by Gillian so that he might overlook the real trackers.

It had to be electronic surveillance. Since E-Tech had kept a tight rein over such technology for the past two centuries, Haddad was most likely utilizing one of the old methods.

Where had the locating transmitters been planted? His clothes? E-Tech had given him a full wardrobe, but it was unlikely that they would have bugged every article. Besides, in lieu of opening modem-accessible accounts through the ICN—an unwise move because of their uncertain status—E-Tech had supplied both him and Nick with generous wads of cash cards. There was nothing to prevent Gillian from stepping into an outfitter shop and purchasing new clothing.

Subcutaneous bugs? Probably. It would have been fairly easy to implant microtransmitters beneath his skin during the stasis-revival process. Haddad appeared shrewd enough to have done such a thing.

Well, no matter When the time came, he would dispose of the tracking bugs. For now, it was best to allow Haddad to believe he had the upper hand.

Gillian wandered aimlessly for several hours, absorbing and correlating the rhythms and anatomy of the city. Irrya was immense. Its structures represented architectures from a melange of Earth societies spanning human history. Buildings echoed their styles as he passed them by.

A sleek granite skyscraper proudly exclaimed: UNITED STATES OF AMERICA. Two wood-veneered pagodas, designed to look as if they had authentic thatched bamboo roofs, politely announced themselves as early Japanese. A bank projected the warm exterior of a Swiss chalet. Soaring apartment buildings, with creeper vines entwined through quaint railed balconies, reminded him of Rio's old section.

A block-long chunk of sculpted marble predated them all. Its rounded columns supported a stone esplanade that was straight out of the Roman empire. ICN was carved in the polished stone above the pillars.

Nick had explained to Gillian about the Intercolonial Credit Net. It was a direct outgrowth of the banking consortiums that had dominated Earth's twilight years. The ICN wielded financial power throughout the Colonies on a scale that the monster corporations of the twenty-first century would have envied.

Gillian made a huge circle and was heading back toward E-Tech when he came to a weird building along the main thorofare.

Huge blue-green block letters spelled out CHURCH OF THE TRUST at an angle across the front facade. The building appeared to be an elegant throwback to early twentieth-century architecture. Parallel speedlines swept across curved arches and rectilinear shapes accented the cream-colored walls. Art Deco had been a rarity even in Gillian's time. The designers of this structure certainly recognized the value of distinction.

There was something else strange about the Church. He hesitated across the street from it, puzzled until the memory surfaced. *Art Deco.* Catharine had once taken him to an old building in New York with the same architectural style. They had gone there for lunch one afternoon. No, it had not been lunch, it had been a show of some sort—a play with real actors. They had sat near the back of the old theater and had watched, had watched . . .

He could not remember. It was strange, sometimes, trying to recall those few precious years with her. Events jumbled together, defied the logical discipline of his mind. There was, of course, an explanation for his forgetfulness. During that short time they had been together, *thinking* had not been a priority. The pleasures of the relationship had been too intense. A whole other level of his being had been involved.

He looked up at the sky, saw huge buildings hanging far above, about to fall on him. Reeling in panic, he clutched the side of the nearest structure for support. His head spun. His hands and feet shook with a sudden chill. His guts ached.

Stupid! I should know by now! I should know not to think of her!

The worst of the vertigo passed. Several people stopped to help, breathing their concerns. He forced a smile, pushed away from them.

"I'm all right. Just a little dizzy."

They let him go. He marched quickly down the street, away from the Church. He had experienced enough for one day. His only desire now was to get back inside the E-Tech building as quickly as possible.

Nick had asked Pasha Haddad for the toughest and meanest volunteers that could be found. Gillian sat on a stool in the corner of the private gym that Haddad had arranged for them to use, observing the volunteers trudging in through the far door. The men and women traded asides with one another and laughed and gave each other hearty smacks on the back. Their mood was good. Gillian did not hide his disappointment.

"Is this the best we can do?"

Nick shrugged and kept studying his portable computer terminal. "Remember, this is a peaceful society. Their idea of intense excitement is to go out and watch a thunderstorm."

Gillian laughed. He felt good this evening and was looking forward to training a new team. Catharine and today's sickness were distant memories.

"How many has Haddad given us?"

Nick stared up at the approaching crowd. "Twenty or so in this first bunch, and he's promised another thirty by the end of the week."

"Do you have preliminary reports on them?"

Nick grinned. "Of course. I know their life stories, including when they first burped and when they last fucked. I'll say one thing for Haddad, he's thorough."

Not thorough enough, Gillian feared. There were now a total of three witnesses to the Paratwa killings. One of them, the young warden who had survived the carnage at the zoo, was being held in secret custody by the Guardians. The other two had been released by Haddad, had managed to outwit E-Tech's tail, and were now officially listed as missing.

Gillian would have liked nothing better than to talk to those people, especially the mother and son, who had actually conversed with the assassin. He could have asked subtle questions, things that neither Haddad nor the Guardians would have considered important. A wealth of information about the Paratwa was most likely contained in those minds. And he could not get at it.

Nick stood up and ordered the approaching volunteers to form a half circle. One of the men made an audible remark about Nick's size. Several of the group laughed. Gillian moved onto the mats and stood before them.

"You have all been chosen to try out for a new E-Tech special forces group. We've prepared a rather harsh little test for you. And if you pass, the training will get worse."

Gillian studied their faces, saw doubts on at least half of them. No one spoke, however. Their machismo was at stake.

"Any questions?" Nick asked.

A black woman stepped forward. "What's the purpose of this special forces group?"

Nick planted hands on hips. "To subdue threats in restrictive combat situations."

"Does this have something to do with the Paratwa assassin?" someone asked.

"No comment," said Nick.

Gillian allowed a condescending smile to creep over his face. "I've been told that most of you are unsuitable for E-Tech's main forces and that all of you possess substandard intelligence. Now these are just the qualities we're looking for—men and women such as yourselves will serve as excellent shock troops in special combat situations. None of you should be ashamed of your stupidity—my assistant and I are prepared to make reasonable concessions during your training period. We will respond at your own level of understanding whenever and wherever possible. Do you understand?"

There was nervous laughter and a few looks of outrage. Gillian targeted one of the angry ones—a big man with a face that looked like it had been formed by hammer and anvil. Gillian moved to within a yard of the man.

"Are you married?"

The man favored his friends with a grin. "Yeah."

Gillian shook his head. "Nick, what do our records show about this man's wife?"

Nick pretended to study his terminal. "When he's not around, she goes out whoring."

"Is she a good whore?" Gillian asked calmly.

The man glowered. "You'd better watch what you say."

"Why? There's no shame in being a whore, provided she's a good one." He smiled and reached out his hand to playfully tickle the man's chin. "Of course, if you're keeping something from us . . . Maybe she's not such a good whore, after all?"

Nick's four-foot-four frame shook with laughter. "I think you're right. It says here that she's even done it with animals . . . dogs, mostly."

The big man's face turned red and ugly. "I didn't come here for this crap!"

"Probably not," Gillian replied. "You're probably here because you can't satisfy your wife at home and you're trying to make up for your failure by showing how tough you really are. Actually, deep down inside, I'll bet you got married just so that you could impress your friends."

Nick laughed. "And the real bitch is, they're probably not even impressed!"

The man took a menacing step toward Gillian. "What is this shit—one of Haddad's reaction tests or somethin'?"

Gillian ignored him and turned to one of the other volunteers, a smaller man with sandy hair. "What's this one called, Nick?"

"Let's see . . ." Nick referred to his hand terminal. "That there is Roger Kensington."

Gillian moved closer, stuck his left foot behind the man's ankle, and pushed him. For a second, Roger Kensington's arms flailed the air. Then he tripped backward and slammed onto the mat.

Without hesitation, Gillian threw a punch to the guts of the next volunteer in line. The man doubled over in agony. Gillian brought his foot up and slammed it into the chest of a burly woman. She grunted and crashed against the man next to her. Both of them sprawled to the floor.

The big man cursed and came up behind Gillian.

"Hey! You care to try that shit on me!"

Gillian whirled. His outstretched foot caught the giant in the side of the face. The man dropped, out cold before he crashed to the mat.

"Anyone else?" Gillian asked pleasantly. No one moved. "How about all of you at the same time?" he goaded.

There were no takers. Nick hid his disappointment by clearing his throat. "Well, people, I'd like to thank you all for coming down here tonight. We're still doing preliminary testing and we have a lot more work to do before our team is assembled. I hope that you all get over your aches and bruises and realize that this was indeed a test of your reactions. You all did quite well. Thanks again for your cooperation. We'll be in touch."

The volunteers milled about for several moments. Confused mutterings filled the gym.

Nick rubbed his hands together and smiled politely. He sounded like a tired party host trying to clear the guests from his home. "Thanks again, gang. It was good of you to take time out of your busy schedules to come down here tonight. Really. We appreciate it."

A couple of the men picked up the unconscious giant. Several of the others helped the battered victims to their feet. Angry faces glared at Gillian as they exited. In a minute, the gym was empty.

"Son-of-a-bitch," Nick muttered. "Not a one! Too bad. Several of them looked pretty good on paper."

Gillian felt energized from the exertion. He jogged in position to drain himself. "Too many inhibitions. It would take months to retrain them."

Nick wagged his finger, looked thoughtful. "Yeah, but maybe they're the best we're gonna get. You're not gonna find anything like the old Earth Patrol Forces in these Colonies. These people haven't had a war for two hundred years. They're not prepared."

"Are you saying we should lower our standards?" He accelerated the pace of his jogging.

"Oh, hell, I don't know. It just might come down to that."

Gillian shook his head. "Are you sure Haddad understands what type of people we need?"

Nick scratched his chin. "He understands as well as he's going to understand. It's just that the kind of people we're looking for probably don't exist, at least not within E-Tech."

"Then what about outside the organization? What about these pirates you've been telling me about?" Such people could be difficult to recruit, but they could prove more suitable.

Nick shook his head. "Haddad looks like he's going to be real stubborn about this. I don't think he'll give us permission to go beyond E-Tech."

Gillian's feet pumped steadily. "Rome has the final say, doesn't he? Maybe you could use your charm to plead our case." He wanted to add: *Either that or we think about doing this on our own.* He did not dare. Haddad probably had the gym bugged. Besides, Nick understood what was left unsaid.

"Yeah, maybe I could convince Rome. And maybe not. It's just that we gotta play by their rules here. We could kill this Paratwa and end up doing more harm than good to E-Tech."

Sweat began to break out on Gillian's forehead. "Do you think the Paratwa's going to play by their rules?"

"Don't feed me that crap!" Nick growled. "I know that a Termi's no pushover."

"If it is a Termi."

Nick paused. "Are you holding something back?"

He began to breathe deeply. "Two murder scenes and three witnesses! Even Termis weren't that sloppy."

"Yeah, I thought about that. But think of the ego trip this assassin must be on. He comes out of stasis and sees that he's the baddest creature alive—he's a walking nightmare in a world of daydreamers. He's bound to feel reckless."

"Maybe. And maybe he's leaving witnesses for a reason."

"Self-exalting arrogance," Nick said. "He wants the attention. Even Termis weren't modest."

"Or maybe he's more calculating than that. More deliberate." Gillian was beginning to heat up. He could not jog in place for much longer. Soon he would have to run.

Nick looked gloomy. "I suppose it's possible. But unless we can talk to those witnesses, we're not going to learn anything further . . . until the bastard strikes again."

Gillian gave a sharp nod. Tiny lesions of sweat broke through the thin fabric of his pullover. "Tomorrow I want to go to Lamalan, the site of the first killing."

"Haddad's people have been over that whole area—quite thoroughly, judging by the reports I've seen."

"We'll go anyway." Gillian broke into a sprint and began to circle the gym before Nick could think of an argument. Legs pumped furiously and his chest heaved, sucking oxygen in controlled gulps; cadences learned long ago. His thoughts drifted.

I move—I am. I want—I take. I see—I learn. I grow—I make. Odd, the things that came back to you from childhood. It was an old nursery rhyme.

He ran with the abandon of the short sprinter; twice around the gym, knowing that he had not even approached his limits. It felt good: his mind, fully locked into the rhythms of the hunt, ages away from pain and loss; his body a hard shield against the past. He experienced that curious feeling of invulnerability that came to him on rare occasions, a physiological high that even the best drugs could not emulate. Nothing could stop him.

I am ready to hunt a Paratwa.

In terror, Paula awoke; aching, enveloped by dry heat, her head pounding from the steady shriek of nearby machinery. She could see nothing, could not tell if she was right side up or upside down. Something across her mouth prevented her from screaming. A wail threatened to rise within her and she knew she would go mad if she allowed that to happen.

I must not give in. The thought calmed her. The events in Moat's shop came back. *The pirates! They injected us with some sort of knockout drug . . .*

Us! Where was Jerem?

She shuddered as a host of unpleasant possibilities blossomed. *Jerem could be dead!*

No! He is not dead. My son is alive! I know this. He cannot be dead. He is alive and he may need my help.

The thought restored calm. *All right. First I must help myself. Where am I?*

The shrieking noise was suddenly familiar. Paula had heard it before, though never this loudly. *Rocket engines! I'm in a shuttle!*

Probably she was in one of the darkened storage bays, directly beside the powerful motors. That would explain the heat. And her lack of a sense of direction . . . *We're in space—there's no gravity! And I can't move my lips because there's a gag across my mouth.*

She felt calmer. And angry.

Jerem could be in here with her. Most storage bays were fairly large. She stretched out her arms to explore. The movement disturbed her delicate tension with the deck. She floated away, gently bumping into a warm flat object with her nose. A quick grab at the new surface proved unwise. She slid away and floated in another direction. Moments passed. Then she felt her bottom pressing against a series of bars.

A ladder! This time she moved her hands very carefully. Her left palm tightened on a rung. Movement stopped.

With her free hand, she tried to peel away whatever was covering her mouth. The gag would not come loose. It felt like a wide band of supple leather, somehow clasped at the back of her neck. She yanked at it several times before giving up.

She turned to face the ladder and began climbing, head first. She had no idea if she was going in the right direction but it was a moot point. If this way did not lead to an exit, the other would.

The ladder ended at a steel hatch. She felt around its rim, located the snaplocks, flipped them back. Brightness blinded her as the hatch motored itself open.

She squinted. A shadow moved, blocking the light. Strong hands grabbed her wrists, hauled her out of the storage bay.

The hands released her. Slowly, her eyes adjusted to the brightness.

She was in the mid-compartment of a shuttle. The Costeau with the scarlet penis tattooed on his cheek stood before her. Piercing green eyes regarded her with an almost polite grin. She sneered at him. The pirate grabbed a pair of friction boots from a rack, shoved them to the deck in front of her.

"Put 'em on." The boots touched the serrated floor, stuck fast. The pirate reached behind Paula and pinched something at the back of the leather gag. It loosened, floated away.

"Where's my son?" she demanded.

"Same place you were." He turned, keyed open an airseal, and disappeared into the forward part of the vessel.

Bastard! She hooked a leg around a sidebar to stay in position while she exchanged her shoes for the friction boots.

Enough light shone through the open hatch to illuminate the storage bay. Jerem floated near the center, kicking and flailing at the air, trying to propel himself toward a wall.

Paula used her hands to walk down the ladder. Jerem calmed

down when he saw that she was reaching for him. Their palms locked. A minute later she had him out of the bay and into the mid-compartment.

She released his gag. His face was red, wet with tears.

"Oh, Jerem!" She hugged him.

"Mom! I'm all right!" He pulled away from her. "It's just that for a while I didn't know where I was or what happened to you." His voice sounded brittle, controlled. "I thought maybe the pirates left us to die out in space or somethin'."

"We're on their ship," Paula soothed. "I don't think they mean to hurt us." Rage welled up inside of her. *No one has the right to terrify my son!*

The rack of friction boots hung beside the compartment's miniature galley. Paula found a pair that fit Jerem. She held him in place while he put them on.

"What do we do now?" he asked.

"Come on." She stepped carefully, making sure that at least one foot was in contact with the deck at all times. Jerem followed her toward the forward part of the shuttle, to the airseal that the pirate had disappeared through.

Her son suddenly pushed off the deck, somersaulted, and landed feet first on the ceiling.

"Stop it!" Paula snapped, then realized she was being insensitive. Jerem had been badly scared and now he was being a boy again and she should be thankful. "I'm sorry."

He grinned. "That's okay. Watch this."

He launched himself more forcefully and performed two mid-air twists before his feet touched the deck beside her. "I learned that in freefall class last month!"

"That's good." Paula stopped at the airseal, twisted the snaplocks, drew a deep breath as it opened.

Three men sat at a small table in what was obviously a rec compartment of some sort. They were playing a game—poker, she thought—with a deck of laminated plastic slabs. Piles of cash cards sat before each man. Two of the pirates she did not recognize, but the third was the lanky black from Moat's shop.

Twangy music, threaded with deep bass notes, filled the background, made their low conversation nearly inaudible. The pirates wore no odorant bags, though Paula could still detect the faint smell of spoiled fish.

The Costeau with the tattoo dropped down from the flight deck above. He landed in front of them. "You hungry?"

Paula glared, wanting to hit him. "Kidnapping is an Intercolonial crime."

The three men at the table looked up from their game and laughed. Penis tattoo grinned at the black man. "Hey, Santiago—looks like we're in trouble again."

Santiago hooked his palms under his suspenders. He sneered at Paula. "I'm just plain fuckin' frightened."

His companions threw back their heads and howled. One of them shouted: "Tell us more, woman!"

Paula spun to face the tattooed pirate. "You're a bastard!" The only thing that kept her from slugging this Costeau was Jerem. If she angered these people, they might take it out on her son.

Piercing green eyes regarded her with amusement. "Yes, I'm a bastard. Now, are you hungry or not?"

"Mom, I'm hungry."

"What do you want with us?" Paula demanded.

The tattoo wiggled as he spoke. "It's a clan affair. You'll find out soon enough."

"Where are you taking us?"

The pirate motioned for them to follow. He pushed off the deck and shot through the open hatch above.

"Jerem, I want you to follow right behind me. And be careful."

Paula launched herself and missed the opening. She had to crawl several inches along the ceiling and pull herself through the hole. Jerem arrowed up to the flight deck in one easy motion.

"Wow!" he shouted.

Visible through the flight deck's narrow band of windows was an incredible sight—two or three hundred shuttles, crisply shining against the blackness of space. The vessels seemed to be orbiting an immense conglomeration of patchwork metal. The scarred object was cylindrical and, judging by the size of the shuttles, looked to be several miles long and about a half mile in diameter. Paula had never been to such a place—Costeaus did not encourage visitors.

"It's a pirate Colony, isn't it, Mom!"

Paula nodded.

A woman sat in the command chair. The tattooed pirate stood by her side. The woman swiveled an instrument panel from her lap and eased it back into the larger framework of control boards.

Black hair was braided into a triplet of ponytails. Narrow lips and heavy eyebrows, both accented in blue, made the oval face appear stern. She was a bit slimmer than Paula, and an inch or so taller. Her green jumpsuit fit like a tailored glove.

She studied Paula's anger for a moment. "We're cruel, yes?"

"You said it."

"My name is Grace. This is Aaron, my brother."

The tattooed pirate gave a gracious nod.

"We are of the clan of Alexander," said Grace. "What you see out there is one of our places."

Paula kept her anger in check. "What do you want of us? And don't tell me again that it's a clan affair."

"My brother and I were instructed to find you and bring you before the lion of Alexander."

"Is that supposed to frighten us?" Paula snapped. "Like it frightened Moat?"

Grace shrugged. "Moat Piloski once crossed the clan, cheated a shuttle crew out of what was rightfully theirs. The lion showed him mercy on that occasion. Moat recognized the consequences of crossing us again."

"And what have my son and I done to you?"

"You are to be brought before the lion. That is all I may say."

"And did the lion instruct you to terrorize us in the process? Gag us and imprison us in a dark bay!"

Aaron smiled and directed his words at Jerem. "Guardians often board our vessels when we're docked in the Colonies. Ostensibly, they search for contraband, but the real reason they harass us is that they do not want us in their worlds. They make our lives difficult whenever possible. On Lamalan, we put you in our storage bay for safekeeping, in case the Guardians boarded. Unless specifically instructed, Guardians generally won't take the time for a complete search. The gags were used in the event you had awakened while they were aboard."

"How long were we asleep?" Jerem asked.

"Almost twenty-four hours," said Aaron. "You were given a minor stasis drug in Moat's shop."

Paula's anger swelled. "We've been in space for a whole day? You could have at least brought us out of storage. My son was petrified!"

Aaron shrugged. "We had other stops to make before coming here. It was best that you remained asleep. We released you from the acceleration straps. You were free to emerge from the bay at any time."

Grace turned to Jerem. "Is it true? You were frightened?"

Jerem responded with a rapid nod.

"And what did you learn?"

"Learn!" Paula exploded. "He's not some test subject for a deep-space probe! He's a twelve-year-old boy!"

Aaron spoke proudly. "One of our children of his age would have taken the learning from such a situation."

It was the final straw—Paula could no longer contain herself. "Oh, yes, you people learn, don't you! You're the scum of the Colonies! There was a wrong done to you two centuries ago and you've made it a part of your damned lives! You wear foul odors when you walk among the outsiders to show your disdain for them and you steal and smuggle and kill and who knows what else! I've got news for you—you could bathe from now until the next Apocalypse and you would still be just as rotten!''

Grace muttered, ''I could send you through the airlock for such talk, woman.''

Aaron chuckled. ''She's gutsy, I'll say that.''

''Too bad she won't allow her son the same privilege. She takes too much pleasure from the maternal leash.''

''You bitch. What do you know about my son.''

''I know,'' Grace whispered, ''that he doesn't know who his father was.''

Paula felt her guts begin to rise. *My god. Moat must have told them.* With an effort, she turned to Jerem, met a look of intense curiosity.

No . . . not like this. Not here.

Jerem began carefully. ''My father was a technician working at an Ecospheric Turnaround base on Earth. He was killed in an accident when I was real small.''

Grace said, ''Tell him, woman. Or I will.''

Paula stared through the windows, wishing she could hide herself in the blackness between the shuttles. Jerem's eyes were upon her—she could feel them without looking. He was waiting for confirmation, waiting for her to repeat the story that she had been telling him since he was first old enough to ask.

''Mom?''

She forced herself to meet his gaze. ''Jerem, your father—I always told you that he was a technician . . .''

Hurt came into his eyes. There was no getting around it, now. She should have told him the truth years ago.

''I was ashamed of your real father, so I made up a story, about him being a technician . . .''

Jerem waited. Grace broke into a faint grin.

Bastards! Paula thought. She took a deep breath. ''Jerem, your real father . . . he was a Costeau.''

Jerem winced, as if he had been slapped. She reached for him. He pulled away from her, violently. "You liar!"

"Oh, Jerem! I didn't want to tell you because I was afraid. I shouldn't have been but I was. I thought it would be easier for you if you thought your father was . . . someone else. At school, if they knew about your real father, your friends, they might have made fun of you . . . made your life difficult."

His face turned cold. He stared out the windows into space. "I don't care."

"Jerem, I . . ."

He grabbed the sidebar above the opening and propelled himself off the flight deck. Paula glared at the pirates.

"Satisfied?"

Grace shrugged. "You live with lies and blame us for truth."

"Typical of a Colonial," Aaron added.

Paula had a host of responses, but her mouth had gone suddenly dry. She could not speak. And all she could see was the hurt on Jerem's face.

Rome arrived twenty minutes early for Wednesday's Council meeting. The others were already in the chamber, seated around the polished table. Lady Bonneville doodled on a large scratchpad, creating doilies with a fiberjet pen. Nu-Lin and Artwhiler studied their monitor displays. Drake spooned beef broth from a huge bowl with such vigor that Rome wondered when he had last eaten.

Lady Bonneville looked up from her doodling and blessed Rome with a pleasant smile. She was a plump matronly woman in her late fifties who served as liaison to the Irryan Senate. Her hair was dyed brown today.

"Rome! How are you? How is dear Angela?"

He flashed a quick smile. "Angela and I are quite well."

The Lady sighed. "Oh, dear, sometimes I wish I could trade places with Angela and simply be away from all this."

No you don't, thought Rome, as he took his seat at the table. Lady Bonneville had been mouthing that line for as long as he had known her.

In addition to her Senate liaison duties, she voluntarily served as Councillor of the Arts. Rome suspected she considered that function more important than her official responsibilities.

Drake shoved his empty bowl to one side and called the Council to order. The status of the Paratwa investigation was of foremost concern. Artwhiler was asked for a report.

The Guardian Commander stood up, keyed the controls of a hand terminal, glanced at his gooseneck screen, then broke into a confident smile. He looked like a freelancer about to go live.

"This investigation is proceeding well. Several promising leads are being explored. With luck, we should be able to capture the Paratwa before it carries out any more sadistic acts."

Rome gazed at the blocky face. *He's lying. He has no leads.*

Nu-Lin hunched forward. "Are you a-ware that no Pa-ra-twa has e-ver been cap-tured?"

Artwhiler's smile expanded. "I am guilty of a figure of speech Naturally, should this creature resist arrest, my Guardians will use deadly force."

"Was dead-ly force used by your Guard-i-ans at the Nor-thern Cal-i-for-ni-a Pre-serve?"

Artwhiler reddened slightly. "Those three brave men died because they were mentally unprepared to encounter such a beast. Their deaths have not been in vain. Their sacrifice has provided a rallying cry for the rest of my Guardians—we will not be caught unprepared again!"

Nu-Lin placed a hand on her neck and gently squeezed the flesh, as if trying to force some emotion from the implanted wafer speakers. "This Pre-serve was un-der Guard-i-an ju-ris-dic-tion. Could you ex-plain to the Coun-cil how a sin-gle crea-ture was a-ble to de-stroy most of the a-ni-mals?''

Rome stared at Nu-Lin, wondered about her anger. The blue eyes held fire.

Artwhiler looked around the table for support, saw none. He cleared his throat. ''I'm afraid that even I could have gone into that zoo and killed those animals without much effort. They were, after all, helpless beasts, confined to a limited area.''

''The Com-merce League feels that you are not ap-proach-ing this threat ser-i-ous-ly. Do you have an-y con-cep-tion of the trade dis-rup-tion cre-at-ed in Nor-thern Cal-i-for-ni-a be-cause of this at-tack? That Pre-serve formed the lo-cal ec-o-nom-ic base—with-out tour-ism, the Co-lo-ny will suf-fer grave-ly. Have you tak-en the time to stu-dy the his-to-ry of these crea-tures? This at-tack was mild com-pared to what they are ca-pa-ble of.''

''I assure you that the Guardians will bring this creature under control.''

''Let us hope,'' said Nu-Lin.

Lady Bonneville turned to Artwhiler. ''Given the time and re-sources, I am certain that the Guardians will triumph.''

Rome glanced at Nu-Lin. She avoided his gaze. Nu-Lin's feel-ings echoed his own, but attacking Artwhiler was not the way to gain Council support.

Drake offered the next surprise. ''I wish to announce a special ICN subsidy for the renovation of Sirak-Brath. That Colony is the heart of the black market and an infusion of well-managed capital should decimate some of this illegal trading.''

This time Nu-Lin looked at Rome, sharing his astonishment.

What's going on here? That was our proposal. Three days ago we made a deal not to introduce such a measure. And now Drake has completely reversed his position!

Artwhiler sat down. ''An excellent idea, Councillor. Next to taking a legion of my Guardians into that sewer and cleaning it out, I can't think of a better way to civilize Sirak-Brath.''

Rome addressed Drake. "It was my understanding that the ICN was opposed to such renovation."

"We have changed our position," Drake snapped.

He's furious, Rome thought.

"The pol-i-cy of this Coun-cil has al-ways been to share the ra-tion-ale be-hind our pro-pos-als. You your-self have pro-mo-ted that pol-i-cy."

Drake stared coldly at Nu-Lin. "I thought the rationale was clear. Sirak-Brath is in need of renovation. And I am not propos-ing that the Council spend anything. I am merely stating that the ICN plans to invest a considerable amount in this project—up to point-seven billion in the current fiscal year. We would like the Council to serve as administrators, nothing more."

Point-seven billion! With that kind of money, you could almost build a new Colony! Everyone shared Rome's bewilderment.

"Surely," Lady Bonneville began, "such a massive investment will bring cries of unfairness from the Senate. After all, the ICN budget has been established for some time now. The Council and the Senate have funded projects in relation to where ICN monies were being directed. To change budgetary strategy at this late date . . ."

Drake interrupted. "Inform the Senate that the ICN has recently completed a special audit alignment. We have restructured our in-vestment program and are now accepting new proposals. That should take some of the sting out of their grievances."

"Perhaps a lesser amount?" Lady Bonneville suggested hope-fully.

"As always, the ICN is open to negotiation. But we intend that the majority of this point-seven billion go toward Sirak-Brath res-toration."

Nu-Lin frowned. "But where is this mon-ey com-ing from? If you are de-priv-ing point-sev-en bil-lion from ICN pro-jects, the Coun-cil may be asked to make up some of these los-ses."

Lady Bonneville wagged her head in agreement.

Drake stared straight ahead. He looked like he had been turned to stone.

"This money comes from our corporate lending program. There has been a major shift in short-term investment strategies. The availability of this money should have no repercussion on this Council."

Nu-Lin shook her head. "Per-haps not. But if you cut off certain cor-por-ate aid, the Sen-ate may be asked to make up the dif-fer-ence."

"That will not happen." Drake spoke with such finality that no one responded.

The black face turned to Rome. "E-Tech has done preliminary work on the details of Sirak-Brath restoration. I suggest that they oversee the project."

Three days ago, Rome would have gladly accepted such a proposition. Now he was suspicious. Drake had ulterior motives that Rome could not begin to fathom.

He needed time. "I vote to table any discussion of a Sirak-Brath restoration for two weeks."

"One week," countered Drake.

Lady Bonneville and Nu-Lin both seconded Drake's motion. Artwhiler gave a slow thoughtful nod.

Drake closed the discussion. "The Sirak-Brath restoration will be on the agenda in one week. The next item for today's session concerns the possible disciplinary action against E-Tech for its failure to inform this Council about the Paratwa. Specifically, E-Tech violated the Irryan charter, chapter one, paragraph seven."

Drake paused and Lady Bonneville jumped in. Their action smacked of a rehearsed piece. Drake and the Lady had come to an understanding.

"I propose," the Lady began, "that E-Tech be given a Council censure and that the matter be relegated to chambers."

Drake nodded. "I second that."

A private Council censure was the mildest of disciplinary actions. Rome was not surprised. Both Drake and Lady Bonneville generally saw the wisdom of avoiding severe intra-Council disciplinary disputes.

Artwhiler stood up. "I would vote for a more severe penalty against E-Tech, but I see that the Council has made up its mind on this matter." He glared at Lady Bonneville, who kept her eyes focused on the Van Gogh cornfield on the opposite wall.

"I do, however, have something to say on the matter of this huge Sirak-Brath investment. At the last meeting, I proposed that this Council fund a major expansion of our perimeter warning system. That issue was tabled until next month—fair enough, since I promised to supply more substantial data at that time. Now, however, there is suddenly a huge amount of capital available from the ICN for . . ."

"That matter also has been tabled," Drake reminded him.

"I'm aware of the status of both these issues. I merely wish to point out that if the ICN has money available, the priority should be defense, not renovation."

Lady Bonneville spoke quietly. "This sounds like a matter that should be settled directly between the Guardians and the ICN."

"No! Our mutual defense is a common priority!"

Drake killed the issue. "Then have your Guardians send a detailed proposal to the ICN. We will take it under consideration."

Lady Bonneville smiled soothingly. "Now, Arty, the Council has agreed to give your project a fair hearing next month. We are all as concerned about security as you are."

Artwhiler sat down, fuming.

Rome thought: *Artwhiler I understand. A slight case of paranoia has always been his trademark. But Drake?*

Something of consequence had occurred within the ICN. The banking consortium had never before made such a drastic change in an established budget; they simply did not operate that way. And for Drake to propose Sirak-Brath's restoration . . .

It made no sense.

Later, after the meeting ended, Lady Bonneville caught Rome at the elevator.

"Dear me!" she began. "These Council affairs are becoming such trying experiences lately." She smiled gamely. "Artwhiler is always so angry. It's good that the more level-headed individuals—primarily you and Nu-Lin—are there to maintain some dignity."

"It's becoming more difficult," Rome offered. He stepped into the elevator with her and gave the command for street level. The elevator thanked him and began its slow descent.

Lady Bonneville shook her head. "And Drake? Goodness! That loan business came as quite a surprise. Perhaps organizational troubles are plaguing him? Could he and the other ICN Directors be feuding?"

"It's possible."

"Or do you think that this funding proposal has something to do with La Gloria de la Ciencia's loan?"

Rome stared straight at her, waiting.

"Well, you *do* know that La Gloria de la Ciencia is receiving a huge loan from the ICN."

Rome had not known. He kept his voice casual. "I heard a rumor."

The Lady smiled. "Not a direct loan, of course. Most of the money is being funneled through the West Yemen Corporation." She eased closer to Rome, whispered in his ear like a conspirator.

"You know what they're saying out on the street, don't you? One of my doormen told me. Many of our citizens feel that La Gloria de la Ciencia must be somehow connected to the awakening of this Paratwa. It makes sense to people. There's a hi-tech assassin on the loose and there's a powerful organization that favors hi-tech. People connect the two. You know how people think."

Rome nodded, letting her know that he did indeed know how people think.

"It's possible," the Lady went on, "that at this time, Drake and the ICN are worried about being too closely linked to La Gloria de la Ciencia."

The argument sounded spurious. He pushed for more information. "How do you know this ICN money is being funneled to La Gloria de la Ciencia?"

Her eyes twinkled. "I have my sources. And the West Yemen Corporation loan is for point six-three billion. A very close figure, wouldn't you say, to the point seven billion that Drake suddenly has available?"

Rome nodded. "I never heard of the West Yemen Corporation."

"You should look them up, and find out whether they're being denied their latest loan."

The elevator reached street level and the doors whisked open. A deserted corridor led to a private exit.

Rome hesitated. "What was La Gloria de la Ciencia planning to do with such a huge loan?"

The Lady smiled. "Financial realities beset us all."

Rome wanted more details but he realized that she had given him all she was going to. Beneath Lady Bonneville's charming manner was a shrewd politician. She had provided Rome with an avenue for exploration. She would not waltz down the street with him.

He said, "I'll let you know what I find out."

She beamed as she trailed him from the elevator. "By the way, you and Angela are coming to my party next week, aren't you?"

"We hope to."

"I'm very excited! The guest list, I do believe, is my best one ever. I am looking forward to an extraordinary evening."

Rome squeezed out a fascinated smile. "I can hardly wait."

Rome found an angry Pasha Haddad waiting for him back at the office.

"Gillian and Nick should be returned to stasis immediately. They possess a brutality that will hurt E-Tech, no matter what the outcome of this Paratwa hunt."

Rome sat down, listened patiently as Haddad related the events of the previous evening. "Where are they now?"

"In one of the spare offices. Should I call them in?"

Rome nodded, hoping this would not take long. A staff meeting with his top aides was needed as soon as possible. Today's Council behavior had to be discussed; E-Tech's ongoing strategy might need to be shifted, modified. It was vital that they learn the reason behind Drake's sudden policy change.

"Howdy do!" drawled Nick. He strolled into the office and hopped up on Rome's desk. Gaudy jumpsuits with movable pockets were fashionable right now; Nick's was crimson, and several sizes too large. For no apparent reason, he had attached all of the pockets to the small of his back. He looked like he had grown a tail.

Gillian wore a gray jacket, dark pants, and a pale shirt. He could have passed for an industrial manager or an ICN banker.

The Pasha closed the door and sternly folded his arms.

Nick grinned. "Daddy says we've been naughty."

Gillian sat down. Haddad remained erect, a statue at the door.

"I'm afraid this is serious," Rome began. "The Pasha told me what happened at the gym last night."

Nick shrugged. "We were just doing our job."

Rome shook his head. "A man was hospitalized—two others were treated for minor injuries."

Nick hesitated. "I don't want to sound callous, but this is the big leagues. Those volunteers couldn't cut it."

"You attacked them and they fought back," Rome argued. "What did you expect?"

Gillian raised his arm and Nick fell silent. *So soft,* Gillian thought. *They still don't realize what they're up against.*

He spoke calmly. "Our methods were harsh, but we learned in five minutes what would have taken an entire evening under more polite circumstances. Those volunteers were unsuitable because they *thought* about attacking me before they attacked me. An admirable characteristic for a civilized human, but not for anyone going up against a Paratwa. While they were thinking, I was knocking them down and hurting them. Such caution would be fatal against an assassin."

Haddad stepped forward angrily. "You did not give my people a chance."

"Neither would the Paratwa," Nick said. "Remember, this ain't no boy scout we're going after."

"Boy scout?"

"Never mind."

Gillian shook his head. "Your people could be taught to react faster, but it would take a long time. And the sheen of consciousness would always be present. They might even learn to attack a Paratwa on sight, but the first time an innocent pedestrian entered the picture, they would hesitate. The Paratwa would not."

Rome saw where the conversation was leading and did not like it. "You want criminals—sociopaths with no qualms about killing."

"Such people would be just as unsuitable, but for other reasons." Gillian kept his tone calm, soothing. "A conscience is acceptable, so long as it does not interfere with basic instincts. I need people whose reaction to being shoved is to shove back. No intervening rationalizations, no guilt, no fear. I need instant anger. I push and they push back."

"For the sake of argument," Rome said, "let us assume that no such people can be found. What would be your next option?"

"There is no option. I would not attempt combat against a Paratwa without an effective team."

"Fortunately," Nick added hastily, "there are such people. You've got to allow us to recruit outside of E-Tech."

"Impossible," barked Haddad.

Nick faced Rome. "Think about it. First of all, we would be further separating ourselves from E-Tech. If things went badly, the organization would not be caught in the middle."

"There are already too many connections between you and E-Tech," the Pasha pointed out.

"True enough," said Nick. "But it would still be an improvement over present circumstances." He pleaded with Rome. "We must have a free hand. It's the only way."

Rome was inclined to agree with Haddad. Despite possible repercussions, they had to maintain some sort of control over Nick and Gillian. "You realize that I still have grave doubts about allowing the two of you to be involved in this investigation in the first place."

Investigation? Gillian wanted to laugh.

Rome continued. "And I certainly don't like your methods, no matter how necessary you claim they are." He shook his head. "You'll have to work within the organization as we agreed."

Gillian leaned back and folded his arms. Cold rationality was the last hope for changing their minds. "No one has ever told you what a fully armed Paratwa is like."

Haddad spoke calmly. "We've studied the history texts."

"Archives are dead—my experience is alive. True?"

Rome nodded. "Go on."

Gillian closed his eyes. "It comes at you from two places— movements are sharp, catlike. A crescent web surrounds each tway, protects it front and back. A window of vulnerability exists at the sides, but even a thruster must be precisely aimed. No hand weapon can penetrate the front or back of the web. Only a multi-port range laser can cut through, and even that would take a few seconds. The operator of the range laser would die in those seconds.

"The crescent web repels gases, so you cannot easily poison the Paratwa. Extremes of temperature and pressure are bearable for short periods of time—survival in a vacuum is even possible for a few seconds.

"The Paratwa carries AV and sensor scramblers, which means that computer and auto-targeting techniques are useless. You cannot electronically lock onto scrambled signals. The creature forces its attackers to utilize direct methods.

"Offensive armaments. While you're trying to get through the creature's defenses, you are undergoing assault from at least four weapons. Two hands hold Cohe wands and two hands bear thrusters. Many creatures also wear muscle-controlled thighpads that can launch a variety of deadly projectiles—fragmentation grenades, gas and concussion bombs, firedarts, bullets, and knives.

"Peripherals—targeting helmets, used to automatically direct firepower when the enemy is not using scramblers; radiation sensors; jetpacks for aerial warfare; acid twisters to splatter a room with burning liquids.

"Experience. A Paratwa assassin has been born and bred for one reason—to kill human beings, as swiftly and as surely as possible. Its whole life has been dedicated to perfecting the means for accomplishing this task. Each creature has trained by destroying hundreds of slave fighters.

"Speed. Possibly its single greatest advantage. Genetically modified neuromuscular systems enable faster reaction times. Training from birth enhances these inbred abilities."

Gillian stopped, studied Rome's uncertainty, played on it.

"According to your own figures, on the average each Paratwa killed over twenty thousand humans. And that ratio occurred in a society that was infinitely more prepared for violence than yours."

Haddad's scalp seemed to be throbbing. "The Colonies are not totally helpless—we have thrusters. We have crescent webs too, although their use is highly restricted."

"It does not matter," Gillian said calmly. "Even if you could match the Paratwa weapon for weapon, you would lose."

He spoke with such certainty that Rome felt convinced, even while a more rational part of him was generating arguments.

Haddad spoke bitterly. "And what is it that makes you so uniquely effective against these creatures?"

Gillian looked at Nick, wanting the midget to answer for him. *It's strange how blind we can be to our own natures. I don't know why I have such skills. An accident of birth, I suppose. I do know that when my parents were killed and I first picked up that Cohe, the wand felt as if it were part of me. I understood the way it was meant to be used.*

Nick gazed at the ceiling. "Gillian is a rare combination of instincts and acquired skills. He is a one-in-a-billion freak."

A freak. Yes, that felt true. *I am a freak.* His guts began to ache. He shuddered.

Rome frowned at Gillian, equating his pained grimace with Nick's casual use of the word "freak."

Gillian perceived the Councillor's error. It amused him. He laughed, suppressing his pain. All three of them looked at him strangely.

"It's rather funny," he lied. "Here we sit, calmly discussing what must be done about a hole in the roof. Meanwhile, we are getting soaked by the rain."

Nick clapped his hands. "Say, I like that! A great analogy!"

Rome spoke soberly. "I'm still inclined to agree with the Pasha. You've got to stay within E-Tech."

Nick hopped down from the desk. "All right, let's suppose we accept your restrictions. What about that Cohe wand you're holding in the archives?"

"If I give you this wand, I will be violating a deep trust."

"If you don't," Nick pointed out, "a lot more Colonists are going to die."

Suspicion lined the Pasha's face. "What happened to Gillian's Cohe?"

Nick answered. "We thought it best not to go into stasis with a wand. You can understand our trepidation. If we had been accidentally awakened and it was discovered that we possessed a Cohe . . . Well, let's just say we wouldn't have won any popularity contests." He grinned brightly. "Besides, we always assumed that when we woke up, there would be Cohes available. We never suspected that E-Tech would manage to almost totally eliminate the most devastating hand weapon ever designed."

"And now," said Haddad, "you expect us to simply hand over one of these weapons to you. I find that rather naive."

Nick winked at the Pasha. "Midgets can be rather short-sighted."

Gillian chuckled.

Haddad turned to Rome, spoke coldly. "Even if it were not a violation of our own laws, we could not give such a weapon to a man who has displayed such ruthlessness."

Rome had made the decision yesterday. "I'll have the Cohe wand brought up from our vaults. The weapon, however, will remain within this building." He avoided Haddad's wrathful stare. "In return, you will work within our organization. You may train your team but you will also exercise a little more restraint in dealing with our people. Agreed?"

Nick bowed gracefully and smiled. Gillian's pose was unreadable.

The midget rubbed his hands together. "Now we're getting somewhere. So! How about a bit of good news to cheer you up?"

"We're listening," said Rome.

Nick pointed at Haddad. "Daddy let us go to Lamalan early this morning like we were promised. Of course, he sent six security people with us to make us behave, but it was still a nice trip. We found these."

Nick reached behind his back and withdrew a pair of tiny black marbles from one of his pockets. He displayed them in his open palm.

The Pasha's eyes widened. "You lied to my people, told them you found nothing!"

Nick dropped the marbles on the desk. They did not roll; they stuck to the surface. "We wanted to save our little discovery for you."

Rome examined the tiny spheres. "What are they? Bugs?"

"You got it! Audio transceivers with dynamic tracking. These little suckers can lock onto, amplify, and transmit a whisper at two hundred feet."

Haddad picked one up, studied it with a frown. "What's their transmission range?"

"About half a mile."

"I assume they're deactivated," said the Pasha.

"I certainly hope so!"

"The Paratwa planted these?" Rome asked.

Nick nodded. "At Paula Marth's. One of the bugs was in her hallway and the other in her gallery—stuck to the bottom of an antique ice cutter." He grinned. "Kinda makes you wonder, huh?"

Haddad spoke carefully. "You're saying that the Paratwa secretly planted these bugs when it visited Paula Marth on the day of the killing. It wanted to find out if she knew anything."

Nick corrected. "It wanted to learn whom she would call to report Bob Max's murder."

"Then she was set up to be a witness," Haddad concluded.

Gillian forced patience. *They're so slow.*

"Of course!" snapped Nick. "After the murder, the creature probably monitored the bugs from the nearby forestlands. Paula Marth called E-Tech and the Paratwa passed that information on to its master."

Rome felt his stomach clench. A sense of foreboding came over him. "And the next day, Artwhiler and Drake knew all about the murder."

"Yup," said Nick. "Sounds to me like whoever is running this Paratwa wants to discredit E-Tech."

"Then Paula Marth is innocent," mused Haddad. "She was telling the truth—she did not inform anyone else about the killing."

"Probably not."

Rome shook his head, tried to make his guts unwind. "These bugs, we have nothing like them. In fact, I doubt if we even have data on how to construct one."

Nick grinned. "They're state-of-the-art technology—pre-Apocalyptic, of course. Probably the plans for them are hidden somewhere down in your data archives. Oh, and another thing. These bugs are self-disintegrating. Another few days and they would have begun to decompose. Handy little feature for eliminating evidence."

Rome asked, "These bugs . . . the Paratwa must have known we would discover them."

Nick squirmed back onto the desktop. "Not necessarily. The bugs were well hidden. We found them only because we had a good idea of what we were looking for."

The Pasha raised his eyebrows. "You knew her house had been bugged?"

"Gillian suspected the Paratwa did not visit Paula Marth just to discuss the antique business. The murder of Bob Max was well orchestrated."

Rome's stomach discomfort increased, yet refused to become outright fear—something that sank teeth into you. The sensation more closely resembled a feeling he had once experienced as a small child attending his grandfather's funeral. It was a helplessness that could never be fully acknowledged. Iceberg agony, Angela called it. Always nine-tenths submerged.

The Pasha, too, was upset by the discovery of the bugs. Rome could tell by the way he chose his words.

"It seems unlikely that the Costeaus are controlling this creature. They would not go to such trouble just to discredit E-Tech. It is not their way."

Rome felt himself tense. La Gloria de la Ciencia? They might go to such lengths to hurt E-Tech. Could this incident be somehow related to Drake's actions at Council?

I'm grasping at the wind. Right now, there were simply too many possibilities. He opened his desk drawer, withdrew a small vial, and swallowed an antacid pill.

Nick asked, "Have you learned anything more about Bob Max?"

Rome raised an eyebrow at Haddad. The Pasha scowled. He obviously had information that he did not want to share with Nick and Gillian.

Haddad spoke coldly. "Bob Max spent most of his time away

from Lamalan, but as yet, we haven't learned much about his lifestyle. We do know he was known among the smugglers. And our deepthroaters intimate that Max was friendly with many pirate clans.''

"But you have no direct links between Bob Max and the Paratwa,'' stated Gillian.

"Not yet.''

"Did Bob Max have any other connections?'' asked Nick. "Political or business friends, maybe?''

"He made fair-sized donations to several political organizations over the past five years. A group urging stronger trade barriers between Colonies and a committee fighting restoration projects on Sirak-Brath were the main ones.'' Haddad paused. "It is quite obvious why a smuggler would consider such causes important.''

"Anything else?'' Gillian asked.

Haddad shrugged. "He was apparently rather wealthy, although we have not as yet been able to unravel all of his financial dealings. He seems to have enjoyed antique collecting for its own sake and had investments in several major galleries throughout the Colonies. He was a lifelong member of the Church of the Trust—a true believer, as they say.''

Nick withdrew a strip of white licorice from his tail of pockets. He slid the candy between his teeth. "Did Max associate with any particular pirate clans?'' Half of the licorice dangled from his mouth, swaying as he spoke.

The Pasha nodded. "Max had most of his dealings with two of the clans, the Alexanders and the Cornells.''

Nick stared at Gillian but directed his words at Rome.

"These Costeaus—as I understand it, they're mainly descendants of the original workers who built the Colonies?''

Rome nodded. "Two centuries ago, when the Colonies were being settled, everyone had to be cleared by E-Tech immigration. It was always assumed that these hundreds of thousands of space workers would return to Earth when their construction efforts were completed. But then came the Apocalypse. The workers couldn't return to the planet.''

Nick said, "Even your most recent history files do not seem to delve into much detail about this matter. It's very strange.''

Haddad folded his arms. "The Colonies—and E-Tech—made a terrible mistake two centuries ago. No one is proud of it.''

Nick continued looking at Gillian. "Rather than implementing some means for slowly phasing these space workers into Colonial society, the powers-that-be rejected them utterly. Most of the workers were banned from settling in any of the cylinders.''

Rome recognized that this discussion was for Gillian's benefit and added: "When these workers visited the Colonies, they were forced to carry identity badges. Their travel was restricted.''

Gillian held up his hand. "You created a second-class citizenry. There are many historic parallels.''

Rome nodded. "The Colonies feared that Paratwa might be hidden among the workers. Some of these construction people put up with a lifetime of prejudice so that their descendants might become full-fledged Colonists. But most of them rejected second-class citizenship. Thousands of their shuttles were converted into homes. They adopted a sort of gypsy lifestyle, wandering from Colony to Colony, seeking temporary work. Many dove down to the Earth's surface, learned to hunt for uncontaminated artifacts that could be sold on the black market. A few of the bolder ones even attacked Intercolonial transports, boarded unarmed vessels, robbed and murdered crews. That sort of thing ended more than a century ago, but by then the Costeaus were firmly linked with piracy.

"These workers divided into clans. Some clans constructed their own cylinders—smaller and cruder than the Colonies, of course, but livable just the same. Other clans chose a particular Colony and moved their shuttles into permanent orbit. A low-tech industrial cylinder—Sirak-Brath—attracted an inordinate number of Costeaus. Today, that Colony is the hotbed, a sort of unofficial haven for them.''

Gillian understood why Nick had initiated this line of discussion. "Interesting," he said, with a trace of boredom in his voice.

Nick popped down from the desk. "Well, we've taken up enough of your time. I want to spend the rest of this afternoon going through some more of your archives." He rubbed his hands together gleefully. "'Cause tonight, if Daddy gives me the car, I'm going out skirtchasing!"

Haddad raised an eyebrow. "Wait for me in the outer office. I'll be along shortly."

Nick clicked his heels together and thrust his right arm upward at a forty-five degree angle. It was an odd salute, Rome thought.

Haddad waited until they left. "My initial feeling remains unchanged. We should return them to stasis."

Rome leaned back in the chair. Despite doubts, he believed that Nick and Gillian would prove useful. "They did find those audio bugs," he argued.

"It is a mistake to give them the Cohe wand. Not only is this a serious violation of our own policies, but if Gillian is truly as capable with this weapon as claimed, the end result could be disastrous. I do not trust their motives."

"I don't either," Rome said. "But at this point, I fear the Paratwa more than I fear them. I am convinced that Artwhiler will not be able to contain this creature."

Haddad allowed his bitterness to show. "And what makes you certain we can contain Gillian?"

That was a good question. Rome wished that he had an equally good answer. "You have them under constant surveillance?"

"Of course. The subcutaneous bugs are operating perfectly. But that merely tells us where they are—not what they are doing."

"It will have to suffice." Rome's mind was made up.

The Pasha swallowed his disagreement. "Do you wish me for anything else?"

"Yes. I'm calling an immediate meeting of the advisory staff. I want all our top people present, yourself included."

"Troubles at Council?"

Rome nodded thoughtfully. *Troubles everywhere.*

The lion of Alexander was a withered old man with fluffed gray hair and a face rippled by age lines. He sat on the arm of a well-preserved davenport; drawing pad on his lap, black pencil clutched tightly in a scarred palm. The silence of his chamber was broken only by the faint scratching of soft lead on paper.

Paula remained at the doorway with her son—as ordered—while Grace and Aaron approached the old man.

The chamber appeared to be a combination of bedroom and study. A small, linen-covered cot lay nestled against the wall several feet behind the davenport. Above the cot, a braided silver stick thrust outward, spread wings, became a dove with a band of fresh red roses clutched in its beak. Two corners held electronic equipment: one a communications console, the other an ancient assembly of music synthesizers. The carpet was tan shag and faintly tattered. A small mahogany desk—an antique worth thousands—sat alone in the center of the room.

Jerem wore a mask of boredom. Under better circumstances, a visit to a pirate Colony would have been a momentous event for him. But since yesterday, when she had told him about his father, he had withdrawn into himself, becoming resistant to Paula's gentle attempts at conversation and showing little interest in the oddities of the tiny apartment where Aaron had imprisoned them for the past twenty hours. Even on the few occasions when he had spoken to her, she detected the strain in his voice; a deep anger festering beneath the surface.

He'll get over it, Paula thought. *I won't blame myself for trying to spare my son pain. I did the right thing by not telling him who his real father was.*

Doubt remained.

Grace and Aaron entered into a whispered conversation with the old man. Voices rose and fell, and although words remained unclear, it was obvious that a disagreement was taking place. Finally, the siblings bowed slightly and retreated.

Aaron's tattoo rippled as he addressed Paula. "The lion wishes to see you and your son alone." The disapproval in his voice told her what the argument had been about.

Grace's dark eyes flashed. "Do nothing to harm him, do nothing to disturb his peace. Displease him in the slightest and you'll answer to me!"

The pirates left the room, closing the door behind them. Paula acknowledged a tinge of fear; she and Jerem were now alone with a man who ruled a Costeau empire.

The lion's voice was strangely youthful. "Come. Sit beside me."

She chose a spot on the far side of the davenport. The old man chuckled as she sat down.

"I have been deodorized and I do not bite, nor scratch. Please—sit beside me."

Paula slid closer, maintained a discreet distance between their bodies. Jerem sat down on her other side.

"I apologize for not being here yesterday to meet you when you arrived. Such was my intention, but duties required me to be out of Colony."

Paula squirmed on the soft cushion, avoided the old man's gaze.

"Do you like it?" asked the lion, holding up his pencil drawing.

Happy children, with meticulously detailed faces, frolicked on a grassy field. A forest of pines rose behind the children and far in the distance, ice-capped mountains probed high into a sharp blue sky. No Colony could boast such a panorama.

Paula did not have to lie. "It's beautiful."

The lion smiled. He picked up an olive pencil and began to darken some of the pines.

"I dreamed this picture, two nights ago. In the dream, I floated down to the field, became one of these children. I was happy.

"When I awoke, I sought to hang onto the dream. The stir of feelings was primal, a hint of an essence that had once been my soul. A time in my life before time carried meaning. I longed to return.

"Alas, there is no going back. The dream pruned as we faced sun; the longing hardened, became an abstract model to be studied, examined by the conscious mind. An imitation of reality."

Pale green eyes locked onto hers. "This drawing—it is an attempt to recapture the glory of those feelings. The colors, the shapes—they come close, but not close enough. Something will always be missing." His eyes wandered, held on her breasts for a timeless moment. "You are a beautiful woman."

Paula crossed her arms. She felt somehow betrayed, lulled by his words into a false sense of security. Anger returned. "What do you want with us?"

"Do you ever have such dreams?" he challenged. "Feel such feelings?"

"Yes . . . not that it's any of your damn business!"

"My eyes, they scare you?"

She kept her voice low, tried to contain her anger. "Your people kidnap us, treat us like slaves, threaten us. Yes, you scare me."

He smiled. "Grace and Aaron. Did they fill you with stories about me? The lion of Alexander, who devours his foes, who is not to be trifled with? Did they warn you about the price of resisting me?"

Paula felt a sudden chill. "With my son beside me, you have the upper hand."

"Why is that?"

Again repressed fury. "You know perfectly well."

He chuckled. "You believe I would hurt your son?"

"I believe a pirate would do . . . anything. You people, you're all . . . the same."

His smile disappeared, was replaced by a look of concern. "The same? The same as your son's father?"

"Shut up about my father!" Jerem snapped.

Paula turned to him. "Jerem! Please." She felt hurt, confused. "Whatever you want of us I will do it. If you want me . . . you can have me. But you must promise not to harm Jerem."

The lion shook his head. "Neither of you will be harmed. You were brought here for questioning—that is all. As for having you, I meant what I said—you are a beautiful woman. But my wife of nearly sixty years satisfies me in ways you could never hope to." He smiled gently. "She brings on my dreams."

"What are your questions?" Paula asked. She felt like lying down and simply crying. An array of emotions, swirling through her over the past few days, needed to be focused.

He seemed to understand. "Please believe me when I say you're both safe here. Such is my wish and the desire of our ruling tribunal. Grace and Aaron . . . they are young, angry like many of our people at the great injustices done to us. But they are good people, who know the difference between right and wrong. And they will obey the will of the clan."

Paula sensed the truth in his voice.

He laid his hands on hers. "I am the lion of the clan of Alexander, but my real name . . ." He grinned brightly. ". . . the one my wife uses, is Harry."

Paula smiled before she could think not to.

"I want you to understand clearly my motives. The questions I wish to ask you—they are very important to the clan. I had to know for certain whether your answers would be truthful."

Paula eyed him warily. "And now you will know?"

Harry smiled. "I did not become the lion of Alexander by accident. You have revealed your feelings, your own truth. When stirred, you glow with honesty."

"She's not honest," Jerem muttered.

"Ahh, but she is. That is not to say she never tells lies. But her reasons for being untruthful are mostly noble and arise from the heart. She seeks to spare you pain. And mixed with that desire is a human frailty—she seeks to lessen her own pain by denying a lost love. Do you understand?"

Jerem responded viciously. "No!"

Paula gazed into Harry's eyes, transfixed. The old man's perceptions were undeniably accurate.

He squeezed her hands. "I am sorry it has been so painful."

Paula looked at Jerem. He turned away. "We'll get over it," she whispered.

"Do not blame your trader friend, either. Moat Piloski is a weak man. His fear of us made him divulge your secrets."

She nodded.

Harry eyed her for a long moment. Then, with the care of the aged, he stood up and slowly walked over to his antique desk.

He could be a hundred years old, Paula thought. She fought back a crazy desire to help him, give his frail body her own flesh to lean upon. Such help would be considered an insult.

And she recognized that her desire to help him had little to do with his age. *He has inspired me.* It was no wonder that such a man ruled a Colony of Costeaus.

Harry picked up another drawing pad from the desk. "The clan knows my fondness for the art of picture sketching. Quite often, I receive messages in the form of a drawing. There are many artists among us.

"A sketch of a scene can often reveal more than video images. The digitized picture throbs with accuracy, but it is cold and dead, lacking the interface of human perception. Video requires the observer to overlay his own feelings onto the scene without the benefit of his full sensory range. I can see the details of the digitized picture, but I cannot hear the background, nor smell the air, nor taste the essence of the place."

Sadly, he looked down at the sketch in his hands. "The drawing, however, reveals these things. I see and taste and feel through the emotions of another human. I understand the reality of the sketched scene."

He laid the drawing pad on Paula's lap. "This picture was brought to me several days ago."

She drew in a sharp breath. Her first thought was to prevent her son from seeing this image of madness. She was too late. A deep frown twisted Jerem's features as he peered over her shoulder.

Reds and yellows dominated the picture, acting as fierce little cursors for the array of human dismemberments. Point of view was from an open airlock—a distorted fisheye peek into a bright chamber overwhelmed by violence. Legs, hands, other unrecognizable pieces of human anatomy lay everywhere. Two bloody decapitated heads stared at each other from opposite sides of the room. A half-naked woman lay on her back on the floor, her arms and legs tightly bound with acceleration straps. The fingers of her right hand had been cut off and stuffed into her mouth.

Harry sat down carefully. His calm voice helped Paula tear her eyes away from the drawing.

"The location of this place is unimportant. Suffice it to say that it is one of our hidden facilities, where stasis-frozen humans are brought for revival.

"Last week, what was thought to be a pair of revivees were awakened at this facility. Terrible weapons—Cohe wands—must have been somehow hidden within the flesh of these creatures. The crew of the shuttle craft, who brought the capsules up from the surface, and the stasis technicians at the facility were all tortured and murdered. This *Paratwa*"—he practically spat the word—"this *beast* tortured and killed eleven of our clan."

"And Bob Max," Paula whispered.

Harry nodded and carefully withdrew the picture from her hands. He stared at it for a long moment before placing the pad back on his desk.

"Always there is a great anger among my people. It is contained, usually, or directed at outsiders. But the anger lurks in the heart of every true Costeau. What was done to our eleven friends has focused that anger, molded it into a force to be reckoned with. I and the tribunal have done our best to temper that rage, but we cannot contain it, nor would we want to. The clan of Alexander must avenge itself.''

Paula shivered. ''E-Tech and the Guardians . . .''

Harry's face hardened. ''They do not matter to us. They will do what they must and we will do what we must. It is a clan affair.''

She regained her composure. ''You've brought us a long way for nothing. My son and I witnessed Bob Max's murder, nothing more.''

A gentle frown fell over Harry's face. ''Nothing more? You have seen, and by all accounts, spoken with this monster. The evil must be described to our people so that they may know their enemy.''

It will do no good, she thought. A chill returned as the image of Smiler and Sad-eyes, standing in front of her porch, flashed into awareness. *At least you know what you're dealing with. This Paratwa is evil.* She doubted whether E-Tech or the Guardians would ever understand that.

Harry continued. ''You are welcome to stay here in our Colony until the deed is done—the creature destroyed. I would advise that you remain, although, if you wish, transport to another Colony will be provided.''

Until the deed is done. They could be here forever.

''My people tell me that both the Guardians and E-Tech are most anxious to talk with you and your son. An Intercolonial search has been announced. A Costeau, in such a situation, would hide in the deepest hole he could find.''

She looked at Jerem. He stoically avoided her gaze.

''For the time being we'll stay here.''

Harry smiled. ''Good. We will make you as comfortable as possible. I'm sure your son will find much to excite him.''

Jerem glared at the old man. ''Pa, uk-fo si-lo ees-la cro-neer.''

The words sounded vicious, obscene. Paula pointed her finger at him, a warning. He glared at her but remained silent.

Harry looked amused. "I do not recognize the tongue, yet I suspect that I've been insulted. No matter. The young, too, must be allowed to speak their minds." He kept staring at Jerem while addressing Paula. "I will send for refreshments and then we will go before the tribunal and a gathering of the clan leaders. You will tell them your story.".

Abruptly, a vision of Jerem's father came to Paula—a bearded caricature, smiling; a relic of better days.

I will tell them my story.

The thought made her feel incredibly lonely.

Gillian and Nick sat in the back of a plush Irryan restaurant, discussing their course of action. Haddad's watchdogs, nibbling on bologna three tables away, remained just out of eavesdropping range. Nick had worn an antibugging device just the same. Haddad was clever—the subcutaneous transmitters proved that.

Nick ordered lobster steak. The waitress assured them that it was fresh, caught just that morning on the sea Colony of Aegean and shipped to Irrya via express shuttle. Nick, propped on a pair of cushions, asked the waitress to deliver three portions to the watchdogs' table, compliments of E-Tech.

The watchdogs pretended to be nonplussed, but it was obvious they were distraught. Their cover was blown. They ate in silence.

Gillian and Nick kept their faces turned toward the wall to prevent lipreading.

"I suggest Sirak-Brath," began Nick. "The place is bursting with pirates, smugglers, hardcore traders. And they're all rather fond of money."

"How much of it do we have?"

The midget grinned happily. "I've tapped into one of Haddad's special security accounts. Hard as hell to trace. We're probably drawing money from the same fund that pays for our little friends over there." He nodded his head toward the watchdogs' table.

"How soon till you're caught?"

"I'd be willing to say we can get away with it for at least a couple of months. And tomorrow I'm going to open a half-dozen new accounts for you, using fictitious names, of course. You'll be able to draw cash in most any Colony."

"These pirates and smugglers—what else do you think they'll respond to?" Gillian did not like the idea of trying to buy their help.

"Well, I doubt whether you'll be able to inspire them through the nobility of your cause. The Costeaus especially are real hardasses."

There were ways to inspire hardasses.

"How will we remain in contact?"

Nick chewed happily on his lobster. "I'll be able to monitor your cash withdrawals. I've worked out a code. If you want to contact me, make a cash withdrawal ending with an odd number. One hour later, I'll be waiting for your call. I've got a list of public phone codes for you to memorize—we'll go sequentially, so that I won't end up using the same phone over and over. Haddad's people would certainly get suspicious of that."

"They'll be suspicious the instant I disappear."

"Sure they will." Nick grinned. "Don't worry, I can handle 'em."

He would, too. Nick was extraordinarily effective.

"And what about the Cohe switch?" Gillian asked. "Are you sure they won't discover that the wand I checked into Security before we left the building was a fake?"

"It looks and feels exactly like the real one. The only way to tell for sure is to fire the damn thing." Nick chuckled. "And I've been doing my best to keep Haddad's people a little wary of doing that. I told them the story about the E-Tech man back in our era who tried to fire a wand and ended up creating a second asshole for himself.''

"I never heard that story."

"I lied. But really, I don't think Haddad's people are going to mess around with that wand. At least until you really disappear. By then, of course, it won't matter."

There was only one other thing bothering Gillian.

"Haddad and I were talking this morning. He casually mentioned the existence of a second computer program in the E-Tech vaults. The Pasha intimated that it had something to do with us."

Nick's reply came just a fraction of a second too late. Gillian was instantly suspicious.

"Yeah, there's a second program. But Haddad was probably just fishing. They located the program at the same time they found the one that led to our awakening. They haven't been able to break in yet. Haddad probably thought you might know something about it."

"Have you tackled it?"

"Nah, I just haven't had the time. Once you're gone, maybe I'll see if Rome will let me take a shot at it."

"It could be important."

Nick shrugged. "Might be. Hard to tell. Probably doesn't have anything to do with our Paratwa problem."

"Maybe I should take a shot at it before I go?"

The fork froze on its way into Nick's mouth. He avoided Gillian's eyes.

"I think it's more important that you assemble a combat team. That's first priority right now."

"Whose priority?"

Nick put down the fork. He met Gillian's stare.

"Don't stop trusting me now, old friend. It's been too many years."

"I could say the same thing."

Nick grinned. "Good. Then let's both trust each other. You go to Sirak-Brath and I'll take a shot at this program while you're gone.''

Gillian nodded slowly. "And when I return, I'll take a shot at it.''

They finished their meal in silence.

Night had rotated into Velvet-on-the-Green. Directly above, a tapestry of stars glittered through the cosmishield glass; pinpricks of light reflected into the Colony by the huge outside mirrors. Gillian smiled. A true view of space did not exist here. According to Nick, the mirrors of this Colony were programmed to capture starlight from random directions in order to enhance the spectral display. The denizens of Velvet-on-the-Green preferred art to truth.

I'm bitter tonight, Gillian thought. The primary reason eluded him. Natural tension? The beginning of a new hunt always brought some emotional turmoil. He had never quite understood it.

Of course, part of his bitterness derived from yesterday's meeting in the Irryan restaurant: Nick's secrecy regarding the second computer program.

What is Nick afraid of? What could we learn from that computer program that could possibly change our actions here?

A Paratwa was on the loose. Considered as an elementary problem, there was only one solution. The creature would have to be hunted and killed, regardless of its breed or its reputation.

Then why doesn't Nick want this program explored? What knowledge lay buried there? Had Nick already broken into the program? It seemed possible. His suspicious answers suggested that the midget knew more than he was telling.

Brighter flares of light paralleled the long strip of glass above him, a scattering of palatial homes along the other two land sectors. The most notable difference between this Colony and Irrya was the density of the human population. Irrya seemed to be almost a solid mass of people; by comparison, Velvet-on-the-Green boasted a miniscule population. Humanity was spread thin here.

It was quieter, also. His boots, cracking against the hard plastic sidewalk as he strode along the city street, sounded blatantly loud, almost harsh. In comparison, everything else around him seemed to whisper. Cars glided along the black thorofare, the few pedestrians he passed spoke in solemn whispers, storefronts hissed their quaint musical enticements. Velvet-on-the-Green loathed the obvious. It was a place of privacy, of cherished secrets.

He supposed that the subnormal G Forces—Velvet-on-the-Green's most remarkable claim to fame—contributed to the relative silence. Due to the cylinder's slower rotation, the gravity was seven-eighths normal. Objects did not impact upon one another quite so hard. Less noise resulted.

And the weaker gravity made Gillian feel physically stronger. *A good place to begin a hunt.*

He arrived at his destination. The five-story structure loomed above him. Outer support girders crisscrossed the dark facade, soaring at odd angles up into the night sky. He did not recognize the architectural style; Velvet-on-the-Green, like Irrya, boasted a wide range of constructions. But the red neon sign above the door was plain enough. The HOME OF SHARED FANTASY had a thousand derivatives; the archetype probably dated back to the dawn of human culture.

Inside, he was met by a tall, ashen-faced man dressed immaculately in a high-collared burgundy tuxedo, striped trousers, and a royal-blue tailcoat.

"Welcome, sir. May I be of assistance?"

"Yes. I would like a woman . . . for about an hour."

"Very good, sir. May I ask the name of your bank so that we can handle the necessary credit transferral?"

"I prefer cash cards."

"Very good, sir. Will this be a relationship based on the popular norm or would you prefer your own variations?"

Gillian grinned. He had never met a pimp's assistant who was so polite. "I am interested in sensual implements—the old-fashioned variety."

"Hmm. Well, sir, I'm afraid our collection isn't that extensive. But we do possess a rather prehistoric accelerator couch. It is complete with transfer sensors, four-level vibratory massage, and a double Diablo enema unit."

"No, that sounds too complicated. How about smaller implements? A good old-fashioned itchystick would be very nice."

The man smiled serenely. "Yes, sir, we have several of those. They're very old, but all in excellent working condition. You may be interested to know that a new line of itchysticks are currently being manufactured by a plant in Delhi."

"I prefer the older types."

"Of course, sir. And do you have a preference as to the lady?"

"No preference." He did need some excuse to get her out of the room, though. He matched the man's smile. "Could she bring along some of her extra underwear?"

"Of course, sir. Will there be anything else?"

"No. That will do."

Gillian paid the desk clerk and was escorted up the plush staircase by a young girl dressed in a bellhop's uniform. She smiled sweetly, handed him the key to room 227, and wished him an enjoyable evening. He gave her a cash card. She curtsied.

The room was neatly furnished; twin bureaus, a dresser with an ornate mirror, white satin sheets rippling on the waterbed. The silky looked to be in her early twenties. Blond hair, blue eyes, nordic features—Gillian was glad she bore no resemblance to Catharine.

"I'm Mocha." She smiled professionally and sat down on the edge of the bed. Her short skirt bunched up to reveal tanned thighs.

Gillian sat beside her. "Do you have the itchystick?"

Mocha opened her handbag, took out a tapered cylinder with a flat glazed plate at one end. "Will this do?"

It would. Gillian even recognized the brand. "And I asked for some of your underwear."

She opened her mouth, let her tongue wander to the edge of her lips. "Undies are so very nice, aren't they? I mean, what would we ladies do without our bras and paste panties?"

Gillian supposed she was trying to arouse him.

She caressed his arm. "You're very tense."

"Your underwear?"

She reached back into her handbag. "How about these?" She handed him five cotton bras and several pounds of colored stick-on bikinis.

He tried to sound impressed. "Oh, they're beautiful."

"They've all been freshly laundered but if you like I can get you dirty ones." Her eyes sparkled.

He shook his head. "I have sort of a fantasy. I'd like you to leave the room for at least twenty minutes—your underwear stays here, of course. When you come back, I'll be ready."

Her eyes narrowed. "Will you be bad while I'm gone? Will you have to be punished?"

He sighed. "No, that won't be necessary."

She shrugged and bounced her hips toward the door.

"Remember," he called. "Twenty minutes. And please knock first."

"Try not to stain the sheets," she chided.

"I'll be careful."

The door closed. Gillian leaped from the bed. He kicked off his boots and stripped away his olive slacks, turning them inside out in the process. They became light wool pants with blue pinstriping. The jacket, too, was reversible—gray nylon crinkled into jet-black leather. He threw his shorts on the floor.

Naked, he picked up the itchystick and lay face down on the bed. The massager vibrated softly in his hand as he ignited its mechanism. He began rubbing it across his buttocks, felt pleasurable tingling as the itchystick's energy field interacted with the nerve endings beneath his flesh.

He slowly caressed one buttock, then the other. Nothing. Next, he tried the back of his thighs, starting at the crease and working downward to the knee.

At about the halfway point on the right leg, he felt a gentle stab. He rubbed the massager past that spot again to be sure.

There could be no doubt. The itchystick's field had reacted to another energy pattern just beneath the surface of the skin. He had found the first of Haddad's subcutaneous transmitters.

He ran the massager across every square inch of skin, paying careful attention to the most likely areas to hide bugs—the groin, between the toes, the armpits. Apparently, Haddad's technicians were unaware that subcutaneous transmitters, located where the flesh was folded or creased, were more difficult for the subject to locate. They had opted for the standard practice of implanting the devices in areas that would not normally be examined by the subject.

In less than five minutes, Gillian located the other two bugs: one on the back of his left thigh and the third near the base of his spine.

Bugs were usually planted in threes and the chance that a second trio had escaped his careful scrutiny was remote. In theory, Haddad could also have backed up the subcutaneous transmitters with intravenous ones. But Nick had accessed E-Tech's security system and had assured Gillian that such a procedure was rarely implemented. Intravenous bugs could sometimes prove dangerous, leading to blood poisoning and a host of related ills.

Gillian's other concern was the possibility that this room might be under surveillance. Camouflaged microcams were the rule rather than the exception within silky palaces. Ostensibly, they were installed for the safety of the prostitutes.

Nick had chosen this particular palace with care. The Home of Shared Fantasy catered to the upper strata of Intercolonial society. Technicians swept the rooms daily, searching for bugs and microcams. The management here prided itself on its discretion.

Gillian withdrew the Cohe wand from what was now his inner jacket pocket. He hoped Nick was right. An unwanted voyeur might get his kicks from watching Gillian caress himself with an itchystick. But that observer could easily become alarmed at the sight of a Paratwa weapon.

From another pocket he produced a roll of anesthetic gauze and a tiny tweezers. He tore off three strips of gauze and slapped a piece over each of the bug locations. Carefully, he squeezed the Cohe, felt the hard egg compress. The tiny needle popped out, ready to focus the destructive light. He squeezed harder. The black beam lanced several feet into the air.

He released hand pressure on the egg. The light dissolved. He repeated the procedure several times, until he felt in control of the Cohe's energy. Then he turned his back to the mirror and craned his neck to stare over his shoulder. He jerked his wrist and squeezed the wand.

Three times, in rapid succession, the black energy whipped up and over his head. Three times the Cohe found its mark. He smelled burned fabric as the gauze covering each of the subcutaneous transmitters smoldered.

The trio of tiny holes burned into his flesh were just large enough for the tweezers. Quickly, before the anesthetic wore off, he probed into the first hole. A minute later he felt the tiny forceps clamp on something solid.

One down. He deposited the minute transmitter on a fresh piece of gauze and attacked the other thigh. He found the second bug immediately and laid that beside its mate.

The third, however—the one at the base of his spine—proved difficult. Again and again he gently speared the tweezers into the anesthetized hole, searching for the telltale hardness. Each time he met with failure.

He debated another burn with the Cohe, but decided to try one more stab with the tweezers. He entered the wound at a slight angle and located the bug just as someone knocked on the door.

"It's me," Mocha called softly.

"Wait a moment! I'll let you in."

He withdrew the final bug, laid it on the gauze, and folded the fabric into a tight ball, which he stuffed into his pants pocket.

Tweezers and Cohe were quickly hidden. He took a step toward the door and then suddenly remembered her underwear. It was still neatly piled on the bed, undisturbed.

Quickly, he staggered the panties in a large circle at the foot of the bed and used several bras to form a pentagram in the center. It seemed reasonably fetishistic.

Mocha entered. She smiled at his naked form. "Say, you're handsome. I've never seen such a gorgeous body!"

Just wait till you see my back, thought Gillian. The anesthetic was starting to wear off and the three holes in his flesh were beginning to burn. At least there was little bleeding—the Cohe had effectively cauterized the wounds.

She closed the door and raised her eyebrows at the circle of underclothing. "Having fun?"

"I haven't had such a good time in ages."

She moved to him, coiled her arms around his waist. "What would you like?" Her voice dropped to a husky growl.

Gillian felt himself tense.

Mocha squeezed, rubbed her thighs against him. "I like just about anything you can imagine. I like a virile man like you, someone with a body—like yours—with snap in it."

Gillian had never heard the expression before. He analyzed. The girl had probably been in this business since puberty. She must be an excellent sexual partner. Nick had said that only the best worked in Velvet-on-the-Green's silky palaces. She would know all the tricks, all the ways to bring him pleasure; the right words, the right movements.

"Relax, honey. Relax and enjoy." Gently, she fingered his penis.

Her knowledge of the male anatomy would be exquisite. She would understand the rhythms of his arousal, know how to blend herself to them. Mentally, of course, she would be somewhere else—thinking about the next client, perhaps, or buying new clothes at one of the shops in this exclusive sector. She was, after all, a professional.

Her other hand cupped his buttocks. Lips touched the base of his neck. "A man of strength." Her voice dropped even lower. "Power snaps from you."

Her hand on his buttocks moved upward, came precariously close to the gauze-covered wound at the base of his spine. He shuddered.

"I love a man like you."

A simple act, he thought. Physically, the process of sexual intercourse was quite simple. An array of sensitized nerve endings were stimulated. For the male, blood flowed into the penis, making it erect. The tissues became oversaturated with blood and then the pressure caused muscle contractions. Orgasm.

"Let go," she hissed.

He grew erect and imagined the flow of blood.

"On the bed," she whispered.

"No. Here." He lifted her and she wrapped her thighs around his waist. In the lighter gravity, he was easily able to support her. Soft hands gripped his neck, fingernails scratched his skin. She leaned back, guiding herself onto him. The skirt bunched at her waist. He found it vaguely amusing that she wore no panties.

I merely have to support her and sustain my erection. When she is finished, I will have been relieved.

She thrust onto him. He closed his eyes and thought about Nick's motives in having him come here.

Naturally, there were other ways to remove subcutaneous transmitters. It was a relatively simple surgical procedure for any well-equipped doctor. Haddad would know that too, and would have immediately tightened surveillance had he suspected Gillian of attempting to remove the bugs. But going to a house of prostitution and using an itchystick and a Cohe wand . . . Well, the chances of Haddad knowing that trick were slim at best.

Mocha gasped and gyrated wildly. He gripped her shoulders to maintain his balance.

Nick might also have procured a jamming device for the bugs. In the long run, though, such a method was impractical. Gillian would be forced to have the jammer on his person at all times and even a temporary power failure would instantly expose him to E-Tech's surveillance. This way was best.

Her strokes became more violent. His penis felt ready to burst.

Actually, the first part of Nick's plan had been carried out yesterday at the Irryan restaurant. They had exposed Haddad's people. Later in the evening, Nick had implemented his diversion. Several men had been paid to gather in the doorway of the restaurant, momentarily blocking the watchdogs while Gillian raced down the street and into a dark alley. The diversion had been successful; Gillian had lost the trackers.

Naturally, he had not really gotten away. The watchdogs had probably gone straight to their car and radioed E-Tech for a grid-map location. With the subcutaneous transmitters, they would know Gillian's exact location to within ten feet. Their next step would have been to notify Haddad of the attempted escape.

It had all been part of Nick's plan. Haddad had reacted as they had intended. Instead of tightening surveillance on Gillian, the Pasha had pulled back his watchdogs, thinking that he was tricking Gillian into believing the escape had been successful. *We'll let him run a little*, Haddad had probably said to Franco. *See what he's up to.*

Mocha cried out, climaxed with rapid thrusts. He set her down on the bed, withdrew.

"You were wonderful," she breathed. Her eyes tried to sustain the lie.

I did nothing. I stood there and you relieved me. My tension level has been lowered. Several days from now, I will repeat the process. If a woman is not present at that time, I will masturbate instead. Either method produced the desired result.

He recalled a time when there had been a difference.

Sex with Catharine had been explosive—a multilevel blending of physical, emotional, and mental energies. For a time, they would soar within one another, oblivious to all but their desires.

It's strange, Catharine. After I've been relieved, I can think of you without being overwhelmed by pain. The mere act of sex re presses the hurt.

There had been many other women over the years. Not all of them had been prostitutes. But none of them had been able to satisfy his deeper needs.

I'm the cause of the problem, Catharine. Somehow, your death dulled the point of my feelings. Once I could plunge into the darkness with hope, joy, sorrow . . . even fear. I could focus an emotion until only it and the darkness existed.

He had lost clarity—repressed that part of himself. To perceive without veils meant to open himself to the agony of his loss.

I cannot look into the darkness anymore, Catharine. I simply cannot do it. He sometimes felt the need to apologize to her for that.

"You have some time left," Mocha said calmly. "I hope you can come back again soon. I think we were great together."

I was great. The anesthetic had worn off. The three holes in his back burned and throbbed.

He dressed quickly and played out the charade. "I was wondering, Mocha . . ." An embarrassed smile came easily. "You see, I'm a married man and well, my wife suspects. You know how it is. She has me followed sometimes and that's why I've changed my clothes. I figure that if I dress differently, I'll have a better chance of not being recognized. Now if I could only sneak out the back door . . ."

Mocha grinned. "There's an exit that leads to an alley. It'll bring you out onto the street nearly two blocks away."

"I'm shocked. I must not be the only married man coming in here."

Mocha threw her head back and laughed. It was not part of the act. Gillian felt a sudden wave of tenderness for her. By rote, he repressed the feeling.

He said good-bye quickly and took the elevator to the entrance floor. The well-dressed pimp's assistant listened attentively as Gillian retold the lie about having a suspicious wife.

"Sir, the back door is always available to our clientele. We also offer a discreet limousine service that can pick you up and drop you off at any location within the Colony. For a rather nominal fee . . ."

"Thank you, but the back door will be fine."

"Very good, sir. Please follow me."

Just before Gillian stepped out into the alley, he turned and profusely shook the man's hand, thanking him for his assistance.

"It is our pleasure to please you, sir. Our doors are always open." The man smiled pleasantly, then closed the heavy steel portal. Gillian heard electronic bolts slamming into the lock mode.

Gillian strolled down the alleyway, pleased with himself. He had not lost his touch. The pimp's assistant was completely unaware that three subcutaneous transmitters were now resting in the bottom of his coat pocket.

In the alley, Gillian completed his transition. Two wads of skin paste melted instantly onto his cheeks, giving his face a fuller look. Skinny lip inserts fattened his mouth. Eyebrow liners darkened his forehead. He tucked his hair up under a brimmed cap and practiced a jauntier walk. Unless Haddad's watchdogs were incredibly alert, he felt sure he could pass within ten feet of them without being recognized.

Naturally, he had no intention of getting that close. With luck, it would take the watchdogs until morning to realize he had parted ways with the transmitters. The pimp's assistant would be in for a surprise.

He followed the alleyway until it bisected a quiet street, then took the street back to the main thorofare. He covered the mile to his destination in good time.

The shuttle port's mezzanine and most of the entrance ramps leading to the below-ground docking bays were deserted. Nick had already procured Gillian's fare, under an assumed name, to Sirak-Brath. There would be no need to deal with any of the ticket or banking machines.

One other notion had compelled Gillian to begin the escape

within this cylinder. According to Haddad's transcripts, the Paratwa had told Paula Marth and her son that it had come from Velvet-on-the-Green. A lie, obviously. But there were over two hundred Colonies and the creature had claimed this one as its home. That could be a clue as to the Paratwa's identity; then again, the assassin could have simply chosen this place at random. Either way, Gillian had wanted to see Velvet-on-the-Green for himself.

A male voice announced the arrival of the Sirak-Brath shuttle. Gillian was about to head down into the flashing entrance ramp when he noticed a small group of travelers at the other end of the terminal. They seemed to be speaking excitedly. Curiosity got the best of him and he moved closer.

They were grouped around a public monitor, conversing in sharp awed whispers. On the screen, a freelancer had just finished delivering a news report. The phrase, *Special Interrupt,* dissolved across the freelancer's face and then the channel returned to its normal shuttle transit reports.

Gillian asked, "What happened?"

A pudgy man with a child in tow glared at him. "This is an outrage. The Guardians are supposed to deal with this sort of thing!"

The child, a girl, nodded her assent.

"This is real trouble!" a woman answered angrily. "The Guardians stay away from real trouble!"

"What happened?" he repeated.

The woman shook her head, furious. "That creature—that Paratwa—just slaughtered a street full of people in Jordanian Paris!"

"A public street," added the pudgy man, as if that fact alone made the murders an outrage. The little girl shook the man's hand, trying to get loose.

"Over thirty people dead," muttered a third voice. "I suppose we should be glad it didn't happen here."

An old well-dressed man shook his head. "Terrible, terrible! Limbs sliced off, people decapitated. Gutters flowing with blood.

The freelancers are promising video direct from the scene!'' He sounded as if he could barely wait to see the pictures.

"The Guardians and the local police didn't even try to catch the bastard!'' proclaimed the woman. "I can't believe they're so incompetent!''

Believe it, Gillian thought.

The pudgy man shook his fist in the air. The little girl winced as his other hand squeezed her wrist. "They should close off every shuttle port in that Colony! No one should be allowed in or out until they find this beast!''

Gillian shook his head. Sealing off a Colony was a doubtful measure at best. The damned cylinders simply had too many ways in and out. And even if the Paratwa was trapped within one cylinder, what then? The creature would either hide until things calmed down or fight its way off the Colony. Probably it would hide. If it chose to escape in a captured shuttle, it would be vulnerable to attack by the Guardians' patrol vessels. If, instead, the Paratwa went underground in a heavily populated Colony, there would be little hope of finding it. The Guardians could not seal off a Colony indefinitely.

"An outrage!'' muttered the pudgy man, as he dragged the girl toward the nearest ramp. "Something must be done!''

Something shall, Gillian promised.

It was noonday on the Shan Plateau, dark and gloomy, sunlight diffused into shadowless illumination by the multiple layers of poisonous smog. Moist ground—almost mud—covered what had once been tropical lands. The teak forests and poppy fields were long gone, indiscriminately vaporized by nuclear terrorists in the twenty-first century. Only a mutant strain of translucent yellow grass had survived. Small scattered patches studded the landscape like warts on the skin of an animal.

A huge rectangular structure—the Church of the Trust's Shan temple—stood on the crest of a small hill, dwarfing the space-suited figure who stood before it. Bishop Vokir raised his hand as if trying to seize the thick air. Hundreds of worshipers, spread out below him along the base of the hill, grew silent.

"You are children of the Spirit of Gaia," he intoned. "You are of this place, of this Earth. You live your bodily existence out there . . ." He pointed a gloved finger up into the smog. ". . . but here dwells your eternal spirit. The path of your travel within this life leads forever downward—to this place, to these roots, to this soil from which life sprang."

"To these roots," they shouted. Five hundred helmeted heads bowed to the ground.

The Bishop touched his control belt and lowered the volume of his projection amps. His voice fell to a reverberating whisper within the helmets of the mourners.

"It is said among the nonbelievers that the Earth is a dead place, that mankind has foolishly destroyed his home in the name of science. Is this possible? Can the root of all life truly be destroyed?"

"No!" they cried.

He added some bass to the projection amps, raised the volume a notch. "Can a planet that gave birth to billions ever be considered a dead place? Is it not true that one who returns to the roots of life cannot help but be reborn?"

They raised their arms and the deep Burmese smog swirled around them. "It is true!"

"The roots are beyond the touch of us mortals." The Bishop closed his eyes and bowed his head. He boosted the tremolo so that his voice seemed to waver. "The roots survive both frost and fire. The roots maintain us. Our Trust is consecrated by these roots."

"Our Trust is consecrated by these roots," the crowd murmured.

"And so it is, and so shall it ever be, for those who live within the *Spirit of Gaia*."

"Amen," they cried.

The Bishop allowed a moment of silence and then switched his control belt to the clerical channel.

"Are they ready?"

"Yes, your eminence," came the voice of a servant.

"Then let it begin."

He looked past the gathering to the train of shuttle crafts resting on the flatlands beyond the hill. Cargo hatches blossomed open like the petals of extraordinary white flowers. Church servants in green spacesuits poured from the ships to form double lines in front of each craft. The mourners turned to observe.

The Bishop touched his control belt and a prerecorded audio loop began the divine Chant of Mourning.

"Blessed are the rootmakers for they maintain the sands of time. Blessed are the dustmakers for they surround the roots and give them strength. Blessed are the rainmakers, for they pour from the heavens and deliver the dust unto the place of all beginnings."

The mourners quickly picked up the rhythm of the words as the Chant was repeated. Dark caskets slithered from the cargo bays and were passed down the long lines of servants. Each coffin was girdled by a ring of blue/green sparklights that strobed the dull sky in tandem with the holy words. The Chant, intensified by passion, grew stronger.

Mourners divided themselves into small groups of pallbearers. The dark caskets were lifted and carried to a large arena ringed by gas torches. With effort, the bearers hoisted the flashing caskets high into the air, over their heads. Bishop Vokir waited until everyone stood within the arena before slowly fading out the Chant.

Glimmering sparklights began to die as the tiny internal batteries succumbed to the poisoned air. One by one, the caskets lost their illumination. The Bishop, even after all these years, still derived a sensory pleasure from watching the caskets, their lights fading,

floating above the helmeted mourners. The vision possessed indescribable purity.

Silence held the gathering as the final words of the Chant dissolved. In the deathly quiet, the Bishop raised his arms.

"Today, on this Earth, on this plateau, we gather for the Conversion of Souls. Today, in this place, we gather with the spirits of
sixty-two of our brethren. Today, in this place, we return the roots
to the dust. Today, in this place, we are the rainmakers."

"We are the rainmakers," they murmured.

"We who maintain the Trust shall know the glory of eternal
life. We who maintain the Trust shall be forever blessed. We who
maintain the Trust shall again walk the Earth and know the Spirit
of Gaia as the kingdom of life."

"We are the undying," they murmured. Weeping could be
heard behind the words.

The Bishop dropped his arms. The pallbearers followed suit,
gently lowering the caskets to the damp soil.

"The kingdom awaits our brethren." Bishop Vokir touched his
control belt and the gas torches surrounding the arena blossomed
into wild snakes of blue and green fire. Slowly, the pallbearers
drifted out of the torched circle.

"Rest in peace," the Bishop intoned, when the arena had been
cleared.

Almost immediately, the ground within the circle began to
move. Damp mud turned milky white as the preplanted fault chemicals grew agitated. Underground tension rods catalyzed the process, creating minature geysers of dark fluid that spouted high into
the air. A fine mist rose over the unsettled arena.

One by one, the coffins upended and sank into the Earth. In a
minute, the entombment was complete. What had been solid
ground was now a bubbling lake of white syrup.

The Bishop uttered the final words of the ceremony without audio effects.

"In this place, let the Conversion of Souls last seven days and
seven nights. Amen."

He turned and marched into the Temple, shutting down his suit's audio inputs immediately. There was no need for him to listen to humans weeping away into the darkness. As always, many would remain at the lake for hours, mourning their dead until the shuttle engines began to whine, signaling imminent departure. Church servants would then arrive to console and gently lead the more distraught mourners to their acceleration seats.

And in seven days, just before the shallow white lake hardened into a burial vault, some of the liquid would be drawn off, pasteurized and sweetened, and bottled for transport to one of the thousands of clergies scattered throughout the Colonies. There, with proper sacrament, it would become misk—holy liquid of the Church of the Trust.

The Bishop stepped into the open airlock and sealed the outer door. Airjet detoxifiers blasted the rubbery shell of his protective suit, scouring away any impurities that might have been picked up on the Plateau.

It was a good religion, he reflected. Aristotle, before perishing in that freak South African disaster, had generated the basic outlines. Theophrastus had added special touches—the burial ceremony and the sacrament of the misk were his contributions. Sappho played with the symbols, the colors, the effects—had brought the religion to life with that curious detachment of the master magician. And, as always, Codrus had excelled in the financial arena.

To the Bishop, profit was the most exciting part of the Church. Today's ceremony had netted an enormous sum, and there were a half-dozen such burials taking place on the planet every day.

The detoxifiers shut down and the inner airlock opened. He unsnapped his helmet, peeled off the radiation suit, and hung the two sections in the corridor closet. A servant in blue robes approached and bowed gracefully.

"Your quarters are ready, your eminence. Shall I send for lunch?"

"No. I shall require an hour of silence. Please see to it that I am not disturbed."

"Very good, your eminence." The servant shuffled away.

Profits. The Church charged a basic fee for each burial, a nominal amount that barely covered shuttle transport costs. But each friend or relative of the deceased, who wished to pay final respects on the surface, was debited additional sums for transportation, suit rental, and detoxification. Earth passports, issued by E-Tech, also produced a slight profit, since the Church was able to buy them at a bulk commodity discount. And as a nontaxable entity, the Church could solicit donations from its members, ostensibly to cover the high costs of Earth burial.

Occasional freelancer exposés hinted at the enormous profits the Church realized on the burial services, but few Colonials were overly concerned. Money was money and even a church was expected to look healthy within the ICN marketplace. The Irryan constitution specifically recognized the Church's right to conduct planetary burials and guaranteed the Church broad travel freedom between Earth and the Colonies. And to the millions of true believers, the Church of the Trust could do no wrong.

The Bishop entered his private quarters and sealed the door. A quick check of his desk scanner revealed that no major disturbances had taken place within the chamber since his last visit, almost six months ago. Aside from periodic scanning by the maintenance techs for outside atmospheric leaks, no one had even entered the room.

That was good. Although the full-time personnel who manned the Church's numerous Earth cemeteries were carefully screened, there was always the possibility that a disloyal servant would come snooping around forbidden areas of a Temple. At most of the sanctuaries, such antics could be ignored. But here on the Shan Plateau, and within the Temples of Finland and Western Canada, Codrus had much to hide.

The Bishop keyed open his desk and placed his hand on the

identification modem built into the drawer. He typed a twenty-digit access code into the terminal. The monitor flashed green.

He entered the chamber's small closet and pushed aside a rack of clothing. The carpet rolled up easily, exposing another hand modem on the bare metal floor. The Bishop laid his palm against that modem and whispered a second access code. Audio sensors reacted instantly. The modem pivoted up from the floor to form a handle. He opened the hatch.

The staircase spiraled down into darkness. Keeping his hand on the railing, the Bishop carefully descended into the subcellar.

The Temples of Finland and Western Canada boasted similar facilities. From time to time the Bishop scheduled himself for funeral services in those places.

Last month he had been to Finland. From a secret storehouse below that Temple, the Bishop had retrieved Reemul's weapons, mothballed two centuries earlier. Crescent webs, scramblers, launch-control thighpads; an entire arsenal of murderous implements had been prepared for the awakening of the Jeek—everything but the Cohe wands. Those, Reemul had taken into stasis.

It was just as well that the Jeek awoke with his Cohes. Codrus had deemed it necessary to destroy the pirates who, under Bob Max's direction, had brought Reemul from the depths of sleep.

It had been relatively easy to get a cryptic message to Reemul shortly after his revival. The Jeek had been ordered to extract the desired information from the Costeaus and then kill them.

Under torture, the pirates admitted to Reemul that they had no knowledge of anyone other than the smuggler. Bob Max had obeyed his primary orders until the end—he had kept his unorthodox ties with the Bishop a secret.

Lights came on automatically as the Bishop descended. At the bottom of the staircase, one hundred and twenty feet below the temple, a small cavern gave way to a metal door, carved into the bedrock. In the center of the door lay a circle of five single-access hand modems. Only the nervous system of an Ash Ock—or its tway—could unlock the portal.

Near the one o'clock position of the circle lay the Codrus modem. The Bishop placed his hand on the plate, allowing the door's complex access system to identify and disarm. While waiting, he found himself, as usual, staring at the other hand modems.

Poor Aristotle. Poor Empedocles. The Bishop had one of those strange thoughts—he reflected on the mortality of his breed. *We are strong beyond human knowledge, but even we are susceptible to the uncertainties of the universe.*

The thought was strange because the Bishop knew that his monarch did not share it. Codrus took into account the possibilities of accident or miscalculation, but deep within, all Ash Ock felt immortal.

The Bishop sighed. *Yet even we grow old.*

He entered an access code into the tiny keyboard beneath the modem. The unit flashed green, clearing him to enter. With a gentle push, the door opened. The Bishop stepped into a place where no human had ever walked.

Paula ran.

The pirate Colony lacked a sense of order. Buildings sat atop one another. Miniature forests opened onto great esplanades that were actually the roofs of other structures. Streets, jammed with walkers and cyclists, abruptly mutated into hallways with ceilings. She ducked through portals that were either entrances or exits—it was impossible to tell the difference.

A few structures lunged haphazardly across the entire diameter of the Colony. Weird elevators shot through these buildings, rotating their occupants at the gravity-free core of the Colony, then plunging to destinations on the opposite side of the cylinder. The small diameter of the Colony dictated a rapid spin rate to maintain normal gravity at the perimeter. The rotation produced a maddening Coriolis acceleration. Straight lines of motion did not exist. Paula's quarters, on the eleventh floor of a complex, contained a sink that blasted water in a curved stream.

Heart pounding, she leaped over a child's tricycle and dashed through an open doorway.

Artificial illumination bathed most of her route but occasional windows of sunlight overwhelmed the quartz/halogen beams. There were no discrete strips of cosmishield glass here; instead, sunlight penetrated the remotest sections of the Colony via complex arrangements of mirrors. By comparison, the geometries of Lamalan were ridiculously simple.

Pirates paused to stare at her as she dashed past them. Children gave chase, thinking Paula was leading them to excitement, relinquishing the pursuit only when they came close enough to see the pain on her face.

Smells assailed her—pungent stabs of garlic from a marketplace blended with the heavy odor of machinery oils a corridor away. Air conditioners shot perfumed sprays into the docking terminals, reducing but not completely eliminating the foul scent of pirates just arriving from Irryan Colonies. The badge of the true Costeau—the odorant bag—was not worn here, but the smell hung in the air. Paula had been told that lengthy exposure dimmed awareness of the odor.

It still stank.

She came to Harry's room and knocked loudly on the door. There was no response. In desperation, she pounded her fists against the wooden portal. Hands seized her from behind, pulled her to the floor.

"Goddamn you! I've got to see him! I've got to see the lion!"

Aaron, garbed in dirty coveralls, stomped down the corridor. The tattoo wormed across his cheek in anger.

"Let me go!" she pleaded. "I've got to see him!"

Aaron gave a hand signal. The guards released her. "Explain yourself, woman."

She stood up shakily. "My son . . . my son is gone."

"Gone where?"

She wanted to cry and scream with anger at the same time. She ended up doing neither. "He ran away," she explained, forcing calmness into her words. "He left a note. He . . . ran away."

Aaron dismissed the guards and then his firm hands gripped her shoulders.

"The lion is out of Colony. He will not return for many days. At any rate, you can't come pounding on his door as you please."

She drew a deep breath, nodded. "I'm sorry. But Jerem's gone. He left early last night, I believe. I didn't find the note till this morning."

"Children run away, woman. Such events do not cause Apocalypse."

"I know, I know. But I beat him." A sob escaped her. "I felt so mad . . . I was furious! I took it out on him."

For the past several days, she had tried to talk to Jerem, to break through his icy exterior, to explain, as gently as possible, what his father had been like and what a terrible thing her marriage had been. She had been young, incredibly foolish, unable to distinguish a man's good looks and charming manners from the bitter soul that lay huddled beneath.

Jerem had listened to her words but his own hurt remained too powerful and he refused to respond—until yesterday, when he suddenly blew up at her. At first she had been glad he was letting it all out. But then his words had turned ugly as he accused Paula of abandoning his father.

His father! That had triggered Paula's wrath.

Stupidly, she had screamed back at her son, telling him what his real father had been like—an opium-addicted smuggler with an ugly disposition, a pirate thief, rejected by his own clan—a man whose only interest in other people was in how easily he could fleece cash from them.

She had looked her son straight in the eye and told him that the happiest day in her life had been when she had learned that his father had been killed in a squabble with some other pirates.

Jerem had listened to her words with frozen calm. Then he had folded his arms and gazed into her face. He had addressed her with complete disdain, as if he were speaking to a machine.

"My father's dead. And it's because you're just a stupid bitch."

Paula had lost all control. She grabbed him and yanked him violently across her knee and spanked him with an uncontrollable fury. Screaming, he had run to his room.

Later, Paula had attempted to apologize. The effort had been futile. Jerem stood before her, body awkwardly rigid, eyes glazed. He refused to listen to her words or to hear the sorrow in her voice.

This morning, when she awoke, he was gone.

Aaron nodded. "What did the note say?"

Paula felt calmer, in control again. "It said that he was going to find a way off the Colony. It said not to try and follow because he wasn't coming back."

"Did he have any money?"

"He stole some cash cards . . . from my clothes."

Aaron looked thoughtful. "Orbital control keeps a record of all shuttle departures. We'll go there first."

"Do you really think he could have gotten on a shuttle?"

"It's the only way to leave a Colony."

Paula swallowed her fear. "But how could he get on board? Wouldn't your people be suspicious of a small boy?"

Aaron regarded her with scorn. "A Costeau of his age is considered man enough to go where he pleases."

"Yes . . . I forgot."

Orbital control was a three-story structure with a glass wall overlooking two small parks. Aaron led Paula up a steep flight of stairs and through an airlock. The third-floor duty room was crammed with communications gear.

A woman with short-cropped hair was on duty in front of a semicircular console. Aaron took a vacant seat beside her.

"Sheila, I need a favor."

"You got it."

"A list of shuttle departures during the night. Say between midnight and seven this morning?"

Paula nodded.

Sheila typed into a terminal and pointed to a paper-feed printer in the corner of the room. Paula recognized the printer as an antique.

"Only five shuttle departures during those hours," Sheila remarked. "Not a very busy night."

"Our luck," Aaron said. He withdrew the printout, scanned it slowly.

"Only two possibilities here. Three of the ships were on special clan business. We can rule them out. They would not have taken on passengers."

"And the other two?" Paula asked.

"One departed for the L4 group. If your son's on that shuttle, he'll still be in transit."

The distant L4 Colonies were mostly science- and research-oriented. Paula felt sure Jerem would not have gone there.

"How about the other one?"

"Sirak-Brath."

She took a deep breath. *I must be calm.*

Aaron studied the printout. "Sheila, another favor. Contact the Sirak-Brath shuttle and ask the Captain if he took on any passengers last night."

Sheila opened a communications channel while Aaron explained. "That ship was only scheduled to dock twenty minutes ago. The crew and passengers may still be aboard.

"It's also possible that your son never got on a shuttle. He could be wandering around here in the Colony. Perhaps his anger will pass and he will return."

Paula shook her head. "He won't cool down so easily. I'm sure of it."

Aaron shrugged. "Still, he may not have found transport as yet. We'll check the main docking terminals next."

Sheila removed her headset. "The Captain's already left ship on Sirak-Brath. But a crewman still on board says that their shuttle carried three passengers."

Aaron rubbed his tattoo. "Ask him for descriptions."

Sheila readjusted the headset, then shook her head. "The crewman says it's none of our business."

Aaron's face flashed anger. "Tell him it's a clan affair."

Sheila shook her head. "He's not of the Alexanders." She paused. "He suggests, however, that he will make the descriptions available to us, provided three hundred bytes are deposited into his account."

There was venom in Aaron's words. "Tell him that he may have his three hundred bytes. Tell him also that should we ever meet, Aaron of the Alexanders will rip his balls off!"

Sheila grinned and relayed the message. She laughed. "He intimates that the money was only a jest. He says that their passengers were a pair of Colonial traders and a young boy."

Paula tensed. "Ask him about the boy."

Aaron gave a nod and Sheila complied.

"He says the boy would not give a name. Tangled brown hair, carrying a small blue and white satchel. Paid cash cards for the fare."

Paula grabbed Aaron's arm. "It's him! Is he still aboard?"

"He left ship as soon as they docked."

She turned to Aaron. "We've got to go there! How soon can you be ready?"

"Easy, woman. I've no intention of going to Sirak-Brath. Other chores await me."

"I've no way to get there, And I'll need your help in finding him."

Aaron turned to Sheila. "When's the next shuttle going to Sirak-Brath?"

"Nothing scheduled till the day after tomorrow. You know how it is, though. A ship could come along any time."

Paula shook her head. "I can't afford to wait. I'll pay whatever fare you want."

He eyed her coldly. "I'm not for sale, woman."

"Then do it for my son," she pleaded. "He's only twelve. In a place like Sirak-Brath, he'll be at anyone's mercy!"

"A pirate child would know to keep out of trouble."

"Goddamn you, he's not a pirate! He's not mature. He's a regular child. He thinks he can handle things, but he can't."

Aaron sneered. "Does his mother fill his head with such ideas?"

"Of course not. But he's not used to being alone. And he's gullible! Look, I've been to Sirak-Brath. I know the kind of people who live there and I know my son." She shuddered. "Some bastard will come along and offer to help and Jerem will believe him. He's used to a fairly honest world, where people say what they mean."

Aaron smiled grimly. "Is he, now?"

Paula dropped her gaze to the floor. "All right, I deserved that. I did wrong by not telling him about his father. I know that now." She raised her eyes to meet Aaron's stare. "But none of that matters. All that's important is that he's in a dangerous place and he's going to need help."

"I'm sorry, woman, but I can't. Our shuttle has other business."

"What the hell is more important than my son?"

Aaron's voice dropped to a whisper. "Eleven dead Costeaus. They're more important than your son. The clan seeks to avenge itself against this beast!"

Paula gave a weary nod. *So. Again, the Paratwa.* "I would like to avenge myself, too, for all the trouble this creature has caused me. It triggered the events that brought me to your Colony." A deep anger took hold of her. "But the Paratwa did not kidnap us and force us to come here. *You* did that! You, Aaron of the Alexanders."

She shook her fist at him. "You brought us here and abandoned us. Maybe, deep down, you're no different from my late husband. Maybe I was right in assuming my husband was typical of a Costeau."

That got to him. His eyes narrowed. The scarlet penis rippled across his cheekbone.

"Prove me wrong, Aaron of the Alexanders! Show me that you know the meaning of responsibility!"

For a moment, Paula thought he was going to draw back and hit her. Instead, a deep scowl curled his lips.

Sheila laughed. "I've never seen the mighty Aaron slapped. You throw your words well, woman."

"Too well," he muttered.

"Then you'll do it?" Paula asked.

Slowly, the scowl dissolved. "All right, woman. You've got yourself a ride to Sirak-Brath."

Relief swept over her. Without thinking, she threw her arms around him and kissed him on the cheek that was not tattooed.

"I said a ride, woman. We'll take you to Sirak-Brath. That doesn't mean we'll scour the Colony for you!"

"Of course not. I wouldn't expect you to."

Sheila laughed even harder.

—from *The Rigors,* by Meridian

A human once approached with an odd request. As was customary, the man knelt between me and lowered his head. He said his name was Peters and that he wished an audience with the great Sappho.

"This is not allowed," I said. I was about to dismiss him when curiosity phased awareness.

"Why do you wish such an audience?"

Peters trembled. *"I want my soul to be overlapped. The people of my domicile say that if one kisses the hands of Sappho, the Gods will bless that person and grant him the power to overlap with another."*

I laughed. *"You think that by kissing the hands of Sappho, you can interlace with another human and become like us?"*

Peters raised his head. *"Yes! We can become whole!"* His jaw sagged and his eyes wavered. Sadness colored his words. *"Of course, the overlap only lasts for a little while. We can never be whole forever."*

I studied this human for a moment, puzzled by his mad fantasy. I decided that it was a matter to be brought before my master. I bid Peters to rise and walk between me and a short time later we entered the hall of Theophrastus.

The two men who comprised my master sat beneath a study grid, observing a holohedral projection of a mutated skygene. I could tell that Theophrastus had separated—one tway pursed his lips, the other revealed subtleties of hesitation above the eyebrows. Often, when my master became stumped in his researches, he split in order to contemplate the problem from dual perspectives.

I stood silently, the human between me, until one of Theophrastus's tways acknowledged my presence.

Peters was urged to repeat his request. When the human had related his strange desire, the tways of Theophrastus stared into each other's eyes and brought on the interlace. A moment later, my united master arose from his chairs.

"This human is either very shrewd or very unstable," said Theophrastus. *"Make an example of him."*

Peters registered only a brief moment of surprise before I killed him. I used one of my Cohes—the lariat technique—a quick decapitation. I grabbed the head from the shoulders before it could bounce across the chamber and I quickly carried both head and *torso from Theophrastus's presence. Naturally, I ordered a human cleanup crew sent in immediately to scrub the floor.*

I summoned one of my chefs and then I took the head and torso of Peters back to his domicile.

I posted notice on the communion channel that by order of Theophrastus, all humans from Peters's domicile were required to dine with me in their cafeteria that evening.

Dinner was not a very satisfying occasion for the humans that night. It was readily apparent that their digestion was being disrupted by the presence of Peters's head on my table. Several humans became ill and asked to be excused.

After the main course, which was excellent—trout fillets dipped in lime sauce, feathered beans with wild celery and rice—after this, my chef wheeled in the torso of Peters on an examination cart. In front of everyone, my chef skinned several large pieces of flesh from the torso, diced the strips with a carving knife, and then stirred the chunks into his own special cranberry sauce.

Peters was served for dessert. The humans did not want to eat their companion but they also did not want to risk angering me. Their dilemma was intelligently solved. They ate Peters.

I made certain that all the other domiciles learned of our special confection. Never again did any human seek to approach Sappho. Peters had been served as a good object lesson.

He was also rather tasty.

Rome felt the excitement as he entered the conference room. A pair of aides from the Science division, seated opposite Begelman at the long table, were carrying on a frantic conversation with the computer hawk. A financial expert and a corporate watchdog—husband and wife—exchanged data on their hand terminals while engaged in a polite, but sharp, argument with an adviser on Senate affairs. Three young aides laughed as an old systems engineer concluded an anecdote. Pasha Haddad wore the expression of a man who has just consumed a large and sumptuous dinner.

Rome took his place at the head of the table. "I sense a staff meeting overwhelmed by good news. Let's have it."

The financial expert loudly cleared his throat. "We have discovered the basis for Drake's turnaround on the Sirak-Brath restoration project."

Perfectly aligned white teeth shone as the financial expert smiled. "What Lady Bonneville told you last week is correct. There was an ICN loan, for point six-three billion, going to the West Yemen Corporation. That loan has now been withdrawn. It is the cancellation of this loan that mainly accounts for the extra money being available for Sirak-Brath restoration.

"We've known about the West Yemen Corporation for quite some time. Their main business is manufacturing shuttle replacement parts for the transit industry. They also have substantial contracts with the Commerce League and the Profarmers Union for a wide variety of medium-tech items—everything from elevators to seeding/harvesters."

The financial expert's wife, the corporate watchdog, continued. "They're a common stock corporation, run by an executive board. That board happens to be almost completely made up of La Gloria de la Ciencia supporters. The West Yemen Corporation has been lobbying against E-Tech technological restrictions for years."

Her husband nodded. "Now the ICN loan—this point six-three billion—was ostensibly to be used for a huge upgrade of West Yemen's manufacturing facilities in several Colonies. But they managed to include enough clauses in their loan agreement with the ICN so that effectively, they could use the money any way they pleased."

Rome frowned. "The ICN agreed to such terms?"

The financial expert smiled. "Drake himself was the prime signatory."

The woman continued. "Now it also turns out that the West

Yemen Corporation, through their common stock offerings, has, over the past few years, acquired a group of silent partners—people who have purchased large amounts of stock but who do all their board voting by proxy.''

"Of course, there's nothing unusual about that," said her husband. "It's fairly common among the major companies."

The corporate watchdog could barely contain herself. "What is unusual is the identity of one of these silent partners."

Rome shook his head. "Someone from La Gloria de la Ciencia?"

The financial expert grinned. "From the ICN's point of view, even worse. This silent partner is, or should I say was, Bob Max."

Rome leaned back in his chair, stunned. "The man who was probably responsible for awakening the Paratwa?"

Haddad spoke calmly. "We have no more doubts about Max's involvement in the Paratwa awakening. Our deepthroaters with the smugglers have confirmed it. Bob Max hired the pirate crew that dove down to Philadelphia and retrieved those stasis capsules."

The financial expert rubbed his palms together. "Drake knew nothing about Bob Max being a silent partner in West Yemen. When he and the ICN found out about it, they went into an uproar. The huge loan was irregular to begin with, since it could be used for almost any purpose West Yemen intended. Coupled with the fact that West Yemen wholeheartedly supports La Gloria de la Ciencia, and is partially owned by the man who just woke up a Paratwa . . ."

"The Sirak-Brath restoration," interrupted Haddad, "was Drake's response to all this."

The financial expert nodded. "Drake knows that this whole mess is going to blow up in the ICN's face. Drake wants to disentangle himself and the ICN. They canceled the loan and made the money available for restoration. Drake automatically scores political points by supporting restoration—something the smugglers on Sirak-Brath, including the late Bob Max, were dead set against."

His wife continued. "The Sirak-Brath project has wide support. Drake is obviously hoping that by putting ICN money into such a universally recognized cause, some of the heat will be taken off his organization.''

Rome gave a thoughtful nod. "Why would Drake offer such an unconditional loan to West Yemen in the first place?"

The financial expert threw up his arms. "That we're not sure of. Unless perhaps Drake and the ICN actually wanted this loan money to be used to finance La Gloria de la Ciencia.''

Rome frowned. Drake had always seemed to take a moderate stance when it came to La Gloria de la Ciencia. Had he changed his policy?

The corporate watchdog folded her hands and hunched forward. "Even with this Sirak-Brath restoration project, Drake is in a lot of trouble. Though it makes no real sense, people are connecting this Paratwa assassin with La Gloria de la Ciencia. Our polls show that La Gloria de la Ciencia has dropped several percentage points in public acceptance since the butchery at the zoo.

"When this West Yemen affair goes public, the ICN will be firmly knotted to La Gloria de la Ciencia's public-acceptance ratio. And our studies show that La Gloria de la Ciencia's popularity will continue to drop as long as this assassin is on the loose.''

"Which could be for quite some time," Haddad pointed out.

Doubt struck Rome. It was not just the ethics of the whole affair, the fact that E-Tech would gain political strength as long as the Paratwa was alive—that he had seen from the beginning. But things were falling into place too neatly.

He studied the excited faces. "How did we confirm all this information?"

"A variety of sources," said the financial expert. "I have my own high-level contacts over at the ICN.''

His wife smiled. "Drake couldn't hope to keep something like this a secret for very long. Too many people involved.''

Rome nodded. "Any ideas why Lady Bonneville told us about this West Yemen Corporation loan? After all, she's a frequent supporter of La Gloria de la Ciencia. And she generally backs Drake to the hilt.''

The financial expert shrugged. "She was probably just trying to score some points on the side with E-Tech. Sooner or later, we would have found out about that loan anyway, along with everyone else."

Rome hesitated. "It seems that E-Tech should realize incredible gains from this whole affair. Does that strike anyone as suspicious?"

Haddad allowed a rare smile. "No."

Everyone seemed to nod their heads in agreement with the Pasha. The corporate watchdog added:

"E-Tech has been losing ground for so long now that I think we've all forgotten what it's like to come out on top. We're instantly suspicious when E-Tech makes a gain—it's so unusual!"

Laughter erupted around the table. Rome did not join in.

It's wrong. We're missing something here.

Begelman waved his hand. "Yes! Yes, I understand your suspicions, Rome. Friday's Paratwa attack—the street killings in Jordanian Paris—two Irryan diplomats were among the thirty-three victims." The programmer's face lit up. "Those diplomats were on their way to a bioconference!"

Everyone looked at Begelman, waiting for him to continue. He just sat there, grinning madly.

One of the young Science aides lowered his head and coughed. "I believe what Dr. Begelman means is that those two diplomats were the most vocal supporters of E-Tech policy attending that conference. Their murder could be construed as a direct attack upon E-Tech."

"Of course that's what I mean!" snapped Begelman.

Rome allowed his attention to wander from face to face. He thought: *Almost everyone at this table is caught up with the idea of victory—Drake discredited, La Gloria de la Ciencia politically crushed, E-Tech realizing a huge gain in prestige—a dream come true.*

He could not shake the feeling that things were all wrong.

I should have asked Nick to be here. The midget seemed to have a better sense of Irryan politics than most of the people gathered at this table. A fresh perspective could be helpful.

The majority of Rome's staff, however, now considered Nick and the runaway Gillian as serious a problem as the Paratwa. He knew that it would not have been wise to allow Nick to participate in a staff conference.

He suppressed his worries. "Do we have anything new on the Jordanian Paris massacre?"

The Pasha shook his head. "As was pointed out, the only notable victims were the two Irryan diplomats. The others were mostly shoppers, unlucky enough to be in the wrong place at the wrong time."

"And the witnesses?"

Haddad shrugged. "The Guardians released all of them within hours of the massacre. Covertly, we questioned several of these people. All told the same story—they heard the screams, saw the black light of the Cohe wands. Then nothing. A street full of bodies and severed limbs was all that remained. No Paratwa."

"It happened too fast," added one of the Science aides. "It's estimated that the entire massacre took less than ten seconds."

Haddad spoke calmly. "The creature probably feigned fright, blended into the crowds that were running in all directions. Guardians were dispatached to cover Jordanian Paris' terminals, but it was several hours before all of the ports were under surveillance. And with this creature's ability to disguise itself . . . The Guardians now assume that the Paratwa escaped from the Colony."

An aide laughed bitterly. "The way the Guardians are telling it, the creature ran away in fear."

The Pasha continued. "The Guardians have also released the young warden who witnessed the destruction and killings at the Northern California Preserve." Haddad nodded toward Begelman.

The computer hawk flapped his scrawny arms. "We secretly questioned the boy. His testimony reinforces our theory that the Paratwa is from the breed of Terminus."

Rome kept his disquiet to himself. *The breed of Terminus? This monster slaughtered thirty-three human beings and we're still ana-lyzing its origins.* He knew he was reacting emotionally. Such knowledge about the assassin was important. *But we should be doing more.*

He asked, "What about Nick and Gillian?"

Haddad stared at the far wall. "Essentially, there is nothing new to report. Nick is still receiving phone calls from public booths at all hours. We suspect that he has worked out some sort of complex timetable for keeping in touch with Gillian. We have tried planting a variety of audio bugs on Nick, but he has, thus far, deactivated all of them. We are tracking him via the subcutaneous transmitters, of course, but these phone calls are elliptically routed and of such short duration that we have not yet been able to initiate an effective trace." Haddad paused. "He is very clever."

"We should do something!" cried one of the Science aides. "Throw this Nick in a holding cell until he talks."

A chorus of agreement rang out. Haddad stared at Rome.

He met the Pasha's glare. "Nick is to be kept under sur-veillance—nothing more."

"How do we know," Haddad argued, "that Gillian is out there 'recruiting,' as Nick claims? These men are mercenaries—hired killers. I do not understand the basis of your trust in them."

Rome declined to answer. Gillian and Nick simply felt trustwor-thy.

One of Haddad's lieutenants burst through the door. "I'm sorry to interrupt, but there's been another Paratwa attack!"

Everyone tried to talk at once. Rome held up his hand for si-lence.

The lieutenant gave a breathless nod. "It raided one of our hi-tech storage warehouses on Oslo. The creature killed our staff and the guards, then burned the building to the ground. It may have stolen weapons—we have no way of knowing. There were explo-sions. Colony officials have declared Oslo a major disaster!"

Haddad muttered a curse.

"There's more. After the creature hit the warehouse, it went to a public park several blocks away and opened fire on the citizens."

Rome drew a deep breath. "How many dead?"

"We don't know. We believe there were only about a dozen of our people manning the warehouse. But the park was hit heavily. They say at least fifty citizens were killed there." The lieutenant paused. "Apparently, most of the citizens were children."

Rome gritted his teeth, fought back a mixture of fury and horror. *Such a monstrosity!*

"Any leads on the creature?" asked Haddad.

"No, sir. It disappeared, just like it did in Northern California and Jordanian Paris. The Guardians sealed all of Oslo's main ports but . . ." He shrugged. "There have been no sightings, as yet."

Rome nodded. He felt certain the Guardians would not find the Paratwa.

Haddad dismissed the lieutenant, turned to Rome.

"The outcry will be massive when word of this latest massacre goes public. E-Tech should be ready to offer all possible assistance."

The financial expert spoke up. "I believe it would be wise for E-Tech to set up a sizable reparation fund. Cash could be made available to the families of all Paratwa victims."

Heads nodded assent around the table. One of the Senate advisers spoke loudly.

"We should prepare to reintroduce defeated legislation, especially those bills pertaining to the expansion of E-Tech technosecurity measures. Irryan Senators who normally oppose us may now be more malleable."

Rome held his anger in check. *Times of turmoil are times of great gains. Yet we must not deaden our feelings toward the horror.* He recalled Nick's descriptions of pre-Apocalyptic life, the hard decisions made by the E-Tech leaders of that era. *Maybe emotional denial is the only way to survive such times.*

But today was not an era of universal destruction and madness. Rome refused to believe that one vicious creature could wipe out two centuries of relative peace. *Hard decisions, yes. But I won't allow E-Tech to feed off the carrion of this Paratwa.*

He spoke coldly. "Within your departments, you may make such preparations. But at this time, E-Tech will take no formal action regarding Senate bills." Rome met the financial expert's stare. "There will be no reparation fund from us. It smacks of patronage, not of real concern for the victims. Regular relief organizations will provide for those families."

The Pasha narrowed his eyes. "Many would not perceive a reparation fund as patronage."

"Perhaps not. But that's what it is."

Haddad lowered his gaze. Around the table, staff members muttered to each other.

Rome felt a sudden chill. *I stand alone.*

There were no other matters of importance. Rome adjourned the meeting, sat silently while the staff filed from the room. By the time they had all exited, he had come to a decision. He opened an audio link to his execsec.

His aide put through his call to Angela at once. Rome explained to his wife that they would be having a last-minute dinner guest this evening. He told her who it was and asked her to make the necessary preparations. Angela, ever practical, inquired as to whether she should place extra cushions on their dinner guest's chair.

Rome thought it would be a good idea.

The thorofare was dirty and the gutters overflowed with refuse. Heavily scarred plastic sidewalks vibrated under a thousand footbeats. People scurried along, bumped one another, fought, shouted, made music into the night. A mad array of odors floated along the boulevard: bubbling cheese and pungent spices—tarragon, marjoram—roasted meat, honeymilk, fresh urine, a scent of lilac. Battered cars, screeching, dodged the waves of humanity that flowed from one sidewalk to another. Gillian felt as if he had come home.

Sirak-Brath was Rio and New York and Tokyo and Montreal and London. It shuddered with life, splattered the more vibrant emotions of the human psyche onto its streets, painted hot flashes across its potpourri of low buildings.

Laser images flickered; mute projections vying for attention, inviting the passerby to enter the shops and dress the best, eat the finest, experience the deepest. Tracking sensors beamed stereophonic messages into the air: mating calls of the merchant. Red coherent light exploded from a clothing store's marquee and formed a hologram of a scarlet woman that moved in cadence with Gillian for ten steps, its silky urgent voice inviting him to spend his cash without delay.

Sirak-Brath was a transplanted chunk of Earth's madness, and its passion. Young men and women, stripped to bikinis, silently danced beneath the glow of a smoky yellow streetlamp. A gang of teenagers, with brown helmets and huge silver stars pinned to their jackets, forced themselves into the deepest concentrations of people, cold eyes searching for opposition. A woman with seven-fingered hands preached the gospel of the Trust. A fat prostitute on the shoulders of a silken robed giant wormed through the crowd, hunting for prospective clients.

And then there were the pirates.

Gillian paused to watch a trio of female Costeaus marching calmly down the center of the sidewalk. Everyone stepped out of their way. A strong feceslike odor emanated from the women but Gillian knew that the odorant bags alone were not responsible for their ease of movement through the crowd. The silver star gang, eight or nine strong, glared at the pirates, but the youths moved from their path just like everyone else.

The three women did not look overtly dangerous. Gillian recognized one source of Costeau strength: the women projected an aura of complete indifference to the rhythms of the street. They moved in their own world, oblivious to the shouting and screaming and selling that crackled the night air. They ignored the madness and passion.

Disassociation alone could not account for such controlled power. Instinctively, Gillian knew that if it came to a fight, the three women would take on any challenge, without fear.

But the ultimate strength of the Costeaus remained their adherence to the rule of the clan. An offense against one pirate was considered an offense against his or her entire clan. Make an enemy of one Costeau and you might find twenty-five thousand of them mad at you.

Gillian had arrived at two more conclusions since his arrival in Sirak-Brath. Costeaus would make excellent fighters; as a people, they possessed that natural fearlessness that came from years of persecution. They would die gladly for a cause, unconcerned about the odds. If motivated, they would go up against a Paratwa.

That motivation was the problem. The pirates would be more difficult to recruit than either he or Nick had imagined. There would be few mercenaries to be found among such a people. They would fight for their own reasons, not for someone else's.

Gillian turned off the main thorofare onto a dimly lit side street. Above him, the sky dissolved from pale blue to red and then into deep violet, all within the space of a minute, as if the sunset programming had been madly speeded up. It was his fourth day within the Colony and such haste no longer surprised him. Night was eagerly awaited in Sirak-Brath.

Two blocks later, the street terminated in a hedgerow. He halted bedside a battered kiosk, read the brief inscription.

The Teddy Carrera Memorial Park covered over a thousand acres of the Colony's Gamma sector. At one time, the park had probably been a well-kept mixture of trimmed hedgerows, small trees, and flowered dwarf grass rolling across the squat hills.

Now, in the dim light, the hedgerows resembled monstrous castle walls, huge oaks and pines looked as if they were trying to grow straight across to the other side of the cylinder, and the hills were mostly barren clumps of dirt. Concrete paths wound through the maze in all directions, occasionally disappearing into confluences of bristling olive hedges. Human garbage lay everywhere, as did an incredible variety of abandoned artifacts. The weirdest sight, only yards from where he stood, was a dilapidated car punched halfway through a hedge, ten feet off the ground. The driver must have been doing well over a hundred.

Gillian took the main path, which wound between a pair of giant hedges. Within seconds, the street disappeared from view and the familiar noises became muted. Darkness enveloped him; starlight reflecting down from the cosmishield glass overhead cast just enough illumination to follow the twisting path. For all intents and purposes, he had entered another world.

He wore mushboots. Their liquid soles, combined with years of practice, enabled him to walk in relative silence. Though he saw no one, a subtle background of human sounds confirmed that he was not alone within the park. From his left came a hint of distant laughter; muffled words rang out somewhere ahead. And beyond the hedgerow off to his right, he heard the faint patter of footsteps.

At night, stay out of the parks!

He had received the warning from a number of people over the past few days—another similarity between this Colony and the great cities of Earth. Most of the warnings had come from drunks, scuddies, heroin addicts, and a host of other narrowly focused individuals. The taverns of Sirak-Brath overflowed with such people.

Pirates and smugglers also frequented the taverns, and many possessed the qualities he was searching for. Most of the smugglers turned out to be too self-centered—unsuitable for Paratwa combat. The pirates had the right attributes; the ones he had met were tough, resourceful, aware of the intricacies of teamwork, and fearless. But they were impossible to communicate with. Several nights of bar-hopping had so far led to nothing but frustration.

You could talk to the pirates, of course, and after a few drinks, maybe even share a story or two. But a cultural wall went up whenever Gillian hinted at his real purposes. Several of the pirates had made it plain that they were available for hire for the right price. Most of them had been unfazed when Gillian mentioned that the work would be extremely dangerous. He felt sure that they would have no qualms about going up against a Paratwa.

But Gillian needed more. That cultural wall had to be broken down. There would have to be a commitment based on mutual trust, not merely an exchange of cash. A combat team attempting to defeat a Paratwa needed a deeper unity.

Whoever had begun to shadow him from the other side of the hedge was noisy in comparison to Gillian, yet sophisticated enough to keep pace. Probably he or she was tracking Gillian with a portable radar scanner. Gillian took that as a good sign. The shadower was fearless enough to utilize restricted technology.

It was likely that the shadower also carried weapons. Should violence ensue, Gillian was prepared. He slid his tongue along the rubber pads fastened to his bicuspids and molars. A snap of his jaw would activate the circuitry, and the device strapped to his waist would instantaneously ignite. The near-invisible crescent web would shape itself to the contours of his body, provide a defensive field capable of stopping all but the most powerful laser weapons.

It was a first-rate web, too. Sirak-Brath's black market offered an excellent selection.

There was also the Cohe wand, now mounted in a slip holster beneath his right sleeve. A flick of the wrist would launch the weapon into his waiting palm.

Naturally, the Cohe could be used only as a last resort. The telltale evidence of the wand would scream Paratwa to every law officer in Sirak-Brath. Gillian had no intention of making this Colony a focal point of the investigation.

RISK EVERYTHING? OFF-COLONY WORK AVAILABLE. FEE NEGOTIABLE.

Three times yesterday and twice this afternoon he had rendezvoused with parties responding to one of his discrete ads. The ads had been placed through a personnel agency and were accessible via Sirak-Brath's major trade channels.

He reasoned that the wording, vague and unusual, should attract an interesting cross-section of people. Thus far, the ad had attracted only those who were vague and unusual themselves. He hoped tonight would be the exception.

Abruptly, Gillian stopped. The footsteps beyond the hedgerow halted just a fraction of a second later. Good. The tracker was fast and alert.

About eighty yards to his left, off the path and away from the hedge, lay a trio of overlapping hills. Today's ad response, relayed through the anonymous machinations of the personnel agency, had instructed Gillian to be waiting at the eastern base of those hills shortly after dusk.

If I were a suspicious person, he thought humorously, *I might believe I'm walking into a trap.*

Still, tonight's rendezvous was worth the risk. He might get lucky and find some recruits with the qualities he was looking for. At the least, it offered a needed diversion from bar-hopping.

All senses were alert now. He fell into a slow shuffle, allowed tension to drain from his body. Tense muscles locked the system into patterns; the calm physique was able to respond with greater flexibility to a wider range of threats. He walked the last few yards to the base of the hills in a state of complete ease.

A skinny figure came into view. The man stood framed against the distant lights of Alpha sector, on a small rise off to the left. Gillian heard movement from behind. He turned his head slightly. The man who had been shadowing him emerged from a cut in the hedge.

"I never risk everything," hissed the skinny figure on the hill. A third man, a squat hulk, eased out from behind a gnarled tree, twenty yards to the right.

Gillian answered softly. "The work requires it."

"Does it now?" The man hopped down the sharp embankment, came close enough for Gillian to see his face.

Bloodshot eyes and a hungry twisting of the mouth betrayed the man's intentions. Gillian suppressed his disappointment. At best, the trio were bottom-line smugglers, looking for a way off the Colony. A likelier possibility was that they were a mug team who used the personnel agency to set up their victims.

A sudden uncertainty touched him. *My last battle was a defeat. I escaped with my life, yet even that was a near thing. Reemul— the Ash Ock liege-killer—destroyed my team and almost destroyed me.*

I made a mistake. Not the battle itself. The Jeek had come upon them without warning, the team had fought well. *No, the mistake was in allowing E-Tech to put us into stasis. I should have assembled another team and gone after that Jeek. I was knocked down and I chose to stay down. Now, two centuries later, I suffer uncertainty—the consequences of my error.*

The man halted five feet away. "So what have you got for us, putty?" The hulk moved to his partner's side. His fat cheeks formed a brittle grin.

Laughter sounded from the other side of the hills. The hulk spit on the dirt.

"Scudclowns," the hulk muttered. "Probably comin' this way."

The skinny man nodded slowly, then smiled. "Nothing to worry about. Aye, putty?"

Gillian matched the smile. "The more the merrier." Over his shoulder, he heard footsteps. The shadower was approaching from directly behind.

The skinny man laughed. "More the merrier, huh? I like that. Pretty sharp putty, you are." The grin turned vicious. "You got money, putty?"

The shadower halted about ten feet away. Gillian turned slowly, saw a bearded man in black clothes, with a sandram clutched in his palm.

"I have money," Gillian replied. It was good that they did not intend robbing him with killing weapons. Skinny and the hulk probably carried low-power, legal thrusters, but they would use them only as a last resort. A few cracks to the base of Gillian's skull with the hammerlike sandram would suffice to part a normal person from his moneybelt.

The men probably wore crescent webs too, but it was considered cowardly to ignite a defensive field unless you were under attack. And from the way these three handled themselves, it was obvious that they had never run into any serious opposition.

Until tonight.

At any rate, he would not have to risk using the Cohe.

The sounds of laughter came closer. A moment later, a fat woman in a shapeless blue dress marched around the base of the hill. Two boys were with her. They appeared to be about ten years old. Each boy carried a huge plastic bucket.

Gillian smiled, began moving toward them. "I really have to be going."

Skinny held up his arm. "I don't think so, putty!" The shadower edged closer. The hulk hunched down, gearing for action.

"Why don't we all just stand right where we are," warned Skinny. "Allow these scuds to pass us by."

The fat woman stopped twenty yards away and glared suspiciously. Then she led the two boys to a pile of nearby trash. Both youngsters bent down and began scooping the refuse into their buckets. One of the boys muttered something and the two of them burst into hysterical laughter.

"Hush!" snapped the woman. Both boys were yanked backward as the woman reined in their leashes. The chains were fastened to dark fabric collars around the boys' necks.

"Move along, scud!" yelled the skinny man. "You're interrupting a business discussion!"

The fat woman sneered. "Vomit and swallow!"

The hulk pointed a thick finger at her. "You better do like we say."

The boys looked at each other and broke out into another fit of uncontrollable laughter.

"Swallow my dildo!" The woman dragged the boys closer. She halted ten feet away when one of the boys fell to the ground in a convulsion of giggles.

The skinny man hissed, was about to speak when the shadower interrupted.

"It's Miss Vitchy," said the shadower. Gillian felt the man moving closer.

"How do you know me?" the woman barked.

The shadower halted beside Gillian. He spoke soothingly. "Everyone knows you, Miss Vitchy. You've got the best little scuddies on the Zell strip. Now it just so happens that this fine gentleman here"—the shadower laid his palm on Gillian's shoulder—"is out looking for a junior scuddie. Aye, putty?"

Gillian nodded. If he played along, there was a chance he could walk away from here without the bother of a fight.

The boy on the ground sat up and rubbed his belly. His face betrayed pain. "I want another swallow," he said weakly.

"Hush!" crowed the woman. She glared at Gillian. The second boy burst into laughter.

Skinny frowned at the shadower. "Hey, what the hell is this? We don't gotta share this putty with her."

The hulk nodded in agreement.

The shadower released Gillian's shoulder. "No sense in being greedy, is there?" He smiled. "By the way, Miss Vitchy, how's your good friend, Urikov?"

Miss Vitchy wrapped a fat palm around the standing boy's neck. "He's one of my best customers!" she exclaimed. "He gets first crack at my young scuddies."

At the mention of Urikov, Skinny and the hulk fell silent. Gillian had heard the name, too. It was usually spoken in fear. The black marketeer was not to be trifled with.

Miss Vitchy glowed with pride. "And Urikov likes the way I keep my scuddies busy, cleaning up the park."

"And you do a good job," mumbled Skinny.

Gillian smiled. Skinny was terrified by the idea that he might have offended a friend of Urikov's.

The woman dragged the boys closer.

"Is it true?" Her eyes wavered between Gillian and the shadower. "You lookin' for a young scuddie?"

"I'm looking for one," Gillian answered. Skinny and the hulk sighed with relief.

She smiled, used her leash hand to reach into a small handbag. The boy on the ground winced as he was pulled up by the neck.

"It just so happens," began the woman, "that I have my listings with me." She withdrew a bright red book and handed it to Gillian.

He opened it. There were at least thirty pages, each pasted with a dozen photographs of children.

"I've got a big operation," bragged the woman. "And my youngies are treated good! I don't overdo them and I don't starve and beat 'em." She tugged gently on the leashes. "Ain't that right?"

The standing boy laughed. The one on the ground whined. "I want another swallow."

Gillian felt sorry for the two boys, and for the others pictured in the book. Most of the children were probably runaways; a few would be kidnap victims, or simply abandoned offspring. This woman, and others like her, took them in, promising affection or money or whatever it took to gain their confidence. After the young victims had been treated to enough drinks secretly laced with scud, their addiction made them easily controllable.

The boy on the ground grabbed at his leash. "Please! I want another swallow!"

Miss Vitchy sighed loudly. "Oh, all right." She withdrew a plastic bottle from her handbag. The boy opened his mouth, waited obediently for the nipple to descend. He sucked greedily. Within seconds, he began to laugh. Miss Vitchy withdrew the bottle, wiped it off, and replaced it in her bag.

The woman shook her head and pointed to the book in Gillian's hand. "You just imagine how much it costs me to feed all my little scuddies. And when I take a pair of them out to clean the park, I gotta have babysitters at home for the rest of 'em."

"Sounds tough," said the shadower.

"It is. Yes, it is." She eyed Gillian. "Found one that you like?"

He paged through the book quickly, feeling anxious to be away from this sickness as quickly as possible. His eyes froze on the last page.

The picture showed a handsome boy with a mop of tangled brown hair drooping almost to his eyebrows. Last week, Gillian had watched a video, made by Pasha Haddad's people, of Paula Marth and her son. The video had been produced when the woman and the boy were in E-Tech's custody, shortly after the first Paratwa killing.

If the boy in this photo was not Jerem Marth, it was his twin.

It couldn't be the same boy, he reasoned. *What would Jerem Marth be doing in Sirak-Brath?*

Then again, Paula Marth and her son had been missing for over a week. And the photograph of the boy was on the last page of Miss Vitchy's book, which meant he was probably a recent addition to her stable.

He showed her the picture. "I like him. What kind of shape's he in? I don't want a scuddie who needs the nipple every ten minutes."

The two boys giggled. Miss Vitchy smiled. "Oh, no, that's one of my newest boys. Why he's hardly been trained properly yet." She corrected herself quickly. "Of course, he will listen to orders. But he only needs the bottle three or four times a day."

It has to be Jerem Marth. A disturbing thought occurred to him. *Could this be a setup of some sort? Could these people know who I am?*

He allowed the paranoid feeling to wash over him, dissolving its energy. *If the boy is Jerem Marth, then this is a coincidence—nothing more.*

He came to a decision. "I want the boy. How much?"

Miss Vitchy licked her lips. "Well, now, he's a good-looking scuddie, isn't he? He's one of my prettiest." She yanked the book from Gillian's hand and showed the picture to Skinny and the hulk. "A pretty boy, isn't he?"

Skinny and the hulk wagged their heads.

"I'll let you have the boy," she said, "for seven hundred and fifty."

Gillian sensed that bargaining was not expected of him. Carefully, so as not to alarm Skinny and his friends, he reached beneath his jacket and slipped off his wide moneybelt. He opened a pouch and slid seven-fifty worth of cash cards into his palm.

Skinny and the hulk eyed the fat moneybelt with unabashed greed. The bearded shadower stepped back two paces, just out of range should Gillian try to swing the belt as a weapon.

He's the most dangerous, Gillian thought. *I'll have to take him out first.*

For a moment, he considered the idea of trying to recruit the shadower. The man possessed some of the basic qualities that Gillian sought: a quick mind, reactions based more on experience than training, a natural alertness.

But the shadower used his talents to beat and rob—he would not be trustworthy. And any man who teamed himself with the likes of Skinny and the hulk betrayed other weaknesses.

Miss Vitchy urged the standing boy forward. With a bright laugh, the youth snatched the money from Gillian's palm. Immediately, the boy handed the prize to his mistress. She counted it twice.

"And now, Miss Vitchy," began the shadower, "we would appreciate it if you would allow us to finish our business with this gentleman."

Miss Vitchy grinned and tucked the cash cards into her handbag. She withdrew a tiny computer slab and handed it to Gillian. "This is your receipt. You come along to my place anytime and your scuddie will be there waiting for you." She wagged her finger at him. "And you take a good look at that program." She beamed. "I wrote it myself!"

Gillian took the slab from her. The label said: *Keeping Our Beautiful Parks Clean, by Miss Vitchy.*

"Come along, boys." She yanked once at their chains and the youngsters burst into another volley of laughter.

Miss Vitchy waddled away with her charges in tow. They stopped several more times, so that the boys could reach down and put litter in their buckets. Finally they vanished behind the base of the hills. Laughter continued to punctuate the cool night air.

Skinny licked his lips and smiled viciously. "Well, putty. Looks like you'll have a scuddie to keep you company after you get out of the hospital!"

The hulk laughed. Gillian feigned fear and stepped away from the shadower. The shadower grinned, swung the sandram up onto his shoulder. He closed to within striking range.

Good. He believes I'm afraid.

Gently, Gillian threw the moneybelt to the hulk, who caught it with a look of complete surprise. The hulk was slow. He would use precious seconds thinking about the moneybelt draped across his palms and considering his next move.

Gillian took one more half-step away from the shadower, compressed his weight, and attacked.

The shadower never had a chance. Gillian's leg whipped up and the side of his weighted mushboot crashed into the man's windpipe. The sandram spiraled into the air. The shadower fell backward, gasping for breath.

Gillian came down easily, pirouetted, and brought his other boot up into Skinny's side. The force of the blow split ribs. With a loud moan, Skinny collapsed to the dirt.

The hulk dropped the moneybelt and fumbled under his jacket. A soft hum filled the air as the hulk's crescent web ignited. Gillian leaped in front of the man, raised his arms overhead, and smashed his fists down through the weak side portals of the deflective energy field.

A normal man would have collapsed under the force of Gillian's double blow, but either the hulk wore armor under his shirt or else his sides were incredibly tough. The face turned ugly with rage. Ape hands reached for Gillian's neck.

Gillian snapped his jaw shut and back-pedaled as his own crescent web came to life. The energy fields touched, interacted with a flash of red lightning, then repelled one another. Gillian, in motion, managed to stay on his feet and ride out the invisible force that was hurling him backward. The hulk obviously had little experience with web fighting. He lost his balance and crashed to the ground.

Gillian regained his footing, stepped forward, and kicked. His boot entered the side of the hulk's web and sank deep into the man's flesh. The hulk gasped. Gillian rammed his arm through the side of the invisible field and flipped the hulk's belt switch, deactivating his opponent's web. The hulk, now defenseless, attempted to raise his head at the same moment Gillian was lowering his arm. Fist met jaw. The hulk's eyes glazed over and he sank into unconsciousness.

In a flash, Gillian came to his feet and surveyed the arena. Skinny lay in a fetal position, arms clenched around his smashed ribs, moaning and crying in agony. The shadower had recovered somewhat, though he was still on the ground, gasping loudly and clutching his neck.

Gillian took no chances. He kicked the shadower in the hip to make sure the man was not faking, then yanked him upright and chopped him on the base of the neck. The shadower collapsed, out cold.

Quickly, Gillian replaced his moneybelt and sprinted after the woman and her charges. It took only seconds to catch them.

Miss Vitchy looked mildly astonished as he jogged by and halted in her path. She reined in the boys while attempting to slip a fat hand into her handbag. Gillian wagged his finger in warning.

"I just came to get my scuddie," he said calmly.

She withdrew her hand and glanced uneasily over her shoulder. "Should we be in a hurry?"

Gillian smiled. "No, those gentlemen are engaged in another activity right now. They won't be bothering us."

Miss Vitchy licked her lips. "My address is on the slab. You can come and pick up your scuddie."

Again, Gillian wagged his finger at her. "I'm afraid I can't wait, Miss Vitchy. I suggest we go get my scuddie—right now."

She tried to sneer at him, but was unsuccessful. There was too much fear in her eyes. "All right," she mumbled. "We'll go and get your scuddie."

Gillian fell into step behind her. He was not certain, but the periodic laughter of the boys seemed even more hysterical than before.

Rome, concentrating, placed the empty wine carafe on Angela's marble coffee table. Pleased by his dexterity, he settled back into the thick cushions of the lounger. "Would you like another drink?"

"Seven is about my limit," Nick drawled. "Small body weight, tiny metabolism. Hell, I'd be drunk in no time and doin' somethin' obnoxious like throwing up on your rug."

Rome rubbed his heel across the den's shag carpet. "Angela would be most upset." He burped.

The midget shoved a stack of Angela's preservative-coated twentieth-century paperback novels out of his way and hopped onto her prized cherry wood desk. Rome was glad his wife had gone to bed.

"That was one hell of a good meal!" Nick crossed his legs

beneath him. "Angela missed her calling. She should have been a chef in Irrya's best restaurant."

Rome nodded carefully so as not to get dizzy. "You complimented her at the supper table. I'm sure she appreciated it."

"Yeah, but I want you to know that it wasn't just a matter of being a good dinner guest. I swear to you, I haven't had spare ribs like that since I was a boy."

"They were synthetic."

Nick did not hear him. His eyes grew distant. "There used to be a saloon in my old neighborhood. My parents would take me and my sister there for supper about once a month. I remember the waiter—a big fat Mexican with a little white cap. He always seemed like he was very happy."

"I didn't know you had a sister."

Nick stared out the den's only window. A few stars were visible in the night sky of the adjacent sector. "She died when she was twenty. A car accident. Three years later, my parents were killed when some crazies set off a bomb in the middle of a department store."

"I'm sorry."

The midget shrugged. "Life can be the pits. That's about the time I bottomed out. After my parents were killed, I went under for the first time, into stasis. My greatest mistake."

Rome shook his head, tried to steer the conversation away from melancholia. "I've always read that the attitudes of the late twentieth century were similar to those of the late twenty-first."

A grim smile touched Nick's face. "No, actually they were quite different. Both eras shared the lust for technological advancement and the willingness to go to war purely for profits. But the people were different. People had changed."

"How?"

"The people had lost something by the end of the twenty-first century. When I was a boy, there was no shortage of social madness, but there were still lots of individuals around who held real values. I'm not talking about the religious revivalists, preaching

God and country. No, I mean people who actually believed in being compassionate and looking out for those who had less—people who saw government essentially as a tool for preventing the strong from crushing the weak.

"But when I woke up in 2086—well, those kind of people just didn't seem to be around anymore. Compassion was a trait that you could order for your new house robot and the strong crushed the weak just for the hell of it." He shook his head sadly. "For anyone still alive who remembered what it was like a hundred years earlier, the world had become a ship lost at sea in a violent storm. Those people, the ones who used to be the true anchors of civilization—they were gone."

An immense sadness threatened to engulf Rome. He sat up. His head began to pound.

Why did I drink so much? I have better self-control than this.

Nick shook his head. "The end of the twenty-first century was pure insanity."

"And what about our era?" Rome asked gravely. "Where do you think the Colonies are heading? What do you really think of us?"

Nick adjusted his position, slid a boot across the desk. Rome reminded himself to check for scratches before he went to bed.

"Well," Nick said brightly, "you have some beautiful women! Did I tell you about that tall blonde I met at the Southern Alpha Industrial Social Club last night?"

"I'm serious."

"So was I, but she wanted me to pay for it." He smacked his open palm against his heart. "I've got pride, you know."

Rome pointed his finger accusingly. "Say it. You think the Colonies are heading for trouble. You think we've lost our anchors."

Nick laughed. "Oh, you're heading for something, all right. But trouble? Who can say."

Anger came. "Don't play games with me. You have a viewpoint culled from three distinct societies over a span of hundreds of years. That gives you a unique perspective.''

"Don't get carried away. I'm only a midget.''

"All right, I'll say it. These are pre-Apocalyptic times. The Colonies are about to enter their own particular version of the final days. Drake and La Gloria de la Ciencia are having their setbacks right now and E-Tech will make some temporary gains. But it's only a respite for us—it can't reverse the larger trends. E-Tech is going to fall. Technology is about to begin its endless ascent all over again. Humanity will grow miserable even while it praises the great advances of science.''

Nick smiled grimly. "It sure looks that way, doesn't it?''

. Rome sighed. "So you agree with me.''

"Yes, I'll confirm your worst nightmare, if you like. But, hell, I'm an eternal optimist. Things could always get better by tomorrow.''

"They won't get better," Rome insisted.

"Who do you think is behind this Paratwa?''

The question caught Rome by surprise. He hunched forward. "You're supposed to tell me that.''

"You must have some suspicions.''

Rome burped loudly. "The common feeling is that La Gloria de la Ciencia has something to do with it. Personally, I believe that they probably did awaken the creature and it got out of control.''

Nick shook his head. "You don't really believe that. We both know it makes no sense. Why should La Gloria de la Ciencia risk such a foolish act?''

Rome shrugged.

"I have a theory," Nick proclaimed loudly. "I've used my extensive skills, culled from three distinct societies no less, to pinpoint the most logical suspect. The person who has gained the most from the Paratwa rampage is you—Rome Franco!''

"That's nonsense.''

"Is it? There have been four known Paratwa attacks. The incident at the zoo we can dismiss from consideration—that was flexing, plain and simple. And Bob Max was murdered to shut him up.

"But now we come to the Jordanian Paris killings. The targets were obviously those two diplomats, both hardcore E-Tech supporters. And in Oslo today—how many dead?"

"The final count was eighty-six," Rome muttered.

"First an E-Tech armory and then a park full of children. Doesn't that tell you anything?"

"It tells me we're dealing with a vicious maniac."

"He's a nasty one, all right. But my point is, can't you see the sympathy that these last two attacks have generated for E-Tech? If I were a demented public relations person, I'd be coming in my pants with excitement. I've calculated that by the end of the week, E-Tech's acceptance ratio will climb a full seven percent throughout the Colonies. Seven percent! When was the last time your organization realized that kind of overnight gain?"

Rome put his weight against the armrests and carefully stood up. "You don't seriously believe I had anything to do with . . ."

"Of course not!" Nick snapped. "But there are other people within E-Tech who possess the wherewithal to carry it off."

Rome felt his face reddening. "You suspect one of my people?"

"What about Haddad?"

"That's ridiculous! The Pasha's been with me for decades. In no way would he condone such actions. Your whole theory is absurd!"

Nick shrugged his tiny shoulders. "Perhaps his duty toward E-Tech compelled him. You and I can't be the only ones who sense that E-Tech has been failing. What better way to turn things around than to release a Paratwa and set it against your own people? The majority of the populace would get behind you, support the organization in its hour of need. And through some careful behind-the-scenes planning, La Gloria de la Ciencia is set up to take a fall at the same time. E-Tech's worst adversary is crushed while E-Tech realizes an immense gain in public acceptance. I couldn't have written a better script myself.''

Rome shook his head violently. ''No! Not the Pasha.''

''He's tried to hinder Gillian and me at every turn.''

''The Pasha's doing what he thinks is best for the organization.'' Rome forced a smile. ''And he's human enough to be suffering some professional jealousy toward you and Gillian. Had we not awakened the two of you, he would have been totally in charge of the Paratwa investigation.''

The midget paused. ''Perhaps someone else, then. E-Tech is a big organization. There are numerous individuals, or small groups of individuals, who could pull something like this off.''

''No.''

''Do you mean: 'No, it's not true,' or 'No, I refuse to consider such a thing'?''

''It's not true. I know my people.'' Rome sat down. His head ached.

''Why did you bring me here?'' asked Nick.

''I thought you might enjoy a home-cooked dinner for a change.''

''Bullshit! You brought me here because you no longer trust your executive staff. You needed to talk to someone outside of E-Tech.''

Rome sighed. ''You're wrong. It's not that I don't trust them. It's just that none of them seem to fully understand the ramifications of these events. Believe me, they're good people. They want what's best for E-Tech. I'm certain that none of them could be guilty of the monstrosity that you're suggesting. But, something's wrong here. This whole affair with Drake and the West Yemen Corporation and Bob Max . . . It feels wrong.''

''That's rather vague.''

''I know. I wish I could explain it better. It's just that I can't help feeling that we're all being manipulated—E-Tech, La Gloria de la Ciencia, the ICN—everybody.''

Nick did not react. He sat quietly for a long time, legs tucked into the lotus position, tiny fingers drumming gently on his knees. After an interminable minute, Rome broke the silence.

"Are you sure you don't want another drink?"

Nick closed his eyes, then opened them and smiled. "No. I should be going."

"Time for another mysterious conversation with Gillian?"

Nick grinned. "It's become quite a challenge. Sooner or later, Haddad's people are bound to catch me and trace the line. After all, he always knows exactly where I am. Subcutaneous bugs are very effective."

"Gillian didn't seem too troubled by them."

Nick chuckled. "Gillian just doesn't like all that attention."

"I've ordered the Pasha to keep you under surveillance, nothing more. Naturally, he will try his best."

Nick hopped off the table. "You could go all the way with us. Order Haddad to leave me alone."

"I can't do that. After what the Paratwa did in Oslo today, I'm now convinced that you and Gillian have as good a chance as anybody for stopping this monster. But I've got to protect E-Tech. The organization can't openly support a pair of . . . mercenaries.

"Do you know that the Pasha and most of my staff think I'm crazy for trusting you and Gillian? And sometimes I think they're right. I start feeling like I'm betraying E-Tech." He shook his head and laughed bitterly. "I find it astonishing to realize that I gave a Cohe wand to a complete stranger. For that action alone, I should resign from the organization. Do you have any idea what the repercussions would be if my behavior were made public?"

"Sure. Two weeks ago they would have hung you. Today, with a brutal Paratwa on the loose, they would praise your courage."

Rome shook his head. "I don't think I'll ever be able to imagine what the twenty-first century was like."

"Don't feel bad. Most people who lived through it couldn't imagine it either."

Rome accompanied Nick to the front door of the house. The midget smiled.

"I really did enjoy dinner. Make sure you tell Angela."

"I will."

Dwarf grass, illuminated by the porch lamps, fell away from Rome's elevated rancher. A path of inset wooden blocks twisted its way down to the street level. Nick's rented car was parked by the curb.

They stared straight up at the display of stars. A half-moon was just coming into view.

"You know," began Nick, "it's never really dark in Irrya." He pointed to the other two livable sectors flanking the cosmishield panels. Both were ablaze with light.

"On some evenings it's cloudy," Rome offered.

"Still, I'll bet you it's never pitch black."

"True."

"On Earth, there used to be places where you could go, outdoors, on a cloudy night and not be able to see your own hand in front of your face."

Rome found it hard to imagine such places.

Nick started down the path, hesitated. He turned. "I'd like to spend tomorrow down in the archives. Could you give me Begelman for the day?"

"I'll arrange it."

"Thanks. And tell Angela I'm always free for supper."

Rome watched Nick's rainbow hardtop vanish around a bend. The cool night air felt invigorating and he stood on the porch for a long time, trying to imagine a world without E-Tech.

Gillian's tiny room at the Hotel Costello consisted of a fur-lined bed, a small dresser with a data monitor mounted above it, a window overlooking an alleyway three stories below, and a rather oddly combined, bathroom/kitchen cubicle. On his first day at the hotel, he discovered that he could stand in the shower and dry himself under the airjets while stirring vegetables in a wok on the ancient thermaltop stove. There was something to be said for convenience.

"I'm hungry," whined the boy. Jerem sat on the edge of the bed, kicking his legs violently against the base of the mattress.

Gillian leaned against the dresser and continued what he had been doing for the past hour: studying Jerem Marth and his growing agitation at being deprived of scud.

"I've got some fresh vegetables boiling," Gillian offered. "A little later, I'll bake some haddock."

"I don't like fish," Jerem stated flatly. "And I don't want vegetables."

"You need strength. You can't live on scud."

"Yes I can." The blue eyes glared defiantly for a moment, then dropped to the floor.

Gillian shrugged. "I told you when we got here—no scud."

"You could go and get some."

"No scud. Be brave. Try and put it out of your mind. If you fight it, things will be easier on you in the long run."

The boy frowned. "Why did you take me away from Miss Vitchy? She always gave me a swallow when I wanted it. She was nice."

"I told you before. You're through with Miss Vitchy."

His legs kicked angrily. "I'm leaving here! Right now!" His eyes wandered from Gillian to the bolted door.

"You're staying."

"I'll start screaming as loud as I can and the patrollers will come."

"No scud. It's over."

He sneered. "What do you care? You shouldn't care whether I drink scud or not."

The boy's indignant tone was a good sign. There was a hint of genuine feeling in his voice. The scud was beginning to lose its iron hold over his emotions.

Jerem reached into his jacket pocket and pulled out a wad of cash cards. "I'll give you twenty-five bytes if you take me back to Miss Vitchy. And I know where she keeps some of her money. She's rich. She's got megabytes! I could show you. You could get more." His legs continued kicking.

"No scud."

In a fit of anger, the boy threw the cash cards at Gillian. They splattered harmlessly against the wall.

"Do you think your mother is looking for you?" Gillian asked gently.

For an instant, pain was scrawled across Jerem's face. He jumped to his feet and kicked the side of the bed. His shoulders quaked with anger. He pointed a finger at Gillian. Instead of shouting, though, he burst into a fit of laughter.

Gillian listened closely, heard the strain; the threads of agony coursing within the scud-induced hysteria. *It should not take much longer.* The boy had gone beyond mere craving, had entered a more dangerous period. Now he would try nearly anything for a sip at the bottle.

The laughter stopped as if turned off by a switch. Jerem smiled unnaturally.

"Could you go out and get me one of those shell steaks? I'll pay for it."

Gillian shook his head. "We're having vegetables and fish."

"If you go and get me a shell steak, I promise I won't pester you about scud anymore."

Gillian answered calmly. "You will not be given an opportunity to get scud. It's over. I can be tricked, but certainly not by a scudclown." He added, "Scuddies are too dumb to trick people."

"I'm not dumb!"

Again, Gillian sensed genuine emotion. The boy's outrage was real.

"No, you're not dumb. Jerem Marth is not dumb. It's the scud that makes you act stupid."

Jerem bit his lower lip. "You just think it makes me stupid, but it really makes me smart."

The boy's lucky, he thought. A new addiction was relatively easy to break.

Gillian kept his voice casual. "If you had been a scuddie for several months, you would really be in trouble. After a time, the body begins to store the drug in the tissues. It becomes more and more painful to stop."

"I don't care!"

"A real scudclown loses all control over his bodily functions. After a while, he has to start wearing a diaper. He dribbles. He grows allergic to several essential food groups. His fits increase, both in intensity and duration, and eventually he reaches the point where he spends more time laughing than he does sleeping. Coronary pressure increases drastically and a heart attack is the inevitable result. Most scudclowns die within six years of beginning their addiction."

This time, Jerem's painful frown did not vanish so quickly. He sat down again.

Gillian pressed. "Do you think your mother's been worried about you?"

There was effort in his words. "She's . . . just . . . a . . . damn . . ."

Abruptly, Jerem clamped his mouth shut. "You're trying to trick me!" Another fit of laughter overwhelmed him. He fell to the floor in hysterics.

Gillian switched on the wall-mounted monitor and accessed the internal files. He needed to find something for the boy to concentrate on.

The instant Gillian turned his back, Jerem leaped to his feet and made a dash for the door. The boy fumbled with the bolt for several seconds, then raised his foot and angrily kicked at the heavy portal. Fuming, he pounded his fists against the wall.

Gillian continued scanning the files. "I modified the lock," he said quietly. "Only I can open it." That was not quite true, but he had changed the mechanism enough to prevent an enraged scuddie from figuring it out.

"Open it!" the boy demanded.

The only internal programs contained in the monitor's processor dealt with utilizing the room's temperature control system and bathroom/kitchen cubicle. The management of the Hotel Costello was too stingy to have included even a basic gaming system.

Jerem wrenched at the door handle. "Open it!" he screamed. "I wanna go out! I gotta get out!"

Gillian remembered the computer slab Miss Vitchy had given him as a receipt for the boy. He pulled it from his pocket and inserted it in the slot beneath the volume control.

Keeping Our Beautiful Parks Clean, by Miss Vitchy appeared on the screen—silhouetted golden letters on a lush background of pine forests, with an ice-capped mountain range in the distance.

"If you don't let me out," Jerem warned, "I'm going to get you in trouble. Real trouble!"

Like most computer programs, Miss Vitchy's was multifunctional, offering the viewer a choice of formats for displaying essentially the same information. Gillian touched the control setting for READ MODE. The colorful title was superseded by a page of standard text.

"Come here," said Gillian.

"Let me out, you bastard!"

He allowed menace to underscore his tone. "Come here."

The boy sneered and gave the door a sharp kick.

Gillian did not want to scare Jerem too badly, but the boy had to be wrenched from his behavior pattern of anger and laughter. "Last chance," he warned. "Come here!"

"Ox-le-me-noi-quid-lo!" the boy said sharply.

Gillian had no idea what the words meant, nor did he care. In a flash, he crossed the room, grabbed Jerem by the elbow and the seat of the pants, and swiftly carried him over to the monitor.

"Put me down!"

Gillian obliged. He set the boy down facing the screen and stood behind him. "Start reading."

"No!"

He gripped Jerem under the chin and directed his head toward the monitor. "Read."

Jerem stomped his foot against the floor. "Let me go!"

Gillian laid his other hand on the back of Jerem's neck and used two fingers to give the skin a sharp pinch.

"Oww!"

"I said read."

"I don't feel like . . ."

Gillian pinched harder. The boy tried to pull away. Gillian tightened his grip on Jerem's chin and pinched him a third time.

"Oww! Let me go!"

He dug two fingernails into the soft flesh and twisted sharply. This time, tears came to Jerem's eyes.

"Oww! All right, I'll read."

"Do it."

The boy rubbed a palm across his eyes and stared at the screen. "Keeping Our Beautiful Parks Clean, by Miss Vitchy . . ."

He paused and began to giggle. Gillian applied two quick painful pinches. Jerem cried out.

"Stop it! I'm trying!"

"Read."

"I can't when you keep pinching me!"

Slowly, Gillian pressed his thumb and forefinger against another hunk of skin. Jerem did not wait for the pinch.

"The Teddy Carrera Memorial Park was established shortly after the founding of this Colony. The Park is the largest within Sirak-Brath. There are some wild animals in the park, but most of them are tame."

Gillian smiled grimly. He wondered if Miss Vitchy intended her tract to be humorous or whether she was simply unaware of its connotations.

The boy continued. "The Park was named after Doctor Teddy Carrera, an Earthman who lived prior to the Apocalypse. Teddy Carrera was a great scientist and engineer who was the guiding light behind Star-Edge, the massive project that sent twenty-six huge spaceships deep into space in order to colonize distant planets. Teddy Carrera himself went on one of the spaceships. He was never heard from again."

Jerem sighed. "This is dumb. I learned all this stuff in school. Why do I have to do this?"

"I like stories. Keep reading."

Jerem paused, then with a slight smile, continued. "In memory of Teddy Carrera and all of the lost star voyagers, the people of Sirak-Brath dedicated this grand park. Teddy Carrera also was a great humanitarian . . . and he also said that everyone should take scud whenever they could!"

This time, Gillian made the pinch long and painful. The boy wailed and tried to twist his chin away from Gillian's unyielding grip.

"I was just making a joke," he whined.

"Not funny. Continue reading—and only what's on the screen."

"Why don't you just beat me like my mom does?" He started to cry. "Everybody is always hurting me. It's not fair."

The feeling was real. Gillian rubbed the back of the boy's neck. "I don't want to hurt you, Jerem. But I won't allow you to be a scuddie."

"What do you care?"

"Let's just say that I have an interest in you and your mother." He eased his grip and Jerem turned quizzically toward him. The boy wiped a tear from the corner of his eye.

"How do you know my mom?"

Gillian hesitated. It would be best to stay as close to the truth as possible. "I'm with E-Tech. We've been looking for you and your mother. We'd like to ask you some more questions about what happened to Bob Max.''

Jerem's eyes widened. He sniffled. "Are you going to take me back to Lamalan?''

"I'd like to. As soon as we find your mother.''

Jerem licked his lips. A fierce grin distorted his features. Gillian wagged a finger in warning.

"If you let out another scud laugh, you'll be pinched!''

The boy's face exposed his turmoil. He wanted to laugh and he knew he dared not. His shoulders began to quiver.

It's coming, Gillian observed. Scud withdrawal, especially for a new addict like Jerem, displayed clear parameters. The boy was on the edge right now—half free of the drug's emotional repression. Jerem's real feelings would serve as a catalyst to bring him the final step away from the scud's influence.

Better methods supposedly existed for addicts to withdraw from the drug. Even in Gillian's era, hospitals had offered sophisticated programs and had boasted of quick and relatively painless paths to scud freedom. But painless ways were not always the best. Gillian knew that to be true even while recognizing his own shortcomings—his fear of descending too deeply into that unremitting sewer of agonies, the memories of his relationship with Catharine. It was unhealthy to repress pain. Inner turmoil should be unleashed, assuming it was possible for one to do so.

And there lies the difference between Jerem Marth and myself.

The boy clutched his sides and bent over. "It hurts.''

"Lie down.''

Gillian helped him to the bed. Jerem began screaming before his face touched the pillow.

The withdrawal did not take long, perhaps ten minutes, though Gillian knew the boy was experiencing a distorted sense of time and that the agony seemed much longer. Jerem's body curled into the fetal position. Tensed muscles fought the waves of pain that made him flop across the bed like a fish out of water. Several times the boy's screams were of such intensity that Gillian felt certain the manager would arrive to pound on the door. No one came, though. Presumably it would take something more direct, like blowing up the hotel lobby, to arouse anyone's interest.

Gillian went to the kitchen and divided the steaming pot of vegetables into two unequal portions. He put the larger plate back on the thermaltop; Jerem would likely have a ravenous appetite when he emerged from the pain.

Two clogged plastic shakers reluctantly provided Gillian's steaming plate with a dash of pepper and thyme. He returned to the side of the bed and forked a mouthful. The beans and sprouts were excellent, but the carrots were a bit underdone. Next time, he would remember to precook them longer.

He stood silently by the bed; eating, hearing the boy's screams but tuning out the emotional intensity that would overwhelm his own psyche if he listened too closely.

Pain triggers pain. The perpetual agony of his own loss lay just a shout away.

Jerem's uncontrollable thrashing peaked. Gradually, his screams lessened, then stopped completely. A long moment of calm brought an almost unnatural silence to the room. Gillian could hear the soft scraping of his own fork across the bottom of the plate.

Jerem sat up. He stared at Gillian for a moment and then turned away in embarrassment.

Gillian threw his plate in the disposer and sat down next to the boy.

"You did well. I'm sure your mother would be proud of you."

"She'll be mad at me." He winced and hugged his arms to his chest.

"Maybe. But it took a fair amount of courage for you to fight through the pain."

He shrugged. "You didn't give me any choice."

"I said 'be brave,' then I gave you a push—nothing more. You did all the work. Don't demean your accomplishments."

Jerem frowned, then without warning, threw himself onto

Gillian. The boy buried his face against the dark fabric of Gillian's pullover and began to sob.

Four Paratwa killings, Gillian thought. *I must renew my efforts at recruiting. I've been lax. I should have been training a combat team by now. Sirak-Brath certainly has the raw material. Somewhere in this Colony there must be pirates whom I can communicate with—break down that cultural wall.*

Jerem hugged him desperately; without fear, without any sense of shame. For the good of the boy, Gillian knew he had to respond. He laid his arms on Jerem's back and patted him gently.

Tomorrow I'll arrange for Jerem's mother to come and retrieve her son. With any luck, Paula Marth and her boy should be willing to relate everything they can remember about the Bob Max killing. I may be able to form a clearer gestalt of this creature I hunt. And then I will put all my efforts into finding a team.

He did not want a rehash of tonight's trouble. *No more cryptic advertisements and clandestine meetings. I'll use a more direct approach.* Sirak-Brath's numerous shuttle ports offered potential opportunities. *A place where people are in transit should produce a wide range of suitable individuals.* He felt surprised that he had not thought of it earlier.

Jerem stopped crying and released Gillian from his grip. The boy stood up and cleared his throat. Gillian sensed effort in the boy's words.

"I know you really helped me . . . and I know that . . . you didn't really have to and all . . . and I know that you're from E-Tech and that you're doing it because it's part of your job." Jerem amended himself hastily. "Not that you don't care and all 'cause I know that you do and . . ." He paused, took a deep breath. "Well, I just wanna say that I wish someone like you had been my father." He blushed and turned away.

Gillian felt his guts beginning to churn. He wanted to say: *Don't throw your feelings at me, boy! Don't try and make me into something I'm not!*

Instead, he got up and crossed to the stove. "I'll bet you're hungry."

Jerem brightened. "Yeah, I'm starving. And before, I wasn't hungry at all. It's really strange."

He presented Jerem with the steaming plate. The boy sat down on the floor and began wolfing down the vegetables. Gillian turned away. His hands were shaking.

I move—I am. I want—I take. I see—I learn. I grow—I make.

Gillian closed his eyes. A vision of Catharine filled the blackness. He opened his eyes, gripped the sides of the dresser, and concentrated on the monitor screen.

Keeping Our Beautiful Parks Clean, by Miss Vitchy. Silently, and without any real interest, Gillian read through the entire tract.

Later, after the boy had fallen asleep on the bed, Gillian lay on the floor. He wanted drowsiness to overtake him. It refused.

Do you remember, Catharine, when we used to talk about having children?

Gillian hopped to his feet. He had no idea why his mind had phrased such a question. He only knew that he had to escape such thoughts. *She's dead. Dead and gone. I must forget her.*

With shaking hands, he switched on the monitor. He read through Miss Vitchy's inane dissertation again.

He read it three more times. Then he tried reading it backward. Somewhere, beyond the middle, close to the beginning, he fell asleep.

Urikov looked around and saw nothing that he liked. *Foolish men,* he thought, *drinking, arguing, dreaming of the circle score—the royal path to riches. They think enough talk will catapult them to luxury.*

He raised a beaker of diluted brandy to his lips and poured the mild liquor over his tongue. *They are nothing but stupid animals, guided by their fears and the whining beat of the music.*

Urikov swallowed the brandy. He listened to the sax/drum duo for a moment. He did not like this tavern's drowsy excuse for entertainment. The music, however, was appropriate for the losers scattered at tables on the dimly lit main floor or perched solemnly at the bar. If Urikov had owned this tavern, he would have had the musicians forcibly removed from the small stage and thrown out into the middle of Sirak-Brath's widest boulevard. He grinned, imagining the fat sax player crushed under a hundred wheels.

Losers one and all. The circle score required intelligence and action.

The main door opened. A tall figure pushed through the beaded curtain of the inner vestibule. Urikov took one look at him and knew that this was the man he was waiting for.

The stranger moved with a casual grace that was far too sleek for a crowd like this. A gray jumpsuit with loose sleeves cloaked the man's frame. Blond hair edged out from beneath a green satin fisherman's cap. He was clean-shaven. Forty, forty-five, Urikov guessed. The stranger scanned the tavern like a robot insecticizer searching for flies.

Urikov licked his lips and grinned. The man's clothes were plain, but his haughty demeanor suggested wealth, prestige.

A rich smuggler from off-Colony? Urikov knew all the prime black marketeers on Sirak-Brath and this man was definitely not local. Then again, he did not look like a smuggler. A corporate trader? Or a retired bureaucrat with enough savings to indulge his darkest fantasies? Urikov took another sip of brandy and wondered if the man had brought the rest of the money with him as promised.

The stranger sauntered past the bar and sat down at Urikov's table. Smiling, the man held out his hand.

"Hello. It is good that we can meet."

Christ, thought Urikov. *The bastard talks like a sitpissy.*

The stranger was not the same man who had contacted Urikov by phone several days ago. That voice had been high-pitched, but sounded mean. Urikov did not really care what a pervert sounded like, of course. The man on the phone had agreed to Urikov's price. The first payment had been delivered promptly via courier. That was all that mattered.

The stranger withdrew his hand when it became obvious Urikov was not going to shake it. The smile expanded. "Allow me to buy you another drink?"

Urikov nodded. The stranger pointed his finger at the main ceiling sensor. A small cylindrical robot emerged from behind the bar and waddled over to their table. Speedtreads stopped rotating. The robot waited obediently for its next command.

"My," said the man, eyeing Urikov's drink, "that looks good. Peach brandy?"

Urikov gave a sharp nod. The stranger grinned like an idiot as he typed his order into the robot's terminal. He popped a wad of cash cards from his vest pocket and inserted the required amount.

A few seconds later, the robot opened its front panel. The stranger grabbed the two beakers of brandy from the robot's serving tray. He patted the robot's dome head as if it were a child.

"You like sex machinery?" Urikov asked. It was usually easy to sell perverts more than they wanted.

The man grinned and handed Urikov his brandy. "No."

The stranger looked like he traveled a lot. "I can get you a small terminal briefcase with good data-storage capabilities. You put it on your lap when you're traveling by shuttle and it looks like you're a businessman at work. But a panel underneath opens up and a cock-grabber snakes into your pants and charges your meat. The machine has seven different settings."

"How fascinating." The stranger peeled open his brandy and sniffed. "Robots are nice, aren't they? So obedient. I wonder why E-Tech has made them illegal?"

Urikov sneered. *Because E-Tech is made up of sitpissies like you.*

The stranger winked at the robot. "It appears as if this tavern is in violation of the law. My, yes! I do hope we don't get raided."

"Why? I've got nothing to hide. Have you?"

Raising his beaker, the stranger took a tiny sip of brandy. He opened his mouth wide and, with the edge of his tongue, gently licked his lips.

Abruptly, Urikov made a decision. He would let this pervert squirm. A buyer who acted this much like a sitpissy deserved to be scared. Besides, a good dose of fear, properly applied, usually produced a better deal for Urikov. If this bastard was as rich as he looked, it should be relatively easy to squeeze some extra money out of him.

Urikov gave a hand signal. A pair of monstrous bald men got up from a nearby table and approached. Dell One laid a huge palm across the back of the stranger's neck. The stranger continued smiling.

The Dell twins had first names, but Urikov preferred to call them Dell One and Dell Two. They did not mind. They were dumb but intensely loyal. Last month, a union grafter had tried to sell Urikov false data on the practice of organized farmland thievery. Dell One had held the man down on a warehouse floor while Dell Two had carefully kicked the grafter's balls up into his chest.

The stranger's grin grew more intense. "Your friend has strong hands."

Urikov smiled. "He likes to break things with his hands. It makes him happy."

Dell Two sat down and laid a thick palm on the stranger's knee. Dell Two squeezed. The stranger chuckled.

"I wish I could get my bodyguard to use his hands more. My. But instead, he just loves blasting away with that thruster of his."

Urikov leaned back and studied the stranger for a moment. He nodded to the Dell twins. They released the stranger.

Urikov had misjudged. The man did not scare easily.

"Would your bodyguard like to join us?"

"No." The grin became fiercer. "He's close enough."

Urikov glanced around the tavern. If the stranger was telling the truth, his bodyguard had preceded him. There were about fifteen losers scattered across the main floor and another half dozen at the bar. None looked like a professional backup.

At a center table, four drunken men traded shouts and laughter. As Urikov watched, one of the burly losers turned his chair toward a trio of giggling young whores in the far corner. The man began making obscene hand gestures. The women tried to ignore him. *Stupid silkies.*

Adjacent to the whores' table sat the only other woman in the tavern: an aging silky, nursing her beer and trying to ignore everyone.

At the bar, two men sat alone. One was built like a miniature Dell twin—squat and broad-shouldered with a stone face. The other, a slender and nervous-looking youth, was garbed like a pirate, wearing heavily stained trousers and a beaten leather shirt. An odorant bag hung from his waist.

Urikov sniffed. The youth was not a real pirate. He did not have the odor. Another loser, playing games.

By mutual agreement, this was one of the taverns that was off-limits to real Costeaus. Of course, if the damn pirates suddenly decided to break that pact, there was not a hell of a lot anyone was going to do about it. Even the Dell twins were not so dumb as to pick trouble with Costeaus.

"Is my package in transit?" asked the stranger.

Urikov turned his attention back to the grinning face.

"It was crated and shipped this morning. It'll arrive tomorrow." Urikov reached under his coat and handed the stranger a small key disk. "This'll get you into my warehouse. All you have to do is show this to my men and pick up your package."

The stranger fingered the key disk. "Is she fertile, as I requested?"

"They tell me she's fertile." *Christ, this sitpissy should run for Governor of Velvet-on-the-Green. What a fuckin' pervert!*

"Is she as young as I asked for?"

Urikov allowed his face to darken. "She's as young as she's going to be. There are goddamn limits to these things. You're talking major genetic alteration and there isn't exactly a huge market—"

"Of course," interrupted the stranger. "Just as long as she's between one and two."

"You gotta take what you can get."

"What if my package isn't at the warehouse tomorrow?" asked the stranger.

Urikov felt a rush of anger. "I don't talk shit, hotface." The Dell brothers inched closer. "When I say something's so, it's so."

The stranger frowned, then burst into laughter. "My, we're tough!"

Stupid fuck loser! If I weren't making such good money on this deal, I'd have the Dells rip your tongue out.

The stranger settled back in his chair. "Do you want the money here?"

No, clonecock, I want us to shuttle to Irrya and have you pay me on the steps of the ICN. What a dumb fuck!

"We're in a rather public place," offered the stranger.

Urikov spoke coldly. "You're giving me money that you owe me, right? I don't see any illegal exchange goin' on." He turned to Dell One. "Do you?"

Dell One thought for a moment. "No," he growled. Dell Two nodded in assent.

Urikov sneered. "So why don't you just lay it on the table where I can see it."

Chuckling, the stranger reached into the vest pocket of his jumpsuit. His hand froze.

A commotion had erupted at the far end of the tavern. The burly loser, tired of pestering the three whores, had arisen from his table. He had crossed the room and was now standing in front of the old prostie. The silky kept her head lowered and her fingers tapped out a sharp rhythm on the rim of an empty seltzer mug.

"This ain't no sitpissy!" shouted the burly loser. "It's a fuckin' silky misfit, dressed to be stern-cocked! We shouldn't let this crap in here!''

The young whores whispered to each other and shook their heads in disapproval. One of them got up from the table and wiggled her ass over to the lavatory cubicle opposite the bar.

The old prostie raised her eyes and stared across the tavern. She seemed to be looking straight at Urikov, or at the back of the stranger's head.

"I oughta hammer a sandram up your ass and set your balls on fire," growled the loser.

"If she's got any, Klaus!" yelled one of his drunken friends from the center of the room. Several of the other men howled with laughter. The man Klaus turned slightly to display a wicked grin.

He spun back to the prostie. "You hear that, shiteater? They want to see if you really got balls under that skirt."

Urikov shook his head. *Goddamn losers.*

The stranger's hand was still frozen inside his pocket. His smile became brittle. Music stopped. The fat sax player and his drummer leaned back in their chairs to watch the show. They took turns swilling beer from a huge mug.

"Stand your ass up, silky!" shouted the burly loser. "I wanna see what you're hiding in your panties!"

Urikov glanced toward the bar and smiled. The squat, broad-shouldered man had spun his stool around and was poised for action.

So that's your bodyguard, eh? thought Urikov. Thrusters or not, the broad-shouldered man did not look like a match for the Dell twins.

"Perhaps," said the stranger quietly, "your men can break this up."

Urikov grinned. "What's the matter? That old prostie a friend of yours?"

The stranger shook his head. "I just don't want any trouble."

"Last chance!" shouted the prostie's abuser. "Either get up and strip or I'll do it for ya'!"

"Rape him, Klaus!" yelled one of the others. "His asshole's probably been stretched enough to take your little cock!"

A heavy round of laughter flooded the tavern. The phony pirate quivered on his barstool.

The stranger tensed. His smile vanished. His voice fell to a whisper. "I'll pay you an extra five hundred if your men break this up."

So, you're a frightened little sitpissy after all! Urikov laughed. "Why don't you get your bodyguard to take care of it for you?"

"I'll give you a thousand," hissed the stranger. "End it. Now!"

"A thousand, eh?" Urikov rubbed his hand across his chin and pretended to consider the stranger's offer.

"No," he said finally. "I think I'm going to let that sitpissy get his ass stretched." He laughed at the stranger's astonished expression. "I didn't like the way you talked to me just now. Maybe if you'd been a little more polite . . ."

The Dell twins chuckled. Tension suddenly went out of the stranger's body. His shoulders drooped.

A chilling scream erupted from the prostie's abuser. The man—Klaus—turned and fell to his knees. From neck to waist, his chest had been slashed open. Dark fluid gushed to the floor.

The prostie was on her feet. A beam of jet-black light whipped from her hand, crossed the tavern, curled around Dell One's neck. Dell One's head flew from his shoulders and plopped to the floor. The decapitated body shook for a moment, then fell backward over a chair.

Urikov's mouth dropped open. One moment, the stranger was seated. The next, he was on his feet. Urikov had never seen anyone move so fast. A thruster appeared in the stranger's left hand. His right palm clutched some tiny object.

A cluster of tiny darts shot out from below the stranger's waistband. The darts pierced the side of Dell Two's cheek. Dell Two grunted, then screamed as the side of his face exploded into flames. He bolted from his chair and tripped blindly over his brother's torso.

Thrusters wailed. Black light crisscrossed the tavern. Urikov knew he should be reaching for his own weapon, energizing his crescent web. He could not. Or perhaps he was trying to and events were simply occurring so fast that his muscles had not yet responded to the survival commands.

It's not real, he thought. *This isn't happening*.

One of the young prosties flew against the wall as the invisible energy from a thruster shattered her ribcage. The men at the center tables jerked like puppets as thruster fire hit them from both sides of the room. Along the bar, black light chopped off arms and heads. The phony pirate leaped from his stool and made a run for the door. The stranger's beam sliced him in two. The top half crashed headfirst into the edge of the bar.

Urikov fumbled beneath his coat, activated his crescent web. He gripped the handle of his thruster and pulled it out into the open. One of the black beams whipped across the tabletop. Urikov stared dumbly at his weapon. The barrel had been sheared off by the disintegrating light. It felt hot. He dropped it.

The sax player got hit in the face by a thruster blast. The drummer gripped his dead companion from behind and tried to use him as a shield. A black beam circled in from behind and punched a hole in the back of the drummer's skull. Both bodies tumbled from the stage.

The lavatory door opened. The young whore emerged shrieking. Two thruster blasts lifted her into the air and sent her body somersaulting backward into the cubicle.

I can't die. Urikov stared at his hands. They were shaking.

The broad-shouldered man, whom Urikov had mistaken for the stranger's bodyguard, had also managed to activate a crescent web. He jerked from side to side, absorbing thruster blasts, twisting his body desperately in an effort to keep the deadly black light from piercing the weak side portals of the web.

With a chill, Urikov realized that he and the broad-shouldered man were the last survivors.

Abruptly, the stranger and the prostie stopped firing. Calmness gripped the tavern.

"He's good," said the stranger.

"Very good," added the prostie. She cackled like a witch.

The broad-shouldered man ran for the door. The prostie's hand flashed. A black beam tore into the side of the man's neck. He gasped. Blood spurted out both sides of his neck, spraying the floor. Some of the blood became trapped inside the web, outlining the front and rear energy crescents in a sea of red. The broad shoulders collapsed, the man hit the floor.

The demon turned its two heads to face Urikov. Urikov felt himself shuddering uncontrollably.

"A million!" he screamed. "Let me live! A million for each of you!" *Each of you! Each of you!* A spasm of laughter threatened to tear itself from his belly.

The stranger laughed. "Don't you wish you had broken up that fight?"

"Naughty!" barked the prostie.

Urikov felt himself gasping for air. "Anything! Anything you want!"

"Lower your web," said the stranger calmly.

"Wha . . . what?"

"You did say *anything,* didn't you? Well, lower your web."

"We'll let you live," offered the prostie.

Urikov reached under his coat and deactivated his crescents.

"Only joking!" cackled the prostie.

Blackness emerged from the stranger's hand. Urikov felt the hot beam touch his forehead. And then it was inside him and he felt nothing.

On the cracked plastic steps of the Hotel Costello, Jerem Marth sat and sulked.

"I told you," the boy whined, "I'm not ready to see my mom yet. Why can't we wait till tomorrow?"

Gillian wondered where the taxi was. He stepped off the curb and gazed up the street in both directions. The darkened boulevard ran east/west, circumnavigating the Colony; one of the few streets that actually crossed the cosmishield strips to link together Sirak-Brath's three livable sectors.

"Can't we at least get something to eat?" the boy pleaded.

"Your mother will be waiting," Gillian explained patiently, for the third time. "If we're late, she might become worried about you all over again."

"I don't care. I want to stay with you a while longer."

"Yes, I know you do." *But you can't.*

Gillian had awakened this morning feeling recovered from last night's torment. Sleep, as usual, seemed to have corralled his pain, fenced it away from his conscious mind. The day with Jerem had passed quickly and he had been able to deal with the boy's emotional demands. But now, Gillian was beginning to feel anxious again. The boy had to go.

It had been dark out for less than ten minutes, yet already the boulevard had come alive with night denizens. Silkies gathered on corners. Aspiring smugglers, laden with trinkets, searched for buyers. Young skin dancers swarmed beneath the streetlamps like moths drawn to the light, their bikini-clad bodies gyrating wildly to whatever silent music clamored through their heads. Two old women, wearing pleated miniskirts and dragging ten-foot aluminum chains, sneered at Gillian and crossed the street to avoid him.

"I won't be glad to see my mom," Jerem stated boldly, "but I will be glad to get off this Colony."

Paula Marth had placed an ad on several of the trade channels, offering a reward for the return of her son. Earlier today, Gillian had spotted the ad and had responded anonymously. A meeting had been arranged through the personnel agency. They were to contact Paula at Kevin's Hide, one of the Colony's largest shuttle ports.

Jerem frowned. "I wonder if my mom is still with those pirates?"

This morning, over breakfast, Jerem had related to Gillian what little he knew about the killing of Bob Max. The boy confirmed what E-Tech already suspected: the Paratwa appeared to be a Termi, a breed Gillian had hunted on several distant occasions. The boy's memory of the tways fit the parameters of a Terminus assassin perfectly.

Gillian no longer felt particularly anxious to talk to Paula Marth about the killing. He doubted she would be able to add anything new to the Paratwa profile. But he did, very badly, want to meet the pirates who had kidnapped Jerem and his mother. The Alexanders had, at the direction of Bob Max, awakened this Paratwa. Eleven of their clan had died as a result. According to Jerem, the clan now sought vengeance.

Hopefully, Gillian had stumbled upon a way to break through that cultural wall. The clan of Alexander might just provide him with his combat team.

Jerem let out a deep sigh. "Are you sure you gave that taxi the right address?"

"Yes, I'm sure."

"Then why isn't it here yet?"

Gillian found himself wondering how Paula Marth would have answered such a question.

With a wail of sirens, two vehicles roared down from the west. The first car, a green convertible, was their taxi. The driver whipped the steering wheel and screeched to a halt three feet out from the curb. Behind him, a wailing police hardtop swerved and shot past.

Gillian wondered what was happening. It was the third police cruiser they had seen in the past ten minutes. And multiple sirens seemed to be emanating from distant areas of the Colony.

The taxi driver wore a space helmet with a modified faceshield; a jagged hole had been sliced through the lower part of the clear panel so that he could talk. The helmet was painted fluorescent orange and labeled Awlspate Shuttle and Taxi Service.

"Where to?" the driver yelped.

Jerem hopped over the door and splashed down in the soft cushions of the back seat. Gillian took the passenger side.

"Take us to Kevin's Hide."

"You gettin' out?" asked the driver, as he accelerated from the curb.

"Getting out?"

"Sure! I would if I could. Christ! If that sonna-bitch killed Urikov, ain't no one safe."

"Who killed Urikov?"

"Christ! You didn't hear?" The driver spun the wheel to dodge a young woman who had stepped into the street without looking. She cursed as they shot by.

"Stupid silky!" screamed the driver.

Gillian repeated his question.

"That damned Paratwa did it. Sonna-bitch slaughtered a whole batch of people over on the Zell Strip."

"When did this happen?"

The driver raised his faceshield and blew snot into his sleeve. "Hell, it's been on the news for the past twenty minutes. Couldn't have happened more than a half-hour ago."

"Take us there," Gillian demanded.

"What? Hell, no, I ain't goin' near that place!"

Gillian allowed his hand to slip under his jacket. He spoke coldly. "Urikov was a good friend. I hope your name won't have to be mentioned—in a bad light—at his funeral."

The driver chuckled nervously. "Hey, putty, no problem. Zell Strip, here we come!"

The driver lowered his faceshield. The taxi accelerated.

"Wow!" Jerem hunched over the front seat. "There must be a thousand people."

The street surrounding the tavern was jammed. Local patrollers tried to keep the surging crowds away from the building, but they were outnumbered and overwhelmed. Wave after wave broke through the makeshift police barriers; each fresh assault brought cheers from the back of the crowd. Directly across the street from the tavern, a tiny third-floor balcony blossomed with a score of onlookers. Under the balcony, at the building's entrance, two swarthy men collected tolls from a long line of people desperate to see the spectacle from a choice location.

The driver swerved into the curb less than a block away from the commotion. Almost immediately, a pair of sleek black and gold cruisers skidded to a halt beside their taxi. Uniformed Guardians hit the street and began jostling through the crowds.

"We're parked in," the taxi driver cursed. "Trust-damned Guardies! Sons of bitches . . ."

Just as well, Gillian thought. He hopped from the vehicle. "Jerem, I want you to stay here. This man will take care of you till I return."

The driver's dark glare slithered into a smile as Gillian smacked a thick wad of cash cards into his palm.

"I'm coming with you," Jerem began.

"No. You stay here. I'll be back shortly."

"But I wanna . . ."

Gillian ignored the boy's protests and leaned over the door to face the driver. "I'm making you responsible for the boy. I want you to keep him here."

The driver grinned and continued separating the cash cards into large and small denominations.

"Hey, I'll watch the boy all night. No problem." He pointed to the corporate label on his helmet. "He's in good hands!"

Jerem frowned indignantly. "Gillian! You're not listening."

Gillian wagged his finger. "I want you to stay here. This might be dangerous."

Jerem groaned. "That's what everyone always says."

Gillian caught up with the Guardians and followed their wedge through the crowd. He made it to within twenty feet of the tavern entrance before a local patroller raised a long-handled sandram to Gillian's chest.

"I'm with them."

The patroller nodded wearily. "Sure. And I'm with god."

Further down the line, an ambulance crew was threading their way toward the barriers. Gillian jostled through the crowd to intercept them.

The lead medic wore a white cloak and a professional grimace. His two companions had portapak stretchers strapped to their backs. Gillian halted in front of the trio and held up his arm.

"Hold it! We've got no need for a stretcher crew here. Who called you?"

The lead medic sighed. "Hey, we're dispatched and we go where they send us."

"Did we call you or did the patrollers?" Gillian demanded.

There was another audible sigh. "Look, I can give you our dispatch number and you can find out."

Gillian shook his head. "All right, never mind. Just follow me and stay close."

They approached the barriers. A burly patroller stepped forward. Gillian fell into step with the lead medic.

He patted the medic on the back. "I just hope you guys brought along plenty of bodybags this time. Hell, there's pieces all over the place."

"Wonderful," groaned the medic.

The burly patroller lowered his sandram and ushered them through the barrier.

So far, so good, Gillian thought.

Another patroller stood guard directly outside the tavern entrance. His hands were busy playing solitaire scramcheck on a hand terminal. He barely looked up as they passed.

Poor security, Gillian mused. He parted the beaded curtain of the inner vestibule and ushered the ambulance crew in ahead of him. The lead medic came to an abrupt halt.

"Jesus!"

"Wait here," Gillian ordered. He was in luck. It appeared that none of the bodies had been moved yet.

A mixed score of patrollers and Guardians swarmed around the victims like hungry flies. Some took measurements, others typed or dictated into hand consoles. In the center of the tavern, several Guardians were setting up an elevated microcam grid. When assembled, the grid would automatically begin rotating, scanning the entire tavern, immortalizing the carnage onto a batch of recorders.

Guardians barked commands at one another and at the local police. Several patrollers openly grumbled at the presence of Artwhiler's people. Gillian could spot no one who looked like he was in charge.

He moved to the center of the tavern and stood under the microcam grid. Relaxing, he allowed his senses to absorb the brutal scene. Images washed over him—the bottom half of a man garbed like a pirate, odorant bag still hanging from his waist; a bone-shattered woman against the back wall of the open lavatory cubicle; a huge bald man with half his face burned away. . . .

Firedarts? Thought intruded upon the process of assimilation. The huge man had been killed by incendiary needles. Termis rarely used firedarts.

Gillian closed his eyes, forced awareness to retreat. When he opened his eyes again, images seemed to explode at him.

Bodies were slumped over tables—thruster victims, hit from both sides of the tavern. A man near the bar had been pierced through the neck by a Cohe. The man was caked with blood. A crescent web had protected him and when he died, the field collapsed, bathing him in his own juices.

Awareness refused to retreat. Gillian found himself unable to stop conceptualizing.

Something is wrong.

He circled the tavern, as oblivious to the Guardians and patrollers as they were to him. In the back of the room, slumped across a low table and clutching a spilled beaker of brandy, lay Urikov. Gillian had no trouble recognizing the black marketeer; the Guardians had thoughtfully fastened a nametag around his wrist. A small hole had been punched through the center of his forehead with a Cohe wand.

On the floor beside Urikov lay a decapitated giant. The head was nowhere in sight. Gillian stared at the bloody neck and frowned. For a long moment, he was unable to figure out what it was that disturbed him about the headless man. Certainly, not the decapitation itself. He had long ago accustomed himself to the aftermath of Paratwa attacks. Most of the assassins were fond of using their wands to slice . . .

Slice! Imagery sizzled into patterns, consciousness arose like smoke over a smoldering fire. A thought branded awareness, providing new direction.

Not a Termi! The Paratwa that had decimated this tavern was not from the Terminus labs.

His hands shook. He looked around the tavern. The pattern of the attack became clearer.

A Termi would have sliced, but the neck wounds on the giant did not come from a slicing beam. The burns were too even. Two beams? Had the giant been caught in a cross fire of Cohe energy?

No! That's not it! Desperate excitement forced Gillian to his knees. He rubbed his hand across the bloody neck, noted the way the flesh seemed to have been scorched well below the spot where the beam had actually touched.

One beam, not two! The giant had been struck by one beam, which had curled around his neck, scorched the flesh, and then, with a slight twisting of the Paratwa's hand, crushed inward from all sides at once. The giant's head had not been sliced off. It had been garroted.

Within the realm of the assassins, the technique was known as the "lariat." Only one breed of assassins had ever possessed such skill with the Cohe wand.

Gillian stood up slowly. Tension knotted every muscle in his body.

Again, he scanned the tavern. Focusing on details brought clarity. He understood. The Paratwa had not come here to kill. Something had gone wrong. A fight had erupted and the assassin had been forced to defend itself. The creature had been caught by surprise, its Termi mask momentarily misplaced. Reaction had been pure, unrehearsed. A Jeek Elemental, in all its terrible glory, had been unveiled.

And Gillian knew its name.

The pattern of the attack came into sharp focus. Details swamped details but a depth of clarity illuminated all the shapes, outlined all the shadows. He knew. There was no disguising the handiwork of this Jeek, not in Gillian's mind. He had met the creature two centuries ago, in a tavern much like this one, in the heart of Boston.

It was the same Jeek who had destroyed his team and who had almost destroyed Gillian. It was Reemul, the Ash Ock liege-killer.

A new rhythm took hold of him, fortifying awareness, driving the agony of Catharine even deeper into his subconscious. He felt endowed with fresh purpose.

This was no longer just a Paratwa hunt. The game had grown in stature. Unfinished business had expanded the stakes.

He walked to the entrance and parted the beaded curtain. The lead medic grabbed his arm.

"Hey! What are we supposed to do? Do you want us to start cleaning up?"

Gillian shook his head. "Stay here. Someone will give you orders."

Without waiting for the medic to respond, he stepped out the door and headed toward the barriers. The crowd seemed to have grown even larger and more unruly. Additional patrollers had arrived. None of them interfered with Gillian's passage.

He ignored everyone. His thoughts were on the future.

The liege-killer. The game had changed, but not just for Gillian. The presence of Reemul led to new possibilities that could affect all of the Colonies. It was conceivable that one or more of the Ash Ock were here.

One of the Guardian cruisers had departed and the taxi driver had managed to free his vehicle and turn it around. Jerem sat in the front seat, giggling as the driver showed him a lewd video on the taxi's dashboard monitor. Gillian hopped into the back.

"Let's go."

The taxi driver shrugged, turned off the monitor, and pulled away from the curb.

"Did ya get to see anything?" Jerem asked.

"Yes. I saw something."

Rome was running late. Lady Bonneville's Friday night party had been scheduled to begin at seven, and it was already close to nine-thirty. Even Angela, a fastidious believer in 'fashionable tardiness,' would have raised her eyebrows. It could not be helped, though. This week's frantic pace of events had thrown Rome into a seemingly bottomless cauldron of E-Tech staff conferences.

A pair of armed servants met Rome as he stepped off the elevator. The men quietly ushered him to the door of the penthouse, then returned to their remote station at the end of the private corridor. Security was tight. He had counted a total of nine guards since entering the building.

"Rome, how good of you to come."

Lady Bonneville wore a sweeping, low-cut gown, patterned in a striking arrangement of Scottish plaids. A set of wrist, ankle, and throat bands, formed of studded brown leather, served to visually trim her plump figure. Today, as at Wednesday's Council meeting, her hair was colored a fashionable bluish-gray and styled into a bun.

She escorted him through the long vestibule before he had a chance to examine the unframed Picasso mounted on the inside of the door.

"I knew you would be one of the last to arrive," she scolded. "And where is dear Angela?" The Lady pretended to look cross. "Shame on you for leaving your better half at home."

Rome smiled. "I'm afraid she's not feeling too well this evening." Angela generally disliked parties and frequently begged off attending.

"Well, you're forgiven." The Lady beamed. "You at least had the good sense to invite that darling little friend of your son's."

Rome coughed. "A friend of Antony's?"

"Now don't pretend you don't know him." She frowned. "You did invite Mr. Nicholas, didn't you?"

"Mr. Nicholas. Oh, yes. Of course."

Lady Bonneville looked relieved. "He claimed to be a good friend of Antony's. He said that he had dinner with you and Angela the other evening." A smile crossed her face. "The guards did not want to let him in, but he made such a fuss that they had to call me. And when he described you and Angela and the inside of your house in such perfect detail . . ."

"Yes, I had forgotten that I invited him. I wasn't thinking." The idea of Nick interacting with this level of Irryan society was vaguely troubling.

The vestibule widened into the main living area, a huge three-tiered chamber overwhelmed by the clamor of multiple conversations. Lady Bonneville did not know the meaning of the word "small." Rome estimated that there were over three hundred people in this room alone.

Someone grabbed the Lady by the arm and led her off into the crowd. Rome sighed. He wanted to talk to Nick but realized, whimsically, that locating the midget in this overflowing mass of humanity could be difficult.

He scanned the assemblage and spotted Drake instead. The Councillor's six-foot-six frame towered over a group of Irryan Senators and trade delegates. As Rome watched, Drake gave a slow nod, apparently in response to some conversational point. The black face looked as it always did—attentive, cold, unreadable.

Rome eased through the crowd, intending to make his way over to Drake's group.

"Greet-ings, Fran-co."

"Nu-Lin!" He smiled, fell in beside the Councillor and her two companions. "As always, you look stunning."

White organdy ruffles cascaded from her thin shoulders, metamorphosing into an orange blouse. The long skirt was fiery red and pleated. Tiny emerald-studded rings protruded from the skin of both cheeks, accenting the implanted wafer speakers that lay directly beneath.

"Dare I as-sume that you are ac-quaint-ed with these two gentle-men?" The blue eyes sparkled.

Rome shook hands with the slim balding man first. "Senator Oberholtzer, how are you?"

The Senator shook his head in mock sadness. "I'm afraid not too well, Councillor. My belief system was seriously shattered upon arriving at the Lady's abode." He gazed at the floor and lightly stomped his foot. "Baseboards made of two-inch-thick mahogany slabs are bad enough, but these paintings . . ." His gaze rose to the nearest wall. "I counted two Picassos, a Renoir, a Haynie, and three Turners." He chuckled. "I used to think *I* was rather wealthy."

Maroon robes swirled as the second man stepped forward. "Lady Bonneville does tend to redefine the meaning of excess."

Rome detected no criticism in the words. He took the extended hand. "Good evening, Bishop Vokir."

The Bishop shook hands firmly, then twined his fingers and allowed his arms to hang beneath the gray sash of the robes. "Councillor Franco, it is good to see you again. It has been about . . . three years? A dedication ceremony for the South Irryan shuttle terminal, as I recall."

"You have a good memory."

"The Church demands it." The Bishop smiled. "I also make extensive use of diary recorders. With some sadness, I confess to the debilities of aging."

Senator Oberholtzer shook his head in agreement. "It's too bad we have to grow old so fast."

"Fast is a rel-a-tive term. Hu-man be-ings, to an ex-tent, de-rive their own life-speeds ear-ly on. An ob-jec-tive of liv-ing should be to re-duce ac-cel-er-a-tive ten-den-cies."

Senator Oberholtzer raised his hand to gain the attention of a passing waiter. "That sounds wonderful, Councillor. What does it mean?"

A cryptic smile touched Nu-Lin's lips. "The pre-A-poc-a-lyp-tics sought to ex-tend the life span of hu-man be-ings. A much more re-a-lis-tic goal would be to de-crease the life-speed. En-a-ble a per-son to more ful-ly ex-per-i-ence each wak-ing hour."

The waiter, girded by a belt-tray, stood silently while Senator Oberholtzer mixed himself a gin and tonic. Rome noted that the Senator poured very little tonic.

"Perhaps," Rome offered, "people don't want to experience every waking hour." He paused until the waiter departed. "At times, life can be boring."

"I couldn't agree more," said Senator Oberholtzer. He raised his drink in a mock toast. "I, for one, do not seek to fully experience each moment."

The Bishop smiled at the Senator. "As a man in your position, I should probably agree. Representing Sirak-Brath certainly appears to be no easy chore.''

Senator Oberholtzer took a long swallow and shook his head. ''I was born and raised in that Colony and I tell you truthfully, the place is a sewer. Everything bad you hear about Sirak-Brath is a lie—the truth is infinitely worse.''

''The ICN fund-ing should les-sen your bit-ter-ness. Re-ju-ve-na-tion will take time, but I sense a day when peo-ple will feel pride in that Col-o-ny.''

''You'll forgive me if I don't share your faith, Nu-Lin,'' said the Senator.

''Faith, at least, can be shared,'' said the Bishop. ''Cynics dwell alone.''

Senator Oberholtzer laughed. ''Have you ever been to Sirak-Brath, Bishop?''

''Several times.''

''And you still maintain it is a human Colony?''

The Bishop hesitated. ''There are roots in Sirak-Brath. Where there are roots, there is hope.''

Senator Oberholtzer finished his gin with a loud gulp. ''Very interesting.''

''The Cos-teaus help breed such neg-a-tive at-ti-tudes, Sen-a-tor. It is their in-flu-ence that must be re-chan-neled.''

Rome jumped in. The threat of the Costeaus was one of the few areas where he sharply disagreed with Nu-Lin.

''There is no solid link between the problems of Sirak-Brath and the presence of the Costeaus. At least not in the past fifty years.''

Senator Oberholtzer glared at Rome. ''No link! Tell that to the daily victims of violence in my cylinder.''

Rome shook his head. ''We must distinguish the pirates from the smugglers and gangs who commit crimes in their name.''

''They're all the same,'' said Oberholtzer. His head scanned the room, searching for another waiter.

Rome faced Nu-Lin. ''I believe the pirates have become a social scapegoat. We blame and curse them for all our troubles.''

"The Costeaus are human garbage," growled Oberholtzer.

Nu-Lin assumed a dispassionate smile. "I would not ut-ter such cur-ses too loud-ly, Sen-a-tor." She nodded toward a trio of men up on the room's second tier. "You might of-fend some par-ty guests."

Rome followed her gaze to the lower balcony. The three men stood apart from other company. Two wore thick gray beards and were garbed entirely in black. The third was a withered figure par-tially hidden by a long gray cloak. He caught Rome staring and his ancient face broke into a faint smile.

"Costeaus?" Rome asked softly.

Nu-Lin nodded.

"Hell of a place for them to be," muttered Oberholtzer.

"Who invited them?" asked Rome.

"I would as-sume our host-ess had the hon-or."

The Senator growled. "Just make sure that Lady Bonneville is reminded to deodorize her penthouse. Some of those pirate smells are so strong that it takes days to remove the stink."

Nu-Lin smiled. "For-tun-ate-ly, these three have been de-o-dor-ized. And they are not or-di-nar-y pi-rates. They are lead-ers, from the clan of Al-ex-an-der. The old one is known as the li-on."

The lion of Alexander? Rome had heard the name before. He had always visualized a more imposing figure.

Oberholtzer waved his empty glass around the room. "Where did Artwhiler get to? If he knew pirates were here, he'd probably throw them out the door himself."

Bishop Vokir drew his eyes away from the Costeaus, faced Rome. "Did you know that the Church of the Trust maintains missions in Sirak-Brath? Thousands of souls come to these places, seeking the salvation of the roots. Smugglers, silkies, addicts of heroin and scud, workers from the outlawed hi-tech labs, even civilians from E-Tech—they all come to be saved." He paused for effect. "I can count on my two hands the number of pirates who have entered our missions within the past five years."

"What would you expect from a batch of crazed killers?" mumbled Oberholtzer.

"I would ex-pect dis-sa-tis-fac-tion, a wil-ling-ness to change. At least a-mong a fair num-ber of Cos-teaus."

"We are not the only Church in the Colonies," the Bishop pointed out. "Yet many theologians from other denominations share our frustrations with the pirates."

Senator Oberholtzer laughed harshly. "What good is complete religious freedom when you're dealing with scum?" He threw a glance to the balcony. The Costeaus had either not heard him or were ignoring his singularly loud voice.

Rome decided to let the argument drop. As far as he was concerned, the Costeaus were to be admired for resisting the temptations of the Church of the Trust. Vokir's religion merely offered another form of escape from the realities of life; more socially acceptable than smuggling or drug addiction, but just as ritualized and habit-forming. Neither alternative offered real change—confrontation with the inner self and the opportunity to conceptualize buried feelings.

It would be political folly to openly contradict the most powerful religious leader in the Colonies. Yet Rome could not resist a slight barb.

He smiled. "It's good that your Church is helping to remove these poor souls from the streets of Sirak-Brath. I should hope that these individuals profit from their rebirths." He stressed the word "profit."

The Bishop smiled gravely. Senator Oberholtzer waved his arm frantically at a waiter halfway across the room.

Nu-Lin covered her mouth and coughed. Rome was not certain, but it seemed as if the Councillor was trying to refrain from laughing.

That was probably very stupid, thought Rome. *I should not risk antagonizing this man.* Bishop Vokir had many allies.

The Bishop stared at the E-Tech Director. *Codrus is right.*

Franco is dangerous. The Bishop hoped it would not be necessary to have Reemul kill the Councillor.

In today's political climate, with the increasing attacks against E-Tech, the untimely death of Rome Franco could easily lead to his martyrdom. Initially, such an event would serve the Ash Ock plan—Intercolonial society would be outraged and more than sympathetic to the E-Tech cause. But Codrus was aware that martyrs often generated unpredictable long-term side effects. The Ash Ock dared not take such a risk, except in desperation.

The Bishop excused himself from the group. "I must get some fresh air." He made his way toward the outer terrace.

It is not fresh air that I seek. He mounted a short flight of stairs and stepped out onto the balcony that surrounded Lady Bonneville's penthouse.

Tonight, no clouds disturbed the Irryan atmosphere. The Colony's other two livable sectors blazed with light. Skyscrapers hung like jeweled stalactites, thrusting their crowns toward centersky. The alternating sectors of blackness served to accent the distant tapestry of streets and buildings. Few stars were visible through the mirrored glass. Distant suns were no match for megawatts of proximate light.

The Bishop sidestepped the flowered terraces and made his way to the edge of the balcony. A few other partygoers stood there enjoying the view. The Bishop chose a deserted section of railing and leaned over to gaze at the street, fourteen stories below.

It is difficult, he mused. *Separation tends to repress the yearning. And then suddenly, social realities require our presence in the same room at the same time.*

The Bishop sighed. Physical distance, by itself, bore little consequence for the tways of an Ash Ock. But standing in the same crowded room, being able to observe the same hundreds of people from two different perspectives presented a formidable challenge. *The desire to link becomes great. Our thoughts drift together.*

He stared at the passage of cars in the street far below. *We yearn for unity to such a degree that even the mirror is not necessary for interlacing. Our awarenesses touch without the complex symmetry of reflected eyesight.*

Fortunately, scenic separation helped reduce the immediate yearning. The Bishop would observe the street for a time and allow his Councillor-tway to continue with the vagaries of social intercourse. They simply could not risk linking.

Not here, not amid this crowd. There are too many dangers.

The chances of Codrus being detected were astronomical. Their monarch certainly would have no real trouble simultaneously communicating through his tways. And yet, there was always that remote possibility of mishap. An unexpected agony, perhaps; a steaming beaker of soup spilled on the flesh of one tway, causing an involuntary cry of pain from the other. The Bishop shook his head. Nothing short of the long-term goals of the Ash Ock were at stake.

Weeks ago, before Reemul's reign of terror had begun, they might have dared the flow into unity and the arising of Codrus. But Reemul's vicious attacks had put a scare into society. Throughout these past days, the Bishop had observed the suspicious looks afforded strangers. Most citizens would never admit it, but their faces betrayed them. People felt helpless before the onslaughts of the Paratwa and they reacted by attempting to make themselves more aware of potential danger. Even Irrya's wealthy upper crust, many of whom were gathered here tonight, was not immune. They possessed greater skill in cloaking their apprehensions, but the fear was present nonetheless.

That fear meant that Codrus's chain of events was proceeding as planned. Reemul was performing well. Only a few more orchestrated kills, vaguely directed at E-Tech, would need to occur and then society would be ready for the final outrage.

Codrus had spent a good deal of time considering the problem of putting Reemul back into stasis and had decided to inform the Jeek of his fate at the same time he told him about the last killing spree. Reemul's anger would be tempered by the knowledge that his final outrage would be one of his greatest challenges. Codrus also planned to schedule the final attack to coincide with one of Reemul's flexing periods. Afterward, with the Jeek freshly satiated, Reemul would be relatively easy to manipulate back into a stasis capsule.

At least that was Codrus's plan. With Reemul, there was always that element of unpredictability.

And Reemul was not the only potential problem. Again, the Bishop wondered whether it was coincidence that three leaders from the clan of Alexander—the clan that Bob Max had used to carry out Reemul's awakening—were here at the party.

Coincidence. It has to be. Still, it would be wise to learn precisely why the Costeaus were present.

The Bishop pulled back from the railing. *Risk is a fact of nature.* To Codrus, the rewards of success would be extraordinary: the second coming—the ultimate domination of the Ash Ock Paratwa over human affairs.

The Bishop smiled. His own goals were more modest.

I will be free to exist as a whole.

Rome located Nick within a circle of Irryan affluence, which included Artwhiler and Lady Bonneville. The midget wore a three-piece suit of blue and gold seersucker, shiny white boots, and a floppy low-brimmed hat imprinted with the double-helix pattern of DNA. He would have looked out of place anywhere.

"And so," Nick concluded, "the salesman says to the farmer: 'But I swear, I didn't know she was your daughter. I thought I was milking a cow!'"

The group erupted. Artwhiler threw his head back and laughed so hard that his chest heaved. The Councillor's medals looked ready to burst from the tight jacket of his black and gold uniform.

Lady Bonneville spotted Rome. Chuckling, she gripped his arm and pulled him into the group.

"Uncle Rome!" declared Nick. "I'm glad you could make it."

Rome looked down at the happy face. He hoped his own smile

did not appear too grim. "Sounds like I just missed another of your entertaining little tales."

Artwhiler's companion, an attractive redhead garbed in a silver lamé jumpsuit, asked sweetly: "Is Councillor Franco really your uncle, Mr. Nicholas?"

"No, my dear. It's just that Rome's son Antony and I have been good friends for so long that I feel compelled to call him Uncle." Nick grinned like a scuddie.

The redhead frowned, then turned and whispered something in Artwhiler's ear. The Guardian Commander shook his head sternly.

"Well, I'm going to ask him anyway," proclaimed the redhead. "Mr. Nicholas," she began, "I hope you don't take offense, but I just have to know. Is your small size congenital or is it related to hormonal deficiency?"

Lady Bonneville coughed. Several of the others turned away.

Nick rubbed his hands together and laughed. "That's a very good question. The truth is, my condition stems from neither of those possibilities."

"Neither?" The redhead looked troubled. "I thought it had to be one or the other."

"No, my dear. A third cause of smallness exists." Nick lowered his gaze and shook his head sadly. "It's very hard for me to admit but the truth must sometimes be expressed, for the good of the soul." He hesitated. "You see, I've been shrinking."

Artwhiler threw back his head and roared with laughter. Most of the others grinned and chuckled.

The redhead looked unsure of herself. "You're joking, right?"

Nick took the redhead's wrist and gently kissed her palm. "My dear, your perceptions are exceptional."

The redhead looked pleased. Rome wondered where Artwhiler had found her.

An ICN banker, with his arm thrown across the shoulders of his petite boyfriend, turned to Nick.

"Sir, is this your first visit to Irrya?"

"Yes it is. Why, a month ago I would never have dreamed such a place existed."

The redhead nodded vigorously. "My first time was a shock, too."

Nick smiled.

The banker continued. "Your impressions of Irrya have been positive then, yes?"

"For the most part."

"And you must have some thoughts on these terrible Paratwa problems we've been having?"

Nick raised his eyebrows. "I do indeed. I find it very strange to see that my hobby has now become major news."

"Hobby?" asked the redhead.

"Yes, for many years I've been sort of an amateur expert on Paratwa history. Those creatures have always fascinated me."

Artwhiler's face darkened. Lady Bonneville afforded Rome a faint smile.

Why is Nick doing this? Rome wondered.

The redhead looked angry. "That awful creature should be caught and put in prison for a long time!"

"Easier said than done," said the banker. He grinned fiercely at Artwhiler.

The Guardian Commander stared straight ahead. "We'll get him."

The banker's petite boyfriend let out an exaggerated sigh. "I certainly hope so! Why, people are becoming afraid to leave their homes at night. No one knows where this mad creature will strike next."

Rome scanned the group. Attention had crystallized since the Paratwa was mentioned.

The redhead nodded. "I know exactly what you mean." She threw her arm around Artwhiler. "Why, without Arty, I would have been scared just to come to this party."

Lady Bonneville soothed. "Now, now, my dear. I assure you

we're perfectly safe here tonight. I've taken extra precautions with security."

"Regular security measures," intoned the banker, "do not seem to daunt this creature."

Artwhiler locked his jaw in anger.

Nu-Lin joined the growing circle. Senator Oberholtzer, carrying a beaker of gin, squeezed in beside her.

"A Paratwa is a nasty problem," said Nick. "Back in the twenty-first century, these creatures were almost impossible to kill."

"Oh, no!" said the redhead. "They shouldn't kill it. Capital punishment is against the law."

"I suspect that the creature will have to be killed during its capture," Nick explained.

Rome wished that he could get Nick away from the party.

The banker spoke. "I've been wondering. What would happen to this creature if the authorities . . ." he glanced smugly at Artwhiler ". . . managed to kill only one of the tways. What would happen to the other one?"

"It would go mad," said Nick. "It would go on a destructive rampage that would end in its death."

"Like being torn in half," mused the banker's boyfriend.

"Something like that. The interlace would dissolve and the surviving tway would be unable to function in a rational manner. Kill one tway and you kill the Paratwa."

The banker smiled and turned to Artwhiler. "Do you hear that, Councillor? It was not even necessary for the Guardians to stop the whole Paratwa. Just send your people after one of the tways."

The Guardian Commander reddened. "This creature is a coward! It knows that it must attack and run or be destroyed."

Nick fingered the brim of his hat. "Have you learned what breed it is yet, Councillor?"

Artwhiler planted his hands on his hips and spoke loudly. "Breed? A meaningless term. My Guardians are trained to remove criminals from society. They do not concern themselves with the criminal's lineage.''

"Well," said Nick, "I've read that when dealing with Paratwa, breed can be of extreme importance.''

"It's a Terminus assassin," said the redhead proudly. "That's what all the freelancers are saying.''

"Freelancers know only what they're told," said Artwhiler with disdain. "Tell them a lie, and they'll report a lie.''

A lobbyist from the Profarmers Union frowned. "Does that mean, Councillor Artwhiler, that you don't believe this creature is from the breed of Terminus?''

Rome watched Nick. The small face scanned the crowd, searching, probing.

Artwhiler sighed in exasperation. "I've already stated, breed is a meaningless dictum. A criminal is a criminal. This particular lawbreaker is more vicious than usual, but its actions stem from the same sociopathic mind set that afflicts other criminal elements throughout the Colonies.''

With effort, Rome kept silent.

Nick shook his head. "A Paratwa is not a member of the species Homo sapiens. Our own rules do not apply.''

"Nonsense!" barked Artwhiler.

The party had grown unnaturally quiet. A sea of faces was now paying close attention to the exchange. Necks craned as guests tried to gain a view of Councillor Artwhiler's antagonist.

"The Paratwa," said Artwhiler, "were a creation of humanity. Therefore, they are part of our species. Only their perversity and lust for blood are alien to us.''

"They do not lust for blood," Nick countered. "They seek power, control over their environment—the same things we humans desire. But they are Paratwa and they've been bred and trained to seek these things at the expense of human beings.''

"Sociopaths," Artwhiler growled. "And this particular one will shortly be removed from society.''

"The Guardians have a new scheme?" asked the banker.

Artwhiler glared at the man. "We are working on a means to stop this creature. I am not at liberty to discuss procedures."

"I've heard it said," began the Union lobbyist, "that this Paratwa could consist of a male and a female."

Rome saw the thinly disguised excitement in the lobbyist's eyes, observed that the look was repeated across the sea of faces.

This creature breeds fascination. Unseen terror drives us to understand the nature of our fears. And there was something else there—an almost primal sexual appetite. Rome could not hide a deep frown.

We are fitting the mold. We are becoming more and more like the pre-Apocalyptics.

Nick gazed at the lobbyist. "Assassins usually were male/male and less often, female/female. But there did exist Paratwa where the tways were of mixed sexes."

"How strange," said the redhead. "I wonder if they ever made love to each other?"

Nick smiled. "Incest between tways was known to occur, but the more common arrangement was for the Paratwa to acquire a pair of sexual partners. Some Paratwa preferred to share one partner."

"A ménage à trois," mused the banker's boyfriend.

"Something like that."

Rome spotted Drake several rows back, calmly observing. Throughout the room, conversations ceased as more and more guests tuned into the exchange.

Nick continued. "For reasons never completely understood by students of Paratwa psychology, many of the creatures became pedophiles."

The redhead frowned. "That's not nice. Children should be left alone."

"We should all be left alone!" someone yelled. Nervous laughter erupted and was just as quickly silenced.

The redhead continued. "These Paratwa didn't have real parents, did they?"

"No," said Nick. "The fetuses were grown in the laboratory. Women were hired to nurse the Paratwa babies, provide the basic physical/emotional bonding necessary for infant survival. But the Paratwa were taught self-reliance at a very early age and were gradually removed from the influence of these surrogate mothers."

"I'm curious," inquired the lobbyist. "If one of these Paratwa consisted of a male and a female, how would it think of itself? What sex would it be?"

The redhead licked her lips.

Nick shrugged. "According to what I've read, the mixed Paratwa usually considered themselves male."

"Chauvinists," suggested Lady Bonneville.

More laughter sounded. Drake eased himself closer.

The banker turned slightly as Drake entered his field of vision. Rome watched with fascination as Drake signaled his man with a casual nod. The banker smiled and turned to Artwhiler.

"Councillor, I've heard it rumored that the Guardians' Paratwa investigation will soon become a joint venture with E-Tech Security."

Artwhiler glared. "I've not heard such a rumor."

The banker caught Rome's eye. "Perhaps Councillor Franco could offer your beleaguered troops some assistance?"

So Drake is preparing to throw his support to E-Tech. Rome kept his expression carefully neutral. *The ICN is warning Artwhiler that the Council needs results. Public pressure is building. The Guardians must stop this creature.*

Nu-Lin drove the point home. "I should hope such mea-sures will not be nec-es-sar-y."

Artwhiler was spared from responding. A Guardian officer squeezed into the circle and whispered something in the Commander's ear.

Artwhiler hastily excused himself and followed the officer from the room. Everyone tried to talk at once; the redhead summed up the general concern.

"I hope that awful Paratwa isn't causing more trouble!"

Senator Oberholtzer staggered forward and pointed his finger at the balcony. "I know why the Councillor's been called away. It's these damn pirates! Arty's probably gonna get help, throw them the hell out."

Everyone gazed upward. The lion of Alexander turned from his companions and stared down at the gathering. He smiled serenely.

Lady Bonneville sighed. "Now, Senator. There is no need to direct your anger at the Costeaus." She met the lion's stare. "They are here at my invitation."

Oberholtzer brought the empty gin beaker to his lips and licked at the rim. He grinned. "My apologies, Lady." The Senator pounded his fist against his chest as if to stop from burping. "But I'm just a simple representative of the people, a man who knows these filthy pirates for what they are."

Tonight, thought Rome, *you're nothing but a drunken fool.*

The lobbyist turned to Lady Bonneville. "I do not wish to pry, my Lady, but I am curious. Costeaus rarely come to Irrya."

Rome observed a curious thing. Nick and Drake were staring at each other; eyes locked together as if engaged in some invisible contest of wills.

The two men ended their silent struggle as Lady Bonneville answered the lobbyist's question.

"I invited the Costeaus here because I thought they'd enliven the party."

The banker, his boyfriend, and several others laughed.

With a smile, the Lady continued. "Actually, for the past five years, the Costeau leaders from the major clans have had an open invitation to attend any of my parties." She raised her head and met the lion's solemn gaze. "This noble gentleman is the first Costeau to ever honor that invitation. I thank him."

The lion of Alexander bowed slightly. He leaned over the balcony and spoke in a surprisingly youthful voice.

"Integration is a meritorious objective. We of the Alexanders welcome you."

Oberholtzer lunged forward. "Lies! On Sirak-Brath, my life has been threatened by these pirate clans!"

The lion met Oberholtzer's glare, then calmly turned his back to the assemblage.

Nu-Lin, red with anger, faced the Senator. "We seek so-lu-tions. La-dy Bon-ne-ville and the clan of Al-ex-an-der have helped break a bar-ri-er here to-night. We seek peace. Your words in-hib-it such i-deals."

Oberholtzer scowled. "My words don't do justice—"

"May I have your attention!" Artwhiler announced loudly. The Guardian Commander stood just inside the vestibule, hands on hips, a pair of stern Guardians at his sides. Party noise faded.

"The Guardians have just learned that there has been another Paratwa attack."

As the room boiled with excitement, Rome turned to where Nick had been standing. The midget had vanished.

"The creature struck a tavern on the Zell Strip of Sirak-Brath. We have no further information at this time." Artwhiler and his men spun and marched back out through the vestibule.

Partygoers formed knots of excited conversation. The redhead whined.

"Who's going to take me home?"

Lady Bonneville patted her arm. "Don't worry, my dear. I'll arrange for one of my chauffeurs to drive you."

Smiling, the redhead turned to the banker. "People with lots of money are so generous."

Bishop Vokir felt worry. A nocturnal breeze whispered across the outer balcony, stirring little crescents of dust at the edge of the flowered terraces. Fourteen stories below, Artwhiler's black and gold cruiser pulled out of an underground garage and silently raced onto the wide Irryan boulevard.

What has Reemul done?

The Bishop watched the Guardian cruiser vanish onto a side street two blocks away. From the main party room came snatches of frenzied conversation.

"Sirak-Brath! Of all places! Maybe the Guardians will be able to seal off that sewer, trap this damn assassin."

"The Guardians will do what they've been doing—nothing!"

"Sirak-Brath! Who knows? Maybe this Paratwa has found a permanent home."

The worry emanating from his tway wafted through the Bishop's psyche, seeking the delicate threads of the interlace, urging the union of mind patterns—the awakening of Codrus. The Bishop easily resisted. It would take a far stronger surge of emotion to overcome his singular awareness.

For now, the Bishop would merely share his tway's concerns. *Reemul had acted without orders.* Flexing could not explain such actions—it was not yet Reemul's time. Most likely, the Jeek had been careless.

As soon as possible, Reemul must be contacted. Codrus would have to ascertain the possible damages. Plans might have to be altered.

But the intrusion of worry was not based solely upon Reemul's actions. The Bishop's Councillor-tway had detected a potentially far more dangerous threat to the second coming.

The little man who claims friendship with Rome Franco's son.

The Bishop felt a cool breeze slap against his robes. *Who is he? He passes himself off as an 'amateur' expert on Paratwa history. He charms. He understands the seduction of words, is conscious of the effect he has on people.*

The little man shared many traits with Rome Franco.

It would be just like Franco to introduce such a random element. By now, the Councillor had to know that Reemul's killing spree was directed at E-Tech. Franco may have even conceptualized the subtler truth: that the Paratwa attacks were designed to enhance E-Tech's popularity throughout the Colonies. Rome would suspect a political opponent of controlling Reemul's rampage.

A parry in the dark. Rome Franco had brought the little man to the party in order to sow suspicions, to warn E-Tech's invisible adversary that the game was known. But Franco could not know who that adversary was. The little man remained a weapon without aim, stabbing blindly into the night.

La Gloria de la Ciencia does not make a big enough target, the Bishop realized. *Franco sees through that sham.*

Still, Codrus had expected that. The plan contained its minor imperfections. And no matter how well Reemul's demise was handled, some Colonists would remain suspicious. Rome Franco would be foremost among them.

Worry still emanated from his tway. Quite abruptly, Bishop Vokir realized that his entire train of thought could be in error. The possibility existed, however slight, that the little man was a stasis revivee from the past.

He could be a real enemy.

Rome said his good-byes, made his way slowly to the door. Twenty minutes after Artwhiler's announcement, the party still throbbed with discussion of the Paratwa. Yet Rome had also detected a change in those last twenty minutes, a relaxation of tensions.

Tonight, we are all safe. Tonight, the creature is far away, on Sirak-Brath.

He wanted to corral Nick, haul him back to E-Tech headquarters. But the midget was nowhere to be found.

Nick had gone too far tonight. His actions should have been cleared with Rome beforehand.

As he opened the inner vestibule door, Rome spotted Nick out of the corner of his eye, leaning against a corridor that led to one of Lady Bonneville's private rooms.

Towering over Nick was the lion of Alexander. They were engaged in an intense dialogue—hands moving in tandem with indecipherable whispers. The corridor was deserted except for the two of them.

Rome felt his jaw tighten. *Tomorrow, I will begin making some demands.*

At a bank terminal near the main concourse of the port known as Kevin's Hide, Gillian withdrew thirty-nine cash cards from one of Nick's secret accounts.

Thirty-nine—an odd numeral. It was his signal to Nick. In one hour, the midget, if possible, would be waiting at a specific phone for Gillian's call.

The system had worked pretty well thus far, although twice yesterday, Nick had been unable to respond. Gillian hoped that the midget was making progress with Rome and the Pasha. This convoluted form of communication was annoying, to say the least. Nick had to convince E-Tech to get fully behind their efforts.

Perhaps Gillian's next call would do the trick. *Once they learn that the Ash Ock liege-killer is here.*

Jerem sighed. "Why can't I convince you that I don't want to see my mom."

"You have convinced me. But you can't always get what you want."

"I never get what I want."

"Come on. Let's go." They stepped out into the main concourse.

The shuttle port swelled with a rich cross-section of Sirak-Brath's most obdurate citizenry. Bare-breasted silkies leaned against shuttle ramps, eyes darting as they sought new trade. Scudclowns howled. Quiet men in dark suits scurried like mice. Guardians and patrollers glared suspiciously at everyone; a trio of C-ray ignors hobbled along, holding hands, vacant eyes seeing no one. The air was filled with the smell of pirates.

Gillian walked behind Jerem, kept a hand on the boy's shoulder to guide him. A swarthy band of old women, uniformly garbed in swirling Mexican skirts, fell into their path and began singing a dirge about the fall of Quetzalcoatl. Gillian steered Jerem out of their way.

He felt the boy's shoulders tense as a laughing scuddie brushed by. The young woman childishly stuck her tongue out at Jerem. She broke into fiendish hysterics when the boy released an uneasy smile. The woman stank—not the distinct odor of a pirate but the more pervasive smell of someone who had not bathed in ages.

"Money for Missy?" begged the woman, stretching out a quivering palm. "Money for . . ." Her voice cracked; she dropped to her knees, giggling.

Jerem unpocketed a small wad of cash cards and shoved them into the scuddie's hand.

"You know where she'll spend that money," Gillian warned.

The boy shrugged. "Maybe someone will help her someday."

Gillian felt a knot tighten his chest. He changed the subject.

"Whether you like it or not, I'm sure your mother will be glad to see you."

Jerem frowned. "Yeah, I know she will. But she'll just be happy because she'll have me to push around again. That pirate woman I told you about—Grace. She understands Mom. Grace said that my mom takes pleasure from the maternal leash."

Gillian chuckled. The boy's words struck him as oddly humorous.

"Was your mother that way?" Jerem asked.

Gillian flashed to a forgotten memory of his own mother—a pale-faced stick figure feeding him citrus-sweetened fiber bars. They were alone on an enclosed porch. He was very young at the time, perhaps three, yet he sensed that the porch was a part of their home. Outside, the moist air was tinged a dull shade of pink, the sky half-blackened by an approaching storm. The thick rain forest surrounding their Kansas home crackled with the sound of distant thunder.

Without warning, the memory disappeared, was replaced by a feeling of discomfort in his guts. He gasped. Terror surged through him—a swell of emotion that rose from his stomach and rooted him to the terminal floor. He released Jerem's shoulders and turned away so that the boy would not see his fear.

I move—I am. I want—I . . . I . . .

Terror became pain, expanding into his chest, coursing through his body like an electric current. He wrapped his arms around himself, clenching in an effort to control the cry that threatened to burst from his lips. A spasm shook him.

"Gillian! What's wrong?"

Jerem's words seemed to physically recede, mutate into a distant cacophony of sounds, intermingle with the general hubbub of the shuttle terminal.

What's happening to me?

His fists tightened. The agony surged down his arms, seemed to explode out the ends of his fingertips. A cry escaped him.

I am in control! He silently mouthed the words, allowed them to tumble through awareness. *I am in control!*

Abruptly, the pain retreated. It collapsed within him, a balloon pierced by a hot needle. The residue of the pain became a ball of sparkling warmth at the base of his spine. He took a deep breath. The ball rocketed up his spine, dissolved.

"Gillian!"

Jerem stood at his side, the young face twisted with worry. Gillian sensed a melange of other concerns from along the concourse. Mixed among them were expressions of cruelty, a range of enjoyments at his agony.

"I'm all right," he breathed. "It's all right."

From beyond the Mexican dirge singers came a flash of golden light.

"Down!" Gillian hissed, yanking Jerem violently to the floor. He clamped his jaw shut, heard the soft hum of his crescent web igniting. A flick of the wrist launched the Cohe into his waiting palm.

The scuddie, screeching out giggles, fell to the floor in a fit of mimicry. She rolled onto her back and kicked her legs high into the air. Her mouth opened wide as if she were trying to keep from choking on her own peals of laughter.

Gillian gazed at the spot where he had seen the strange flash of light. There was nothing; only the endless movement of people across the terminal.

He shuddered. "Did you see that?"

"See what?" asked the boy. The worry seemed fixed to Jerem's face.

Gillian stood up. "It was nothing, I suppose. Just . . . nothing."

"What did you see?"

"Nothing." He slid his tongue along his upper left molars, located the tiny web deactivator, rubbed it twice in quick succession. The crescent fields dissolved. He slipped the Cohe into the pocket of his leather jacket. He felt reasonably certain that no one had seen the weapon. And anyone who had heard the faint hum of his web would not be unduly alarmed. Crescent webs were illegal, but tolerated—at least in Sirak-Brath.

Still, there were patrollers and Guardians everywhere tonight, no doubt in response to the tavern killings. Gillian had been lucky none of them had taken notice of his episode.

Episode? He stifled a harsh laugh. The word did not exist to describe what had just happened to him.

Quickly, before they attracted more attention, he led Jerem away. The scuddie staggered to her feet. "Money for Missy?" she begged. "Money for a poor lonely little girl." Her laughter echoed as they retreated.

"Ramp forty," Gillian said, eagerly pointing to the descending treadway. "That's the one."

Jerem's eyes did not leave Gillian's face. "What happened to you? Some kind of epileptic attack or somethin'?"

They stepped onto the deserted ramp, fell into the flow of the moving treadway as it burrowed toward the outer shell of the Colony.

Gillian shook his head. "No. It was . . . a reaction. Something to do with an old injury."

"What kind of injury?"

"An old injury. It's very complicated." Gillian had not the faintest idea of what had occurred. *I must speak to Nick. He might know.* The midget possessed some medical knowledge. He had helped Gillian with ailments in the past.

But never anything like this.

"Are you sure you're all right?"

Gillian forced himself to smile at the boy. "Yes, I'm really all right." Whatever had befallen him had passed. All that remained was a cold memory of his actions, a dull confusion. He knew better than to dwell on the incident, to probe for reasons.

Three massive shuttles came into view at the base of the ramp. They rested side by side in the huge storage bay. Their outer shells were pockmarked and scarred and all bore clan markings on their short stubby wings.

One airlock was open. A powerful-looking black man stood beneath the hatch.

Jerem stiffened. "That's Santiago—one of the pirates who kidnapped us in Moat Piloski's shop. He's Aaron's friend."

Gillian nodded. They stepped from the treadway and walked toward the shuttle. The pirate turned and called to someone inside the craft.

Jerem's face twisted into a deep frown. The boy's concern over Gillian had been displaced by his own fears.

"I still don't want to see her," he argued.

Gillian said: "You'll be fine. Be brave."

Paula sat in the corner. She scrunched her legs up to her bosom, gripped her knees and hugged. On the other side of the shuttle's main compartment, Aaron and Grace argued loudly. It was their third battle of the night. Paula had lost count of the grand total of fights; these last few days in Sirak-Brath seemed to have increased both the frequency and intensity of the sibling war. Only the cause of the fights remained clear.

Grace wagged her head angrily toward Paula. The triplet of braided ponytails whipped across the pirate's shoulder.

"How many more false hopes must we endure, brother? This mad infatuation of yours must end. Her son is her own problem, not a lifetime quest of the Alexanders!"

Aaron's tattoo seemed to crawl across his cheek. His voice remained a low growl. "I am responsible."

"So she has said. And you have been foolish enough to believe her."

"We will remain on Sirak-Brath until we find the boy."

Grace raised her arms. "*I* command this vessel."

"And I command *you*, sister! By age, by skill, and by order of the lion. This ship goes where *I* say."

Grace sneered. "By order of the lion. How dare you! You have disobeyed the lion's and the tribunals' directives. You have lost sight of our mission."

"Our mission is to destroy the creature that murdered our kindred. That creature has been here, on Sirak-Brath. The lion cannot fault us."

"A lucky coincidence for you, fool brother!" She laughed bitterly. "And why do we sit in the shuttle port awaiting the beast's arrival? Hah! We should be out hunting . . ."

"Hunting what?" Aaron shouted. "Have you been deaf? This monster will not be trapped by attacking its shadow. It is a creature of motion. It kills—it moves. By now, it is probably in another Colony."

"Then command us, dutybound brother! Command us to another Colony!"

Aaron hesitated, glanced at Paula.

Paula shuddered. *I will find my son!* She squeezed her arms together, crushing her legs even more tightly to her breasts. *I will find him.* Nothing else mattered.

Aaron turned back to his sister. "We will wait a while longer."

"A while longer! How long, Aaron? Until this woman spreads her legs again for you?"

"That is none of your concern!"

Grace laughed. "You accuse me of being deaf, yet you remain totally blind. This outsider leads you by the cock and you stumble after her like a toddler."

Aaron's voice was barely a whisper. "Enough, sister. My heart remains clear."

Grace shook her head in amazement. "Poor blind Aaron. Guided by his heart. Hah! A leashed child, ruled by his emotions."

Kindness entered Aaron's words. "Sometimes, dear sister, you too would be better off being ruled by your emotions."

Grace glared at him for a moment. Then she turned violently away and climbed up the ladder to the control deck.

Aaron sighed. "I should not have said that last thing."

"You were angry," Paula said. "She'll understand."

He shook his head. "Grace is right. I have lost sight of our mission."

"Yes. I suppose you have."

"It would be best for all if I gave the shuttle to my sister—gave her command."

Paula nodded.

"I could remain on Sirak-Brath with you until we find Jerem."

Paula unclenched her body and wrapped her arms around Aaron's neck. She inhaled deeply. Aaron wore no oderant bag, but the smell of the Alexanders permeated his shirt. Over the past days, Paula had grown accustomed to that raw odor. The fish-smell had taken on new meaning, had become a symbol for closeness, for a sense of place. She nibbled at his neck, wanting him to make love to her again.

Gently, he pulled away. She waved her arms helplessly, fought back the tears.

He smiled gruffly. "I want you on our terms, woman. Not because you mourn for your son."

"I know." A sob escaped her. "It's just that I thought—I really thought that Jerem would come tonight. That man sounded so sincere . . . and he described Jerem perfectly . . . and he said he would bring him to us."

Aaron gripped her shoulders. "Enough! There have been other disappointments since we docked. You know what many of the people in this Colony are like. They will do or say anything for the right price."

"But the man *described* Jerem! He must have . . ."

Aaron soothed. "The man could have met the boy briefly. Or he might have known Jerem on Lamalan. Anything is possible."

She sniffled. "It's just that I really felt tonight . . ."

"Then don't lose hope yet. The man said seven-fifteen and it is only minutes after eight. They may simply have been delayed."

Paula nodded. "Do you think . . . Do you think they may have been . . ." She clamped her mouth shut. The thought was too frightening to put into words.

Aaron understood. "I do not believe that Jerem could have been in that tavern on the Zell Strip. I know of that place. It is doubtful that a boy of his age would have even been permitted to enter."

She forced a smile. "I guess it's lucky he's not a pirate child."

Aaron chuckled. He helped her to stand. "Come. We'll go."

From outside the shuttle came a shout. Paula felt her heart race. *They're here!*

A moment later, Santiago stepped through the open hatch. Behind the black pirate walked her son. Paula felt hot tears coursing down her cheeks.

"Oh, Jerem!" She ran forward, threw her arms around him, crushed him to her. "Oh, I missed you so badly! I was so worried!"

He felt stiff in her arms. Paula released him from her iron hug and tried to stare into his downcast eyes. "Are you all right? Did anyone hurt you?"

"Are you gonna beat me again?" He raised his eyes as he spoke, fastened his attention on some invisible object above Paula's head.

"Oh, Jerem! I love you! Of course not!" She shook him gently. "Jerem! It's me! I was angry with you that night but that's past. It's over. And it won't happen again. Not telling you about your father was wrong. And hitting you—that was wrong. I'm sorry."

Aaron laid his hand on Jerem's shoulder. "That doesn't go for me, boy! Old enough to run from flames—old enough to face fire. You cost my crew time and effort searching this Colony."

Jerem pulled away from Paula and backed toward the open hatchway. For the first time, Paula noticed the tall, leather-jacketed man who stood there beside Santiago. Sharp gray eyes met her gaze. She frowned as her son wrapped his hand around the man's wrist.

Aaron spoke coldly to the stranger. "We thank you for returning the boy."

The man stood silently. *He wants something*, Paula thought. *A reward.*

Aaron nodded. "You brought the boy. The clan of Alexander is in your debt. You are free to make a demand of us."

Gillian stared at the man with the scarlet penis tattooed on his cheek. He sensed strength in the pirate, fearlessness, a focusing of energies on the moment at hand.

The other pirate, Santiago, kept his attention focused on Gillian's hands. The black Costeau looked completely relaxed. His arms hung freely, inches away from a carved and dirty sandram drooping from a thick belt. A sheathed knife lay strapped to his right leg above the knee.

Excellent, Gillian thought. *He's prepared for violence.*

Gillian laid his hand on Jerem's shoulder. Tension appeared on the face of the boy's mother.

"I make no demands," Gillian said carefully. "Merely a request."

Aaron came forward to the center of the compartment. He was about to speak when a woman came into view from the upper deck. She descended the ladder in quick steps, a triplet of dark ponytails thrashing from side to side.

"Guardians," she hissed. "They're boarding all the shuttles in Kevin's Hide!"

Aaron turned to Santiago. "Quickly! Hide the woman and boy in the storage bay. The Guardians may not bother with a complete search."

"Hah!" the woman cried. "Don't deceive yourself, brother. These Guardians search for the Paratwa. They will not be daunted. They will look everywhere a person could hide."

Aaron nodded sharply. "You're right." He turned to Paula. "If asked, you are my wife. Jerem is our son." To Gillian: "You are a friend of the clan, seeking transport on our vessel."

A series of sharp tappings sounded on the hull of the ship. Aaron motioned to Santiago. The black pirate left the compartment and headed for the airlock.

"Where are the others?" Aaron demanded.

Grace held her head proudly. "I sent David and Alfonso to the Zell Strip."

"Fool sister! Did you think they would catch this beast?"

"I sent them to acquire information," she snapped.

Gillian made a decision. These pirates reminded him of the hardened warriors of the old Earth Patrol Forces—the international legion responsible for quelling uprisings across the globe during the final days. It was from their ranks that he and Nick had recruited their Paratwa team.

He released Jerem and withdrew a kerchief from his jacket, unfolding it in his palm. Quickly, he bundled his Cohe wand into the rag. He twisted the weapon's tiny switch to safety-lock it, then knotted the kerchief.

The outer airlock opened. Footsteps sounded in the midcompartment.

Gillian held up the kerchief. "I have one request of your clan. The object I hold here must not be found by the Guardians."

Aaron nodded. "Grace, hide it in the false control panel."

Gillian threw it to her. The pirate woman leaped onto the ladder, catching the kerchief with one hand. She scrambled up to the control deck.

Excellent! Gillian thought. *Reactions based on the necessity of the moment.* He could barely conceal his pleasure.

Santiago reentered the compartment with three Guardians. The officers carried thrusters.

"I'm Lieutenant Sparden," cracked their leader. The man pointed his gun at Aaron, snorted disdainfully at the strong odor permeating the shuttle. "Sirak-Brath is under martial authority. Your vessel will be searched. All crewmembers will assemble here on this deck. Immediately!"

One of the Guardians aimed his thruster at the ladder as Grace climbed down.

"The rest of your crew?" demanded the lieutenant.

Aaron shook his head. "They're not here. They're in Colony."

Lieutenant Sparden grunted. "All of you—stand in the center. Face the outer walls with your backs to one other. Strip naked and throw your clothing away from your bodies."

Gillian watched Grace and Santiago turn calmly to Aaron. The tattooed pirate gave a subtle nod.

Gillian smiled. *Good discipline. And they betray no fear.* Even with thrusters aimed at their bellies, Gillian knew that the pirates would have attempted to overcome the Guardians had Aaron signaled differently.

Paula felt intense anger take hold of her. "You have no right to do this to us."

"Shut up. Into the circle and strip."

"No! You have no right!"

The lieutenant aimed his thruster at her head. "Strip or I'll do it for you." The officer allowed a grin to spread across his cheeks.

Paula stiffened. *Bastard!*

She stood in the circle with her back to the others, staring at the wall while she removed her clothing. Pasha Haddad's warning came to mind. He had said it would go badly for her and Jerem should they be caught by the Guardians.

At least these men aren't looking for us. The Paratwa is uppermost in their minds.

The lieutenant examined each of them while his men stood guard. When it was Paula's turn, he circled her naked body and then, satisfied she carried no concealed weapons, reached down and patted her bottom. With effort, Paula held her temper.

Gillian stood calmly as the Guardian searched him. The lieutenant completed his quick inspection and then moved to Santiago, the next man in the circle.

A poor examination, Gillian reflected. Paratwa could easily insert Cohe wands into their rectums. The lieutenant should have had each of them bend over for a more complete search.

Next, one of the Guardians examined their clothing, checking for weapons and ID. As he located information cards, he typed data into a boxy terminal strapped to his left arm.

"Any problems?" asked the lieutenant.

The man hesitated, pointed to Gillian. "He has no ID. These three—" he motioned to Aaron, Grace, and Santiago "—are Costeaus, all with clear records."

"And the woman and boy?"

The man frowned, typed another batch of data into his terminal. A moment later, he broke into a smile.

"Paula and Jerem Marth, both wanted by us for questioning."

"Concerning what?" asked the lieutenant.

"The man shook his head. "No further information. It's classified."

Gillian watched the Guardian officer sigh and roll his eyes. It was the reaction of a man accustomed to dealing with an unwieldy bureaucracy.

"All right," said the lieutenant, "get your clothes on." He turned to one of his men. "Search the ship." The officer hustled from the compartment.

They dressed quickly. The lieutenant waved his thruster toward Gillian, Paula, and Jerem.

"You three are to come with us for questioning."

Everyone remained silent until the other Guardian returned. "Shuttle's clear," said the officer. "No one else is aboard."

A poor search, Gillian mused.

The lieutenant turned to Aaron. "You're to have this vessel off Sirak-Brath within thirty minutes."

Aaron's face darkened. "Several of our clan have not yet returned."

"Too bad. You've got thirty minutes. We're clearing the scum out of every port in this Colony. Be glad you're not being arrested."

Gillian's own goal was clear—he had to stay with the pirates. It would probably work out better if the Guardians took Paula and her son. They would be a burden to his plans.

He turned to the lieutenant. "My name is Gillian. I work for E-Tech Security. I report directly to Pasha Haddad. I am on special assignment with these pirates and it is vital that I remain on this vessel."

The mixture of truth and lies might just be convincing enough to the Guardians. The key was Haddad. Although there was strong friction between E-Tech Security and the Guardians, Nick had intimated that the Pasha was highly respected among them.

The lieutenant studied Gillian for a moment. "Prove it."

Gillian pretended to glance at a clock over the hatchway. "Right now, you should be able to reach Haddad at this number." He recited a phone code.

The lieutenant nodded to the man with the terminal strapped to his arm. The officer keyed the number, then covered his ear to heighten the volume of his tiny lobe receiver. His eyes widened as he spoke into the terminal.

"Yes. Pasha Haddad, please. . . . He's not? . . . No, no message. Yes, thank you. . . . Uhh, no I would rather not give a name. . . . Thank you."

The Guardian broke the connection. He looked surprised. He stared at the lieutenant.

"Well?" demanded Sparden.

"That was the private line into Rome Franco's office."

Gillian shrugged. "The Pasha was supposed to be there. I guess something happened. Your best bet now is to dial into Irryan headquarters and have him paged."

The lieutenant gave a slow, thoughtful nod. For a moment, Gillian suspected that the Guardian was going to demand another phone code. Gillian did not know another phone code. The only one he had memorized was the one from Franco's office terminal. And he had only taken the trouble to remember that number because Nick had earlier been spending so much time with Franco.

The Guardian officer faced Gillian. "I still want this shuttle off Sirak-Brath within thirty minutes."

"No problem." Gillian avoided Aaron's wrathful stare.

It worked. The Guardians obviously did not want to waste time trying to track down Pasha Haddad within the vast labyrinth of E-Tech headquarters. Gillian had access to Rome Franco's private line. That was reason enough to believe his story.

Paula laid a hand on her son's shoulder. They fell into step with the Guardians. Jerem pulled away from her. He turned to Gillian.

"Can't you do somethin'?"

Gillian shook his head. "I'm sure you'll be released shortly."

Paula did not relish the idea of another uncomfortable period in custody. But it would be bearable.

I have my son back.

She looked at Aaron, saw the mask of rage distorting his tattoo.

"Please, Aaron. Don't do anything rash. We'll be fine."

She saw how her words calmed him, extinguished some of the

fire in his eyes. She forced a smile and then turned and led Jerem through the hatch. The Guardians followed.

Gillian called out. "Jerem!"

With a sulking glare, the boy turned. "Yeah?"

"Remember. Be brave."

They vanished from view. A sharp crack vibrated through the compartment as the airlock slammed shut.

Gillian smiled at Aaron, Grace, and Santiago. His expression was met by hostile frowns.

Now comes the hard part.

Santiago withdrew the sandram from his belt. Grace and Aaron moved closer. Gillian held out his hands in a gesture of peace.

Aaron stopped two paces away. "Why does a man from E-Tech Security wish to remain with us?"

"I need your help."

"Indeed! And what makes you think for an instant that the clan of Alexander would help anyone from E-Tech?"

"We both hunt the same enemy."

Grace scowled.

"What enemy would that be?" Aaron asked calmly.

Gillian knew that he could not lie to these people, not if he expected them to risk their lives with him.

"His name is Reemul. He is of the breed of Jeek Elementals. He has killed less than two hundred people within your Colonies, but on the Earth of two centuries past—my Earth—he was responsible for perhaps thirty thousand murders. He is one of the worst of the Paratwa assassins—vicious and clever, a hunter of not only humans, but also of other Paratwa. Reemul will be difficult to stop."

Gillian observed looks of surprise, disbelief, a trace of bitter humor on the lips of the woman.

"I was awakened from stasis, by E-Tech. Two hundred years ago it was my task to hunt and destroy these creatures. I had a team. We were successful against every Paratwa we went up against. Except one. Reemul."

He paused. "I intend to remedy that."

Aaron laughed sharply. "A wild story!"

"But true."

"And you seek the assistance of pirates? Why?"

"I sense you have had experience with violence. You're better trained, more prepared than E-Tech Security or the Guardians. Your feelings and thoughts are more unified; your muscles obey without question, without the intervening shell of the overly civilized human being."

"You suggest we're not civilized," Grace snapped.

"It was not meant as an insult."

Aaron smiled. "And why should the clan of Alexander wish to hunt this Paratwa, this Reemul?"

"Because Reemul tortured and killed eleven of your clan."

"Ahh! The boy has filled you with childish stories."

"Not stories," Gillian countered. "The truth. We both know that. So let's waste no more time on deception."

They need a demonstration, he thought. *Words will not be enough to convince them.*

"Throw this fool off the ship," Grace argued. "We don't need . . ."

"You do need!" Gillian said harshly. "Make no mistake—if you find this Jeek and attempt to go up against him, you will die. Gloriously, perhaps, and with honor to your clan. But you will be dead and Reemul will be alive. That is fact."

Santiago swung the sandram onto his right shoulder and closed in on Gillian.

Aaron sneered. "The clan of Alexander seeks no help in this matter. We settle our own scores."

"Then you'll die. Oh, there's always the possibility of luck—fate may intervene and you may have your shot at Reemul." Gillian added sarcasm to his words. "But only a complete fool relies solely on luck."

Fury twisted Aaron's features.

Fighting is the only way. If I defeat these pirates, I may earn their help.

Gillian forced a mocking laugh. "Come! Throw me off your vessel! Show me the skill of the Alexanders!" Then, lowering his voice, he allowed deadly threat to replace boasting. "And I will show you your weaknesses."

Santiago swung the sandram. Gillian crunched his jaw, felt his crescent web ignite. The sandram struck the invisible field and bounced away as if it had encountered a rubber surface. Gillian twisted, threw his foot sideways into Santiago's guts. The pirate doubled over.

Aaron charged, slapping his palm against his chest to ignite his own crescent web. Grace leaped toward a wall cabinet.

She goes for a weapon!

Gillian turned sideways, watched Aaron match his movement. *Good. He's fought with a crescent web before.*

They stood side to side, a pace away from each other. Grace tore open the storage cabinet on the far wall.

Gillian observed that Aaron was studying him. The pirate appeared to be searching for a way to kick or punch through Gillian's weak side portal. *Either that, or he's waiting for his sister to bring out a gun.*

Gillian lectured. "First lesson. In hand-to-hand web combat, never wait for reinforcements."

Gillian dropped to the deck, barrel-rolled forward. Red sparks flew as their webs touched and repelled each other. Gillian was merely rolled in the opposite direction along the floor. But Aaron, standing, found the bottom of his web shoved violently away while the upper portion remained motionless. His legs flew out from under him and he crashed to the deck.

Grace yanked a thruster from the cabinet. She flipped the sprocket to the armed position and took aim.

Gillian came to his feet, tucked his arms behind the web's protective front crescent, leaned his body forward. The thruster wailed loudly in the confined space of the shuttle compartment.

Gillian took the blow on the chest, felt his body jerk upright. He now had a precious second while Grace's weapon recharged itself. He dove toward her, bellyflopped on the deck. His front crescent compressed as he hit the floor.

Grace's second thruster blast shattered harmlessly against Gillian's rear crescent. The weapon's discharge compressed him even further against the deck, working to his advantage.

Like a rubber ball, he bounced violently up off the deck and hurtled headfirst in his original line of motion, toward Grace.

She never got off a third shot. The top of his web, where the front and rear crescents came together in a dull point, plowed into the woman's chest. With a loud gasp, Grace flew backward. Her thruster dropped to the floor.

Gillian landed on top of her. He rolled away, snatched the thruster and fired at Aaron, who was just getting to his feet. The tattooed Costeau, still off-balance, caught Gillian's blast square in his web-shielded chest. He curled backward, crashed to his back.

Santiago, charged, sandram raised. Red sparks bristled; he, too, had activated a web. Gillian waited until the enraged pirate was almost on top of him before diving to the floor. He fired upward.

Santiago took the thruster blast directly under his chin. At such close range, the weapon carried enormous power. The portion of the web beneath Santiago's jaw compressed violently. His head flew back as if a huge fist had crashed into his jaw. He dropped to his knees. The black face stared blankly at Gillian for a moment, then his eyes glazed over. He fell forward into unconsciousness.

Enough, Gillian thought. *I've hurt them worse than I intended.* He allowed himself a grin. *They fought better than I expected.*

The amount of training they need will be minimal. It will just be a matter of redirecting some of their energies, showing them a few tricks.

Grace lay on her back, breathing deeply. Santiago was out cold. Aaron staggered to his feet, eyes locked warily on the thruster in Gillian's hand.

Gillian spoke calmly. "What I've just done to you is nothing compared to what a Paratwa would do. It holds two Cohe wands, two thrusters, and is protected by webs. Its consciousness exists in two locations simultaneously. Its instincts are to kill.''

Aaron breathed deeply. Fire still burned in the pirate's eyes, but his fury appeared to be tempered by a grudging acknowledgment of what Gillian had just done.

"There is a way," Gillian said. "A way for myself and a small team to take on a Paratwa. There is a method. The Paratwa is an incredibly violent opponent, but it has weaknesses. I know of these. I can show you. Together, we can kill this beast."

Aaron pulled himself erect, rubbed the back of his neck. "And if we refuse?"

"I obviously can't make you help me, and I know I can't buy your assistance." He shrugged. "If you refuse, I'll leave and keep on searching until I find those who are willing."

With a slow thoughtful nod, Aaron tapped his chest, de-energizing his web. Gillian lowered the thruster, sprocket-locked the weapon, and threw it gently to the pirate. Aaron caught it with an easy motion.

Gillian de-energized his own crescent web, heard the hum die to a whisper, then vanish. Aaron heard it too. The pirate slowly raised the gun, aimed it at Gillian's chest.

The thruster is sprocket-locked. It will take him a moment to unlock and fire. I will be able to reenergize my web in time. He smiled. *Aaron would know that too.*

For a moment, Gillian studied the pirate's face. Then, with a grin, he turned so that his back was to Aaron. Across the compartment, Grace had managed to sit up. She was staring at Gillian with a curious intensity.

Gillian spoke carefully. "If you wish to fire, Aaron of the Alexanders, then do it now. When we go up against a Paratwa, our trust of each other must be complete, absolute. There can be no suspicions."

He heard a sound, turned. Aaron lowered the gun and threw his head back. The red penis quivered across his cheek as he roared with laughter.

Gillian had not really taken a chance in turning his back to the Costeau. He had known how Aaron would react.

The pirate's laughter subsided. He grinned wickedly.

"Well, Gillian of E-Tech. I believe you have got yourself a team."

Rome kept pace with the Pasha's swift stride as they marched through the vaults toward the prime data-retrieval section. Haddad looked grimmer than he could ever recall.

Rome shook his head in disbelief. "How could it walk into a Guardian station and kill forty-four armed men and women?"

"We believe one of the tways allowed itself to be arrested on a minor smuggling violation. The other tway then entered the building and opened fire. More than that, we can only speculate."

"And seven of our own people?"

The Pasha stared straight ahead. "They were on special assignment in Kiev Alpha. They were working with the Guardians, trying to break a local smuggling case."

Rome shook his head. *It attacks a Guardian station but makes sure that E-Tech people are also killed.*

The sixth known assault by the Paratwa fit Nick's scenario perfectly. Once again, public sympathies would flow toward E-Tech. *And the Guardians have been made to look foolish, unable to even defend one of their own Colonial stations.*

A door vaulted open as it detected their presence. They passed through without slowing down.

"I wonder how the creature got off Sirak-Brath?" Rome asked.

"Artwhiler swore that his Guardians sealed all of Sirak-Brath's ports immediately after last night's tavern killings. They claimed to have searched every departing shuttle."

Haddad shrugged. "Fodder for the freelancers."

"Partly true. Artwhiler is certainly known for making wild claims and appearing foolish later. But still . . ."

The Pasha spoke coldly. "On this point, I agree with Nick. There is little chance of preventing this creature from traveling between Colonies. The Guardians may have searched every shuttle still in port and they may have boarded every vessel that departed Sirak-Brath before the ports were sealed. But what good are such actions?

"To begin with, the Guardians have no idea who they're looking for. There is no visual ID on the Paratwa. And Nick suggests that the creature might split itself—the tways could board different shuttles and rendezvous later. The Cohe wands are the only sure giveaway. And these weapons are tiny enough to be hidden almost anywhere.

"And imagine all the groups that the Guardians would be wary of offending. Private corporate vessels would certainly undergo only perfunctory searches. Medical and local patrol shuttles would be completely ignored. The Irryan Constitution protects religious travel between Colonies. Even under a state of martial law, the Guardians would be extremely careful about interfering with such rights."

The door at the end of the corridor snarled, "Identify." They stuck their hands against its body-sensor.

"Proceed," it grumbled, sliding open.

Inside the cramped data-retrieval section, Nick and Begelman stood side by side, studying a twin set of access screens. The midget broke into his patented smile as Rome and Haddad entered.

"How do!"

It was Rome's first opportunity to see Nick since last night. "Your behavior at Lady Bonneville's needs explaining."

"Granted, some of my jokes were a bit old."

"I'm not kidding, Nick."

Begelman gripped Nick's shoulder. "Look!" The computer hawk waved his scrawny hand at one of the monitors. "Another pattern!"

Rome ignored the interruption. "This creature has now attacked the Colonies six times. Almost two hundred people have been murdered!" He heard his own voice budding with anger and he knew, deep inside, that the focus of his rage should not be Nick. But he could not stop. "We've allowed you and Gillian wide parameters, which you have continually abused. We have even tolerated Gillian's disappearance. But your behavior at the party last night cannot be treated lightly!"

The midget continued studying the monitor. "I was acting in a perfectly rational manner at the party. What I did was necessary."

Rome felt his anger harden. "What you did last night was unforgivable. You dabbled in a complex political arena of which you know little—an arena, I might add, that has taken me a lifetime to master, at least to the point where I know when to keep my mouth shut."

Nick turned to him gravely. "And what if I told you there was probably an Ash Ock at that party."

For an instant, the only sound was Begelman, whacking his fingers against a pair of keyboards. Each wiry hand typed rapidly into a different terminal while his head scanned back and forth between the two screens.

Rome slumped down on a cushioned stool, his anger transformed to shock. "What . . . are you saying?"

Nick explained. "A few days after we were awakened, I began to have some funny suspicions about this whole mess of yours. But I had nothing concrete until Wednesday evening, when I had dinner with you and Angela. That night, you confessed to me that you felt everyone was being manipulated—E-Tech, the Guardians, La Gloria de la Ciencia, everyone."

The bright blue eyes seemed to bore into Rome. "Two hundred and some odd years ago, I heard people confess the same uncertainties in the same tone of voice. Oh, the organizations at that time were more complex and the structure of society was vastly different. But the subtle elements—the fears, the confusions—those things rang true across the centuries. Fear and confusion are the visible trails left by the Ash Ock, evidence of their existence.

"For the past three days, Begelman and I have been accessing the history of your Colonies."

"Patterns!" shouted the programming hawk. "They're here, in almost all our records."

Nick smiled grimly. "Patterns. Some of them so ethereal that they almost defy conceptualization. It's only when they're added together and cross-referenced that they begin to make sense."

Begelman flapped his arms. "The patterns are base-yielding re-fractive—nondirectional, but visible against a Cheslarian social grid."

"Mathematically," Nick explained, "they're extremely complex."

Begelman looked disturbed. "That's not necessarily true."

Rome held up his hand. "I gather what you're trying to say is that you've found indications of social manipulation. You blame this on the Ash Ock." He sighed. "Historians have been through our records before. I couldn't begin to tell you how many examples of so-called manipulation they've uncovered."

"Not like these," said Nick. "For instance, we've found evidence that the long-range planning goals of the ICN have frequently run counter to the banking consortium's espoused policies. This has been going on periodically for nearly two hundred years."

"Unethical, perhaps, but certainly not unusual."

Nick grinned. "We've identified four distinct time periods throughout the ICN's history—periods when the consortium's largest profit ratios have occurred. During each of these time-frames, the ICN has deliberately—*deliberately*—thrown money away. There is no other way to describe the process. They have invested in projects that every sane financial expert of the era declared hopeless. They have made huge charitable donations at times when the Irryan Senate had enacted the strictest legislation against tax incentive credits. And we're talking large percentages, way out of line with normal banking policies.''

Rome spoke wearily. "You are from the pre-Apocalypse. You've lived for too long in a society where the twin gods of profit and progress determined all human activity.'' He shook his head. "Did it ever occur to you that the ICN, during these eras, might have been run by civic-minded people—people who invested in projects or made donations because it felt like the right thing to do for the Colonies?''

Nick dismissed Rome's theory with a wave of the hand. "During these four time periods, I believe that the tway of an Ash Ock controlled the ICN.''

"That's absurd.''

"Ninety-one years ago, during one of these periods, the Council of Irrya proposed a major investment—a project to revitalize the surface of the Earth, to remove the poisons and make the planet hospitable for humans again.''

"I'm aware of that proposal,'' said Rome.

"Then you must also be aware that the ICN refused to go along with the plan. Instead, they proposed financing Colonial renovation. They sank huge sums into the upgrading of buildings, refurbishing of mirrors and cosmishield glass, et cetera. Almost all of those expenditures were completely unnecessary. The original cosmishield glass was designed to last a thousand years.''

"Engineers disagreed,'' Rome argued. "Refurbishing had supporters and detractors.''

"True. But the end result was that E-Tech's planetary revitalization project was effectively halted.''

"Nonsense! We established bases, began Ecospheric Turnaround. That goes on to this day.''

Nick pointed to Begelman's terminal. "The evidence is here. Ninety-one years ago, the ICN effectively put a stop to any major revitalization of the Earth. They refused the necessary funding. E-

Tech was forced to pursue the project on its own, with a fraction of the financing that the ICN could have provided.''

Haddad spoke quietly. ''You are suggesting that the ICN has systematically, over a period of two centuries, used its financial strength to block E-Tech?''

Nick wagged his finger. ''With Earth's revitalization, yes. But hindering E-Tech has not been their main thrust. Indeed, they have most often acted in ways that complemented E-Tech policy. No, what the ICN has effectively done over the centuries is halted progress in general—by making sure that money was not available for growth.''

Rome felt exasperated. ''All this proves is that the ICN, and other organizations, supported the prevailing social views of those eras. E-Tech's very purpose is to limit unchecked growth.''

Passion colored Nick's words. ''You say they supported the prevailing social views. I say that the ICN, to a great degree, *controlled* those views. I say that at least one of the Ash Ock Paratwa has been manipulating your social structure since the time of the Apocalypse. I say that he has used the ICN as the primary means of accomplishing this control. I say that this Ash Ock has never stopped plotting the domination of humanity!''

Rome shrugged. Nick's theory was ludicrous. ''The ICN has always been a conservative organization. Ninety-one years ago, they simply did not believe that Earth revitalization was a financially worthwhile project.''

Nick bubbled with excitement. ''A conservative organization? Yes, the ICN's been a conservative organization throughout its history, except for these four time periods during which, in banking terms, they went mad.''

Rome was growing tired of the argument. ''So the ICN went through a radical period. That's not unusual. Over the long term, most organizations go through such cycles.''

Nick smiled. ''Not unusual, huh? What if I told you that each of these four time periods ended with the Director of the ICN dying in such a way that his body could not be identified?''

Rome took a deep breath. "What do you mean?"

"I mean that two Directors perished in shuttle crashes where the bodies were not recovered. One Director supposedly committed suicide by stepping into a thirty-megavolt solar grid. He was incinerated. The fourth died in a fire, burned beyond recognition.

"There's more. All four of these men came from large urban Colonies. All four had families in which the parents died relatively young. None of them had brothers or sisters. None of them had any close relatives, other than their parents. And none of them ever got married. Does all that suggest anything to you?"

Rome shook his head. His stomach began to burn and he wished he had brought his antacid pills along.

The midget continued. "Did you ever study a process called 'sapient supersedure'? It was real popular back in the good old twenty-first century. If you wanted to become, let's say, a banking executive, and you didn't feel like wasting the time going through all that schooling and all those years of hard work, then you found someone who was almost there—someone who had his degree and who had a few years of banking under his belt and who everyone realized was a real hot shot, headed for the top.

"After you found this person, you studied him, learned his history, got a hold of his records and his biocharts, and prepared yourself to replace him. As long as you were nearly the same size, the surgical alterations were rather basic. It was a time when people were constantly changing their appearances. There were surgeons everywhere who could shape your flesh into any form you desired.

"The internal alterations and the biorhythmic and brainwave camouflaging were a bit trickier, but the technology existed for those who could afford it.

"After you had been properly altered to look like the banking hot shot, you had him killed in such a way that his body could not be identified. Then you took his place. The whole process was a bit more complicated, of course, but essentially that's what happened."

Rome caught the Pasha's eye, knew that Haddad shared his thoughts. *This can't be true. This sort of thing occurred on Earth, during the height of human madness. Supersedure ended with the Apocalypse.*

Nick went on, relentlessly. "We only learned about a supersedure when the substitute made a mistake. During the final days, when this vicious craze was at its height, E-Tech conservatively estimated that four out of every five substitutions went undetected."

The midget paused. "My point is, there were some basic rules of success for the supersedure process. Your victim should come from a large City, or Colony, where it was generally easier to retain anonymity. The victim should have a few, if any living relatives; the fewer family ties, the better. And substitutes tended not to marry.

"Now, the Ash Ock, they mastered supersedure from the beginning. They were very good at it—a fact that E-Tech didn't learn until it was too late."

"The patterns are here!" screeched Begelman, caught up in the throes of Nick's excitement. "There is manipulation! There are patterns!"

Rome turned to Haddad. The Pasha wore a curious expression.

"A few weeks ago," began Haddad, "I would not have believed any of this. But today, with the Colonies threatened by this creature . . ." He hesitated. "I don't know."

"Ahh, yes," said Nick. "The creature. Late last night, Gillian finally reached me. Our creature has a name."

Nick told them about the tavern, about Gillian's discovery of Reemul, about the slain pirates and Gillian's recruiting of Aaron's people. Rome's stomach felt like a hot oven.

With deliberate calm, the Pasha crossed the room to an unused terminal. He began typing.

Rome thought, *This can't be true.*

"There's other evidence," argued Nick. "Recall the subway tunnel under Philadelphia where Reemul was found. That was no run-of-the-mill stasis operation. It was an entire train, complete with power-generation equipment and fuel to last centuries. The tunnel was effectively sealed at both ends.'' Nick wagged his finger. ''A powerful organization was responsible for Reemul's entombment.''

Haddad began reading from the monitor screen.

''Reemul. Breed: Jeek Elemental. Sex: male/male. Date of births: circa 2067 to 2073. Birthplace unknown. Popularly referred to as the liege-killer.'' The Pasha tapped the keys, jumped to a new file, continued.

''A free mercenary until circa 2090. At that time, believed to have been recruited by the Ash Ock. Believed to have served the royal Caste until the Apocalypse of 2099.'' Haddad paused. ''No confirmation of death.

''2091—believed responsible for assassination of four Cardinals of the Holistic Catholic Peace Foundation in Mexico City. 2093—believed responsible for detonating a controlled nuclear device in the Novosibirsk Communist headquarters building. Nine hundred killed. 2094—responsible for slaughtering over a thousand settlers in the Antarctic Reclamation Areas. 2094—responsible for the so-called Parliament Purge in London. One hundred and twenty-eight members of the British House of Commons slain along with two hundred and fifty-nine army regulars and seventy-eight civilians.

''Known to have murdered sixteen Paratwa of mixed breeds between 2094 and 2097. Believed responsible for numerous other Paratwa killings during that timeframe, all at the discretion of the Ash Ock.''

Rome's thoughts wandered as he listened to the Pasha's words. *Political manipulation via the ICN—could it be? Could an Ash Ock have been controlling our society since the time of the Apocalypse?*

Haddad continued. ''2096—trapped by a U.S. Marine commando brigade within the city limits of Pensacola, Florida. Escaped, killing one hundred and eighty-eight soldiers.'' The Pasha stopped. ''The listings from 2096 on are more frequent.''

Nick spoke quietly. "Toward the end, Reemul's masters kept him busy."

Rome stood up. "Is Gillian absolutely certain it's Reemul?"

"In matters of Paratwa identification, I've learned to trust Gillian implicitly. He's never been wrong.

"As to the Ash Ock," Nick continued, "I have no more doubts. The patterns and the manipulations are real. I don't know whether we can prove this to you or to anyone who lacks deep training in the particulars of probability matrixes and social grids. But we're convinced."

Begelman nodded vehemently.

Nick stared up at the ceiling. "It's likely that during these four time periods, an Ash Ock came out of stasis, perhaps via a timer-controlled Wake-up system. By means of supersedure, one of the tways of this Ash Ock infiltrated the ICN and eventually assumed control of the organization. The purpose of this control was to limit technological advancement—in essence, to support E-Tech's policies.

"By periodically controlling the purse strings of the ICN, this Ash Ock was able to forestall the natural growth patterns of society, inhibit those forces within humanity that continually strained against artificial limits.

"After this Ash Ock felt that humanity's growth patterns were again under control, he arranged for a reverse substitution—some-one who would take the Ash Ock's place in a prearranged death."

Haddad nodded. "The four ICN Directors, they were last-min-ute substitutes. Their bodies were destroyed."

"Exactly. Then the Ash Ock probably returned himself to stasis for another forty or fifty years until it was time to check on society and make sure that E-Tech was doing its job." Nick smiled. "Oh, yes. There's a fifth time period. An Ash Ock is manipulating your society right now."

Rome looked around the room, feeling suddenly alienated from everything and everyone. He forced himself to look at the midget.

"This whole thing . . . it's too fantastic! How could an Ash Ock have gotten away with such substitutions again and again?"

Nick held up his hand. "The most terrible mistake we made two centuries ago was in underestimating these creatures. No one dreamed, until it was too late, that the royal Caste could so effectively infiltrate and manipulate human society."

"If all this is true," Rome argued, "then why? The Ash Ock— in fact all the Paratwa—were the sworn enemies of E-Tech. They were technofreaks. Why would they want to limit technology?"

Nick brought his gaze down from the ceiling. He hesitated. "I don't know. Not exactly.

"I do know that the royal Caste were bred and trained to seek power. In pre-Apocalyptic society, they assumed positions of responsibility throughout the world. One of the tways of Aristotle, the Ash Ock who perished in a South African firestorm, was the Prime Minister of Free Brazil. His tway was a South American energy magnate. A tway of Codrus, we learned too late, had been a powerful member of the World Bank until his *'disappearance'* in 2096.

"Now within your Colonies, the power structure is more concentrated than anything Earth ever imagined. Irrya rules completely. Your Council and its representative organizations, a handful of powerful industrial brokers and a few religious leaders—they essentially control the Intercolonial decision-making process. Irryan Senators and Colonial Governors are freely elected, but it is these appointed Irryans who wield the real power.

"The Ash Ock possessed remarkable ambition and that fanatical perseverance found in history's most destructive monarchs. Within Irrya's concentrated power structure, I am certain that an Ash Ock would be able to infiltrate the highest echelons.

"Remember, too, that technology today is a mere shadow of what existed two centuries ago. This Ash Ock would still have access to many of the lost sciences. Combine high technology with an extremely potent intellect and anything is possible."

Rome felt his hands clench. "You're saying that an Ash Ock could right now be sitting on the Irryan Council."

"Yes." Again, Nick hesitated. "But not both tways. I don't believe that this Paratwa would risk having its tways together in public for extended periods. In such situations, the Ash Ock would experience difficulties with the interlace. When the tways are together, the urge to link becomes inordinately powerful. In a social situation, the tways would try to keep away from each other."

Haddad suggested, "The tways would assume complementary positions of power?"

"Exactly. Each tway would utilize supersedure to gain control of a particular organization. But they would remain in two different social spheres."

The midget rubbed his jaw. The blue eyes opened wide. "The Ash Ock were not just five randomly gifted Paratwa. Their breeders foresaw that in order for the five to rule together, each had to be specialized—five cogs in a machine, each one necessary for the machine to function at its highest level.

"Aristotle, who we are certain perished, was the master politician. We can be thankful that it is not him we're faced with. It's likely that Aristotle would have created far more subtle methods of manipulation.

"Empedocles, also known to be dead, was the youngest of the five. He was to have been some sort of military figure, an overlord, ruling over the assassins."

Rome nodded. "And the three who were never accounted for?"

"We know Theophrastus was a scientific genius, excelling in pure research. He wielded his secret influence within the world scientific community.

"About Sappho we knew nothing. He, or she, remained a shadow presence."

Nick stared at a rack of terminals across the chamber. "The fifth Ash Ock is Codrus. His specialty was banking. On Earth, it was Codrus who was responsible for raising the funds to finance the Ash Ock's rise to power."

"So Codrus is the one," Rome said.

"I think so." Nick turned to Begelman, who was again lost in a melange of flashing monitors. "The patterns we discovered and the fact that the ICN has been responsible for this manipulation makes me fairly certain. A tway of Codrus, secretly ruling the ICN, fits all the known facts."

"Drake," suggested the Pasha.

Nick shrugged. "He's certainly leading the pack of suspects right now. But we can't be sure."

"If this is all true," asked Haddad, "then why did Codrus awaken Reemul?"

Nick stared at Rome. "To change the direction that Colonial society is heading in today, to make sure that restrictions are maintained on science and technology.

"I believe Codrus realized that in our present climate, the ICN alone could not stop this tremendous resurgence in science and technology. So Codrus awakened Reemul and sent him on a killing spree."

Rome nodded. "With the attacks directed against E-Tech."

"Exactly. For the purpose of making E-Tech into a victim, thereby engendering its popularity. When E-Tech gains in stature, science and technology are brought under greater control. And Codrus has also arranged for E-Tech's foes to be dealt severe blows.

"Because of that West Yemen loan business, La Gloria de la Ciencia receives a financial setback. They were probably going to use that loan money for expansion of their programs. And because Bob Max turns out to be a major shareholder in West Yemen, La Gloria de la Ciencia gets even more intimately linked to the assassin. The net result: La Gloria de la Ciencia's growing popularity is checked. They lose their power base.

"The ICN loan money is redirected—toward Sirak-Brath. The money is not used to expand technology, but merely to renovate a depressed Colony."

Haddad gave a solemn nod. "The same sort of thing that happened ninety-one years ago, when Earth revitalization money was redirected into rejuvenating the Colonies.''

Nick grimaced bitterly. "Yes. But I think that ninety-one years ago, there was another reason why Codrus did not want the planet redeveloped. I'll get to that in a moment.

"But I want to make sure you see the whole picture first—E-Tech becomes more popular, the ICN is stopped from funding scientific development, La Gloria de la Ciencia is disgraced . . .''

"And the Guardians," Rome said calmly. "They're made to look foolish because they can't stop Reemul.''

Nick smiled wickedly. "Yes. The Guardians, too, are brought down a notch. And let's not overlook the coup de grace, which I'm sure is scheduled to occur shortly.

"The Council of Irrya, fuming because Artwhiler's Guardians cannot bring Reemul under control, will turn the responsibility for stopping the assassin back to E-Tech.''

"Drake hinted as much at the party last night," said Rome.

"Naturally, E-Tech will quickly and successfully end this threat. Reemul will be located and destroyed by your Security forces. Of course, Reemul's body will probably be burned beyond recognition during the battle, but the Cohe wands will be found nearby. And the murderous rampages will stop. Everyone will be convinced that E-Tech truly ended the threat of the Paratwa.'' Nick paused. "The real Reemul, of course, will be returned to stasis. He's too valuable to waste.''

Rome shook, invigorated by rage and wonder. "This whole thing has been a complete setup from the very beginning! Reemul planted those bugs at Paula Marth's gallery in the hopes that she would contact us after she witnessed Bob Max's murder.''

Nick nodded. "Codrus planned Max's murder with great care. Codrus knew it was likely that Paula Marth would only contact E-Tech following the killing. Max was working for Codrus, of course, and being Paula's neighbor, he was able to tell Codrus all about her. She was perfect. An antique dealer with indirect links to the black market would never deliberately involve herself with the

Guardians or the local patrollers. When she witnessed Max's murder by the Paratwa, she called E-Tech.

"Reemul, monitoring the bugs, confirmed that fact to Codrus. Codrus leaked the information to Artwhiler or Drake." Nick smiled brightly. "Another variation suggests that Artwhiler or Drake is the tway of Codrus, in which case leaking the information becomes redundant."

Rome laughed bitterly. "I'm beginning to accept these fantastic speculations, but I have to draw the line somewhere. Artwhiler as a grand manipulator of civilization I cannot handle. The man does not have it in him."

Nick shrugged. "Who knows? Maybe Artwhiler is an incredibly gifted actor. But you're probably right. Artwhiler controls the Guardians but in terms of wielding real power, he's the most limited member of Council. This Ash Ock would not aspire to such a restrictive position.

"At any rate, during the Council session, Artwhiler accuses you of trying to cover up the Paratwa killing. And so, through a chain of events, E-Tech is removed from an investigation that would have normally been within its province. Codrus gets an opportunity to discredit the Guardians, by having them eventually fail to stop the assassin."

"Such manipulation," murmured the Pasha.

Nick hopped up onto a console beside Begelman's keyboards. "Yes sir! The Guardians fail to score. They fumble the ball. E-Tech picks it up on their own five-yard line. E-Tech runs for the touchdown, winning the game with only seconds to spare!"

The midget smiled faintly. "E-Tech is destined to become the hero of the Colonies. In a short time, your organization will have enough popularity to pass any new legislation it wants, tightening the controls on science and technology for decades to come. La Gloria de la Ciencia will have its fangs pulled. Codrus will be pleased."

Rome sat back down on the stool. He felt drained. *Does consis-*

tency have a source? Yes. There is a beginning for that which does not change.

But I was wrong when I thought the Irryan Council formed that beginning. We have merely been a tool, hammered and forged by others. We have been pawns in an Ash Ock game.

His guts unwound. He felt something akin to a sense of elation—an awareness that he had never experienced. It was as if a veil had been lifted; the hard truths, once only peripherally glimpsed, were now exposed to full view.

He faced Nick. "You said earlier that you had a theory about why this Codrus has done these things. Why has he manipulated us across the generations? Why does he want E-Tech to remain strong?"

Nick squinted. "What if the Ash Ock have instituted a long-range breeding program? What if there are secret bases where a new breed of Paratwa are being created? Bases that have never known any restrictions on scientific advancement?"

Haddad spoke with a trace of disbelief. "A breeding program lasting two centuries?"

"Yes. Remember, the Paratwa are not of our species. Never forget that! And the Ash Ock . . ." Nick hesitated. "The Ash Ock, in particular, would not grow disenchanted with a breeding program lasting hundreds of years."

Rome had the feeling Nick was going to say something else. But Haddad interrupted.

"Where would such bases be hidden? Not within the Colonies?"

"Probably not," said the midget. "Not when there's a large nearby planet that is virtually uninhabited."

"Earth?" Rome shook his head. "Certainly not on the surface . . ."

"Underground, at bases prepared by the Ash Ock before the Apocalypse."

Haddad gave a thoughtful nod. "It could be. There's little enough activity on the Earth—our Ecospheric Turnaround facilities, a few Guardian installations, the Church of the Trust burial temples, some specialized industries.'' He frowned. ''And ninety-one years ago, when the ICN refused to support Earth rejuvenation . . . that was done to prevent these secret bases from being discovered?''

Nick grinned. ''If a major Earth rejuvenation had begun, by now the surface would be crawling with Ecospheric Turnaround bases. The Ash Ock facilities might have been accidentally discovered. Codrus could not allow that possibility.''

''And what about the pirates?'' asked Rome. ''They're down there all the time, illegally hunting antiques. Do you suspect the Costeaus of being involved?''

Nick shook his head. ''No. I doubt the Ash Ock could have recruited them.''

''Pirates awakened Reemul,'' Haddad pointed out.

''Yes, but those pirates worked purely for profit. It was Bob Max who hired them.'' Nick flashed a grin. ''And there lies our key! Bob Max—the first victim.

''Begelman and I have compiled a list of about thirty of Irrya's most powerful citizens, most of whom were at Lady Bonneville's last night. We are going to begin scanning their pasts, searching for inconsistencies, for signs that a substitution has occurred. But unless this Ash Ock has been incredibly sloppy, the best we can hope for is to narrow down the list, eliminate some possibilities.

''Bob Max, though, is another story. He's the one we'll concentrate on.''

Nick smacked his hand on the console. ''Bob Max was killed because he knew one of Codrus's tways. I'm sure of it! This Ash Ock cannot dare to have middlemen—the risks would increase geometrically. Our manipulator would deal directly with the humans that he needed to carry out his tasks.''

Rome nodded. ''If that's true, this Ash Ock would have had to be certain of Bob Max's trust.''

''Yes.''

Haddad frowned. ''How do we know that it is only Codrus we

are faced with? Could not all three of these Ash Ock have survived the Apocalypse? Perhaps all three have used sapient supersedure to infiltrate our society?"

Nick nodded. "Probably all three of them *did* survive. The other two—Theophrastus and Sappho—could be alive down on the planet. Or they could be in stasis. But the nature of the manipulation we've uncovered suggests that we're dealing with just one Ash Ock—Codrus.

"Codrus's job would be to hinder the growth of the Colonies until the Ash Ock were ready to release their newly bred army of Paratwa. The Ash Ock would want to make certain that human society was stable enough before their new generation of conquerors took control.

"The Ash Ock would have learned from their mistakes. The final days would have reinforced the lesson that a stable society is far easier to control than a culture where scientific advancement is running wild, where the social fabric is being sheared by constant change."

The Apocalypse never really ended, thought Rome. *It was merely postponed.*

He was surprised by the strength of his own voice. "We'll need hard facts to back up all these allegations. We'll need ammunition to throw before the Council and the Senate."

Nick patted Begelman on the shoulder. "We'll get it. Like I said, Max is the key. Somewhere, somehow, Bob Max is connected to this Ash Ock. When we find that connection, we'll be able to act."

Rome nodded. "E-Tech will do whatever is necessary."

"You'll end your surveillance of me and allow Gillian to do his job?"

"Yes."

"But trust has two directions," pointed out the Pasha.

"Yes it does," said Rome.

The midget shrugged. "You're right. I've been holding things back all along. I've still not told you everything."

Rome said, "You can start with your conversation last night with the lion of Alexander."

"Ahh, that! I just wanted to find out why the lion came to Lady Bonneville's party after having turned down invitations for years.

"He's a shrewd old man. He wouldn't tell me exactly why he was there. But I got the strangest feeling that his suspicions are similar to ours. The Alexanders also believe that someone in high places is controlling Reemul's reign of terror. The lion came to the party to see if he could learn anything."

"And the second computer program?" Rome demanded.

Nick's eyes pleaded. "I've got to ask you to trust me a while longer on that. There's a reason."

Rome stared at him for a moment. "All right. A while longer. But there will come a day . . ."

"There'll come a day when you'll learn everything." Nick's expression darkened. "But on that day, you just might wish for the relief of ignorance."

"The Achilles' heel of the Paratwa can best be understood by analogy."

Gillian spoke from the center of a spacious mat-covered arena—a brightly lit corner of the same Irryan gym that he and Nick had used to test Haddad's volunteers fifteen days ago. Gillian had ordered changes throughout the rest of the gym. A low drop ceiling of unlit strip panels and a series of movable wall grids combined to produce twisting corridors and a potpourri of enclosed spaces. Sparse lighting cast heavy shadows; against the warm amber glow of this training arena, the adjoining bedrooms and halls remained wells of darkness.

In the center of the training arena stood Aaron, Grace, and Santiago, attentive and wary. They had good reason to remain alert. Over the past four days, Gillian had been slowly introducing them to the rigors of the Shane/Ammon technique—an instructional program practiced by the old Earth Patrol Forces. Long dry lecture periods were broken up by unexpected attacks. Done correctly, Shane/Ammon training produced unusually alert fighters. And the technique weeded out trainees who suffered from easily frayed nerves.

There were no problems in that regard. The pirates accepted extremes of tension as a way of life. They had adapted quickly to Gillian's techniques.

In the back of the gym, on a high stool, sat Nick. He wore a bright yellow jumpsuit. A remote terminal was strapped around his neck. At his side, Pasha Haddad, stone-faced, still masking his displeasure at the presence of the pirates, observed. Haddad was cooperating only because Rome Franco had ordered it. The Pasha still did not fully accept the unsuitability of his own Security people. For the fourth day in a row he was here to see why the pirates were different.

Nick and Haddad wore active crescent webs; the faint hums were clearly discernible throughout the quiet gym.

Gillian continued. "Our analogy is the magnetic compass. It was a common Earth tool until the more sophisticated directional sensor made it obsolete. Are you all familiar with it?"

The pirates glanced at one another, making sure that their attentions never completely shifted away from Gillian. Aaron expressed the group answer with a sharp nod.

Good, Gillian observed. *They function more and more as a unit.* Four days of intense training had gotten across to them the overriding importance of teamwork.

"Now imagine a compass having two needles perpendicular to one another, one of them north/south, the other east/west. Consider a Paratwa assassin in terms of this special compass. One tway is the north/south needle and the other is the east/west. This perpendicular relationship is analogous to the way in which a Paratwa actually functions. The very nature of the interlace that forms the Paratwa's single consciousness prescribes that the tways are ninety degrees out of phase with one another.

"Applying this special compass analogy to the realm of combat, we can imagine the Paratwa as two wildly spinning compass needles—always perpendicular to one another but forever in motion, the needles always pointing in different directions, not limited to north/south or east/west. In addition, although the needles rotate synchronously, they are given to abrupt changes in speed and direction. The only constant is that ninety-degree relationship between the two needles.

"To effectively fight a Paratwa, we must stop those compass needles from moving, freeze their motion so that the needles align themselves north/south and east/west. We must *directionalize* the assassin. In theory, this is very simple: we protect ourselves against the creature's first violent assault. Then at the earliest opportunity, we align ourselves so that we attack one tway and defend against the other."

He watched their reactions, saw the tattoo ripple over Aaron's frown, saw Santiago drift into an uneasy smile. Grace allowed contemptuous disbelief to play across her angled cheekbones.

"Attack one tway," he repeated. "Defend against the other.

"In theory, simple—in practice, difficult to accomplish without being killed."

Only Santiago laughed.

"If the Paratwa can be *directionalized*—forced into a situation where one tway must defend while the other's only option is to attack—then the assassin's greatest single advantage is effectively neutralized. The Paratwa, able to fight from two locations at the same time, is in essence forced to respond as two separate creatures. One tway has no choice but to defend itself against the attackers; the other tway automatically becomes the aggressor, but discovers that the enemy is not fighting back." Gillian permitted himself a faint smile. "We are merely defending ourselves.

"The assassin has been directionalized. An option that makes the Paratwa such a deadly opponent is bypassed: it cannot shift offensive/defensive tactics from tway to tway, confusing us. Also, half of its arsenal is hopefully put out of commission. The tway under attack cannot use its Cohe wand and thruster with any degree of accuracy, providing our attack is fierce enough.''

Aaron chuckled. "This, Gillian of E-Tech, is your great secret? This is what we've waited four days to hear?''

"Yes. This is the Achilles' heel of the Paratwa.''

Grace and Santiago laughed openly. Pasha Haddad frowned. Nick ignored the commotion, burying his face in the viewscreen of his portable terminal.

"Of course, this technique is not very effective unless someone—in this situation, me—can match the attacking tway's skill with the Cohe wand. Even one tway with a Cohe can wreak terrible havoc.''

Gillian smiled at their disbelief. Then he drew his thruster and fired at Aaron.

Three sets of jaws clamped down, three crescent webs ignited. Aaron tucked his arms behind his protective shield and took Gillian's shot without flinching. Even without a web, the controlled discharge was barely potent enough to knock a man off his feet. For training purposes, they used only low-power thrusters.

Santiago and Grace tucked close together, drew their weapons and fired at Gillian. His own web easily repelled the double blast.

"No!'' he shouted, reholstering his thruster. "I told you before. For today's session, you are to consider me as one tway and Nick as the other!'' He pointed to the back of the arena. Nick held up his hand and gave a friendly wave.

"Attack one tway—defend against the other! Since I, the Paratwa, initiated the attack, your only option was to flow into the nature of my assault. The parameters of my attack were very clear. I was firing at you; therefore you should have put your shields to me and fired at Nick, who was only defending!

"You failed to directionalize your enemy. You allowed Nick

and me to determine the nature of the combat. All of my options were left open while yours were severely limited."

The pirates lowered their webs. Grace scowled. "I do not see the necessity of . . ."

"Quiet! You made a mistake. Don't attempt to rationalize it! In combat against a Paratwa, you would be dead."

Her eyebrows flared, her jaw tightened with anger.

Grace is the weak link, he reminded himself again. *There is rage bubbling within her. It could erupt and defeat the mind/body rhythms at a critical time.*

Four days ago, as their shuttle headed here from Sirak-Brath, Gillian had spoken to Aaron in private and had broached his doubts about Grace. It had been a weird discussion, out of sync and eventually maddening.

At first, Aaron had made things sound very simple.

"She is my sister. She is of the clan. You will train her along with Santiago and me. She will be there when we earn our vengeance and destroy Reemul."

"Your sister may not be suitable," he had argued.

"How can she not be suitable? She is of the clan."

"I was speaking in terms of temperament."

"So was I."

Gillian had tried another tack.

"Grace seems to anger easily. It's possible that during combat she will allow her rage to run wild. She could lose her sense of discipline and become a threat to the stability of the team."

"Her rage is a part of her," Aaron granted. "But lose her sense of discipline?" He had laughed. "She might. And maybe your leg will fall off during combat. Who can say?"

"I'm talking about something very real, Aaron. Your sister could end up destroying all of us."

"So could you."

"I don't want her on the team," he had said with finality.

"That's obvious."

"There must be other clan members who would gladly take her place."

"Yes, many of them."

"Then it's settled. Grace is out. You'll call your leaders, have a batch of recruits sent to train with us in Irrya."

Aaron had displayed puzzlement. "Why would I call my leaders? And why would we need a batch of recruits? You're only asking to replace Grace."

"We would screen your people, pick out the best candidates."

"Grace is the best."

"Aaron, you're just saying that because she's your sister."

"Of course."

He had kept his own anger carefully under control.

"I do not want her on the team. She is out. I will not train her."

Aaron had finally become perturbed. "You come to us, ask us for help. You talk of teamwork, yet you try to divide us."

"I am trying to put together the best possible team. I am trying to ensure our survival."

"You have the best possible team. You have Grace, Santiago, and me."

"Are you saying that I either train the three of you or none of you will cooperate?"

"How could it be any different?"

"How do I know that the three of you are the best possible teammates without seeing other Costeaus?"

Aaron had shrugged. "If you wish to go elsewhere, go. You asked us for help—we accepted. I do not see what is so difficult to understand about this."

And that had been Gillian's first real lesson in clan etiquette. The pirates remained firmly bonded to the overall goals of the Alexanders while maintaining a strong sense of individuality.

Reemul had tortured and murdered eleven members of their society. The entire clan was sworn to vengeance. But Gillian had only convinced Santiago, Grace, and Aaron to help him. Therefore, only Santiago, Grace, and Aaron *would* help him. He had not earned the assistance of the clan of Alexander, but merely of three individual members. Even Aaron and Grace's other two crewmen, whom they had been forced to strand on Sirak-Brath, were not involved in this pact.

He sighed, returned his full attentions to the arena. *I am stuck with Grace. I must temper my criticism, help her to control her anger.*

He continued. "Grace, Santiago—though you did not directionalize me, you did act swiftly. Aaron—never forget that whenever possible, tuck into line with the team. Remember that the Cohe wand can whip at you from any direction. With active crescent webs, each of you has two weak areas—your left and right side portals. With webs touching, two people effectively eliminate half of their four target areas.

"Also, remember to practice shifting your thrusters from hand to hand. You must become fluidly ambidextrous.

"Now, tell me about the Paratwa. Santiago—what does it mean when the tways change attack planes?"

The black pirate responded instantly. "When one tway moves to a higher or lower elevation, then the tway still at your own elevation is preparing to spinsaw."

"Aaron—define spinsaw."

"The tway at your own elevation will crouch and come up on his toe, go into a skater's spin with the Cohe arm outstretched. He does this mainly to confuse. The black beam will whip around the room and seem to be everywhere at once."

"Grace—in reality, only one part of the Cohe beam is deadly."

"The extended part of the beam—the final fifteen to twenty inches. The rest is harmless, nothing but the trailing light of the projected energy."

"Aaron—real purpose of spinsaw?"

He hesitated. "To confuse . . ."

"No! That is a secondary purpose. Santiago?"

"To force us sideways, throw our front crescent shield toward the path of the whipping beam so that the other tway can get a straight shot into our side portals.''

"Correct. Grace—power source for the wands?"

"Thermal heat from the hand, pressure on the surface of the egg, plus rechargeable internal batteries.''

"Battery life?"

"A full ten minutes at constant power,'' she quoted.

"Yes. And since the Cohe is rarely turned on for an entire ten minutes, the actual life of the weapon is more in the neighborhood of twenty to thirty minutes, still far too long for us to take advantage of in combat.

"Aaron—Reemul holds the Cohe in which hand?"

"Both tways are right-handed.''

Gillian nodded. Reemul had given away that useful bit of information over two hundred years ago, in Boston.

He tried a more complex question. "Santiago, what tactic should we employ, taking advantage of Reemul's right-handedness and our goal of directionalizing him?"

Santiago stared straight ahead, lost in thought.

"Aaron?"

The pirate slowly shook his head. His sister broke into a smile.

"We should try," Grace began, "to come at the tway we are attacking from his right side. The hand that holds the wand is then exposed through the weak side portal of the web.''

"Excellent.'' Grace did have her redeeming qualities. In mental agility, she was probably the sharpest of the three.

"Santiago—what position should we avoid at all cost?"

"Never allow ourselves to come between the tways. Keep in motion so that both tways are always within our field of vision.''

"Aaron—what would you do if the rest of the team were killed, and you were knocked down and without weapons?"

"I would deactivate my crescent web and play dead.'' He paused. "Then I would die.''

Gillian nodded. "Probably. But the tactic is real, based on the actions of survivors. During combat, the Paratwa is operating at heightened awareness, its advanced neuromuscular system working at blinding speed. It registers the enemy in terms of motion and attacks all forms of movement. The possibility exists, however slight, that if the assassin were forced to quickly leave the scene of combat, a person playing dead might be taken for dead. That person could survive.''

He continued quickly, not wanting them to dwell on thoughts of defeat.

''Grace—what is our best terrain for combat?''

''Wide-open spaces. Such an environment gives us a better chance of keeping both tways within our field of vision.''

''Santiago—range of the Cohe wand?''

''At full power, about forty yards.''

Gillian yanked out his thruster and fired at Grace.

Jaws crunched, webs ignited. Grace jerked forward, met the blow. Aaron and Santiago spun on their heels, drew thrusters, fired at Nick and the astonished Pasha.

In a line, the three pirates, webs touching, sidestepped rapidly across the arena. Aaron and Santiago kept firing at the grinning Nick while Grace, in the fully protected center position of the line, shouted commands.

''Left! Hold! . . . Right! Faster! Left! . . . Hold!''

Grace kept up the string of orders, kept them gliding in tandem, making sure that Gillian never strayed from her peripheral vision. Nick swiveled his stool to keep his front crescent facing the barrage of thruster blasts from the two men.

Gillian halted the attack and lowered his weapon. ''All right. That was very good.''

Nick chuckled. Pasha Haddad allowed himself a faint smile.

Good indeed! thought Gillian. Haddad, their severest critic, was not easily impressed.

Gillian glanced at the wall clock. *Almost four hours since we started this session. It's my time to be alone.*

''We'll take a fifteen-minute break. When I return, we'll have another practice period with the wand. Your defensive tactics against thrusters are excellent, but you still need more work against my Cohe.''

Aaron grinned fiercely. "We look forward to that!"

Gillian left the arena. He walked rapidly through a twisting corridor to the room where he had spent the past four nights.

Spartan furnishings—a table, two chairs, and a cushioned airbed—broke the severity of the small darkened compartment. He closed the door, sat on the edge of the bed, and waited.

It came gradually, as it had every four hours for the past four days.

First, a delicate tingling, seemingly from within his skin. Then slices of memory, discrete fragments, dissolving into one another.

Fragments—places he had been, events he had experienced, all manner of ancient reality, all dripping with indescribable feeling.

And then they were gone. The memories whistled through awareness and vanished, losing themselves once again in the flux of his subconscious. He tried to hold on, tried desperately to cling to images representing a time when his thoughts and feelings were one and the same. But he could not retain them. As each memory dissolved, he felt a sense of loss and a grim recognition that he existed today as a mere shadow of what he had once been.

And finally, utterly predictable after four days of experiencing it, came the flash of golden light. This time, the bright light originated from his left side—a blinding instant of luminescence, then nothing, a return to normalcy—the bed, the chairs, the semidarkness of the small room.

The golden light burst from different locations each time, but other than that, the periodic eruptions remained identical. Once every four hours the sequence repeated. Even in sleep, he sensed the eruptions were occurring. Strange dreams, impervious to later recall, ended in showers of gold, like spring rains on a virgin forest.

A knock sounded. Nick opened the door, peeked in. "Is it over?"

Gillian nodded. The midget entered and closed the door behind him.

"Any different this time?"

Gillian shook his head. "The same."

Nick pushed one of the chairs closer to the bed and sat down.

Gillian folded his hands. "Do you think Jerem could have been right? He said it looked like I was having an epileptic fit."

Nick shrugged. "Possible, I suppose. Do you feel ready to visit a doctor yet?"

"No."

"The sensations that come before the light, the memories. You are totally unable to recall them?"

"Totally." He did not allow Nick to see how truly dismal that made him feel.

Nick spoke cautiously, almost stumbling over his words. "Any memories of . . . Catharine?"

"Not since the attacks started." Gillian allowed himself a smile. "So far, that seems to be the only blessing. I can almost think of her without growing depressed, or worse."

"Good. Any ideas about why these eruptions are happening?"

Gillian frowned. "Not really. And yet, I get the strangest feeling at times . . . hard to describe, really."

"Try."

"Well, it's just that . . ." He stopped, shook his head. "I don't know. I don't even know what the feeling is, not exactly. Something to do with what my life could have become, something to do with life in general, maybe. Life here in these Colonies.

"I guess it's a kind of displaced nostalgia. Catharine and I could have had a good life here in the Colonies. And yet . . . I don't know." He spread his arms. "Irrya! It's everywhere around us and it's so big. It's alive with possibilities we never had on Earth. And not just this Colony—the other cylinders, too. There's something different, a dispassion that allows for a kind of freedom we never had on Earth." He shrugged. "It's hard to explain."

Nick gave a slow nod. "And Sirak-Brath?"

Gillian's mood broke. He chuckled. "No, I guess there are exceptions to every rule. Sirak-Brath—that place is more like the Earth of our day."

"And you were getting ready to leave Sirak-Brath when you had the first attack."

Gillian nodded excitedly. "Yes! I hadn't thought of that."

Nick paused. "These attacks—any impairments in your functioning, either before or after they occur?"

"Not that I'm aware of."

Nick leaned back in his chair. "Then you'll just have to make sure that you're alone every four hours."

"That shouldn't be too difficult. The attacks only last for a few moments. No one will have to know."

"Just make sure you don't run into our Jeek friend at one of these four-hour intervals."

"I'll be careful."

They sat quietly for a time. Gillian's thoughts drifted to the training.

"Do you think they're doing well?"

Nick frowned.

"The pirates, I mean."

"Oh, yeah. Real well. They caught on to your training techniques even faster than the team did two centuries ago."

Gillian nodded. "Another week and I think we'll be ready."

"You can't take that long. Reemul might be back in stasis by then. Rome and I believe that the murder spree is almost over. If we risk waiting too long, we could lose our shot at the Jeek." Nick sighed. "We came up with a plan. Rome is going to implement it at today's Council meeting. We may be able to draw Reemul out into the open as early as tomorrow."

"Tomorrow? No, we're not ready. We won't be ready to face him."

"C'mon, Gillian! You know from experience that the fighters who were the easiest to train made the best team members. These pirates are naturals. They're fanatics, willing to die for a shot at Reemul! Aaron, Grace, and Santiago are ready."

Gillian shook his head. "We need more time."

"That's just an excuse. We both know the score here. You're the one who's going to do the real fighting. The team provides backup; they're flankers, nothing more. They're there to distract the Paratwa, give you the opportunity to kill it."

"This is no ordinary assassin we're going up against."

"That shouldn't matter."

"It does."

Nick folded his arms. "You honestly think that these pirates aren't ready?"

"Aaron and Santiago, perhaps. I still have my doubts about Grace."

Nick stared. "She seems very quick."

"She is. It's just that she may lose her discipline in a tight situation. She may allow her anger to overwhelm awareness. She could be a threat to our mission." He shrugged. "And with her brother fighting beside her . . . Well, if something happened to him, she might lose complete control."

"But that could happen the other way around, too. If Grace were killed, Aaron might go to pieces."

Gillian shook his head. "Aaron's too well disciplined."

"So is Grace."

He sighed. "I've had this argument before, Nick. I look at Grace and I see a woman who could destroy me."

Abruptly, the midget tensed. He shifted his weight in the chair. "What's wrong?"

Nick shook his head. "Nothing."

He's lying. I've never seen him look so agitated.

Nick took a long deep breath. "So what are your plans for Grace?"

"I guess she stays. If you say that we might have to confront the Jeek as early as tomorrow, I don't have much choice, do I?"

Nick appeared to study him for a long moment. When he spoke, his voice was barely a whisper. "No, you don't have any choice."

Nick's voice rose to normal volume as he quickly changed the subject. "Tell Aaron that I found out about Paula Marth and the boy. The Guardians are still holding them, but they've been transferred here to Irrya. The Guardians won't allow visitors yet. But Haddad is using his influence. He's at least certain they're being treated well."

Gillian hesitated. "By this time, the Guardians must know all about me. Jerem was along when I investigated the tavern killings in Sirak-Brath. He's bound to have talked. E-Tech may have some explaining to do."

Nick smiled. "Yes. In about an hour, I expect that Rome Franco will be confronted in the Council chambers by a very angry Artwhiler. I wish I could be there."

"You're not worried?"

"Do I look worried?" Nick's grin expanded. "You just reassure Aaron that everything is going well with his woman. Tell Aaron that Paula and Jerem will probably be released within a few days. And tell him also that I've spoken with the lion. Harry says that the tribunal gives full approval to, and I quote, 'E-Tech's assistance to Aaron's mission against an enemy of the Alexanders.' That's one way of putting it, I suppose."

"Harry?"

"Harry, the lion of Alexander." Nick grinned impishly. "He's still in Irrya. I've spoken with him several times since Friday night's party. Harry's an interesting old fellow. I believe you'd like him. We're having dinner together this evening."

"Did you find out anything more from him about those eleven murdered Costeaus? Aaron's been tight-lipped. He says that it's none of my business."

Nick shrugged. "The way I figure it, Bob Max, at Codrus's direction, passed a secret message to Reemul via the pirates. I believe the message contained a hidden code, ordering Reemul to destroy his benefactors. After all, these Costeaus had seen the Jeek naked, without disguises. The pirates would have run a medical examination. They had seen too much. They had to be killed.''

''And the torture?''

''Reemul was probably just being thorough. He wanted to make sure that no other pirates had witnessed his Wake-up. And knowing Reemul, there was probably a degree of pleasure involved in his actions.''

Nick hopped off the chair. ''I guess that's it. The Pasha and I are leaving for a while. I have to meet with Begelman. If you like, Haddad will send over one of his people to act as a practice dummy.'' The small face brightened. ''By the way, that was an interesting experience, being shot at. Remind me never to try it again!''

The midget winked, opened the door, and briskly strode out into the dimly lit corridor.

Gillian sat still for a moment, staring into the shadows.

I should have asked Nick about the second computer program. I forgot.

Actually that was not true. *I remembered it while he was sitting here.* But it no longer seemed so important.

Besides, Nick always had a tendency to play with information, to withhold crucial data until the last moment. He enjoyed pulling the strings—he probably had Rome and the Pasha half crazy by now.

The thought amused Gillian.

Still, it would be best to pry the information about the second program out of Nick's devious mind. Tomorrow, perhaps.

He straightened and stretched his arms almost to the drop ceiling.

And I'm keeping secrets, too. I didn't tell Nick that sometimes I find myself staring at Grace. Sometimes, if the lighting is right and the woman is wearing a certain expression, she reminds me of my dead love, Catharine.

Today, in this chamber, I am truly alone.

Rome sat stiffly in the Council chair, his fingers tapping a vague rhythm on the polished surface of the round table. The prism chandelier, set to its lowest illumination, hung like a glittering spider, spinning a web of beams into the far corners of the room. A Rockwell Kent illustration received barely enough light to distinguish faded colors. To its left, Van Gogh's cornfield lay within deep shadow.

The door opened; a blaze of corridor glow rushed in. Nu-Lin entered the chamber, followed by Drake.

"Fran-co!" She smiled in surprise. "The dark-ness does not become you."

Rome molded his cheeks into a smile and hoped that he did not appear too unnatural. "I was resting, preparing for the meeting. I've not been sleeping well lately."

Nu-Lin, Councillor of Intercolonial Affairs. Born 2243 on the Mann Strip of Leipzig Colony. A small family, parents and one sister, all deceased. Rose to rank of Governorship in 2278. Served six years, then emigrated to Irrya to assume high position in the Commerce League. Within three years, developed radical program leading to reorganization of the League and the breaking up of monopolistic interests within the Profarmers Union. In 2288, appointed Commerce League President and permanent representative to the Council of Irrya. Never married.

Drake flashed his hand at a wall sensor, brought the room illumination up to normal. "Hungry, Rome? Nu-Lin and I were about to order."

"Nothing, thank you."

"A stimulant perhaps? We'll need you alert at today's meeting."

Yes, I'm sure you will.

Drake moved his massive frame back into the corridor and yelled for a chef-servant. Nu-Lin sat down.

"Trou-bled?"

She was too clever to be fooled by his excuse about needing sleep. He shrugged. "Artwhiler—he could be a problem at today's meeting."

"Why?"

Rome lifted his head, met the regal chin, the gleaming blue eyes.

Cold eyes, he noted for the first time. Her face displayed warmth but the eyes betrayed her. They reminded him of the little ice droplets used to chill Pocono wine.

He felt himself grinning. *My imagination runs wild. Nick's suspicions have infested me.*

It couldn't be Nu-Lin.

She looked at him oddly for a moment. Then her features relaxed into a delicate smile. "Art-whil-er will not be a prob-lem. We have the votes to de-feat him."

Good. She misunderstands.

Drake returned and took his seat at the table. "Skewered lobster and rice, bathed in pineapple juice and flavored with misk."

"It sounds de-lec-ta-ble. I must al-low you the choice of lunch more of-ten, al-though I hope the in-take of misk re-quires no re-li-gious cer-e-mon-y."

Drake rumbled, "We won't tell Bishop Vokir of our sacrilege."

They laughed together. Rome felt a chill sweep up his spine. With effort, he contained the shudder.

I must control myself. No matter how difficult, I must act un-suspecting. If one of them is indeed an Ash Ock tway, it must not be alarmed.

Their laughter faded. Drake turned to Rome.

"I found your little friend intriguing, certainly a welcome addition to the Lady's party. Nicholas is possessed of a rich humor."

"He knows how to tell a joke." *Why does Drake talk about Nick?* The Councillor seldom initiated trivial discussions.

"I hope he's enjoying his stay in Irrya."

"Yes, he seems to be." *I must be careful not to place exaggerated value on innocent remarks. I'll drive myself crazy, seeking out hidden meanings in all manner of conversation.*

Drake adjusted the snake supporting his armrest terminal and began typing. His face blanked, as if turned off by a switch; the smile cauterized to an effigy in black stone.

His history is more complex than Nu-Lin's. There would have been even greater opportunity for a successful substitution. Drake, like Nu-Lin, was unmarried and had no living relatives.

Elliot Drake had been born in Irrya. He had begun his financial ascent as a private banking officer, a position that eventually led to an ICN appointment as an Accounts representative. But at that juncture, he had not risen any further within the organization; instead, he had, perhaps deliberately, begun moving laterally through the ICN's complex framework, achieving initial success as a loan analyst. Later, he became an Intercolonial Projects troubleshooter, traveling to over a hundred and thirty Colonies within a three-year period. His phenomenal performance at that job launched him directly to the ICN Directors' Board. In another four years he became their chairman.

The question remains—are Drake's talents those of a human being or of a Paratwa?

Artwhiler sailed into the chamber. His black and gold uniform, as neatly creased as ever, counterbalanced a face riddled with turmoil. A pace behind the Guardian Commander came a young chef-servant, carrying two covered bowls. Artwhiler took his seat as the boy carefully placed the bowls in front of Drake and Nu-Lin. Exiting quickly, the servant almost bumped into Lady Bonneville.

Today, the Lady wore a simple white dress. Her hair had not

changed since Friday evening. The bluish-gray bun still rested on her head like an inverted nest.

She beamed. "Dear me! I thought I was early!" She sat down beside Artwhiler.

Delicately, Drake uncovered his bowl and forked a tiny slab of lobster. He held the steaming portion under his nose for an inordinate moment. His huge mouth gaped, closed on the meat. He swallowed.

"Meeting is called to order."

Everyone waited. Drake forked another portion, repeating the ritual. Smiling coldly, he laid down the utensil.

"First item of business, the Paratwa problem." He turned to Artwhiler. "Have the Guardians made any progress?"

Artwhiler stood up and brushed a speck of lint from the front of his uniform. "We have many promising leads . . ."

"Of course, but have you made any real progress in finding a way to stop this monster?"

"My Guardians are working long hours," Artwhiler snapped. He took a deep breath and tried to calm himself.

"We have conceived a plan for which I need this Council's approval. When the beast strikes again, we intend to declare a total state of martial law. We would completely seal the affected Colony, stop all shuttle traffic, isolate the enemy. Then we would send several Guardian divisions into the quarantined cylinder—they would root out and destroy the Paratwa."

Nu-Lin glared at him. "That is ab-surd. What if the Co-lo-ny were large, Irr-ya, for in-stance? There are fif-teen to twen-ty million peo-ple here."

Lady Bonneville nodded in agreement. "Arty, you would probably just force this Paratwa underground. It would hide out until the quarantine was lifted. After all, the Sirak-Brath isolation was something less than successful. And to stop all shuttle traffic for a long period . . . goodness! You know the Colonies are highly interdependent. If trade were halted for any length of time, you could destroy a Colony's economic base.''

"The Com-merce League would nev-er stand for it."

"It's not feasible," agreed Drake.

Artwhiler barely contained his fury. "Raw force is the only way to stop this killer!"

Drake shook his head. "Four days ago, this creature walked into your Guardian station on Kiev Alpha and slaughtered dozens of your people. I don't believe that 'raw force,' as you put it, is a solution."

"You have a better plan?"

"I believe E-Tech has been on the right track. We should seek historically proven methods for fighting this Paratwa."

Artwhiler boiled. "The Colonies are not the same as Earth!"

Drake ignored him and turned to Rome. "I would like to see a joint investigation. E-Tech Security should be . . ."

"E-Tech Security has already been operating a secret investigation!" Artwhiler stormed.

It's coming, Rome thought. The first part of Nick's plan was unfolding.

Artwhiler spoke with disdain. "E-Tech has gone against the will of this Council from the start. Rome and Pasha Haddad have awakened a man from stasis—a man from the pre-Apocalypse, a killer who earned his living by slaying Paratwa!"

"An ex-cep-tion-al in-di-vid-u-al," Nu-Lin murmured.

Rome carefully observed the Councillors' reactions. He learned nothing. Nu-Lin, Drake, and Lady Bonneville all seemed surprised.

"Is this true?" asked Drake.

Rome hesitated. *I must appear unwilling to share this information.*

"Well?" demanded Artwhiler.

Rome nodded slowly. "We did awaken a man . . . an adviser." He expanded on the lie. "This man was brought from stasis before the Council removed E-Tech from the Paratwa investigation. It seemed best to take advantage of his knowledge.''

"Knowledge? Hah! E-Tech immediately released this killer into the Colonies. My Guardians discovered this man, this Gillian, on a pirate shuttle in Sirak-Brath, just after the Zell Strip murders. Also on that shuttle were the two witnesses to the Bob Max killing. I might add that those witnesses had been originally detained by E-Tech Security, from which they conveniently escaped!''

Rome shrugged. "You probably won't believe this, but Gillian also outwitted our surveillance. He's been acting mainly on his own.''

Artwhiler laughed harshly. "One of the witnesses informed us that Gillian entered the Zell Strip tavern immediately following the murders. Later, aboard the pirate shuttle, this hired killer gave my officers the private number to your office, Franco. *Your office!*''

Rome let out an audible sigh. "Gillian had my number, yes. But he was out of contact with E-Tech for a long period.''

"Lies!''

Drake frowned. "You disobeyed the decision of this Council?''

"If you wish to split hairs, yes. But E-Tech initiated no formal investigation into the Paratwa problem. We merely studied options. Gillian has acted almost entirely of his own volition. Pasha Haddad and I will swear to that.''

Artwhiler sneered. "Naturally!''

Hesitation entered Nu-Lin's speech. "You say that this Gil-li-an hunt-ed and killed Par-a-twa? I nev-er heard of such a thing.''

Rome came alert. *She probes for more information! Could she be the one?* His heart pounded. *I must stay calm. She asks a general question that demands a general response.*

"E-Tech located Gillian through our archives. We were researching Paratwa history. There had been rumors from centuries ago about a special team, trained to kill. Gillian says he was their leader . . . and the only survivor.''

"In-ter-est-ing.''

"Nonsense!" barked Artwhiler. "It would take scores of men to kill one of these beasts!"

"Gillian says he can do it. And I've seen his abilities demonstrated with weapons. He possesses great skill."

There—I've revealed what needed to be revealed. If Nick is right, and an Ash Ock indeed sits at this table, then I've just given it cause for alarm.

The Ash Ock will remember Gillian's secret team, Nick had said. *They will remember that little band of humans who, against all odds, hunted down and destroyed assassins from the deadliest breeds. A member of the royal Caste will not permit Gillian to survive. One more victim will be added to Reemul's list. But this time, the team will be ready. Gillian will be ready.*

In theory, the idea of using Gillian and the pirates as bait to draw Reemul out into the open seemed sound. But Rome found himself sharing some of Artwhiler's doubts.

Gillian and three pirates—could they really kill this assassin? Despite Nick's assurances, it did not seem possible. Reemul had butchered forty-four armed men and women on Kiev Alpha. And the Jeek's history abounded with even more terrifying examples of mass slaughter.

"Where is this Gillian right now?"

Lady Bonneville's words yanked Rome from his reverie. She wore an innocent expression but her question bristled.

I must answer, though I must again appear reluctant. And then he thought: *Lady Bonneville? Could she be the tway?*

He stared at his blank monitor screen. "Gillian is presently . . . within Irrya."

Nick had said: *It's only necessary to tell them what Colony he is in. That will be enough of a clue. Reemul will do the rest.*

Drake appeared to have lost his appetite. He shoved the unfinished bowl off to the side.

Lady Bonneville glanced at Artwhiler, who was still fuming. Then she turned back to Rome.

"Goodness! I sometimes wonder if we're not our own worst

enemies here in this chamber. I believe the ancient term for such behavior was cloak and dagger.''

Rome sank back into his chair. He folded his hands, pretended to be lost in thought. Finally he spoke.

''It's true that Gillian has been helping us, although, as I've said, he's acted mostly on his own. Nevertheless, technically, E-Tech has violated the Council's directive not to involve itself in the Paratwa investigation.

''However, I must point out that E-Tech recognized from the beginning that a Paratwa assassin was a far graver threat than this Council was willing to acknowledge. Thus, we acted accordingly.''

He switched on his monitor, read the prepared statement.

''At this time, I formally request that any E-Tech violation, past or present, in the matter of the Paratwa investigation, be relegated to chambers and that all such violations be summarily dismissed. I further request that E-Tech be immediately placed in full and complete authority for all present and future investigations into Paratwa-related matters.''

Artwhiler turned scarlet. He looked ready to explode.

Lady Bonneville frowned. ''Your requests are a bit extreme.''

''Agreed,'' said Drake. ''You cannot seriously expect this Council to grant carte blanche to E-Tech.''

''I can and do expect it.''

''I be-lieve we are be-ing threat-ened.''

Drake hesitated. ''You would defy this Council?''

Rome spoke calmly. ''I would go before the freelancers and announce that this Council has hindered the natural course of the Paratwa investigation from the beginning. I would point out the historical rationale for E-Tech to be in charge of such matters. We would, with popular support, launch our own investigation, fully independent of this Council.''

Rome met Drake's cold stare. ''E-Tech would also call for an immediate Senate inquiry to look into the actions of this Council regarding the matter of the Paratwa's awakening. We would point out certain curious connections between ICN loans, the West Yemen Corporation, and Bob Max. La Gloria de la Ciencia's role in this affair would also be closely examined.''

Drake reached across the table and retrieved his bowl. He dug in, wolfing down a huge glob of rice.

Rome smiled. He found himself deriving pleasure in seeing Drake so upset. *The ICN is not accustomed to being thwarted. Drake has gotten his way for too long.*

Abruptly, the huge Councillor laid down his fork. Cold eyes panned the table, halted on Artwhiler.

"The Guardians must acknowledge this request."

"Request?" Artwhiler spluttered. "This is absurd! We are not going to end our investigation because E-Tech demands it!"

"But your in-ves-ti-ga-tion has been a com-plete and ut-ter fail-ure."

Artwhiler stood up. His hands shook. "This . . . Council . . . has . . . no . . . right . . ."

"We have every right," said Drake. "I call for an immediate vote to honor E-Tech's formal request. Lady Bonneville?"

The Lady stared at Rome, nodded her head.

"Nu-Lin?"

"I vote yes."

Artwhiler stormed from the chamber.

Rome thought, *Drake understands political necessity. He sees the choices and he makes the decisions.*

"I hope Arty doesn't do anything rash," offered Lady Bonneville.

"He won't," said Drake.

Artwhiler would be in a rage for weeks, but the Guardian Commander would not defy a Council vote. Not when he realized popular support—and Drake—were against him.

"The Paratwa is now E-Tech's responsibility," Drake announced. A grim smile twisted the corners of his mouth. "Let us hope you can do a better job than the Guardians."

We will, Rome thought. *E-Tech had a secret helper.* Even if

Gillian failed, the Ash Ock would arrange for E-Tech to end the threat of Reemul.

The meeting had gone much as Nick anticipated.

The Councillors will understand E-Tech's boldness, Nick had said. *They will understand the relationship between the killings and E-Tech's huge popularity gains. Some of them will be puzzled as to why this crazed assassin has directed its attacks against E-Tech. But they will consider it inevitable that your organization, suppressed for so long, will take advantage of the situation, make strong demands, flex new muscles.*

Codrus, too, will understand. He will be pleased that his plan is working and that E-Tech is again becoming a strong force within the Council. Hopefully, Codrus will not suspect that we are aware of his presence.

Rome had doubts about that. But Nick had been right so far.

"Next item of business," said Drake, turning to Nu-Lin. "A brief update on Commerce League trade sanctions against the pirates."

Rome thought, *Yes, I have doubts. But those doubts pale beside the righteousness of my anger.*

He stared coldly at the three remaining Councillors. *And I swear by E-Tech that if a Paratwa sits within this Council, I will see an end to its manipulations.*

Bishop Vokir's overture for an evening of solitude had been translated by the priests into ecclesiastical demand. Throughout the Church, the offices and meeting halls had been emptied; even the night maintenance techs had been routed from their bedrooms, driven to other accommodations. All doors had been sealed and code-locked.

From the back of the chapel, the Bishop drew a deep breath and smoothed his robes. Adopting an expression of grim disapproval, he stalked down the main aisle toward the altar. Distant gray-blue slabs—nightlights mounted from the ceiling—cast a muted glow across the front of the chancel. Reemul waited beneath the steel lectern, silhouetted against the gently wafting curtain of shiny misk hoses.

Both tways wore braided long-sleeved pullovers: one red, one white with pale stripes. Shuttle pants, hot pink, drooped from their waists like airbags and vanished into heavy mushboots. The shorter tway, in red, leaned against the lectern, playing with a darkened jewel light on one of the feeder tubes. The other tway stood with his head raised, the nipples of a half-dozen misk hoses jammed obscenely into his mouth. He grinned in the semidarkness, looking like some kind of pale white demon hanging from the ceiling.

The Bishop halted ten feet away. He tried to imagine the Church hysteria that would result if one of the priests entered the chapel right now. The misk tubes were sacred; they were suckled upon only by worshipers during formal services. Misk was the very lifeblood of the Church of the Trust. Reemul, with the tubes in his mouth, was guilty of one of the worst forms of desecration.

"You're making this very difficult," said the Bishop. "We could have met in my office."

The shorter one came forward. "I grow weary of repeated experiences."

The Bishop stared into the sad soft eyes, nodded slowly. "You fear treachery. I could have prepared my office, set traps. That is what you think."

The eyes pretended to smile. "My. You're so distrustful. Why would I think that, dear Bishop?"

The Bishop hesitated, read the menace in Reemul's words. *I should not have criticized him so harshly for the Sirak-Brath killings. That criticism, combined with Codrus's demand that he re-*

turn to stasis, has pushed him to the edge of a critical mode. I must be cautious. He could kill me if I say the wrong thing.

"I'm glad you could come to Irrya so quickly," the Bishop offered.

Baggy red sleeves came together. The tway clapped his hands once in mock delight, then stuck out his tongue and licked at the air. The taller one, mouth crammed with feeder tubes, managed a distorted chuckle.

The Bishop continued quickly. "We have much to talk about. New factors have come to light. I may have to ask you to perform an extra kill."

Red arms flayed. The tway came up on the balls of his feet, pranced forward. "Oh, my! I'm to be allowed an extra kill! I won't be put back in stasis quite so . . . soon. My. Thrills! You are so generous, Bishop."

He might kill me no matter what I say. The Bishop felt no personal fear, just a sense of illogic at the possibility of his own death. *I must defuse his anger, guide him away from the critical mode.*

"This extra kill. You may find it especially interesting."

The tway sneered. But a vein of curiosity exposed itself: two sets of eyes scanned the Bishop's face.

The Bishop turned, gazed at the massive chrome pipes that backdropped the altar and curved upward to become the chapel ceiling. He forced a smile, allowed humor to tinge his words.

"There is a man, an old acquaintance of yours. Let's see. If memory serves me correctly, you last met him in a Boston tavern, two hundred years ago."

Reemul froze.

"Think hard. You may recall."

"If you are testing me . . ."

"Reemul!" The Bishop pointed his finger at the shorter tway. "I do not test you! I have never found the need to test my most effective weapon! I say to you that one of E-Tech's soldier-hunters survived the fire in Boston that night. This man went into stasis. Like you, he has now been awakened.''

The shorter tway lowered his arms, fell into repose. For an instant, the Bishop thought Reemul was going to attack—a Jeek at rest mirrored a Jeek poised for assault. But the moment passed. Subtle tensions departed.

The critical mode is repressed. He is stable again.

"Is it possible," asked the Bishop, with as much innocence as he could muster, "that one of those soldier-hunters survived?"

Both tways nodded. The taller one spit the misk tubes from his mouth. They swung against the other hoses, set the entire curtain rattling.

"Their leader."

"He was trapped by the fire," continued the shorter tway.

"I thought the flames got him . . ."

". . . but perhaps not."

The Bishop hid his anger, responded calmly. "It's probable that he's put together a new team. They're here in Irrya."

So, Reemul. You knew that this man could have survived the fire, yet you failed to inform me of the possibility.

Reemul the fool! Your pride distorts your good sense. You could not admit that you might have failed in your mission. And so you fed false information to an Ash Ock!

The Bishop breathed deeply, forced calm. *And the Sirak-Brath incident? Do you hold back more data from me?*

He kept his voice free of criticism. "Regarding the Zell Strip killings—you claim you were forced to defend yourself. Could you have left signs, exposed your real identity?"

Both tways laughed.

The Bishop translated. *He's not sure. He may have given away the fact that he's a Jeek Elemental, a breed known for serving the royal Caste. In one act of madness, Reemul may have shattered his carefully arranged masquerade as an assassin from Terminus labs. Rome Franco and E-Tech may actually suspect the presence of an Ash Ock!*

It was a sobering thought.

Codrus may have to make drastic changes in the plan.

The Bishop folded his hands to hide his tension.

"Tomorrow, I want you to set a trap for this man. Do it in such a way that his team is forced to come to you."

Reemul nodded.

"Kill his team. Kill all witnesses. But this man from the past, I want you to take him alive. Use whatever methods you deem appropriate. I need information from this individual. I must learn the extent of E-Tech's knowledge regarding us."

Reemul hesitated, then grinned. The Bishop acknowledged a new concern.

"It will be difficult, yes?"

In tandem, the tways shrugged. The taller one spoke.

"This man—he was skilled in the use of the Cohe. He'll be hard to capture. I may have to kill him."

The Bishop nodded slowly. So be it. There were other sources of information.

Perhaps E-Tech's Security Chief, Pasha Haddad, could be taken. Tortured and murdered by a Paratwa, Haddad would make a fine martyr. Codrus would get his information and the Ash Ock cause would be advanced in the bargain.

"Do what you must," said the Bishop. "But if by some means you can take this man alive, drain him. Learn everything—his past, his relationship to pre-Apocalypse E-Tech leaders. I want to know who put him into stasis and who awakened him." The Bishop hesitated. "And find out if he knows anything about a friend of Rome Franco's. A midget."

Reemul grinned. The taller tway grabbed a single misk tube and inserted it between his lips. He sucked deeply.

"Is it addictive?" asked the shorter tway.

The Bishop frowned, caught off guard by Reemul's sudden change of subject. "The misk? No, it's not addictive. Just a mild barbiturate, mixed with spices."

"It tastes like something Sappho would have created."

344

"She was responsible for some of its flavorings." *This is not the first time he has mentioned Sappho. Why?*

Delicately, the tways moved together. They reached out and held hands. They spoke in stereo.

"She was very creative. She understood the flows between levels of my spirit."

The Bishop studied the Jeek. *I've never heard him speak this way before.*

"She understood the simplicities. She made me . . . understand my needs."

Was there some connection between Sappho and Reemul that I never knew about?

The Bishop felt an intense pressure grip his muscles.

The whelm!

In his final moments of awareness, the Bishop realized what was happening. The interlace, glistening with power, was forming without his or his tway's consent. An unconscious recognition by the Bishop was forcing Codrus to arise and abstract the Bishop's melange of data into concrete theory. And the superior conceptual abilities of Codrus was forcing the Bishop and his tway to interlace. It was a dialectic unique to the Ash Ock.

And this whelm was even more unusual. Generally, it could only be brought about during one of the Ash Ock's regulated flexing periods; even then, the whelm usually required the presence of a life-threatening situation.

Codrus completed the interlace, reveled briefly in his wholeness. He stared out through the Bishop's eyes.

Spirit of the Caste! How could I have been so blind? How could I not have seen it?

Sappho had taken Reemul as a lover!

During the final days, Sappho had sexually linked with many of the assassins. On a purely sensual level, he understood her antics. But Sappho's impulses usually had deeper roots. Why she had seduced Reemul, Codrus could not begin to fathom.

The Jeek's motives, however, were clear.

"Ahh, Reemul. I see that you have a desire. But your desire is such that only a long sleep can bring the possibility of fulfillment. Do you agree?"

The tways released hands, pulled away from each other. The taller one withdrew the misk hose from his mouth and carefully laid it against the other tubes. He narrowed his eyes and stared at the Bishop.

Yes, my Jeek. You perceive that you are no longer speaking to Bishop Vokir.

Codrus continued. "Do you wish to meet Sappho again?"

"I am not sure," said the shorter one. There was real doubt on his face.

"I suspect that she desires you again. There have been hints." *And until now, I never perceived them as such! Ahh, Sappho. Were you being shrewd or merely playful?*

The shorter tway argued. "She may not be worth a long sleep."

Codrus laughed, making sure that the display of humor was strictly limited to the Bishop. His Councillor-tway was in a public place right now—open emotions could not be shared.

"Not worth it! Reemul, you speak in circles. A spiritual profluence marks the Jeek Elementals. You deny your own destiny!" And Codrus thought: *He has no choice, of course. He's different from the others.*

"I am really beginning to enjoy the Colonies," boasted the taller tway. "Such opportunities!"

"Reemul, they would kill you eventually. It might take years, but sooner or later they would develop the desperate courage. Time would be your enemy.

"Go into stasis peacefully. Befriend time. Awaken into an age where you will be afforded your rightful glory. For when you emerge, the royal Caste will be there to honor you. Sappho will be there to honor you."

The Jeek laughed. "You twist words, Codrus. You do it most beautifully."

"Truth cannot be twisted. Sappho will be there."

Codrus observed subtle hesitation on the Jeek's faces. He pressed. "And you will not return to stasis unfulfilled. The Colonies will suffer a final outrage. Five days from now, you will flex—with all the potency at your command! You will enter the Irryan Senate building here in Irrya and you will destroy as many of the Senators as possible. There are six hundred forty-two of them, Reemul, plus guards and civilians." He smiled. "That should be enough of a flex to satisfy even you. And remember, you will be destroying not just humans but an entire power structure of their civilization. For as long as they record history, they will remember the Senate Massacre of 2307. You will become legend!"

The sad-eyed tway hissed and stuck out his tongue. The taller one danced forward, pirouetting, his hands swishing through the air.

Good. I have excited him. The crisis point has been passed. Reemul will now go willingly back to stasis. I have infected him with the dream of the Second Coming. Like all of us, he now senses a future grander than the present.

It was a good time to add a positive reinforcer.

"Reemul—I almost forgot. That package you desire. It's been picked up from Urikov's warehouse on Sirak-Brath. It arrived in Irrya this afternoon, on one of the regular Church transports.

"Where would you like it sent?"

Reemul's eyes betrayed his lust.

Was sex with Sappho as exciting? Codrus wondered. *How does an Ash Ock compare to one of your little monstrosities?*

The taller tway stopped dead in his tracks, like a robot with a burned-out power supply. A hot smile creased its face.

"Send the package to the Skeibalis Inn here on Irrya."

Codrus nodded. "Naturally, you will properly dispose of your little treat." Reemul's perversion was not unique—even some humans suffered the lusts of pedobiparauterophilia. But the Jeek's toy could give E-Tech another trail to follow. It was best if the evidence were destroyed.

"There will be a fire," said Reemul.

"Good. And when you have crushed E-Tech's little band of warriors, contact the Bishop. He will arrange for you to stay in one of the Church's retreats here in Irrya until it's time for your most glorious act."

Reemul, sensing his audience was over, ambled out the side doors on opposite sides of the chancel. Codrus waited until he heard the click of the code-locks resealing the portals. Then he closed the Bishop's eyes and allowed his prime concerns to erupt.

Fact: I did not know Sappho and Reemul were lovers.

Fact: I did not suspect Reemul of withholding information from me.

Fact: Recently, I have made drastic mistakes with the ICN.

Fact: during the final days, I may have grossly underestimated the intelligence of E-Tech. They may have been more aware of the royal Caste than I ever acknowledged.

I grow more stupid with each passing year. I was not created to spend most of my life as two separate creatures. I am Codrus, Ash Ock of the royal Caste.

Yet by serving our cause, I must deny my true existence, allowing only rare moments of monarchical consciousness.

Prolonged separation is a disease. Like a human male, denied feminine companionship over a long period, I suffer a dissipation of wisdom. Intellect loses its keen edge.

He opened the Bishop's eyes. *And next will come self-pity. That cannot be allowed.*

The Bishop must make another journey to the Earth's surface. As soon as possible, I must confer with Sappho and Theophrastus. I must call on their wisdom to make up for the loss of my own.

He felt a stab of jealousy. *They are the lucky ones. They live the way an Ash Ock was meant to live. They are forever free to be complete, their vision unmarred by constant duality. Do they understand my suffering? Do they empathize with the sacrifices I have made?*

—from *The Rigors*, by Meridian

One evening, upon emerging from a flexing chamber, I encountered a young Paratwa. She was an Ash Joella—one of the new breeds—sixteen years old, a squat redhead and a tall nordic blonde, both tways garbed in plain white coveralls. She was in charge of the human cleanup crew: eight men and women carrying body bags, waiting patiently for her command.

"You are Meridian." There was a trace of defiance in her words. She snapped her fingers and the cleanup crew scurried past us and into the chamber. I heard them grunt and mutter as they began the thankless task of disposing of the humans I had cut apart with my Cohe.

"Was it a good flex?" she asked.

"It was," I replied. "Several of them fought well. Had they not been criminals, I would have seen to it that they were honored throughout the domiciles."

"Do you always flex against humans?"

I nodded, marking the criticism in her voice. "You disapprove?"

"No. Humans must understand that they will be killed if they break our laws. And the flexing chamber is dual-efficient. Not only is sentence carried out, but one of us is allowed to satiate our natural urges."

I smiled. The source of her displeasure was now clear. "You have not yet been permitted the luxury of the flexing chamber."

"I have not," she said bitterly. "When it's my time, they send me to a forest to kill rabbits!"

"Patience, young one. Someday you will be allowed the richer joys."

For a moment, she was silent. And then: *"They say that the great Meridian has even flexed against other Paratwa."*

Had this female been more mature, I would have placed myself on the alert. There was a hint of challenge in her sarcasm.

"Yes. I have flexed against other Paratwa."

"They say that none here could defeat you."

Attuned to her thoughts, I laughed.

"They say that only one Jeek ever had the power to withstand you in open combat . . . perhaps even destroy you."

"Who could that be?" I mocked.

"The liege-killer—Reemul!"

Humans began emerging from the chamber, dragging body bags. They dumped them into a large six-wheeled disposal cart.

I understood, of course. The young needed their heroes, their rebels. To the Paratwa who had never known him, Reemul symbolized a wild sort of freedom. His actions were legendary. He was their myth; a counterweight to the reality of their structured lives.

I smiled. *"May I tell you something about the Reemul I have known?"*

She tried to disguise her excitement, failed. *"Of course."*

"He was insane."

For a long moment, she stared at me. Then she whirled around and began yelling at one of the humans.

"You! Hurry up with that trash! We haven't got all day! Work a little faster or next time your friends will be putting you into bags!"

Disappointed, I turned and walked away. If she had laughed in my face, or at least challenged my statement, I would have understood. But she had taken my appraisal of Reemul at face value.

I sometimes wonder what we're going to do with these new Paratwa.

Santiago killed the headlights and squeezed their hardtop up against a curb two blocks from the address. The black pirate stepped out into the barren street. He extended his legs and twisted his lanky frame into a rapid series of deep knee-bends. Gillian dismounted onto damp sidewalk.

Down here, at the southernmost end of Irrya's seventy-mile length, where boulevards terminated or became stretches of alley, a fine cool mist hung in the air, condensing on the windshields of scattered parked cars. Squat dirty buildings and stunted pine trees, the latter bent wickedly as if by disease, rose from the edges of vacant lots. Few people roamed the dark streets. Halfway up the block, a skinny woman in tight pants, gazing suspiciously at Gillian and Santiago, slithered along the windowless facade of a three-story warehouse.

Abruptly, the woman broke into a run, disappearing into a grimy modular apartment. Gillian supposed she felt safer inside.

Two thousand feet away, dominating the vista, stood the wall, the southern end of the Colony, the cessation of this inner world.

Santiago finished his warm-up. The pirate separated the velcro strip on his baggy vest and yanked out his gun. Gillian reached into the front pouch of his own windbreaker, encountered dryness and the soft plastic handle of a high-powered thruster. Satisfied with its placement, he withdrew his hand and examined the Cohe nestled in its slip-wrist holster beneath his baggy right sleeve.

"A real slum down here, huh?" Santiago grunted, replacing his thruster. "And the Irryans say it don't exist and the freelancers spout the lie across the spectrum. Everybody thinks Irrya is the perfect Colony."

Gillian merely nodded. "I've never been this close to the end of a cylinder." His words sounded odd, muffled by the damp air.

On a few clear days, he had seen the north and south poles from E-Tech headquarters. But at such distances, the vista provided little inspiration. Down here, the southern plate, six miles in diameter, a shadowy gray monstrosity laced with feeder pipes and pockmarked with small industries, created more blatant psychic demands.

He could almost imagine himself on Earth, standing at the base of a soaring cliff that drew his sight ever upward until vision and sheer rock plunged together into the clouds.

But there were no clouds here, only the mist—a purplish flatness to the air, nearly invisible, distorting the light from Irrya's other livable strips, blending the distant illumination into soft glowing patches as if eyesight were perpetually out of focus. Alternate sunstrips remained black depths, huge slabs of nothingness. Only the massive southern wall held the vista together, capturing the starless voids and the glowing patches of light and fusing them into a whole.

Santiago smeared the condensing moisture off his forehad.

Gillian said, "I didn't know there was rain scheduled for today."

"No rain. In the big cylinders, it's always wet at the poles."

"Why?"

"I don't know. Something to do with air currents, I suppose."

About three miles up the face of the giant wall, near the center, a wreath of hazy yellow lights ringed a series of bulging spires. It looked like an ancient circus tent seen from high above.

Santiago followed his gaze. "That's Irrya's main freefaller hotel. I was there once, a long time ago. I had a silky, but it wasn't all that great. I like to feel some weight when I'm fucking. You can't feel anything in zero G."

Gillian activated his neck transmitter. "Aaron? Grace?"

Aaron's voice sounded clear in Gillian's earclip. "We're in position—about a block and a half east of the address."

"Good. Pasha?"

Haddad spoke calmly. "My people are ready. We have forty units within a twelve-block radius of you. The nearest public shuttle ports are covered. The point teams still have nothing to report."

E-Tech Security had placed the building under distant surveillance. For the past two hours there had been no outside activity—no one had been seen entering or leaving.

We hunt Reemul and he hunts us, Gillian mused. *He sets the trap and we walk into it, knowing it to be a trap. In theory, that gives us the advantage.*

He motioned to Santiago. "Let's do it."

"Good luck," said the Pasha, in a tone of complete indifference.

Santiago poked a hand under his vest and gripped his thruster. They began walking down the street toward the southern wall, toward the address.

"I hope this is it," Santiago muttered. "I don't think I can take another false alarm."

Gillian shrugged. Tonight was the third time that Nick had ordered the team out. It almost seemed like an eternity since he and Nick had sat together in the training gym, discussing the nature of his periodic imagery attacks. That discussion had taken place only yesterday.

Gillian's attacks—intense memories juxtaposed with lost feelings—still slammed through his awareness every four hours. Each attack still culminated in the familiar flash of golden light.

And I'm getting too used to them. The imagery has created some sort of dialectic within me. I am becoming morbidly fascinated by the attacks, looking forward to these brief plunges through my own dissipated dream world.

After this is over—after Reemul has been dealt with—I'll have to see a doctor. I can't spend the rest of my life being mentally blasted six times a day.

A harsh whisper sounded in his earclip. "Gillian of E-Tech," mocked Aaron. "Reassure us. Tell us again that this beast is not simply waiting to blow us into the vacuum."

Santiago laughed. Gillian allowed himself a smile.

"Reemul will want to kill me face to face. I'm sure of it. He won't use explosives, at least not while we're alive.

"Now—no more talk. He may have planted audio bugs outside the building. He may be listening for us." Remote sensors were unlikely, but it was best to be on the safe side.

Two false alarms. This morning they had entered a deserted shipper's terminal and this afternoon, a rundown restaurant catering to Irryan smugglers.

Twice we have gone into buildings expecting to find Reemul waiting for us. Twice we have found nothing.

Scores of reported Paratwa sightings had been pouring into E-Tech every day. The Guardians, no doubt, had also received their fair share. All were investigated. Most reports originated with good citizens who mistook their new neighbors for the Paratwa assassin. A few sightings were the work of cranks.

Nick was now coordinating all reports through E-Tech. He was operating under the assumption that among the sightings that had come in since Wednesday's Council meeting, when Rome Franco had revealed Gillian's presence, one would be a trap set by the Jeek. Nick's screening process had produced the two sightings they had investigated thus far. The less likely prospects had all been turned over to Haddad for regular investigation.

He and Santiago rounded a corner and stopped. The address was halfway down the block, nestled between two other decrepit buildings. The Skeibalis Inn: four stories tall; craggy white exterior reflecting the pale light from a pair of streetlamps. A warm glow came from behind a panelshade on the third floor. All the other windows were dark.

Aaron and Grace came into view at the far end of the block.

Gillian and Santiago activated their crescent webs, accelerated to a trot. Aaron and Grace, approaching from the opposite direction, also picked up speed.

Gillian registered the empty street, allowing details to saturate awareness, subconsciously searching for any datum that looked out of place. The block whispered no obvious clues. Before them, the southern wall, closer and more gargantuan than ever, seemed to breathe the cool mist down onto the area, washing dark buildings under a spray of fine blue particles.

I have thirty-five minutes, Gillian thought. *Plenty of time until my next imagery attack.*

He drew his thruster. Santiago drew his. Down the block, the siblings followed suit.

Gillian felt a sudden excitement—a sense of boyish wonder at the fine blue mist, the monstrous wall, at the brother and sister now only thirty paces away, coming on fast, in step, Aaron's face a mask of determination, Grace stone cold.

Excitement peaked. *She looks like Catharine . . . the way she strides, the soft flush beneath her cheeks, the flared eyebrows, the furrowed brow.*

This is it!

He snapped his wrist, felt the Cohe splat against his open palm, needle projecting.

This is it! There were no outright clues but he knew—certainty shot through his body like a scream. Senses, hyperalert, transmuted a rich gelatin of information into a clear profile.

Reemul! It's his kind of place, his medium. He's here!

"This is it!" Gillian hissed. "I'm sure of it!"

The four of them came together outside the entrance. Red lightning flashed as their crescent webs struggled, repelled. They moved forward as one, slammed against the thick door, Gillian flicking the Cohe, black energy shearing off the hinges, feeling it crush inward with a groaning of metal. They burst into the lobby of the Skeibalis Inn.

Three men. One behind the counter—a desk clerk. The second—a tall freefaller in black adjustor suit with tight gray helmet, sun visor hiding his eyes, seated on a bench to the right of the clerk, motionless. The third—an older man, on the floor of the small rectangular lobby, on his back, grunting with the exertion of sit-ups.

"Thirty-four," panted the older man, ignoring their intrusion, raising his chest, palms locked behind his balding head, slamming elbows into kneecaps. "Thirty-five," he groaned.

"What the hell's this!" screeched the bearded desk clerk, coming out from behind the wooden counter. His right hand clutched a sandram.

Aaron pointed his thruster at the clerk's head; Grace and Santiago aimed their weapons up the dark stairwell off to the left; Gillian kept his eyes on the silent freefaller and on the doorway behind the counter.

"What the hell do you think you're doin'!" screamed the clerk, raising his sandram.

"Put it down," warned Aaron quietly, "or I'll vacuum your brains."

The clerk came up on the balls of his feet, hesitated. He lowered his arm, dropped the weapon. It hit the carpet with a dull thud.

"Thirty-six," huffed the old man, obviously nearing his limit. He lay on his back for a moment, struggling for breath.

Gillian pointed the Cohe toward the old man. *We crash into a building and this crazy keeps doing exercises!*

"Get up."

The old man jerked his chest off the floor. "Thirty-seven," he wheezed.

Grace, eyes on the stairway, risked a quick glance over her shoulder. "He's an ignor—look at his eyes. He's out of touch."

"Yeah," said the clerk arrogantly. "He's just an old ignor. So take what you want and get the hell out and leave us alone."

"We're here for the Paratwa," said Gillian.

The clerk froze, eyes riveted to the Cohe needle protruding from Gillian's fist.

"Someone called E-Tech," Gillian barked. "This person reported that a Paratwa was living in this building. Was it you?"

The clerk licked his lips. "Hey, there were these two guys. I reported 'em, sure. They were weird, all right. Never sayin' nothing to each other but always looking like they know what the other one's thinkin'. It was spooky. Sure, I reported 'em." He held up his hand. "Hey, look—no trouble, all right? I don't know anything about this, you know? If they come back . . ."

"When did they leave?" demanded Gillian.

"Hey, I don't know. Early this afternoon, I think. They're never here much anyway. Always in, then right out again."

Aaron pointed his thruster at the tall freefaller who sat calmly against the wall. "Is that right?"

The freefaller twisted his head to face Aaron. The heavy shield cloaked his eyes, but the faint outline of a nose and mouth were just visible above the breathing vents, where the translucent plastic came closest to his flesh.

Another ignor? Gillian wondered.

The semimechanical suit, dull black rubber on the outside, with an inner layer of sensors to translate body motion into amplified energy, rustled in the chair. Gillian recalled Nick telling him about freefallers—men born and raised in zero G, shuttle gypsies, nearly helpless in the full gravity of the Colonies. The adjustor suits provided some compensation for their complex physical, and psychological, weaknesses.

"Is he an ignor?" Gillian snapped at the clerk.

"Hey, he's my brother, all right? He ain't no ignor! He just don't like to talk to strangers, all right? So let him alone."

An ignor. The clerk's too ashamed to admit it. Gillian motioned to Aaron. "Do it."

The pirate leaned over, rammed a tiny needle into the freefaller's neck, at a spot where the material of the adjustor suit was extremely thin. Gillian kept his thruster aimed at the worried clerk.

"Hey! What the hell are you doing?"

The freefaller's head dropped forward as the drug took effect. Aaron crossed the lobby, stabbed a second needle into the old man's arm.

"Thirty-eight," puffed the old man. His eyes glazed over. He collapsed into slumber.

"Just a stasis needle," Gillian assured the clerk. "They'll be asleep for a few hours."

The clerk raised his hand. "Hey, you can't give me one of those! I get a reaction to stasis drugs. It might kill me, I swear! I mean, tie me up or somethin', but don't give me no . . ."

"Relax," said Gillian. "You're coming with us. We want to see the room where the two men have been living."

The clerk licked his lips, stared at the unhinged lobby door. "Hey, what if they come back?"

"Don't worry," said Aaron. "We have people watching this building."

Gillian grabbed the clerk's arm, pulled him to the stairwell. "You have the key?"

The clerk nodded. "Yeah, I got it. Christ, stop pushing me!"

They moved up the steps as a group, the clerk out in front, Santiago marching backward covering their rear, protective webs humming loudly in the dark firewell, red sparks dancing as crescents occasionally touched. They passed the second-floor firedoor, headed up the next flight. The clerk led them out into the third-floor corridor, a dank graffiti-splattered shaft terminating forty feet away against a supporting I-beam. The hallway fronted four rooms, two doors on either side.

The clerk pointed to the first door on the left, whispered, "That's it."

Gillian nudged his thruster into the man's back. "You first."

The clerk hesitated, then pulled a tiny keypad chain from around his neck, typed 3A-open, moved to the door, smacked the keypad onto the modem plate. There was a sharp click as the door slid back.

Gillian leaped through the portal, twisting, shifting his crescents from side to side, making himself a difficult target, weapons ready to fire at the slightest motion.

Nothing.

Aaron and Grace tumbled in behind him. Santiago pushed the clerk into the room, keeping his thruster aimed at the bearded face.

The room was a twenty-foot square lit by drop ceiling panels. A solitary window fronted the street. The bathroom/kitchen cubicle was as tiny as the one Gillian had lived in on Sirak-Brath. The cubicle was open. *Empty*.

A lump on the bed, under the covers.

A pair of hot pink shuttle pants lay over the back of the room's only chair. A dresser, steel-gray, scratched and dirty, huddled in the far corner. Next to the king-sized airbed, a large plastic shipping crate, its top missing, spouted a series of thin tubes that trailed under the white sheets, into the lump.

Grace pointed to the bed. "A body?"

Gillian frowned, crossed the room. Inside the shipping crate, the thin tubes coiled together, shafted into a gray box with display monitor and indicator lights. He recognized the machine—a portable life-support system.

Carefully, he drew back the white sheets, exposed the pale elfin face of a young girl, maybe five years old. Her eyes were shut and her face looked pained. The tubes of the life-support system ran into a discolored patch of skin beneath her left armpit. Gillian pulled the covers the rest of the way down, already knowing what he was going to find.

As he exposed the monstrosity, Grace let out a tiny cry. Aaron cursed.

Directly beneath the sternum, the tiny girl began to grow wider, began to divide in half. Her torso split into two sets of hips, two discrete crotches, four tiny dangling legs. Three of the legs looked broken. Both vaginas were torn and bloody. She was barely alive.

"This Paratwa beast!" Grace spluttered. "It deserves a fate worse than death!"

Gillian reached into the crate, switched off the mutated girl's life-support functions, allowed the pathetic creature to die quickly.

He had seen such perversion before. In the rampant madness of the final days, both Paratwa and humans had practiced this particular degradation. The sickness had even acquired a name— pedobiparauterophilia, an appetite for freak children with twin vaginas.

"My," said the clerk. "I guess he likes them between one and two."

Gillian registered the slight change in the clerk's tone, knew— in one horrible instant—that they had been tricked.

"It's a trap!" he cried, turning, raising his Cohe, seeking a target, knowing that he was too late.

The drop ceiling exploded in a blinding shower of light, dust, and splintered tiles. The second tway plunged from above—a spread-eagled demon—thruster screeching, black light whittling the air. The tway crashed onto the bed beside the freak girl, somersaulted violently across the room, legs extended, slamming into Aaron's chest at the same instant black light bit through the pirate's shoulder. Aaron's face recorded a moment of utter shock. Then he flew backward through the window and vanished into darkness.

Gillian hit the floor, whipped his Cohe up at the clerk. The beam dissolved harmlessly into the tway's front crescent. The clerk, grinning madly, snatched the thruster from Santiago's hand and shot the startled black pirate in the side of the head. Santiago's face caved in. He crumbled to the floor.

Grace fired at the clerk, missed. Gillian leaped to his feet, moved toward the shattered window, thruster whining, trying to get out from between the two tways. Grace spun, dodged a blast from the clerk, twisted her body directly into the path of the other tway's deadly beam.

Her face registered surprise as the beam lanced through her midsection.

She looked at Gillian—deathshock tempered by the faint begin-nings of a sardonic smile. She closed her eyes, acquiescing. She became a shower of golden light.

The room exploded, transformed itself into a netherland of distorted images. Gillian moved through a haze, through a melange of inner and outer worlds, a floor, a bed, a shattered ceiling, intense memories—jagged reflections, like the light from a madly gyrating prism, spinning too fast. He glimpsed a chair—it flashed gold. Black streaks whipped around him. He jerked his body, automatically dodging the beams. He heard the whining of thrusters and he heard a man, screaming with pain. He wondered who it was, then realized the scream was coming from his own mouth.

The window!

He dove out into the mist, plunged toward the street, ever so slowly, seeing a car, a building, Aaron's body crumpled on the sidewalk three stories below. He jerked his head up, bellyflopped hard onto the pavement, front crescent absorbing most of the shock, but not enough. Ribs cracked.

He gasped for breath. *Move! Move!*

Up—onto his feet—staggering—running. A beam of black death shot past his head, gouged through the sidewalk two feet to his left. Thrusters crackled. He twisted, dove into an alleyway, away from the torrent of destruction pouring from the window. A beam spiraled around the corner, nailed him in the back, its energy harmlessly absorbed by his rear crescent.

Another alleyway came into view, at right angles. Guts aching, he ran into it. No beams followed.

He continued running, through other alleys, past desolate buildings, and onto an unpaved street drowning in rain puddles.

The maniacal screams stayed with him. He tried to shut his mouth, make them stop, but he knew he had no control.

He wished Reemul would catch him and end the screams.

The lion of Alexander reminded Rome of death. His withered
frame, shaped by a gray cloak, hung over the arm of the chair like
one of those nutrient sacks drooping from the shoulder of an ancient farmer. His eyes were half-closed and his breathing sounded
labored. Rome had been assured by the lion's helpers that the old
man was in fine physical condition.

Irrya's morning light suffused Rome's office. He avoided the
old man's gaze, scattered his attentions to a potted juniper shrub,
an uncluttered bookshelf, the comconsole beside his desk that
seemed to draw more light to its casing than any other object in the
room. Avoiding the rhythms of the old man's voice proved more
difficult. The lion possessed a youthful tone and his words, ripened
with clarity, seemed to draw Rome toward a vortex of emotion.

I have no time for sadness today.

The lion said, "Grace was my great-grandniece, Aaron my
great-grandnephew. As children, I recall watching them play.
Fighting, always fighting, but always making up with each other
afterward. Grace had a temper even then. On one occasion I remember seeing them wrestle—in a shuttle, in zero-G. Pawing and
thwacking each other like kittens, banging into bulkheads, unconcerned about being bruised. . . .

"When they were young, I made sketches of them." His eyebrows crinkled into a smile. "I have a fondness for drawing. My
wife says that I draw to say things that cannot be said. That is
partially true. But the sketch resonates with more than mere communication. It forms a window into dreams."

The lion shifted his weight, pulled a bony hand out from under
his cloak.

"I save all of my drawings. When I return home, I must locate the ones that I made of Grace. I must reacquaint myself with her. I must make her real once again and then I must say good-bye to her. Her death was unjust but our parting must not be.''

The lion waved his hand, forced Rome to meet his gaze.

''You perceive me as overly sentimental?''

Rome hesitated. ''We must all acknowledge our grief.''

The old man sighed. ''When Grace was in her teen years, she took a lover. He was from another clan and this aroused jealousy among some of our own young, who lusted for her. A fight erupted one day between her lover and two young Alexanders. It was a stupid fight, as most fights are, but fueled by the passions of the young, the dispute accelerated into real violence. Grace's lover and one of the Alexanders were killed.

''Grace never fully recovered from her loss. From then on, she remained impartial to suitors.'' The lion paused, studied something behind Rome, above the windows. ''Grace never acknowledged her grief. She twisted it into anger. Perhaps in time she would have sought out the deeper emotions and recovered her poise. Who can say?''

Rome nodded stiffly. The lion stared at him for a long moment, then chuckled.

''But here I babble, taking up your important time with my own sorrow.''

This old man speaks with such honesty. He expresses authentic feelings while I wonder about his hidden purpose in wanting to see me. Perhaps I dishonor both of us.

Rome spoke. ''Your people . . . their deaths may have been in vain. I don't know. But I do know that the Colonies owe them gratitude.''

The lion sat up straight. ''Grace and Santiago died opposing evil. Among the Alexanders, there is no greater sacrifice. They will be honored.''

The intercom twanged.

''Sir—Nick is here. He says he must see you immediately.''

''Send him in,'' Rome said.

With effort, the lion rose from his chair. "I will be returning home shortly. I would like Grace and Santiago—and Aaron—to make the journey in my shuttle."

"Of course."

Nick barreled through the door. The midget wore sleeveless nylon coveralls and a chartreuse shirt with balloon shoulders. His face displayed an array of emotions: torment, weariness, and something else.

Excitement?

Rome kept his voice casual. "Any word?"

Nick squeezed his palms together as if he were trying to crush some tiny object. "Nothing. We can't find Gillian anywhere. Haddad's people questioned a local woman, though. She claims to have seen a man running away from the building. The description fits Gillian."

"Running away. . . ," mused the lion.

Nick turned. "Harry, it's not what you think. If Gillian ran, then it's because he thought the others were all dead. Remember, there was no reason to believe Aaron was still alive. Even the medics who arrived on the scene thought he was gone."

"Has Aaron regained consciousness?" Rome asked.

Nick shook his head. "There's no guarantee he will."

"Can he be moved?" asked the lion.

Nick hesitated. "Probably. But we'd like to keep him here a while longer. If he wakes up, he might tell us what happened."

The lion remained silent.

Nick sighed. "Most of the building was gutted by the fire that Reemul set, but the destruction was not as total as the Jeek probably wished. We were able to run some autopsies.

"The Inn's fourteen residents were dead before the blaze got to them. We believe Reemul entered the building earlier in the day, killed all the tenants except for a pair of ignors, and then had one of his tways disguise itself as the desk clerk. Reemul probably placed the two ignors in the lobby, used them as a background for his little charade.

"It was a bold move. Reemul must have felt quite sure of himself. He took an awful chance in splitting up the tways. Gillian and the team might have confronted the clerk down in the lobby."

"A demon is always shrewd," murmured the lion.

"We believe the actual combat took place in an upstairs room. The fire originated there. Grace and Santiago—their bodies were badly charred. Some sort of hi-tech incineration device was placed on the bed and used to set the blaze. The area immediately adjacent to the bed became so superheated that it melted straight down through the floor."

Nick hesitated. "There's nothing to indicate that Reemul was destroyed in the fire. We have to conclude that the Jeek got away."

The lion hobbled slowly to the doorway. "I must go." He turned to face them. "I will wait in our shuttle for Aaron, Grace, and Santiago to be brought aboard. And should you require further assistance from our clan . . ."

"Of course," said Rome. "Thank you for the offer."

The lion paused, then smiled. "I judge from your voice that you are merely being polite."

He opened the door. "But who can predict the future? E-Tech and the clan of Alexander have flowed together once. A stream tends to repeat its course."

The door closed. Rome turned to Nick.

"Now, what couldn't you tell me in his presence?"

Nick gripped the edge of the desk. "Begelman and I, we think we've discovered the identity of one of Codrus's tways."

Rome took a deep breath. "Who?"

"I believe, Rome, that it's time you and I started going to church. They say that the sermons of Bishop Vokir are most inspiring."

It was early morning. Gillian sensed he was nearing the outskirts of Irrya's central political district, the home of E-Tech headquarters. If he kept jogging at this pace, he would arrive there—to safety—within an hour. He could have secured a taxi, but he did not trust himself to sit still. Even though his body ached, his cracked ribs especially, it was best to keep moving.

The buildings on this street all seemed alike, their roof eaves slanted at the same angle, their front solarium panels glimmering with the same intensity as morning light splashed from the identical sheets of curved glass.

I've been running for most of the night. He felt surprised by the realization.

At some point, within those shallow moments separating the darkness from the dawn, his body had stopped screaming.

The boulevard flowed east/west. At this hour, it was not yet saturated with pedestrians. Most of the buildings housed first-floor retail shops and were just beginning to open their doors for business. Gillian, with a fascination he could not control, found himself peeking through display windows as he ran along the sidewalk.

In one store, a woman, kneeling, carefully arranged electronic antiques on an elevated platform. There were massive video-cassette machines, a vegetable cloning apparatus, two sleek, fully programmable wall scrubbers, and a host of other objects that Gillian could not identify. The woman glanced up at him and smiled. She exploded into a rainbow of golden sparks.

Rapid-fire images blasted into his head—twisted memories of Catharine, reshaped and modified by current sensory data, as if the interface separating his consciousness from the outer world had been torn away.

No longer were his imagery attacks predictable, four-hour excursions through familiar terrain. The assaults had lost whatever logical base they might have once possessed. He had become a victim of brutal and random forces.

They are all out searching for me. Reemul is on the hunt. So is E-Tech. Nick will be computing probability grids, trying to predict where I will turn up. The Guardians want me for questioning. So do Irrya's local patrol forces. I'm not safe anywhere.

He passed a sweet shop, its display window brimming with chocolate fudge squares and eclairs and delicate spiral crumb buns baked in the gravity-free environment of centersky. The sweets glistened with logic—with a pattern he could dimly sense, as if they were all part of some great wondrous exigency, urging his body to consume them as a whole.

I'm going mad. Only his recognition saved him from plunging over the edge.

An early shopper, a matronly woman in a black skirt, carrying two small packages, suddenly appeared in front of him. She smiled pleasantly and moved to step from his path. A pair of golden tentacles burst from her shoulders, reached out for him. Her face mutated into a mockery of familiar females—Grace, the prostitute Mocha, countless Earth women—all variations on a theme, all external projections of his lost love, Catharine.

He raised his arms, backpedaled, tried to protect himself from the greedy tentacles. "Get away from me!" he screamed.

The woman became real again; her face a mask of fright. She dashed by. Gillian controlled a wild urge to reach out and tear the black skirt from her hips. He did not want to hurt her. He only wanted to possess some of her clothing.

Nick will know how to help me. I'll be back at E-Tech shortly. He recalled that a long time ago, on Earth, Nick had helped him through a similar crisis. Dimly, he remembered the sense of confusion he had experienced back then; "a dichotomy of the soul,"

Nick had called it; Gillian's mind and body gyrating away from each other, away from the real world, toward incredible living dreams. He shuddered. Back then, his plunge through a spectacle of visions had terminated in a place inhabited by deadly women.

Nick will help me.

He stopped in front of a woman's clothing shop, fascinated by the full-sized energized mannequins dancing behind the thick glass. One robot wore a maroon and black dress. It swirled across her hips as she pirouetted along the display floor.

Catharine used to have a dress like that. The thought soothed him, a wave breaking against the shores of his madness, cooling to the touch. *The dress is real. It is more than fabric and color; it is a symbol of something that was once mine.*

He had to have it. The shop door detected his presence, opened. He crossed the threshold.

A dapper man in a tailored one-piece suit, his face overwhelmed by a gray mustache, approached. Gillian pointed to the dress. "I want that one."

The clerk regarded him silently. Gillian was faintly aware of how disheveled he must appear.

"Sir, that particular item sells for twelve thousand and fifty."

"Get it."

The clerk smiled. "Of course, sir, but I must run your credit . . ."

"I have cash cards."

"Of course, sir. And would you like the dress delivered or would you prefer to take it with you?"

"With me."

The clerk nodded. "Of course. And do you want it gift-wrapped or specialty-boxed?"

Gillian felt himself quaking with anger. *Stupid man! Do I look like I have all day to stand here and answer your questions? Can't you see that I need that dress?*

A thought ripped his awareness. *This clerk! He's trying to trick me!*

"Sir," the man repeated. "Do you want it gift-wrapped or . . ."

Gillian gripped the man by the collar and rammed his thruster into soft belly flesh. The clerk went pale.

"Get the dress!"

The clerk, shaking, mumbled, "What . . . size?"

"How should I know what size? You're the expert." *Stupid ignor!* Gillian shoved his gun deeper into the man's belly.

The clerk looked ready to faint. "I'll get you . . . any size you want." His voice came out in a whisper.

"I don't want any size! You're trying to trick me!"

"No . . . no . . . I swear! Please don't hurt me!"

Gillian laughed. "Don't hurt you? What could you possibly know about *that* subject? I could tell you things about hurt you couldn't imagine!"

"Oh, yes! Oh, yes!"

"Do you know what I did to the last person who tried to cross me?"

The clerk shook. "Oh, no! Oh, no!"

"So! You're not trying to cross me, huh? Liar!"

"Please, sir," the clerk sobbed. "I don't know what you're talking about."

Gillian pondered for a moment. Then it came to him. *This frightened little man—it's all part of a clever performance. He's a Paratwa! He might even be a tway of Reemul!*

"So, Jeek! You thought you could trick me again! You underestimate me! You don't know the extent of my powers!"

"I could learn," cried the clerk.

"Ignor! I haven't got time for this!" Abruptly, Gillian recalled that he had to be at E-Tech headquarters as soon as possible. He could not remember exactly why, but he knew that it was important.

He shoved the clerk toward the display window. With quivering palms, the man switched off the mannequin's power unit and stripped the robot. Gillian, snarling, grabbed the dress from the clerk's hand. He rammed his thruster back into the man's belly.

"Now, Jeek! I want you to lead me straight to your dressing rooms!"

The clerk, gasping, desperate to please, wagged his head.

Gillian prodded the man with his gun. "And I want to get a good look at myself. So make it a dressing room with a big mirror."

I have fallen, thought Rome. *A line no longer separates my consciousness, my synergy of life, from the actions of the pre-Apocalyptics. At this moment I am like them; filled with a desire to slaughter my enemy and grow stronger by such action. For I wish—I truly wish—to kill a man.*

Rome corrected himself. *My enemy is not a man.*

If Nick and Begelman were right—and Rome had little reason to doubt them—Bishop Vokir was the tway of an Ash Ock Paratwa. As such, the Bishop represented a far worse threat than Reemul.

The Jeek, however brutal, remained a distinct foe. Reemul brought horror to the Colonies, but it was the horror of a wild and rabid animal. Bishop Vokir secreted deeper poisons. Whatever disparagement Rome felt toward his religion, the Bishop had come to symbolize hope for millions of Colonists. But Vokir, the Ash Ock, was a betrayer of that hope. He was a betrayer of the future. Rome knew of no greater sin.

And I wish to kill him.

He said nothing to Nick and Begelman. He did not know how to share such a disturbing passion.

The three of them sat in the data vaults and reviewed the plethora of evidence.

Begelman spoke excitedly. His fingers, out of habit, slashed at a keyboard. "This Bishop is no dummy. His temples are scattered all across the surface and he's clever enough to add variance to his visitation patterns. But over a period of sixteen years—since the Bishop took control of the Church—the matrix yields three major distortions."

"Time and again," Nick continued, "he's journeyed to these three particular temples: Western Canada, Finland, and the one located on top of the Shan Plateau. And these three temples are among the few that actually date back to the pre-Apocalypse."

With effort, Rome played the devil's advocate. "Maybe the Bishop just has a keen sense of history. Maybe he simply prefers the more ancient places."

Begelman squirmed with excitement. "When you coordinate Bob Max's recent whereabouts with the Bishop's, and overlay the grids, there are five match-ups. Bob Max attended five surface burials in the past six months—two on the Shan Plateau, two in Western Canada, and one in Finland."

Nick snapped his fingers. "Each time, Max used false ID and made slight alterations in his appearance. But he wasn't as careful as he should have been. Begelman and I created a program to scan through the millions of surface passports issued to the Church by E-Tech over the past six months. Five times the computer came up with definite photo matches, identifying Bob Max under his disguises."

"The Bishop," added Begelman, "was naturally doing the eulogizing at those particular temples during Max's visits."

Nick said, "We also have indirect evidence that Bob Max attended many worship services in Irrya. Those services were also led by the Bishop. And if that's not enough of a coincidence, we have evidence that Max was granted free transport on Church shuttles. A man, formerly a pilot, says that Max had carte blanche to go wherever he pleased. This shuttle pilot claims that those orders came from high up in the Church hierarchy."

Begelman rattled his fingers on the keyboard. "Taken in tandem, the odds against all these occurrences are better than three-point-two million to one."

"No way we're talking coincidence," added Nick. "With the Bishop as a tway of an Ash Ock—Codrus, probably—everything falls together.

"Bob Max was a devout believer in the Church of the Trust. He was also a professional smuggler. The Bishop must have convinced Max to engineer the awakening of the Paratwa by telling him he was performing a service to the Church. Max was sold on Vokir's idea of redemption."

Rome nodded. "He would have felt compelled to do anything the Church asked of him."

"Exactly. Of course, Max had to be killed once Reemul was awakened. He knew too much. And Max may have talked once he figured out that his precious Bishop had tricked him into awakening a Paratwa."

Rome shook with anger. "And this Ash Ock—this Codrus—also arranged to have Max become a shareholder in the West Yemen Corporation?"

"Yes," said Nick, "in order to set up this whole chain of events, to divert the ICN loan money and discredit La Gloria de la Ciencia."

Begelman smacked his hand against a monitor. "And consider the way this Reemul has been able to move from Colony to Colony without the slightest trace."

"Bishop Vokir," said Nick, "has the entire Church transportation fleet under his command. Reemul probably disguised himself as missionaries or as a couple of priests. The Guardians would not dare search such individuals, not unless probable cause existed. Reemul could board a Church shuttle wherever he pleased and be whisked from Colony to Colony."

Rome nodded. "And these three Earth temples—you really believe that the Ash Ock are using them for breeding labs?"

"I think so. I believe that the Paratwa are creating a new army beneath the surface."

''What real proof do we have for any of this?'' Rome asked.

''None,'' admitted Begelman. ''Everything is circumstantial.''

Nick stood up. ''But everything ties together perfectly. The Church of the Trust came into existence during the final days, shortly before the Apocalypse. What a perfect cover for the Ash Ock! They knew the end was near, they knew they had to have a long-range program—a safe house for the future. They created a religion that not only provided a strong source of funding for their projects, but also, through the ritual of Earth burials, guaranteed them continued access to the planet.''

Nick shook his head. ''I should have seen it! I spent years studying the Ash Ock and their methods. I should have perceived that a religion provided one of the easiest ways of manipulating society.'' He paused. ''The more I look at the Church of the Trust, the more I see a concoction reeking of the Ash Ock.''

Rome frowned. ''If Bishop Vokir is indeed Codrus, what about his other tway? Do you still think it's Drake?''

''He's the logical choice. But we can't be certain.'' The midget smiled grimly. ''When we get our hands on the Bishop, though, we'll find out in short order. A little unfriendly persuasion and the bastard will tell us who his other half is.''

Rome's lust to see Vokir killed vanished. It was as if a plug were suddenly pulled; a stopped drain again permitted free flow.

''Nick, understand me clearly. All the proof in the world won't make me condone torture. I will not stoop to Vokir's level.'' And he thought: *The idea of torture has released my real feelings. Brutality and horror—they are like a magnet thrust into the soul, polarizing natural human emotions. They permit us to rationalize any form of injustice.*

Nick grunted. ''Well, you're sure as hell not going to find out who the Bishop's tway is just by asking him!''

Rome hesitated. ''I'm not even certain we can arrest Vokir, not without something more definite.''

''I don't think we should arrest him either,'' said Nick.

Rome studied the small face. "You have something in mind?"

"Maybe. Remember, we don't simply want to stop Codrus and Reemul. We've got to find out what's in those three Earth temples. A surprise raid . . ."

"That's out of the question. Even if E-Tech were to agree to such an outrageous violation, I'm not sure we could pull it off. Many of our own people are devout members of the Church of the Trust. They might warn Vokir or refuse to take part in such a raid. Worse yet, without the Council's approval, Artwhiler's Guardians would view an E-Tech raid as an act of terrorism. In Artwhiler's present state of mind, he would probably take offensive measures against us."

Nick smiled coldly. "I said there should be a raid. I didn't say that E-Tech should take part in it."

Before Rome could respond, the door flashed open. Pasha Haddad entered with a disheveled and strangely garbed figure. For an instant, Rome did not recognize the man.

"Gillian!" Nick's face lit up, then twisted into a frown. "Gillian . . . your clothing?"

Gillian wore dark trousers, a windbreaker, and on top, a maroon and black dress that swirled gently across his hips. Rome studied the dirty face, saw the tension, the clenched jaw muscles and the uplifted cheekbones, as if Gillian were trying with all his might to prevent his head from exploding. The glazed eyes warned Rome that he was looking into madness.

Haddad explained calmly. "He wandered into the building a few minutes ago. He's been very cooperative. We were able to disarm him without any trouble."

Nick crossed the room. "Gillian! Do you recognize me?"

Gillian stared down at the familiar face. He tried to smile. "Nick. Good to see you, Nick."

Rome felt pity. Gillian's voice sounded flat, devoid of all human qualities. The killing of the Costeaus had obviously unhinged him.

Nick led him gently by the arm, sat him down beside a blank terminal screen.

"Can you tell us what happened?"

"What happened," Gillian mused. The question was very complex. He did not understand.

Nick backed away. "We were worried about you. Do you know . . . where you are?"

Gillian looked around, saw that they were surrounded by computers. One of them began to bleed—bright gold fluid poured from the keyboard and dripped down the side of the console. He closed his eyes.

The golden lightning flashed. He shuddered. Abruptly, he remembered why he had come to E-Tech. *Nick is here. Nick will help me.*

He opened his eyes. "You have to help me."

"I will," Nick soothed. "We're all going to help you. But you have to talk to us. You have to tell us what happened."

"Everything happened."

"You have to be more specific, Gillian. To begin with, why are you wearing a dress?"

Gillian ran his hand along the smooth fabric beneath the collar. He began to shake. "I don't know. I had to have it. I had to put it on."

"Why?"

"Because I needed to touch it, to remind me of . . . her." Gillian felt his chest heave, as if some great force were trying to burst from his lungs.

They're trying to trick me! He roared to his feet, aimed an accusing finger at Nick.

"You're the one! You've been deceiving me all along! I know it! You can't fool me anymore!"

The Pasha withdraw a tiny needle from his coat and eased into position behind Gillian. Rome considered calling for a Security squad. Even unarmed, an out-of-control Gillian could be too much for them to handle.

Abruptly, Gillian's shoulders sagged. The threat of violence seemed to pass.

For a long moment, Nick stared at Gillian's twisted features. When the midget finally spoke, it was with deep compassion.

"Gillian, you're right. I've lied to you from the beginning. And I can't allow it to go on. I can't deceive you any longer; you've come too far."

The delicacy of Nick's words betrayed truth. Rome knew that the midget was not merely using psychological persuasion to subdue Gillian's madness.

Gillian swallowed hard. "You can't know what it's like. I loved the most beautiful woman in the world. Don't you understand? I lost the most precious love a person could have. She's gone. Nothing can bring her back! Nothing can replace her!"

"You're right," said Nick. He turned to Begelman. "That second computer program—call it up."

Gillian felt a sob wrack his body. "She was so beautiful," he whispered. "She was my life. I lost everything when I lost her."

"Lost who, Gillian?"

He shuddered. "Her! Catharine—my wife!"

Begelman typed. The first cryptic question of the second program appeared on the monitors.

HOW MANY SEEDS IN A WATERMELON?

Nick reached up, put his hand on Gillian's shoulder. "I want you to sit down at the terminal here and run this program. It's important."

"Nothing's important!" he cried out. "Do you really think I care about a computer program? Do you really think some machine is going to make it better for me?"

"It's important, Gillian. Please believe me. You'll find . . . answers."

Again, Gillian felt his anger erupt. "Answers? What do I care about answers? You still don't understand. I lost her! I lost Catharine! There are no answers! She's gone! I lost her!"

Nick's eyes grew misty. "Yes, she's gone. But Gillian, my friend and my companion, you have to learn the whole truth."

"The truth!" Gillian screamed. "The truth is that she's dead! My wife is dead!"

Nick took a deep breath. "No, Gillian. The truth is you were never married."

Rome knew—in one terrible instant, he knew. *I should have realized it the day we awakened them.*

Gillian snarled. "You're out of your mind! You don't know what you're talking about!"

Rome saw the pain on Nick's face and realized how hard this was for him.

"You were never married, Gillian. Catharine was not your wife. She was your tway."

Lightning flashed before Gillian's eyes. The whole room burst into a savage display of golden faces, enveloping him, swallowing awareness. He threw his arms in front of his face.

"No . . ." Gillian found that his voice had become a mere whisper, alone and separate from him. "You don't know what you're saying."

"Run the program," ordered Nick.

Gillian shuddered. He felt hands grip his shoulders, guide him back down into the chair. He opened his eyes. Letters sparkled on the screen.

"You don't know what you're saying."

"Run it!" shouted Nick.

I'm going mad! In some odd way, the thought soothed him. *Yes, that's it! I'm no longer real. I'm insane.*

He stared at the screen and the letters melded, became words, a sentence.

A question.

HOW MANY SEEDS IN A WATERMELON?

It was a silly query. He smiled at his own cleverness as he typed a response into the machine. THERE ARE A LARGE NUMBER OF SEEDS IN A WATERMELON.

The second question appeared. WHY IS LOVE OF FAMILY CONDUCIVE TO THE FORMATION OF LESS RIGID SOCIAL INSTITUTIONS?

Gillian frowned. This program is stupid. He typed: ANSWER DEPENDS ON SPECIFIC FAMILY AND SPECIFIC INSTITUTION.

The screen blanked. Then:

FAMILY IS YOUR OWN. INSTITUTION IRRELEVANT.

Gillian shook.

"He's running it!" squeaked Begelman. "The program is responding to him!"

Nick did not reply. He was staring at the floor, lost in some deep sadness.

Gillian felt terror. *My family! My family is dead!*

A voice came from within, denying his thoughts.

Not dead, said the voice. *How could something that never was be dead?*

He escaped the terrible feelings by plunging into the next question.

DO GRAY CATS HAVE CLAWS?

The answer came unbidden. YES AND NO, he typed.

I used to have a gray cat. Catharine declawed it so that it would not scratch. . . .

For one horrifying instant, Gillian felt as if he had ceased to exist. He lost touch with his body; no weight, no muscles, no sense of legs or arms or hands or a chest or a beating heart—nothing.

And then his body returned, in turmoil. Agony tore through his guts; his ribs, aching since yesterday's escape from the Skeibalis Inn, felt as if they were being splintered. He cried out and pushed himself away from the terminal. His head fell sideways. He retched violently.

A powerful force—some inexplicable urge—made him turn back to the keyboard and call up the next question.

Nick raised his head from the floor, whispered, "It's got him. The program has control. He's committed to run the entire sequence."

And Rome recalled what Begelman had said about the program. It would take six hundred years to run!

WHY ARE THERE NO TROPICAL RAIN FORESTS IN KANSAS?
Gillian shrieked. "No! I don't know the answer!"

Begelman whispered. "Mnemonic cursors?"

"Yes," said Nick.

Rome frowned. "What are you talking about?"

Nick spoke like a condemned man.

"The program interacts with Gillian on multiple levels. On the intellectual plane, the questions stimulate his curiosity. At the same time, on a purely emotional level, some of the questions key into suppressed feelings. They awaken his hidden pains.

"Then there are the mnemonic cursors. They exist within the deepest fabric of Gillian's consciousness. They are control data—discrete packets of information, genetically implanted by E-Tech at the time this program was created. These mnemonic cursors are keyed by the syntactic makeup of the questions themselves. As Gillian reads, he subconsciously triggers his most powerful and basic urges. It's as if he is being starved. Only by answering the questions can he hope to satisfy this artificially created hunger."

"He's been deprived of all choice," muttered Haddad.

Begelman wagged his head in agreement. "The mnemonic cursors are more powerful than any cerebral or limbic-system patterns. Neither his intellect nor his emotions can override them."

"They are chains," said Nick, "linking him to this program, forcing him to run the entire sequence even though he desperately wants to stop. His body is being sent signals—this program represents food. He must respond."

Gillian sobbed. "I don't know the answer!"

Yes you do, said the inner voice.

He typed: TROPICAL RAIN FORESTS CANNOT EXIST IN KANSAS. BUT I CAN EXIST IN A RAIN FOREST AND IN KANSAS AT THE SAME TIME. I CAN BE IN BOTH PLACES. THEREFORE, RAIN FORESTS CAN EXIST IN KANSAS.

He screamed as the memory came back to him. *They sent Catharine, my tway, to Kansas. They kept me at home, in the rain forest, in Brazil. We were very young. It was the first time they had ever separated us. We awoke—as one—but frightened because we could not see each other. They told us that they wanted to make sure we could still maintain the interlace over a great distance.*

We did it. It was easy. We were never apart. We looked up at the sky and we saw Kansas and we saw the rain forests of our home.

Gillian screamed, a weird yell; a mixture of triumph and pain.

Rome faced Nick. "You did the impossible. You kept one tway of a Paratwa alive after its other half had been killed."

"We did it," said Nick. There was guilt in his voice. "E-Tech caught Gillian's Paratwa in a raid. A combat unit killed Catharine, his tway. Gillian was knocked unconscious.

"When he awoke, he was a madman. E-Tech, myself included, made the decision to try and keep him alive. After all, we reasoned, he was unique—the first tway ever captured." Nick's words grew bitter. "We were overcome by our excitement. The things he could tell us . . ."

WHAT ARE THE TWO NICEST ASPECTS OF HAWAII?

Gillian, still shrieking, typed desperately.

THE SUN ON THE WATER. THE SAND BENEATH OUR FEET.

An early feeling. Separateness. Our tutor took us to the Hawaiian Islands. We were barely toddlers. I enjoyed the setting sun, frothing waves against red sky. Catharine delighted in the wet sand sticking between her toes. We looked at each other, laughing, overcome by this wonderful new feeling of being apart.

We stared into each other's eyes and brought on the interlace, became whole again. We did not even need a mirror. From that moment, we knew we were different. We could be either one or two. We could exist in both worlds.

Rome said, "You lied to Gillian. You created an artificial past for him."

The midget laughed harshly. "Yes. We created a wonderful security blanket, using the most modern techniques. Hypnotic trances, submnemonic probes—we drugged him with painkillers and then we questioned him, learned all about his life. Then we created a whole new existence for him. We hid the real Gillian behind a wall of lies. We implanted false memories. We told Gillian he was human. We performed cosmetic surgery and completely altered his appearance. We twisted all of his hurt and anger in order to make him into a functioning killer."

"Hard decisions," muttered Rome.

"Yes . . . hard decisions."

"You spared him pain," offered the Pasha.

"True enough. But even that wasn't done to help Gillian. We needed a tool to fight the Paratwa. Here was a warrior trained from birth, skilled with the Cohe wand. We gave him the incentive to seek vengeance. We told him that Paratwa assassins had killed both of his parents, and later had murdered his adoring wife, Catharine. We turned him against his own kind."

Gillian cried out. Agony tore through him, wave after wave of searing pain. Awareness of the room contracted until only suffering remained.

Questions continued to flash across the screen. His fingers smacked the keys, responding automatically. Some dim part of his consciousness, that inner voice, recognized that the program no longer carried intellectual or emotional meaning. Everything had become much simpler. He was a sealed crate and the program was a sledgehammer, smashing him open.

Nick continued. "We molded him to our image. We dammed the tide of his own feelings. But we knew that someday, that dam could burst. We knew that his real feelings, his real agonies—buried within—could someday seek release. So we implanted the mnemonic cursors and created this computer program.

"There is an old human saying: 'Time heals all wounds.' I don't know if that can be applied to Gillian or not. But we gave him the chance to find out. If he lives through this program, then he will be himself, freed of our manipulations. He will be nothing less than a fully conscious tway."

Again, Nick released a bitter laugh. "But we did not create the program for Gillian's benefit. We did it to relieve our own guilt. We of E-Tech needed our own painkiller—something to help us live with the knowledge that we were capable of being just as cruel and manipulative as the Paratwa.''

Gillian was suddenly enveloped by the golden light. He jerked upright in the chair.

Death.

The enemy had overrun the base. Combat platoons descended from the skies and poured from the jungles, thrusters wailing, slaughtering lab workers and scientists and trainers alike. He and Catharine—separate—retreated to the meditation chamber, a warm hexagonal room at the edge of the compound.

There was no need for words—they said good-bye with smiles. For the last time, they gazed into each other's eyes, creating the interlace.

Gillian felt his Paratwa emerge from the meditation chamber into the hot noonday sun of the clearing. Crescent webs sparkled in the humid air. Their Cohe wands lashed out at the nearest soldiers, bringing death, cutting a swath of destruction through the ranks of the fighters until hundreds lay dead.

But there were too many—thousands—with reinforcements arriving constantly. And Gillian sensed, in those final moments, that these human warriors fought with a determination bred of deep hatred for the Paratwa.

Catharine's shield twisted the wrong way; a powerful blast penetrated her side portal, lifted her off the bloodstained grass. . . .

Gillian screamed as that terrible moment returned—his death, the slaying of his Paratwa, and he knew that he had descended to the very core of his pain. The interlace, ripped in half, disappeared, and a golden inner light, with the intensity of a thousand suns, impossible to perceive yet impossible to ignore, overwhelmed him. And then something hit him from behind and the golden fire choked, became embers of gray; dissolution.

Silence.

*   *   *

Rome watched Gillian emerge from the pain. Tension seemed to have disappeared from him. The gray eyes looked sharp and clear, free of madness. But his hands were still flashing across the keyboard. In some unconscious way, he was still responding to the program.

Nick spoke tentatively. "Are you . . . all right?"

Gillian stared at Nick and for a moment, the midget met his intense gaze. Then Nick turned away.

"I'm sorry, Gillian. I'm sorry it happened. I'm sorry . . ."

"Stop blaming yourself."

Nick raised his eyes.

Gillian looked at the midget and perceived his own tragedy from a new perspective.

"Don't feel guilty, Nick. You did what you had to do. You saved my life. Back then, I could not have survived the pain. You gave me a chance to function as a singularity, a chance to become something more than a tway, to acquire the strength to someday face my truth."

Nick grimaced.

Rome frowned. The screen still flashed questions and Gillian's hands continued to answer them. He appeared to be completely unaware of the process.

Gillian shuddered with excitement. Released from the agony, he felt as if he had been reborn; his mind drifted in a clear stream of new thoughts, each thought waiting to be snagged and examined.

Flexing! That's what started it!

Eagerly, he turned to Rome. "My flexing urge came back. It was Sirak-Brath. That Colony reminded me of Earth, triggered my hidden needs. And the boy, Jerem . . ."

Gillian shook his head, amazed that he could have been so blind. "Jerem Marth brought my emotions to the surface. He triggered feelings in me that I had suppressed since Catharine died.

"As a young Paratwa, I learned a special way to flex. Rather than hold back the urges until they threatened to burst out, I was taught another method—to allow the flex at periodic intervals, four-hour intervals. That's what came back to me! Jerem triggered feelings in me that I could neither acknowledge nor restrain. He forced my mind back into the old contours. Those four-hour flashes of memory precisely corresponded to my old flexing urges!''

Nick spoke softly, without looking at Gillian. ''Yes, that's what it was. The real you coming back.''

Gillian shouted, caught in the throes of another insight. ''Grace—she reminded me of Catharine! When Grace was killed, it was like Catharine dying all over again. That's what threw me over the edge! All the pain began to come back—I couldn't handle it.'' He shook his head. ''No wonder I went mad.''

A sudden sadness washed over him. ''Grace helped me to take the final step. It was through her death that I was able to . . . return.''

He felt sudden anger. He remembered the men of the old Earth Patrol Forces, whom he had trained and taken into battle against the Paratwa; men who had fought and died under his leadership; men who had been, for a short time, his friends. And he remembered yesterday: the Skeibalis Inn—Grace, Aaron, and Santiago.

E-Tech shaped me into a weapon to be used against my own kind—to hunt and kill Paratwa. Back then, I had no choice. I thought I was avenging my parents; as a Paratwa, I never had parents. The woman I thought to be my wife was actually my tway. My real enemy was not the Paratwa—it was the humans.

But I have changed. I have truly experienced life in both worlds. I have been Paratwa and I have been Gillian—not merely a separated tway, but a human, alone and unique. And now the choices I make will be of my own free will.

Haddad caught Gillian's attention. ''What was your real name?''

Gillian answered with a smile. ''Why, it was Gillian, of course. As tways, we used other names, but Gillian and Catharine were our secret names, known to no one but ourselves.''

Rome frowned. "I believe the Pasha was inquiring about your Paratwa name."

Gillian looked down at the keyboard. Abruptly, he became aware that his fingers were still typing. *I'm still running the program!*

He felt a mixture of shock and amusement. He turned to Nick. "It appears that this program has a sizable number of mnemonic cursors. I don't seem to be able to stop."

The midget had recovered his poise. He answered calmly.

"You can't stop until you run the entire sequence."

"How long is that going to take me?"

"About six hundred years."

Gillian laughed, then realized that Nick was not joking. "You've designed a shortcut, I trust."

"Of course. Just answer the Pasha's question."

Gillian smiled. "I thought I did answer it."

"No," Nick corrected. "You were asked what your real name was—your Paratwa name. You did not respond."

Gillian scowled. He felt as if they were toying with him.

"Think about it," said Nick. "Consider why you can't remember your name. Consider that this program will take six hundred years to run and that there is no way for you to stop the sequence nor escape from this terminal. You're trapped, Gillian. Until you allow yourself to remember everything, you're a prisoner of this machine."

Gillian tried to stand up, tried to slide his chair away from the terminal. He could not. His hand, slapping against the keys, prevented any escape. No matter how he tried, no matter what thoughts he filled his mind with, he found that he could not move away from the terminal.

He grinned. "Nick, this is crazy."

"Your name," prodded the midget. "Tell us your name."

He frowned. "Honestly, Nick, if I could remember I'd tell you. But I don't recall ever having a Paratwa name."

"Then sit there for six hundred years."

Gillian chuckled. "You've put me in another impossible situation, Nick. I obviously can't sit here for six hundred years."

He stopped. The inner voice returned. *That's not true. You can sit here for six hundred years.*

And he knew it was the truth.

Six hundred years. The figure itself seemed to possess some meaning. *Six hundred years—it's a number that was once important to me.*

He spoke slowly, the words coming to him as if out of a dream. "I . . . can . . . live . . . for . . . six hundred years."

His muscles quivered. He felt some deep spirit come to life—a cellular passion—winding through him, full of growth. His awareness registered the sensation, conceptualized.

The earlier part of the program unlocked my experience of Catharine's death, the killing of our Paratwa. But E-Tech had much more to hide from me. They had to disguise my life as well as my death. That required a deeper narcosis. The very essence of my existence—my true identity—had to be buried.

"I can live for six hundred years."

He remembered. The truth did not come as a flash of agony; it was more like coming out of a long sleep. He simply woke up.

The mnemonic cursors recognized the return of Gillian's full consciousness. The program shut down. He pulled his hand away from the keyboard and stood up.

Rome, Haddad, and Begelman stared at him with confused expressions. Only Nick understood.

Sadly, Gillian shook his head. He spoke slowly, as if out of a dream.

"My breed had special gifts. We were more than just mere Paratwa. We were an experiment in cellular protraction, a defiance of entropy. Our minimum lifespan, barring unnatural causes of death, was estimated to be six hundred years."

Begelman's eyes widened. Haddad shook his head in disbelief. Rome recalled Nick's warning. *There'll come a day when you'll learn everything. But on that day, you just might wish for the relief of ignorance.*

The day had come. Rome understood. There was only one possible explanation. "You were of the royal Caste," he whispered.

"Yes," said Gillian. "I was Empedocles of the Ash Ock."

On Rome's office monitor, the lion of Alexander appeared older and less dignified than he had this morning, in person. When the lion spoke, his weathered skin crumbled into a moving mosaic, a rough gridwork of deep creases and mottled flesh, dancing across shallow cheeks like ancient cornfields in the wind. Removed from the lion's presence, Rome suffered even greater difficulty trying to fuse the Costeau's youthful voice with his mannequin of a body. Speaker and words would not blend properly, remained two distinct entities.

"You ask much of us," uttered the lion. "I would have to assemble our tribunal and the clan leaders, present your request. Such action would take time. I have just now arrived back home; other clan leaders still remain out of Colony. In any event, the clan might consider your request an invitation to our own genocide."

"You must convince them otherwise," said Nick. "And you must do so with haste."

The midget stood beside Rome, his tiny hand clutching the leather arm of the desk chair. Office lights had been dimmed, shade panels darkened to their maximum effect, the glass wall made opaque to the Irryan night.

On the screen, the lion shrugged. "You cannot guarantee that my people will not become scapegoats."

"It's a possibility," admitted Nick.

"What you have told me thus far, this fantastic story—the Church of the Trust as a force of destruction, Bishop Vokir as a Paratwa of the royal Caste, a new race of Paratwa being bred under the Earth . . ." The lion hesitated. "Even if these things are true, I could say that they are not the problems of the Alexanders."

"Yes, Harry, you could say that." Nick wagged his finger at the screen. "And we both know you'd be lying. Through Bishop Vokir, Codrus commands Reemul. It was the Bishop who gave the order to murder and torture eleven of your clan. It was the Bishop who was ultimately responsible for the deaths of Grace and Santiago.

"We need your help and we need it quickly. I'm afraid this Paratwa rampage is almost over. Codrus has what he wants—E-Tech officially responsible for the Paratwa investigation, the Guardians and La Gloria de la Ciencia disgraced. We believe Reemul will be sent on one more killing spree, some final atrocity that will arouse the ire of all the Colonies. Then the Jeek's death will be faked and the real Reemul will be returned to stasis.

"We must raid those three Earth temples without delay."

Rome added, "E-Tech cannot become directly involved in this raid. I would have to go before the Council and obtain permission for such a constitutional violation. And as Nick explained, there's a good chance that Vokir's tway sits on the Council. If the Bishop gets even the slightest hint of our suspicions, whatever lies within those temples could well be placed beyond our reach."

The lion shrugged. "E-Tech could launch such a raid without Irrya's permission."

"True enough. But if I chose to send E-Tech troops, the chances are high that the Bishop would be forewarned. Many of my people belong to Vokir's Church. They might feel compelled to alert him. In addition, an action of this sort lies beyond the normal activities of E-Tech Security. I'm not sure we could pull it off."

The lion smiled thinly. "You mean to say that your people are not skilled as raiders, like the Costeaus?"

Nick interrupted. "Rome did not mean it as an offense."

"I'm aware of his meaning. No offense is taken. But you must realize what an extraordinary position you would be putting my people in. If you are wrong—if the Bishop is innocent and there is nothing hidden within those temples—the Guardians would have reason to launch an all-out assault against the Alexanders. I suspect that Councillor Artwhiler even entertains such an idea."

"He probably does," said Rome. "There is no doubt you would be taking a great risk. If the raid doesn't succeed, the Alexanders will become scapegoats. And E-Tech will not be able to do much to prevent that. I fear that we'd be too busy explaining our own involvement. We would suffer just as badly as you."

The lion's flesh crinkled in anger. He shrank away from the screen. "You would suffer? Indeed! And what would be the price of your suffering, Rome Franco? Would E-Tech have to bury its dead in the poisonous ground of a forsaken world?"

Nick started to reply, but Rome placed a hand on his shoulder, urging him to remain silent.

This man will tolerate nothing less than bare truth. I am not dealing with a Councillor or a Senator now—men who are accustomed to the speech of politics, the subtle manipulations and deceits. I am speaking to a Costeau.

He gathered his thoughts and met the lion's gaze. "I was being callous. I apologize.

"But I won't apologize for suggesting that others risk their lives in this cause. I am the leader of E-Tech and as such, it is my responsibility to end this threat. I will use whatever means at my disposal to accomplish this, including sacrificing the lives of Alexanders.

"These Paratwa comprise a grave menace, not just to the Alexanders and E-Tech, but to every human being alive, and to the future of humanity.

"As individuals, the Paratwa were ruthless, with a total disregard for human life. But organized under the Ash Ock, they were truly frightening. Those of the royal Caste were—*are*—dedicated to the enslavement of our species. They are the enemy. They must be stopped."

Rome felt himself shaking, possessed by an anger that he could only dimly comprehend. Words seemed to fly from his mouth; harsh sounds, alive with a force of their own.

"And when I say to you that I would sacrifice your people, I feel a hatred of myself, burning inside. Because it makes me like *them*—like the Paratwa and like the humans of the pre-Apocalypse and like all the other men and women throughout our history who ran away from their own pain and suffering, who gave up their own feelings, in the name of conquest, or progress, or civilization, or a better world for tomorrow. I despise myself for having to decide who lives and who dies! I despise the forces that conspire to strip me of my humanity!"

Rome stopped, out of breath. He caught Nick staring at him, the small face flushed with compassion. On the monitor, the lion had grown very still.

Rome shook his head. "This thing is necessary. It cannot be ignored." He stared into the ancient eyes. "We need your help."

The lion spoke calmly. If he had been swayed by Rome's passion, he did not show it. "I will see what can be done, Rome Franco. I promise nothing."

The lion broke the connection. The screen went blank.

Nick patted Rome's arm. "I've never heard you speak so well."

"I don't often get the chance. There don't seem to be too many people willing to listen these days."

"There's me."

"Yes, there's you."

Not for the first time, Rome was aware of the ironies of the situation. Runaway technology, in the form of the Paratwa, was now being perceived in a harsher light. The Colonies were crying out for E-Tech to put on a new mantle of leadership. Yet through E-Tech's seeking of new technological limits, Codrus—if that was indeed who they were dealing with—was allowed to widen the scientific gap. As E-Tech became stronger, the Paratwa gained ground, came closer to their ultimate purpose—the conquest of humanity.

It must end. The Paratwa must be crushed, once and for all.

He sighed. There were other, more immediate problems to face. "How's Gillian?"

"Better. I was with him before I came up here. He's still . . . contemplating . . . his new existence."

"Did you talk to him about assembling another team?"

"It wasn't the time."

Rome nodded. A man who had just been awakened to the fact that he was once a Paratwa of the royal Caste, with a lifespan of six hundred years, certainly had much to think about.

Six hundred years. That was the hardest part for Rome to accept. *What greatness the pre-Apocalyptics were on the verge of!* Through their science, they had answered one of humanity's oldest fantasies. They had discovered the fountain of youth—a way to extend the span of human life.

If they had only discovered a way for humanity to live in peace with itself.

He thought about Codrus—this unknown Ash Ock—and about his manipulation of the ICN over the past two centuries.

Codrus didn't have to go into stasis from time to time. He didn't have to emerge into new eras, begin a fresh climb to positions of control. He's been alive the entire time, existing within our society since the days of the Apocalypse.

What long-term goals these Ash Ock must possess! Their incredible manipulations, the whole concept of sapient supersedure, none of it now seemed so difficult for Rome to accept. A creature with a lifespan measured in centuries would be capable of the most profound insights, be undeterred by plans that might take hundreds of years to fulfill.

Nick brought Rome back to the darkened office.

"Gillian adapts quickly. He'll probably be ready to assemble another team fairly soon."

Rome frowned. "It's probably best if Gillian rests for a few days. He should stay here in our building and recuperate."

Nick shrugged. "He may want to go out, walk the streets."

Rome kept his voice casual. "I think he should stay put. Reemul might be waiting for another shot at him."

"Probably. But if that's the case, the Jeek won't let a little thing like E-Tech headquarters stop him." Nick's eyes widened with sudden understanding. "Ahh. You're not worried about Reemul. It's Gillian."

"Yes."

Nick smiled. "Gillian would not betray us. Believe me."

"You don't know what he'll do, Nick. Not really. He's just learned, after all these years, that he's not a human being. His tway—his Paratwa—might be dead, but his feelings are alive again. He may start thinking about how human soldiers murdered his other half and how he was manipulated by E-Tech into turning against his own kind."

"No," said Nick calmly. "Gillian is one of us now."

"I'd rather not take the chance that you're wrong."

Nick frowned. "All right. I'll ask him to stay put, at least until after we raid those temples. But you're wrong about him. Gillian is not a Paratwa anymore. He's a human being."

Rome did not answer.

Paula gauged her footsteps with care; in the lightened gravity of this section of the Costeau Colony, too much sprightliness of gait could send her crashing up into the ceiling. Jerem seemed to be having no problems in the corridor's sub-G environment. He walked evenly at her side, boots cracking loudly against the worn plastic floor, his blue eyes focused straight ahead.

They had spent the last ten minutes undergoing a gut-wrenching series of lateral and vertical movements inside an unfettered elevator. Paula had no idea of their actual position within the mad scheme of the pirate Colony. The hospital of the Alexanders was apparently located within a building that plunged across the entire diameter of the cylinder. She knew only that they were high up, close to centersky; the lessened gravity made that obvious.

Her son's mop of tangled brown hair had been trimmed and looked neater than it had in months. The haircut had been given two days ago, at Jerem's request, by an aging Guardian barber. The man had bragged that he was also responsible for cutting the hair of Councillor Augustus J. Artwhiler.

Paula tried to catch Jerem's attention with a smile. "I guess you could do some pretty good freefaller tricks in this gravity, huh?"

"Only if I wanted to."

Their week-long captivity by the Guardians, in Irrya, had not been as bad as everyone had warned her it would be. Even the Guardian Captain who had grilled Paula and Jerem throughout the week had been reasonably gracious in providing for their needs. Because of the brutal slaughter of Guardians in Kiev Alpha, official interest in Paula and Jerem had waned. No one seemed to care much anymore about their encounter with Smiler and Sadeyes.

But their captors had shown a remarkable fascination with Jerem's encounter with that man—Gillian. And it was during one of the interrogation periods that her son had first broached the extent of his adventures on Sirak-Brath.

Paula had been mortified. An almost insane anger had overwhelmed her; the thought of Jerem taking scud made Paula want to strangle the old woman who had forced her son into addiction. She had demanded that the Guardians arrest Miss Vitchy immediately.

The Guardian Captain, just before ordering their release yesterday, had promised that his people on Sirak-Brath would look into the possibility of action against the scud woman. Paula had heard enough bureaucratic jargon in her time to know that Miss Vitchy had nothing to worry about.

Jerem asked, "When can we go and see Gillian?"

Paula sighed. She felt distressed enough over her son's relationship with this E-Tech man; she had no intention of willfully seeking Gillian out, no matter how Jerem felt about him. Gillian had saved her son from the clutches of Miss Vitchy and Paula was grateful. But that did not change things.

"Jerem, I've told you at least five times so far. We're not going to be shooting all over space looking for this man."

"Why not?"

"And I'm getting tired of this argument. I've explained my feelings to you this morning during the shuttle flight. This Gillian works for E-Tech and he has something to do with the hunt for this creature. I don't want us involved with him. Period."

Jerem whined, "Then I'll go look for him myself. That's better than staying here with you in this stupid pirate Colony."

Paula restrained an urge. She knew the urge was wrong, and she knew that such urges in the past had led to much of the current troubles between her and her son. Nevertheless, she truly wanted to smack him.

The hospital corridor opened up into a central hub. A tall, white-garbed nurse sat behind a circular desk. The man looked up from his data monitors as Paula leaned against the counter.

"Yes?"

"We're here to see Aaron Ramos."

The nurse pointed down one of the eight corridors that fed into the hub.

"Room five-seven. Aaron is allowed thirty-minute visits. As little excitement as possible. If he begins to tire, please leave at once."

"Thank you."

Jerem followed Paula down the dimly lit corridor. The door to room five-seven slid open with a touch to its sensor panel.

Aaron lay on his back, buried up to his chest under a thick layer of sheets and blankets. Paula was thankful that the hospital room overflowed with modern apparatus; she had half-expected a pirate medical center to resemble an antique exhibit. Even the permeating Costeau odor was absent here, hidden by the strong smell of disinfectant.

The bed was motorized and contour-adjustable. A life-support system hung from the ceiling, complete with microcams and bodily-function scanners. A vital-sign bracelet encircled Aaron's left wrist. Opposite the bed, a thirty-inch monitor was tuned to an orbital control channel; a stream of shuttle departures and arrivals flashed across the screen.

Aaron looked up as Paula entered. The scarlet tattoo squirmed across his face; a wolfish grin spread from ear to ear.

"About time you got here, woman."

Paula pushed off the floor and hopped ten feet in the lightened gravity. She landed at the side of the bed. She gripped Aaron's hand and squeezed.

"Ouch, woman! Remember, I'm an injured man. I've got a shattered leg, cracked ribs, and I ache all over. Not to mention the hole that's been burned through my shoulder."

Paula fought back her tears. "They say you're going to be all right."

"They tell me I'll survive."

She took a deep breath. "I'm sorry about the accident. I'm sorry about Grace, and Santiago."

"Accident?"

She nodded. "When the Guardians released us yesterday, we called Sheila at orbital control. She told us about the three of you being caught in that shuttle explosion."

Aaron grunted. "We were caught, all right."

He looked her in the eye and told her the truth, about their brief training under Gillian and about their unsuccessful encounter with the Paratwa.

Jerem, listening from the doorway, moved closer. "Is Gillian all right?"

"Yes. I hear he only suffered a minor injury."

Paula sighed. She felt as if nothing could surprise her anymore. It had been three weeks since that fateful day when they had witnessed Bob Max's murder, a primal event that seemed to have somehow linked her to the fate of this Paratwa. Everywhere she turned, the creature seemed to intrude upon her life.

Jerem stepped closer to the bed. "Gillian fought the Paratwa?" There was awe in his voice, and pride.

Aaron squinted. Paula sensed anger, though Aaron kept his tone level.

"We fought. We lost. My sister and Santiago died."

"I'll bet ya Gillian was too quick to be caught!"

The anger flashed openly. Aaron's tattoo rippled. "You should have more respect for the dead, boy."

"Don't call me boy."

"Jerem!" Paula snapped.

Her son turned to her with a look of pure wrath. But he remained silent.

A faded grin touched Aaron's face. "So, *boy*. You think you've done some growin' up. You think Sirak-Brath has made you tougher and stronger."

"Gillian made me tougher and stronger."

"Did he, now? Well, he's tough and strong, no doubt about that." Aaron turned slightly, winced with pain as his shoulder touched the bed. "Do you like hunting and killing, boy?"

Jerem sneered. "As much as you do."

"Oh? You think I liked fighting that creature, risking my life?"

"You did it, didn't you?"

Aaron nodded. "I did it because it had to be done. Sometimes you have to stand up to evil. Sometimes you have to make justice."

Jerem said nothing.

"Do you think I'm tough, boy?"

"Yeah, I guess."

"Tougher than the Paratwa?"

Jerem shrugged.

"Well, I'm not. I was burned straight through the shoulder with a Cohe wand and I was thrown out a window, three stories up. The fall almost killed me—I was barely conscious. But I remained awake long enough to see the Paratwa come flying out of that building and chase after Gillian."

Aaron suddenly reached out. He gripped Jerem by the arm and yanked the boy closer to the bed. Jerem squirmed, trying to break the pirate's viselike grip.

"I was scared, boy. I thought the Paratwa was going to finish me off, but it didn't. I survived only because I lay there on the sidewalk and pretended I was already finished. I played dead, boy, hoping that the bastard wouldn't kill me. And do you know why?"

Aaron pulled Jerem toward him until their faces were only inches apart.

"Do you, boy? Do you want to know why I lay there, playing dead? Do you want to know what I thought about? I thought about your mother, and about how much I was beginning to care about her and about how good she's made me feel. And I thought about never seeing her again and that scared me. A painful death—that I could accept. What I couldn't accept was never seeing your mother again."

Paula let go of her emotions. Tears coursed down her cheeks. Aaron released Jerem. The boy backed awkwardly away from the bed, his face twisting into a deep scowl.

Aaron squeezed Paula's hand. "I love you, woman."

"Typical of a Costeau," she cried. She leaned over the bed and threw her arms around him. Gently, aware of his pains, she hugged him.

"I must be a fool," she sobbed. "I only seem to fall for Costeaus."

"You've got good taste, woman."

She stood up, used the corner of Aaron's bedsheet as a handkerchief. She wiped her face and then turned to her son. Jerem stood in the farthest corner of the room, his arms clutched tightly across his chest.

Aaron spoke quietly. "Tough and strong is good, boy. We all need that. But we need a lot more. You can't carry your anger with you forever. You'd be wise to think about that."

For a time, Jerem stood in the corner, silently frowning. Finally, he took a tentative step toward them.

The door slid open and the male nurse charged into the room.

"Aaron! The news! It's all over the spectrum!" The man rushed to the monitor and switched it to one of the major freelancer channels.

A young woman in a green blouse, seated behind a multiconsole desk, was reading:

"Less than an hour ago, a squadron of shuttles, believed to be from the clan of the Alexanders, attacked and took control of three Church of the Trust burial temples on the surface of the planet. Early reports indicate that fighting has taken place between temple personnel and the Costeaus and that casualties have occurred."

Aaron shook his head. "Have we gone mad?"

The nurse threw up his arms in a gesture of helplessness. "They're saying that the lion ordered the attack. They're saying something about finding secret installations buried under these three Church temples. The Colonies are in a total uproar! But the worst part is that Artwhiler went live two minutes ago and announced that he was sending a fleet of Guardian ships to surround our Colony. They're threatening to blow us up if we don't immediately withdraw from the surface!"

Aaron tried to sit up. His face twisted with agony. Paula gently pushed him back down.

She chided. "You're not going anywhere. I don't care if the universe is ending. You're staying in this bed."

The nurse nodded. "You can't help, Aaron. You wouldn't get ten feet without collapsing. That shoulder . . ."

Aaron glared at them but remained under the covers. "What are we doing about the Guardians? Have we sent our ships out?"

The nurse shrugged. "The lion has ordered us to take no action."

"No action? We should fight!"

"Shh!" hissed Paula.

The breathless young freelancer continued. "We have another special announcement, this time from E-Tech headquarters here in Irrya."

She spun sideways, whispered to someone off camera, then turned back. "We're picking up the E-Tech feed. We're going live to the office of Councillor Rome Franco, Director of E-Tech."

Franco's aging round face faded in over the image of the young freelancer. The Councillor nodded to someone off camera, then began speaking in a clear, solemn voice.

"A short time ago, the clan of Alexander initiated an offensive action against three Church of the Trust burial temples scattered across the face of the Earth. This action was carried out with my full consent. It was at my urging that the clan of Alexander attacked these three temples.

"The specific reasons for the attack shall be made clear very shortly. For the moment, I can only say that I and several of my executive staff made discoveries indicating that these three Church of the Trust burial temples harbored a grave threat to the peace and security of all the Colonies. The nature of this threat made it vital that the temples be raided without delay. Because E-Tech has many loyal members of the Church of the Trust, and because extreme secrecy was of utmost importance, it was decided that an outside agency should carry out the actual assault.

"A short time ago, after being made aware of the nature of this grave threat to the peace and security of the Colonies, and under my direct orders, a shuttle fleet from the clan of Alexander descended to the Earth's surface with the purpose of establishing complete control over the temples located in Finland, Western Canada, and upon the Shan Plateau.

"This assault has been successful. These three temples have now been secured. Thankfully, no Church of the Trust personnel have been seriously injured. But, tragically, there have been fatalities among the Costeau raiders. And when I say tragically, I mean the word with all my heart, for the clan of Alexander has done something for which we in the Colonies may someday owe them a great debt of gratitude."

Franco paused, then stared intently into the camera.

"A short time ago, Councillor Artwhiler ordered the Intercolonial Guardians to launch a counterattack against the three temples that have been secured. Councillor Artwhiler also gave orders that the home Colony of the Alexanders was to be surrounded and destroyed if the Costeaus did not immediately retreat from the Earth's surface.

"I urge that Councillor Artwhiler refrain from such terrible actions. I urge that Guardian forces everywhere be given orders to hold off until the evidence of this grave threat against Intercolonial security is fully revealed. We expect, within the next several hours, to make clear the reasons for this unprecedented attack against the three Church of the Trust facilities."

Aaron managed to prop himself up. "Alexanders attacking burial temples under E-Tech's direction! I don't understand such madness. But I do know why Franco has gone public. Artwhiler and the Guardians—they're actually serious about destroying our Colony!"

Paula squeezed his hand.

Franco continued. "At this time, I have one final announcement." His voice grew even more solemn.

"E-Tech Security has issued a warrant for the immediate arrest of Bishop Vokir of the Church of the Trust. There are presently four charges drawn up against Bishop Vokir and at least fifteen more charges are expected to be issued within the next twenty-four hours.

"Bishop Vokir is presently accused of murder, conspiracy to commit murder, genocide, and conspiracy to commit genocide. If you have any knowledge as to the whereabouts of Bishop Vokir, please contact E-Tech Security.

"Thank you for your attention."

The picture jumped back to the profile of the young freelancer. Her mouth hung open. She was apparently too stunned for words.

Paula shook her head in disbelief. "Bishop Vokir . . . murder and genocide? What's this all about?"

Aaron looked grim. "I don't know. But we'd better hope it's resolved before Artwhiler carries out his threats."

Rome sat alone in his darkened office.

If there is a point of no return, we have gone far beyond it. We are committed. There is no turning back.

He had not yet wanted to announce E-Tech's role in the temple raids. He had certainly not wanted to force a confrontation with Vokir before they had clear evidence to use against the Bishop. But Artwhiler had left him no choice.

The Guardian Commander intended to regain control of the three secured Church temples at any cost. He had surrounded the Colony of the Alexanders with a fleet of armed shuttles. Minutes ago, when Rome began his live transmission, Artwhiler had been preparing to launch dual attacks—against the temples and against the Alexanders' home Colony. Thousands of innocent people were being threatened.

We made a mistake. We did not think Artwhiler would react so aggressively.

Of all people, I should have known.

Artwhiler had taken his removal from the Paratwa investigation as a personal humiliation. He would not allow himself to be humiliated a second time.

Private pleas to Artwhiler had failed. It was almost as if the Guardian Commander did not care why Rome had arranged for the Alexanders to raid the Church temples. Artwhiler perceived the pirate actions as some sort of opportunity to regain his lost dignity.

Madness.

Going public had been a desperate measure on Rome's part. By admitting E-Tech's role in the raids and by ordering the arrest of Vokir, Artwhiler was forced to consider the consequences of his actions. Hopefully, he would hold back his Guardians, at least until after the Council meeting.

Rome thought about what had not been publicly announced.

The three coordinated raids had gone smoothly enough. Costeau vessels had touched down simultaneously at the temples on the Shan Plateau, in Finland, and in Western Canada. Church personnel manning the temples had been surprised by the landings, then astonished when armed pirates had come charging into their sacred domains. The temple servants had put up no real resistance, however, and no serious harm had befallen them. The worst injury had apparently occurred in Finland when a Church maintenance tech, in his excitement, tripped over an airlock portal and fractured his ankle.

The Church personnel had been imprisoned in their bedrooms while the Alexanders, using heavy-duty scanning gear provided by E-Tech, searched the temples.

Almost immediately, secret stairwells had been discovered in all three locations, leading down from the Bishop's private offices. Each stairwell terminated in a small cavern. Each cavern boasted a metal door carved into bedrock. Each door contained a circle of five single-access hand modems.

That discovery had relieved the last of Rome's doubts.

Unfortunately, the metal doors and the surrounding bedrock had resisted all attempts at penetration. Ultrasonics, x-rays—nothing had worked. In Finland, the Costeau crew had decided to pierce the door with beam cutters. In Western Canada, they opted for diamond/thermal drills, set in the surrounding bedrock. The Costeaus on the Shan Plateau resolved to wait and see which method worked best before attempting penetration; they proved to be the luckiest of the three groups.

In Finland and Western Canada, immense explosions had ripped through the underground facilities, blowing holes straight up to the surface and rocking the temples so badly that they were yanked from their foundations. Whatever lay hidden beneath Finland and Western Canada had been totally annihilated. And fifteen Alexanders had perished.

Rome shook his head. *We warned them that the Ash Ock might have set traps. We asked them to wait. We told them we had a safer way to get through the portals. We told them that the Ash Ock might rather see their handiwork destroyed than have it fall into enemy hands.*

But with Artwhiler threatening to blow up their home Colony, the Alexanders had been in no mood to tarry.

Rome closed his eyes. Gillian and Nick were already on their way down to the Shan Plateau. *They must get through that door. We must have evidence to present to the Council.*

The fate of the Colonies depended on it.

"Well," said Nick, over his intercom, "I guess it's show time."

The midget turned away from Gillian. He chuckled as he faced the grim array of spacesuited pirates who stood poised behind them in the shallow bedrock cavern, one hundred and twenty feet below the Shan Plateau.

They did not really need the protection of spacesuits. The cavern was free of atmospheric poisons, its closed air-circulation system secretly linked to the temple above. But once they opened this portal . . .

Nick's theory that a breeding lab lay beyond the door—a huge installation where a new army of Paratwa was being created—dictated the presence of purified air. Gillian had his doubts, not so much about the presence of air as to the existence of a breeding lab. That the Ash Ock would have maintained a trio of fully manned centers beneath the Earth for over two hundred years seemed improbable, especially in the light of what had just occurred in Finland and Western Canada. Two centuries of work would not have been destroyed with such complete indifference. Something else lay beyond this portal.

"I gotta tell you," Nick drawled, "this is the biggest goddamn door I've ever seen."

Several of the pirates laughed. Most of them merely stared at the tiny spacesuited figure huddled next to Gillian in front of the imposing gray portal.

They lost fifteen of their friends today, Gillian thought. *The other temples were booby-trapped. And there's no guarantee that when I place my hand on this modem and open this door, we won't suffer the same fate. The Ash Ock may have constructed more subtle traps to prevent illegal entry.*

It didn't hurt that Nick was trying to cheer everybody up.

Gillian stared at the circle of hand modems embedded in the metal door.

Five modems. He closed his eyes and formed a picture in his mind. *A circle of five.*

Since yesterday morning, when he had learned his real identity, memories, unfettered by pain, had been returning. He had already recalled a rash of events from childhood.

The process of recall proved very strange. He found that the clearer recollections emanated from those times when he and Catharine had been linked together as Empedocles. Somehow, that seemed backward to Gillian. He felt that his own discrete tway memories should have been easier to recall.

It was a mystery whose solution would have to wait. They did not have much time. Artwhiler had not backed down.

Following Rome's public announcement, the Guardian Commander had modified his position to allow the Alexanders three hours to retreat from the surface. If they had not left the temples within that time, Artwhiler vowed to launch a full-scale shuttle attack aimed at regaining control of all three Church facilities. Concurrent with that action, the Guardians would fire the first rocket barrage at the home Colony of the Alexanders. For the Costeaus, it was a no-win situation.

Which means we have less than thirty-five minutes to get through this door, find out what's inside, and then return to the shuttles and blast off.

Gillian depressurized his spacesuit, broke the wrist seal, and pulled the thick rubber glove off his right hand. With his eyes still closed, he raised his bare palm toward the circle of modems.

A circle of five. That was important to me once. Somewhere, ages ago, someone told me about the significance of this circle.

His mind needed no more prompting. The memory, already on the edge of awareness, exploded into full consciousness.

Aristotle, my contact with the other Ash Ock. He was a pair of brutish-looking males—and the only one of the royal Caste I was ever allowed to see. He used to visit me in Brazil, gauge the progress of my training, make sure that I was being properly tutored by the scientists, who by that time were under the dominion of the very Paratwa whom they had created.

One day when I was young, still a pair of preteens, I was alone with Aristotle, our four bodies facing one another on the hot sand beside the quiet jungle stream. One of Aristotle's tways picked up a stick and drew a rough circle in the sand and said to me that I must remember it always, for it was the sphere of the royal Caste.

"First," said Aristotle, "comes Codrus, oldest of our breed,

financier of our cause.'' And Aristotle marked Codrus's position by scribing an X just past the one o'clock spot on the circle.

Aristotle's tways then burst into laughter as he marked his own position on the circle, between three and four o'clock. Still chuckling, he said that he could not understand how such a great political genius like himself had been given such a mediocre position on the perimeter of greatness. And I had laughed with him, but uneasily, for I was too young to understand what he meant.

Aristotle slashed an X at the very bottom of the circle—six o'clock—and he said that that represented Sappho. And he would say no more, for he never talked about Sappho, no matter how hard I pestered him.

"Theophrastus, master of the hard sciences, occupies the fourth spot on the circle," said Aristotle, drawing the X between eight and nine o'clock. "Remember, young one, that it will be Theophrastus whose inventions will someday free us from the crushing burden of human beings.'' When Aristotle said that, a thrill coursed through my bodies and I felt momentarily overwhelmed by a joy I could not describe.

"And finally," Aristotle said, with a twinkle in his eyes, "we come to Empedocles, youngest and fairest of them all, the child who will someday grow to be our protector.'' And he drew a tiny X near the eleven o'clock position.

The memory vanished. Gillian opened his eyes and placed his bare hand on the fifth modem, near the eleven o'clock position of the circle. He repeated the access code that Aristotle had made him memorize that day on the beach.

The modem flashed green. He yanked his glove back on, re-pressurized his suit, and pushed the door inward.

"Here we go," muttered Nick.

Gillian flipped the spring-mount on his left wrist and felt the thruster fly into his hand. He charged into the darkness, not knowing what to expect, but wishing again that he did not need to function within the limitations of a spacesuit. Worst of all, the bulky suit glove defeated the subtle hand pressures needed to effectively use the Cohe. He had been forced to store the wand in one of his belt compartments.

Sensors detected him. Ceiling panels faded up to full illumination.

Nick leaped in behind him. The midget came to a bewildered halt at Gillian's side.

"What the hell do you call this?"

The pirates poured in, thrusters ready to meet any threat. But like Nick, they halted in confusion just inside the door.

They stood within a relatively small chamber, circular in shape, about twenty feet in diameter. The low ceiling offered a standard lighting grid. In the center of the room, a desk, molded from gray plastic, supported a pair of data consoles. A small armless chair stood before the desk. But it was the surrounding circular wall that astonished them.

Except for the portal where they had entered, the circumference of the chamber was an uninterrupted layer of some sort of thick translucent membrane. At least fifty pale green orbs, each the size of a golf ball, floated randomly within the clear gel. Tiny flagella projected from each opaque bubble. The orbs wiggled and pulsed, slowly propelling themselves through the ooze.

"Are they alive?" asked one of the pirates, her thruster aimed warily at the nearest section of wall.

Nick broke into a deep frown. "They seem to be."

With fascination, Gillian watched two bubbles haphazardly encounter one another. For a moment, nothing happened. Then flagella whipped violently. The orbs immediately reversed direction and moved away from each other.

Gillian shook his head. "This is no breeding lab."

Nick looked upset. He stared down at the plastic floor, then up at the illuminated ceiling grids, ten feet above. "There's got to be more to the facility. Another chamber, above or below us, or on the other side of this wall."

Gillian had his doubts. "I think this is it." He crossed to the desk in the center of the room and examined the twin keyboards and dual monitors, a Paratwa arrangement.

The terminals appeared to be standard models, no different from those Gillian had known back in the twenty-first century. Microcams were mounted above the monitors for teleconferencing. But between the two keyboards stood a thick black toggle switch. It was not labeled.

Gillian pointed to the switch. "Any ideas?"

The midget scowled. "I haven't the faintest idea what it's for." Nick kept his eyes warily on the pulsating green bubbles, as if he expected them to leap from the gel and attack him. "Maybe it blows up the whole goddamned planet!"

Gillian smiled. Nick did not like his mysteries this mysterious. "Well, we don't have time for any careful experiments, do we? Let's give it a try." He threw the switch before Nick could stop him.

The screen came to life.

CONTACT POSITION FORMULATING.

"Something's going on," whispered the midget, with a nervous tremor in his voice.

All around them, the suspended bubbles shook violently, blazing through a wild rainbow of colors. After about fifteen seconds, the process stopped. The spectral mutation stabilized itself. Each bubble had grown to twice its normal size and each had turned a dark shade of blue.

"Well, that was fun," muttered Nick. "Now what?"

Before Gillian could respond, the screen came to life again.

DOPPLER CORRECTIONS INITIATED. COORDINATES SYNCHRONIZED.

There was a short pause in the readout. Then:

CONTACT IS BEING ESTABLISHED.

"Doppler corrections!" said Gillian excitedly. "That's the frequency shift between two points in rapid motion. We're in motion—the Earth is moving through space. So are they!"

Nick twisted his lips. "You mean they're up in the Colonies?"

"No! Don't you see?" Gillian could barely contain himself. Insights flooded awareness. He knew what this chamber was used for.

Theophrastus! Aristotle said it was you who would free the Paratwa! And you did it!

Gillian motioned to Nick and the pirates. "Quick! There's no time to explain. All of you back away from the front of these terminals. It says that contact is being established. Whoever comes on that screen will be able to see the person transmitting from this end!"

Gillian replaced his thruster and depressurized his suit. He removed his helmet, then sat down in front of the monitor. Nick and the Alexanders shuffled to the sides of the chamber. They could still observe the screen but they remained outside the viewing locus of the terminal's microcams.

They moved just in time. Status lights ignited above the keyboard. The letters disappeared. A face dissolved onto the screen.

An elegant woven tapestry served as a backdrop for the man who appeared before Gillian. His hair was blond and shiny and just long enough to cover his ears. Short bangs hid most of his furrowed brow. The face was clean-shaven and utterly calm. Alert green eyes betrayed no surprise.

He studied Gillian for a long moment. Then he smiled.

"May I help you?"

Gillian wanted to laugh. *He's expecting an Ash Ock, Codrus probably, and a complete stranger—me—shows up instead. And now he's going to try and bluff his way through a conversation and find out what the hell's going on.*

Gillian matched the pleasant smile. *It won't work. I'll be doing the bluffing. I have the advantage. You have no idea who I am. But I recognize you.*

The face on the screen was that of a tway. He was a Jeek Elemental, an assassin from the same breeding labs as Reemul.

The memory returned in full. *Long ago, when I was just a child,*

Aristotle brought me to you for the first time. In the beginning, you were his servant alone, but later you became chief lieutenant for all of the Ash Ock.

It was you who trained me to be a fighter. It was you who taught me to use the Cohe wand, to master the mind/body rhythms of the assassin. It was you who made me into the deadliest of the Ash Ock, the one destined to become their overlord and protector.

Gillian said, "Hello, Meridian."

The tway registered a slight shock. His eyes wavered.

Meridian quickly regained his composure. "I'm afraid I'm not familiar with that name."

Gillian laughed. "You don't recognize me, Meridian? Well, I shouldn't be surprised. I've had several facial alterations since Brazil."

This time, Meridian squinted. Gillian imagined that the Jeek's other tway was already summoning help—his Ash Ock masters.

Gillian added, "I'm afraid that Codrus is indisposed right now."

The tway gave a wary nod.

So! Nick is right! It is Codrus!

Gillian chuckled, enjoying the game. Another memory came to him.

"Remember, Meridian, the time that you became angry with me because you said I wasn't paying enough attention to my training. And you threatened to punish me by waiting till I had separated and then locking me in different rooms and breaking all the mirrors so that I couldn't interlace. And I laughed at you and I made you kneel down and I whispered in both your ears my great secret— that I, alone among the five, never, ever needed the mirror for interlacing!"

Gillian found himself laughing as he recalled the story. "That was my little secret, Meridian. I never told anyone else about it. Did you?"

The tway's jaw dropped open. He did not even try to hide his astonishment.

"Who . . . are . . . you?"

Gillian mocked his words, in the same manner he had mocked them as a child. "Who . . . am . . . I? I'm surprised, Meridian. I always liked and admired you, especially the quickness of your mind. But you're rather slow today." And he thought, *It's true. I did like and admire you. You were always a good companion to me—harsh, but fair.*

"You taught me much, Meridian, and not just the tricks of the assassin. Next to Aristotle, you were my best teacher."

"Empedocles?" the tway whispered.

Gillian nodded. *Close enough to the truth. I can't let you know about Catharine. I can't let you see that I've been reduced to a mere tway.*

"You . . . were killed." Meridian clamped his jaw shut. His face betrayed total confusion.

"That was the E-Tech story," Gillian explained, mixing truth with lies. "They naturally did not want it known that they had captured one of the royal Caste. I was too valuable a prize to dangle in the public eye."

Meridian shook his head. "Where is Codrus?"

"At this precise moment, I don't know where the Bishop is." *And neither does anyone else.*

Gillian smiled at Meridian's discomfiture. He decided to take a chance. "And the Councillor-tway is up in Irrya preparing for a meeting."

Meridian nodded solemnly. Gillian caught Nick's excited gaze from the side of the room.

So! It's true! Codrus's tway is indeed an Irryan Councillor!

You reveal much, Meridian. A few more steps and we'll have it all.

Gillian kept his own tone neutral, allowing none of his excitement to show.

"And where are Sappho and Theophrastus? I assume your tway has summoned them by now."

A faint smile touched Meridian's lips. "You are being observed."

"Good," said Gillian. "It's best that all hear what I have to say. By the way, Theophrastus, my congratulations to you. A faster-than-light transmitter is quite an achievement. I'm fascinated by the way you've utilized organic molecules in this invention. It's truly a magnificent breakthrough."

Gillian held the smile on his face even while a chill swept through him. *And what other breakthroughs have you made? Surely not faster-than-light travel. Not yet, at any rate. You would have had to concentrate your efforts—there were not enough of you to push back the limits in all fields of science. You would have put most of your energies into communications and weaponry.*

Meridian's face suddenly took on a glazed faraway look.

Someone is speaking to his tway, Gillian observed. *Sappho or Theophrastus is giving him orders, no doubt.*

Awareness returned to Meridian's features. "If it is truly you, Empedocles, you have much to explain."

I've got to keep them off balance. I need more information. I've got to learn which Councillor is Codrus's tway. And I have to find out exactly where this transmission is originating from. We must know how much time we have left.

Gillian laughed arrogantly. "It's not I who must explain, Meridian. It is you who does not seem to understand that Codrus has badly bungled this entire affair. I was hoping it wouldn't be necessary for me to become directly involved, but I was left no choice. I'm going to have to kill Reemul. I'm afraid it's the only solution."

Again, Meridian betrayed his confusion. "But Codrus said that . . ."

"Codrus has been lying to you. Two hundred years of living alone in human society has enfeebled him."

Meridian started to speak, then thought better of it, or else was ordered to keep quiet. His face assumed a hard pose. "We must speak to Codrus. At once!"

"Don't waste your time giving me orders, Jeek! I'm not a little boy and girl anymore, learning to use my wands by slicing branches off those chestnut trees outside your New Hampshire farmhouse!"

Meridian remembered the occasion. His eyes softened. "Empedocles, we are . . . confused." He hesitated. "Where did you come from?"

Gillian mixed lies with truth. "From stasis, of course. That's where E-Tech put me before the Apocalypse. They awakened me when Reemul started his rampage. Naturally, they had no idea who I really was." Gillian forced a laugh. "They thought they were awakening a pair of programmers who might help them design a probability grid for tracking down the assassin."

Meridian frowned. Then he burst into a volley of questions. "How did you learn about Codrus? How did you get into the communications room? Why do you say that Codrus is bungling the adjustments? Why won't you let us speak to Codrus?"

Gillian gave a shrug. "I told you. Codrus is unavailable right now. As for the adjustments, well, for one thing, the Bishop does not cover his tracks very well. That's how I found out about these three communications facilities. And it's been fairly simple to detect Codrus's blunt hand behind Reemul's actions." Gillian shook his head in mock disgust. "It's a shame Aristotle perished. He understood the subtleties of manipulation far better than Codrus ever will."

Meridian was watching Gillian very carefully now.

I'm not going to get much further with this. He's getting too suspicious.

"Empedocles, if it is indeed you, you must allow us to speak with Codrus."

"I told you, I don't know where the Bishop is. And it would be too awkward to bring the Councillor down to this transmitter right now. He's too well known."

Meridian froze. Gillian could have kicked himself.

How stupid can I be! In the back of my mind, I was so sure that Codrus's tway was Drake that I referred to the Councillor as if he were a male!

The look on Meridian's face told Gillian that he had guessed wrong. *It's not Drake! The Councillor-tway is female! Nu-Lin . . . or Lady Bonneville!*

Gillian tried to gloss over his mistake. "From now on, I'll be handling this affair. You'll deal directly with me."

Meridian said nothing. His face was a mask of complete indifference.

It's done. I blew it. I'll get nothing more out of him. But at least we've narrowed the identity of Codrus's other tway down to two possibilities.

There was no point in continuing with the transmission. Meridian would reveal nothing further. And Gillian was liable to give away too much if he kept talking.

"Good-bye for now, Meridian." He hit the switch. The Jeek's face dissolved. The suspended bubbles abruptly shrank to their regular size and slowly mutated through the color spectrum until they had assumed their normal shade of pale green.

"Well," said Nick, "I'll be a son of a bitch!"

That was putting it mildly. Gillian motioned to the Costeaus. "Let's get back to the shuttles and get out of here. We don't have much time."

It was now vital that Codrus be captured as soon as possible. Under no circumstances could the Ash Ock again be given the opportunity to contact Meridian and the others.

Gillian put his helmet back on and repressurized his suit. He hustled Nick and the Alexanders out into the bedrock cavern and then resealed the heavy door. He glanced at his suit clock. They had about twenty minutes to get off the planet. They would make it under Artwhiler's deadline. He was not worried about that.

He turned to Nick as they waited in line behind the Costeaus who were starting to climb the spiral staircase.

"Begelman and a research team must be allowed to come down here. They have to figure out this transmitter and calculate how far away Meridian is. We've got to learn how long we have before the Paratwa get here."

Nick shook his head. "Getting Artwhiler to agree to anything right now is going to be difficult."

"I'm not worried about Artwhiler. He'll be very cooperative once he learns what we've discovered."

"And what about Codrus?"

Gillian smiled grimly. "When we get back to the shuttle, I want you to call Rome. Tell him we're coming to his Council meeting.

"Tell him we're going to expose an Ash Ock."

Each perceptible movement; every hesitant breath, every sigh and every shrug; each nuance of expression on the faces of the two Councillors, however slight, caught Rome's attention. He sat stiffly upright, frozen in his seat, trying desperately to control the impulse that made him want to gaze unabashedly upon Nu-Lin and Lady Bonneville. He feared that at any moment both of the women would turn on him, outraged by his intrusive stares, demanding an end to such rudeness.

One of them would have a legitimate complaint. The other would know why Rome could not keep his eyes off her.

And soon this Council will learn the truth.

He hoped Nick and Gillian knew what they were doing.

With an effort, he turned away from the women and forced himself to concentrate on Drake and Artwhiler. The shouting match had been going on between the men since the meeting began.

"You cannot do such things!" Drake bellowed. "You cannot!" The huge Councillor slammed his fist down on the polished table with such force that his empty soup bowl twirled on its edge and vibrated noisily.

Artwhiler, face and neck flushed, hands gripping the beveled edge of the table as if he were going to rip off a portion of it, rose from his chair.

"You and the rest of the ICN are idiots! You've lost all perspective."

"Perspective!" Drake snapped. "You threaten to blow up a pirate Colony—an action that could start an Intercolonial war—and you accuse us of losing perspective? You're losing touch with the real world, Councillor."

"Am I? Costeaus willfully attacked one of our most respected Churches and you wish to treat the incident the way you would treat a banking error. Stick to your ledgers, Drake! Let the Guardians do their jobs."

Drake wagged his finger at him. "You cannot—I repeat, *cannot*, threaten the peace and security of these Colonies. That is not the function of your Guardians."

"Don't tell me the function of my Guardians!" Artwhiler screamed. "We exist to maintain law and order throughout the Colonies! And we will eliminate any pirate criminals who try and disrupt that law and order!"

Drake's face registered a series of angry expressions. It was as if he were trying each on, searching for one that fit the best, that conveyed the true extent of his rage. He settled on a brutal glare that made the dark flesh above his eyebrows pulsate. When he spoke, his words emerged in a deep growl.

"Councillor Artwhiler, do you have any idea of the repercussions that would have resulted had you attacked the clan of Alexander's home Colony? Do you have any idea as to how the other Costeau clans would have reacted to such an attack? Do you have any real conception of what millions of enraged Costeaus would be capable of doing to our society?"

Artwhiler threw back his head and laughed. He addressed his remarks to the top of the chandelier. "When a criminal commits a criminal act, the law takes action. The law does not sit back and worry about what that criminal's friends will do.''

Drake sighed. Abruptly, the anger left his face. ''No, Councillor, it's obvious that you don't understand the significance of your actions.'' He paused. ''Perhaps the time has come for the Guardians to have new leadership.''

Artwhiler returned his gaze to the table. Words spluttered out. ''How dare you! By what right do you threaten my position? I am a Councillor of Irrya and I am Supreme Commander of the Intercolonial Guardians! And I am beginning to resent these gross attacks on my ability!''

Rome shook his head. *Does he understand Drake's meaning? Does he understand that the ICN can have him removed?*

The ICN tolerated Artwhiler's occasional fanaticism only because the Guardian Commander generally supported Drake's views. But if the ICN Directors' Board decided that Artwhiler was no longer serving their cause, they would threaten the Guardians with such severe financial sanctions that Artwhiler's own people would force him to resign.

Rome felt sorry for Artwhiler. *Perhaps he doesn't even understand the nature of his power. Perhaps he doesn't see that he's only a pawn here.*

A sudden chill swept through Rome. *And we're all pawns in someone else's game.*

The scrambled communication had arrived from Nick's shuttle only a few hours earlier. The message had been simple, the implications terrifying.

Make room. Gillian and I are coming to your meeting. The one we seek—she is an Irryan Councillor. Happy hunting. Nick.

Artwhiler lurched back into his seat. ''This Council is ignoring the fundamental issue—that Franco and E-Tech did willfully order the clan of Alexander to take control of three Church of the Trust burial temples, for reasons we cannot even begin to guess. I'm still waiting to hear Franco's explanation for these incredible constitutional violations.

"And this other nonsense: hidden underground facilities, the issuing of an arrest warrant for Bishop Vokir . . ." Artwhiler pounded the table like an outraged schoolboy. "This Council seeks to remain blissfully ignorant of the fact that E-Tech constitutes the real threat here—not the Guardians!"

Rome stopped feeling sorry for Artwhiler.

Drake began calmly. "We are all anxious to hear E-Tech's explanation, which Franco has promised to provide at this meeting." The Councillor's voice rose in pitch. "However, explanations will be of little comfort to us if an Intercolonial war breaks out while we sit here!"

"You overestimate these pirates," Artwhiler muttered.

Drake locked his palms together and lowered his voice. "In that matter, Councillor, you express the minority opinion. The rest of us feel that the pirates, if aroused, do indeed constitute a grave threat. We are pledged to deal with priorities here. And our first priority is the rapid defusing of this situation.

"Now, I understand that your shuttle fleet has not departed from its position around the Alexanders' Colony?"

"Your information is correct," Artwhiler said bitterly.

"The fleet remains, even though the Alexanders have retreated from the Earth temples?"

"There is no telling what these pirates will do next! We must maintain a club over their heads until we are sure they have been brought back into line."

Drake nodded, and then spoke as if he were addressing a slow child. "Councillor, here is what I want you to do. I will say this plainly and clearly but I will say it only once. You are to contact Admiral Waterson, who is in command of those shuttles orbiting the Alexanders' Colony. You are to order the Admiral to disperse his fleet. You will give that order from these Council chambers and you will do so immediately.

"If you refuse, then I shall contact Admiral Waterson myself and command him to carry out the wishes of this Council."

Drake paused. "If you entertain some notion that Admiral Waterson, or any of your other ranking officers, will remain loyal to you and disobey a direct order from the Council of Irrya, then by all means refuse.''

Lady Bonneville jumped in, soothing. "Arty, the crisis is over. The pirates have retreated from the temples. There is no logical reason for us to continue to threaten their home.''

Artwhiler glared at her, then turned his gaze on Nu-Lin.

"The si-tu-a-tion must be de-fused. Lat-er, we can dis-cuss sanc-tions a-gainst the Cos-teaus.''

And Rome thought: *Later, sanctions against the Costeaus will be the last thing on anyone's mind.*

Artwhiler started to speak, then changed his mind. He clamped his jaw shut. His face still bubbling with rage, the Guardian Commander keyed his terminal and opened an audio link to his headquarters.

"Get me Admiral Waterson—at once!''

It took only a few moments for Artwhiler to contact the Admiral and order the shuttle fleet to pull back.

Lady Bonneville heaved a sigh of relief. "Thank goodness. Now perhaps we can turn to the real issue at hand." She lowered her head and gently rubbed her temples. Her massive beehive hairdo, layers of red streaked with gray, looked like it would drop off if she leaned forward any further.

Drake folded his arms. He stared coldly at Rome. "I believe, Franco, that you are now prepared to offer an explanation for your actions?''

"I am. With the Council's permission, I would like to have two witnesses brought into these chambers." He waited for Nu-Lin or Lady Bonneville to object, but it was Artwhiler who raised his voice.

"We should not waste our time listening to E-Tech minions.''

Rome interrupted. "These men have been to one of the raided Church temples. They can explain better than I what this is all about.''

Drake hesitated, then glanced at Nu-Lin and Lady Bonneville. Neither of the women made any objections.

"Bring in your witnesses."

Rome keyed his terminal. The door opened. Nick and Gillian strode into the chamber.

For once, the midget had dressed conservatively—gray trousers and a black turtleneck shirt. Gillian wore baggy pants and a crinkled maroon leather jacket.

Rome hoped the door had not been programmed to scan for Cohe wands. Although Gillian would have been forced to check his thruster at the security desk, it was entirely possible that the esoteric Cohe had escaped the door's detection system. He hoped Gillian was still armed.

Rome had one more chore. He addressed Haddad on the terminal and typed in the word-command—SECURE. A moment later, the Pasha flashed an acknowledgment.

Five hundred E-Tech Security troops had just been given the order to surround the Irryan Council building and prevent anyone from entering. With Reemul still on the loose, there was no telling what might happen once they exposed Codrus.

"Howdy," Nick drawled.

Lady Bonneville smiled thinly. "Well, Mr. Nicholas, it would appear that your expertise extends beyond the realm of party jokes."

"Yeah, you could say that."

Codrus had interlaced prior to the start of the Council meeting. Deteriorating affairs had cried out for unity.

But when the door opened and the two men entered, Codrus knew—in one gestalt instant he knew—that the Ash Ock adjustment, that minor correction in the social flow, had backfired. He knew that there was indeed a real threat to the Second Coming.

The incredible shock of today's events: the invasion of the three secret transmission chambers, the fact that E-Tech knew exactly which three temples housed the installations, the knowledge that E-Tech had connected the Bishop to Reemul's violence and that they might even be aware that the Bishop was an Ash Ock tway . . .

Codrus had been stunned. He had been forced to reappraise the entire sequence of events since that day, years ago, when the Bishop had recruited Bob Max. Codrus had been forced to conclude that somehow, perhaps through the careful scrutiny of Church records, E-Tech had managed to link the Bishop with Bob Max. He had acknowledged his own possible carelessness in dealing with the smuggler; that admittance, in and of itself, proved a bitter pill to swallow.

But until this moment, Codrus had truly believed that the situation could be saved and that his Councillor-tway remained safe.

I should have acted sooner. I should have urged Reemul to capture Haddad without delay and drain the Security Chief until I learned the extent of E-Tech's knowledge. I hesitated because Theophrastus and Sappho warned me not to kill Haddad, that his death could lead to martyrdom and that martyrs all too often generate unpredictable long-term side effects.

Codrus felt a touch of bitterness. *In this, I should have followed my own course. Theophrastus and Sappho were wrong. And I will pay for their error.*

He knew—logic dictated—that the little man walking toward Drake had emerged from stasis. He knew that the midget was a real enemy from the past.

Codrus locked his gaze on the little man's companion—the soldier-hunter, the one called Gillian—and for a moment, his troubles receded and he found himself utterly fascinated by the man's delicate movements; the casual way his arms swung at his sides and the way his calm gray eyes slowly panned the chamber, seeing everyone and looking at no one, as if the eyes were under the control of some remote scanning machine inside his brain. And Codrus understood why Reemul had twice been unable to kill this man, though he knew he could not bend his thoughts into words.

There was an aspect to this Gillian that defied description. Codrus had never before seen such a human.

With a mad grin, Nick hopped up on the empty chair next to Drake. He stood on the seat's plush fabric, hands on hips, surveying the Council.

"Well now, I hope you don't mind my shoes on your furniture, but it's a little hard to see what's going on from way down there." He pointed to the floor.

Drake spoke coldly. "You are here to provide information. Please provide it. The Council has much business to attend to."

Nick chuckled. "I'll just bet it does, yes sir! Well, the truth of the matter is, Gillian and I came here to do a little more than just provide information. I'm afraid by the time we're finished, we're going to have upset the whole apple cart, if you catch my drift."

Rome observed the women. A faint grin expanded Nu-Lin's shallow cheeks. Lady Bonneville frowned; the age lines on her forehead stood out sharply.

Nick said, "I suppose we better start at the beginning."

He told them about his own history, as an E-Tech programmer during the final days, and about the special team that had been assembled to hunt down the Paratwa assassins. He told them about the three Ash Ock who had never died and who possessed life spans measured in centuries. He told them about how the royal Caste had recruited Reemul, the liege-killer, and he told them about the process of sapient supersedure and how the Ash Ock had assumed the identities of Earth leaders, in the days of the pre-Apocalypse. And he told them what the Earth had been like in the midst of such madness.

When he finished, Drake shook his head. "Six hundred year life spans? This is nonsense."

"El-e-gant-ly put."

Lady Bonneville chuckled. "Dear Mr. Nicholas, you do tell stories."

Artwhiler frowned and said nothing.

Undaunted, Nick grinned. "All that I've told you is just background, you understand. The real story begins during the final days, in the last decade of the twenty-first century, when the Ash Ock began to realize that their dream of conquest was about to be brought to a jarring conclusion.

"Now they were of the royal Caste, and they were not going to let a little thing like the Apocalypse interfere with their plans. So they got together, studied the options, and concluded that humanity was going in two directions, both of which were up, away from the planet.

"The two great hopes for the survival of the human race were the Colonies and the starships, and under the circumstances, both options must have looked pretty good to the Ash Ock. But option one—life in the Colonies—had some severe disadvantages. The major problem was E-Tech and their rigid tests for Colonial immigration. Now the Ash Ock knew they could pass those tests and make it up to the Colonies, but they also must have realized there was no way that they were going to get their army of Paratwa up to the cylinders. It was just not feasible that thousands of assassins would be able to slip by E-Tech's security precautions.

"But the starships—ahh, there was a more viable option. The Star-Edge project was not under the direct control of E-Tech; it was ruled by the remnants of what had once been the planet's respected scientific community. The scientists and engineers who were building the starships needed funding for their colossal project and with the growing worldwide distrust of technology, money was tight."

Rome listened, fascinated. He saw that the others were listening with equal attention, except for Gillian, who had not taken a seat and who was slowly circling the perimeter of the huge table, his eyes facing the center, observing them all.

Nick continued. "The Star-Edge scientists went public, offering salvation among the stars—a chance for those who could afford the price. For exorbitant fees, Star-Edge sold berths on the great starships. Thousands of wealthy citizens who had been denied immigration to the Colonies snatched up this chance to get away from the doomed planet. And in that way, Star-Edge made enough money to complete the construction of the great ships, in Earth orbit.''

Nick smiled. ''Now if there was one thing the Ash Ock had, it was money, lots of it. And Star-Edge, desperate for funding, would not have looked too closely at many of their wealthy applicants, for they had to complete the project and they could not afford to turn away the richest offerings. And so, over the space of several years, a wealthy army of Paratwa assassins, under the direction of the royal Caste, infiltrated the project and guaranteed themselves a trip to the stars.''

The starships! Rome thought. *Is it truly possible? Had the Ash Ock and an army of Paratwa assassins escaped into space two centuries ago?*

Nick went on. ''Most of the passengers journeyed in stasis, of course, it was a long trip to the star systems they set out to colonize. But Sappho and Theophrastus remained awake. A hundred and seventy years ago, when the starships were well beyond our solar perimeter, the Ash Ock woke up their army and took control.

''The last messages to reach the Colonies hinted that fighting had broken out and that several of the vessels had been destroyed. I believe that was a ruse. I believe that the Paratwa overran those vessels with little resistance and then sent messages back to Earth indicating that turmoil and revolt threatened the destruction of the whole fleet.

''And then, with the Ash Ock—namely, Theophrastus and Sappho—in control, and with Paratwa assassins in command of every vessel, that fleet of ships continued their journey.

''Eventually the ships would have arrived at the targeted star systems. Perhaps the Paratwa even colonized planets according to the original Star-Edge plans. Who knows? But we do know that for over two centuries, Theophrastus and Sappho would have remained awake and free to continue their program of scientific advancement, going beyond the technology of the pre-Apocalyptics.

Science without limits, out among the stars, unfettered by the re strictions of E-Tech.

"The Ash Ock's long-range plan for the sublimation of humanity would have been carried out, in miniature, aboard those starships. The thousands of surviving humans would have been enslaved by the Paratwa, put to work, bred and domesticated and no doubt forced to carry out all menial tasks, leaving the Paratwa free to work on their primary goal—the advancement of technology to a point far beyond the level reached by the pre-Apocalyptics.

"Their overall goal, of course, was to return to Earth someday and, with their superior technology, accomplish what they had failed to do two centuries ago—conquer humanity."

Drake shook his head. "If this bizarre tale of yours is true, which I have not been convinced of, then what does it have to do with Bishop Vokir and his Church temples?"

The midget grinned. "Ahh, we come to the most interesting part of all!

"The third Ash Ock who survived the Apocalypse—Codrus— remained in the Colonies. His job was to make sure that human civilization maintained tight scientific controls so that when the Paratwa returned from the stars, they would not be met by a culture as technologically advanced as their own.

"Codrus was to make sure that E-Tech remained the powerful guiding force that it was when the starships took flight over two hundred years ago."

Nick nodded toward Rome. "In the E-Tech vaults, a short time ago, we discovered the evidence of Codrus's manipulations. At least four times in the past, through sapient supersedure—killing a human and replacing him with a tway—Codrus was able to rise to the top position at the ICN."

Nick turned to Drake. "The ICN was the most logical choice for Codrus's manipulations. There was no sense in infiltrating E-Tech; they already shared the Ash Ock goal, at least for human society. Besides, it was the ICN who've always held the real power in the

Colonies. It was the ICN who've decided where most of the money was going to be spent.''

Rome could see Drake's face tightening, as if invisible hands were slowly squeezing the black cheeks together.

"Four times," continued Nick, "Codrus took control of the ICN and steered its course away from scientific and technological progress. Four times, over the space of two hundred years, Codrus managed to stem the inevitable tide we sometimes refer to as human advancement.

"But in our era, Codrus miscalculated. For whatever reason, he was not able to implement supersedure and assume a leadership role at the ICN. He was forced to acquire a lesser position.

"For Codrus and the Ash Ock, it was a big mistake. They underestimated Drake and the ICN. They failed to perceive, until it was too late, that the current leadership at the ICN—Drake, with the full support of his Directors' Board—were determined to remove all limits on science and technology.'' Nick stared calmly at the huge Councillor. "It's been Drake who's been secretly supporting La Gloria de la Ciencia, funneling money to them, helping them to achieve widespread popular support, financing their rise to power. It's been Drake and the ICN who've been secretly responsible for the decline of E-Tech.''

Drake's face rippled with suppressed anger. He refused to meet Rome's eyes.

"The dam was about to break—science and technology were about to run rampant throughout the Colonies. The hi-tech spiral was about to begin again and Codrus was not in a position to stop it. But the dam had to be shored up. E-Tech had to remain strong. Drastic measures were called for.

"Enter Reemul—the Jeek assassin—put into stasis by the royal Caste before the Apocalypse, left behind, probably along with a few other assassins, in case Codrus should ever need special assistance.

"We can all see the effects of Reemul's murderous rampage. E-Tech is growing stronger again, and people are being retaught the same hard lesson they first learned two centuries ago—science and technology require limits."

Rome glanced at the others, read looks of surprise, bewilderment, disbelief. Gillian continued to circle the perimeter of the chamber. *A hungry carnivore*, thought Rome, *seeking its prey*.

"Through a complex arrangement that made Bob Max a shareholder in the West Yemen Corporation, Codrus managed to bring disgrace to both the ICN and La Gloria de la Ciencia." Nick turned to Artwhiler. "The Guardians, unable to stop Reemul, also suffered a loss of credibility."

Artwhiler reddened.

"Codrus's mission was almost accomplished. Through his actions, the pendulum was about to swing back again, toward more stringent social controls by E-Tech."

Drake pressed. "And Bishop Vokir and the temples?"

"Bishop Vokir is one of the tways of Codrus. Beneath those three temples are faster-than-light transmitters, invented by Theophrastus, no doubt, well before the Apocalypse. Codrus and the Paratwa who journeyed to the stars have never lost touch with each other."

Nick explained the nature of the evidence in E-Tech's vaults that linked Vokir to Bob Max.

Drake shook his head angrily. "Have you actually seen these faster-than-light transmitters?"

"Two of them were booby-trapped and exploded as we tried to enter, killing the Alexanders." A cold grin spread across the tiny face. "But we got into the third one. We activated the transmitter and had a rather interesting conversation with an Ash Ock lieutenant, a Jeek Elemental named Meridian."

How? thought Codrus. *How could they have gotten into the transmitter?*

The safeguards, designed by Theophrastus himself, were faultless. Illegal entry would cause an explosion that would totally annihilate all evidence of the facility. Only an Ash Ock could penetrate those chambers.

It made no sense.

Nick continued. "Through trickery, we were able to confirm most of our speculations. One tway of Codrus is indeed Bishop Vokir. The other tway is an Irryan Councillor."

Nu-Lin shook her head. "Ab-surd."

"Is it?" Nick licked his lips and suddenly compressed his body. He leaped from his chair and landed at Lady Bonneville's side. Startled, she jerked upright. A vicious smile distorted the midget's face.

"Lady Bonneville, I have a question for you."

Nervously, she folded her hands together and laid them on top of the polished table.

"Over two weeks ago, at the end of a Council meeting, you provided Rome Franco with information about the ICN's involvement in the West Yemen Corporation—about how Drake was secretly funneling money through that corporation in order to finance La Gloria de la Ciencia."

She nodded slowly. "Yes, I seem to remember doing that."

"Why did you leak that information to Rome? After all, you've generally been fully supportive of La Gloria de la Ciencia yourself."

The Lady spoke slowly.

"Contrary to this Council's belief, I do not—nor have I ever—fully supported La Gloria de la Ciencia."

Drake scowled.

"It's true that I've been mainly opposed to E-Tech over the years. I've always wanted to see more scientific research and a gradual lessening of this cultural stranglehold that E-Tech has had us in for over two centuries." She shook her head. "But there have to be some limits. I wish only to see a better balance between E-Tech and La Gloria de la Ciencia."

She turned to Drake. "Your way is wrong, Elliot. I don't think we've acquired any great fountain of wisdom since the days of the Apocalypse, but we have learned some things. There must be a balance. It is our job to maintain it."

Nick laid his hand on her shoulder. The Lady did not flinch.

"One more question, Lady Bonneville. Where did you get that information about the West Yemen Corporation?"

"My sources must remain confidential."

Nick shrugged. "It really doesn't matter. We know that the information was leaked by someone in the Commerce League."

Gillian stopped his circling, halted directly behind Nu-Lin. Rome studied the woman; regal chin and pale white cheeks, the cold blue eyes dancing with amusement.

Nick pointed his finger at Nu-Lin. "Meridian gave away the fact that Codrus's other tway was a woman. With Drake cleared, that left you as the only other real possibility. Lady Bonneville was never much of a suspect. Even if she didn't grant her total loyalties, she's been a consistently strong supporter of the ICN and La Gloria de la Ciencia. No Ash Ock would disguise itself *that* well.

"But you, Nu-Lin—you've been E-Tech's vigilant friend on the Council all along. It was you who stood by E-Tech in their darkest days. It was you who engineered the political defeat, five years ago, of Councillor Artwhiler's plan for a series of deep-space probes that would have served as a perimeter warning system—a system that might well have alerted the Colonies to the Ash Ock's return from the stars.

"It was you, as head of the Commerce League, who have consistently pushed for a solution to the so-called Costeau problem, seeking to rid Sirak-Brath of their influence, seeking to keep the pirates far outside the mainstream of Colonial life. For you know that when the starships return, when your conquering army of Paratwa assassins enter the Colonies, the pirates will have to be isolated and destroyed."

Nick faced the other Councillors.

"The Ash Ock are shrewd. They will not conquer merely by

raw force, which would only serve to unite people against them, but with the subtler tools of the vanquisher: bribes, promises, great rewards for those humans willing to cooperate. But the Costeaus today are an aloof subculture of Colonial society—renegades living by their own harsh standards. An invading army of Paratwa assassins would only serve to infuriate the pirates, unite them even further. Under Ash Ock reign, the Costeaus, millions strong, would form the basis for a guerrilla army—fearless warriors planting the seeds of revolt throughout the Colonies, inspiring millions of other humans to join them."

Nick shook his head. "The Ash Ock would have to deal harshly with the Costeaus. The pirates would have to be annihilated. And the more removed they were from mainstream culture, the easier such genocide would be."

Nu-Lin arose. "I do not quite know how to re-act to these pre-pos-ter-ous ac-cu-sa-tions."

"You can begin," said Nick, "by giving us a date—the year that the Ash Ock starships will reenter our solar system."

Nu-Lin turned to Drake. "These ri-dic-u-lous in-sults have gone far e-nough. I de-mand that these two men be re-moved from cham-bers."

Gillian laughed. Rome started to speak but in one blinding motion, Gillian moved to Nu-Lin's side and slid his Cohe wand up under her jaw. She gasped as the needle touched her flesh.

Artwhiler roared to his feet. "Let her go!"

"Sit down," said Gillian, "or I'll kill her."

The words were spoken with such utter calm that even Artwhiler had no trouble reading Gillian's intentions. Frowning, the Guardian Commander resumed his seat.

"The date?" demanded Gillian, pushing the point of his needle into her neck until it almost punctured the skin.

Codrus raised his head, locked eyes with his tormenter, knew what he should have known ages ago; that no human hid behind those sharp gray eyes, that no human hand gripped the delicate Cohe with its sharp needle.

So simple. I should have seen. We all should have seen. The soldier-hunter was the tway of an assassin. Somehow, in defiance of all theory, E-Tech had found a way to keep a tway alive after the death of its other half.

Gillian met the cold blue eyes. "I'm going to ask you one more time. When are Sappho and Theophrastus scheduled to reenter our solar system?"

Nu-Lin remained silent.

"Make no mistake, Codrus. Continue with your charade and I will end it. I will squeeze this wand and send the Bishop to hell."

Codrus perceived the cold sincerity behind the words, knew that this man—this tway—would indeed destroy him. Neither logic nor lies nor the other Councillors would stop Gillian. Either Codrus admitted that Nu-Lin was a tway or else a detailed autopsy would later expose the truth.

I am finished. Acknowledgement led to a decision. *My life is over. But I can still serve our cause. Two days from now, Reemul will enter the Irryan Senate chambers and destroy representatives from every Colony.*

Even with the Colonies now aware of the Ash Ock and the Second Coming, the net effect of a Senate massacre could still serve to dampen technological growth.

And I must learn everything I can about this Gillian. The Bishop, before he is forced to surrender, must pass the information on to Reemul. This time the Jeek must not fail. He must kill this soldier-hunter.

Codrus directed his words at Gillian. "You be-trayed your own kind. Now you are nei-ther hu-man nor Par-a-twa."

Rome let out a sigh. *And you, Nu-Lin, friend for countless years—you have betrayed something beyond both human and Paratwa loyalties. You have betrayed the future.*

Lady Bonneville and Artwhiler shook their heads, stunned. Drake's mouth fell open. His voice emerged in a whisper.

"Nu-Lin, this cannot be true."

Codrus smiled. "Do not be too a-larmed, Coun-cil-lors. The

Par-a-twa do not de-sire a fu-ture marred by war and vi-o-lence. We will rule some-day. That is in-ev-i-ta-ble. But hu-mans will share our world. We do not seek your de-struc-tion.''

Nick smiled grimly. "We'll share, all right—like cattle used to share a farmer's fields, until it was time for them to be trucked to the slaughterhouse. Thanks but no thanks, Codrus. You're the product of human madness. You're a human mistake, nothing more, nothing less.''

Gillian stared into Codrus's cold blue eyes and saw himself—his future—what he had been programmed to become. He perceived what the soul of an Ash Ock encompassed. *Nick is right. We were created out of human madness.*

He continued staring, feeling himself being drawn into those tiny pools of blue, sucked across some infinite border into another reality. Just before he broke eye contact, at the instant he yanked his gaze away from her, the Councillor's face melted into a shimmering golden cloud, alive with order, with possibility. And suddenly Gillian understood. He perceived the deeper meaning of the golden flashes. He knew where he had to go and what he had to do.

Smiling coldly, he withdrew the Cohe from her neck. "We're waiting, Codrus. How many years till they return?''

Codrus knew there was no sense in lying. E-Tech could not be prevented from studying the transmission chamber beneath the Shan Plateau, calculating just how far away the returning starships were.

"Our ves-sels are fif-ty-six years from the Co-lo-nies." He allowed Nu-Lin one last charming smile. "Give or take a few months, of course.''

Fifty-six years, thought Rome. *In fifty-six years, the Colonies must be ready.*

Gillian said: "Codrus, I am of your breed. I am the tway of Empedocles.''

Knowing it was true, Codrus laughed. The sound emerged from Nu-Lin's wafer speakers as harsh crackling.

So, the final irony of my failure, the final piece of the puzzle. He understood how E-Tech and the pirates were able to enter the transmission chamber beneath the Shan Plateau. A renegade tway of the royal Caste! It was now more vital than ever that Reemul destroy this Gillian.

He knows us. He knows our ways. Fifty-six years from now, he could prove to be a terrible foe for Sappho and Theophrastus.

For an instant, Codrus considered trying to snatch the Cohe from Gillian's hand, kill the traitor himself. Even as the idea took shape, he perceived it as folly.

Gillian—Empedocles—had been trained by Meridian himself. He had twice escaped from Reemul's grasp. *I would never make it. He would slay me. The Bishop would plunge into madness.*

The thought of death did not particularly disturb Codrus. But the idea of only one tway perishing generated a vague sense of fear. *I may have to face that nether-death. I may have to face being torn in half.*

Gillian pulled away from Nu-Lin and sat down in the adjacent chair. He kept the Cohe clutched in his fist.

"Codrus, I give you a choice. Your death—at least the death of Nu-Lin—here, now, in this chamber. Or the immediate surrender of Bishop Vokir to E-Tech authorities." He glanced at Rome and the other Councillors. "There is no capital punishment within the Colonies. I suspect that if the Bishop surrenders, you would probably be put into stasis—indefinitely."

Gillian smiled. "Still, Codrus, you would be alive. Who knows, perhaps fifty-six years from now, when your people return, freedom could be won. You might be thawed. The future, after all, remains somewhat unpredictable."

"And what is the price for spar-ing my life?"

"Reemul."

Codrus laughed. "Even if I de-sir-ed, I could not give you the Jeek. He re-mains rath-er in-de-pen-dent." Codrus relaxed his body, preparing for the worst. "I'm a-fraid you will have to kill me."

Gillian raised the wand. Rome drew a deep breath, saw Nick and the other Councillors hunch forward, eyes glued to the tiny needle that projected from Gillian's fist. The chamber became a rigid tableau, poised to be shattered.

Gillian broke the tension. He lowered the wand and turned to Nick. "I can't do it. I can't kill, not like this, in cold blood. The Colonies have changed me. Paula has changed me." He shrugged. "I'm sorry, Nick. I can't do it."

Frowning, the midget turned away.

Rome kept his confusion to himself. Paula? It sounded like Gillian was admitting that he had fallen in love with Paula Marth. But how could that have happened? According to Nick, Gillian had only met her once—and then only briefly.

Gillian turned back to Nu-Lin. "You're lucky I'm no longer of the royal Caste, Codrus. You're lucky that I have discovered human feeling." And he thought, *What lies I tell! I have discovered feelings, yes. But they are neither human nor Paratwa, they are some unique melange.*

I have truly lived in both worlds.

"Codrus, I will not—cannot—slay you. But I could arrange for you to be turned over to the Alexanders." He glanced around the table. "I do not think your fellow Councillors would object."

Angry scowls twisted the faces of Drake and Lady Bonneville. Artwhiler, who looked barely able to contain himself, slowly rubbed his fists together.

Rome went along with Gillian's ploy. "Codrus, this Council would not interfere were you to be turned over to the pirates,"

Gillian nodded. "One hour, Codrus. If you haven't surrendered the Bishop within that time, we'll allow the lion of Alexander to deal with you."

A bitter smile twisted Nu-Lin's lips. "And Reem-ul?"

Gillian shrugged. "He won't surrender, of course. But you could trick him."

Codrus thought, *Yes, I could trick Reemul. But I won't.* "What is it that you wish me to do?"

"Before the Bishop surrenders to us, he is to contact Reemul. He is to order the Jeek to perform one more kill. Tomorrow afternoon, perhaps, here in Irrya. We'll work out the final details shortly."

Drake rose, leaned his bulk against the table. He addressed Gillian. "There will be a trap? You will be waiting for this assassin?"

"Yes."

Smiling coldly, Artwhiler turned to Rome. "My Guardians will naturally offer every assistance. We will help you set this trap."

Rome glanced at Nick. The midget wore a deep scowl.

Something's wrong, Rome thought. *Gillian is lying.*

Codrus allowed resignation to play across Nu-Lin's face. *Yes, there will be a trap. But it is Reemul who will set it.*

Gillian's attention wandered from the table. He stared at a painting on the far wall, a vivid cornfield, streaked with gold. *This time, Jeek, I will face you for my own reasons.*

In the Church sanctuary three miles from Irrya's north pole, Bishop Vokir finished packing a small suitcase. Even as he closed the lid, tripping the locks, he recognized the inherent inanity of his actions.

I have no need for personal items. E-Tech will remove them from me the instant I surrender.

Still, it kept a part of his mind occupied. He needed a touch of fantasy right now.

The door to his small bedroom sprang open. Reemul's tways slithered in.

"My," said the shorter one. "This really isn't necessary, Bishop."

The Bishop sighed. "Please don't argue. We both know there is no choice."

"A rescue attempt could succeed."

"They would kill Nu-Lin," he said firmly. "They might even kill you. E-Tech will be ready. A rescue would be doomed to failure."

The taller tway sat down on the edge of the bed. He smiled. "So you will go willingly into their clutches."

"Not willingly, Reemul. But I will go." The Bishop stared at the taller tway.

"No heroics, Reemul. Surrendering to them is my only chance for survival. You must carry out my wishes. You must destroy Gillian. I told you how to locate him. I told you about the feelings he expressed for the woman, Paula Marth. You must find her. Threaten her life and you will force him to come to you—on your terms."

"She is not at her home on Lamalan."

The Bishop hesitated. "How do you know that?"

"I had one of your Church servants check her house."

He nodded. "Be wary of using the Church network after I'm gone, Reemul. E-Tech will waste no time infiltrating our temples. Now that they know of the Church's role, you will no longer find safety within the Trust."

The tways laughed. "My. I won't be safe. Goodness!"

The Bishop turned away. *Certainly I do not look forward to captivity. But there are compensations. Once and for all I will be removed from this mad Jeek.*

"Go to Lamalan," the Bishop said. "Plant new bugs in Paula Marth's home. Use long-range transmitters and a phone patch. Monitor from a distance, from another Colony. She must return home eventually. When she does, take her. Gillian will come to you."

Both faces smiled. The shorter one said, "But why wait, dear Bishop? Tomorrow they set a trap for me. I should not disappoint them. Besides, they may be very upset with Codrus when I do not show up.''

The Bishop had given that problem much thought. *Yes, I promised the Council that I would bring you into their trap. They will be angry. They may indeed turn me over to the Costeaus. Or perhaps Gillian will change his mind and slay me himself.*

It was no use worrying.

"Reemul, two days from now the new Senate session begins. I expect most of the Senators will be in attendance for the opening ceremonies.'' He paused. ''It is vital that you perform that kill. After you destroy the Senate, you may do as you wish. But until Monday, take no unnecessary risks. Do not be foolish enough to prance into tomorrow's trap.''

The Bishop picked up his suitcase and walked to the door.

"The arrangements have been made for your return to stasis. Remember, Reemul. The Ash Ock will arrive fifty-six years from now. Carry out your final two assignments—destroy Gillian and the Senate—and then go to sleep.'' He smiled from the doorway. "I am sure you will enjoy being awakened by Sappho.''

The Bishop turned and marched from the room, his thoughts already shifting to his own coming ordeal.

It may not be so bad. They may simply put me into stasis. That possibility offered a slight requital.

I will be free to exist as a whole.

Paula stepped from the car, paid the driver in cash cards and watched her son drag the suitcase from the taxi's rear compartment. Three weeks of being on the run had forced the two of them to acquire a moderate assortment of new clothing.

The driver turned his car around and headed back the way he

had come, zigzagging and bouncing along the narrow blistered road until his taxi vanished into the surrounding forests. Paula stood silently for a moment beside the small decorative fence.

Her house appeared strange. Nothing had been altered, at least not that she could tell. The flowerbed, the railed porch, the gently slanted roof with its cedar shingles—all appeared as she remembered. But the house seemed different. Perhaps it was today's weather: bleak sky, a warm gentle breeze whipping thick nickel-colored clouds across Lamalan's three sunstrips, blocking the other livable sectors, limiting vision.

Or perhaps I realize that this is no longer my home.

She had returned to set things in order and to arrange for the transportation of her gallery to the Alexanders' Colony. Two days at most. Then she and Jerem would shuttle back to Aaron's cylinder for good. She smiled, thinking of the pirate. Aaron's injuries would require at least another month's hospitalization but Paula would be there at his side, helping him, caring for him.

She already missed him.

Tomorrow she would go to New Armstrong and contact the Lamalan Realty Commission and get permission to put her house on the market. She could handle the actual sale long-distance, through an agent. And tomorrow she would also visit the trader district and drop in on Moat Piloski.

She held no grudge against the smuggler. Moat's fear of reprisals by the Alexanders had made him act in his own best interests, and she wanted to let him know that everything had turned out for the best. With some amusement, she looked forward to seeing Moat's reaction when she told him that she was going to marry another pirate—the one who had abducted her, no less.

Jerem said, "They got the window boarded up."

She followed her son's gaze, stared past Bob Max's decrepit yard, saw the rigid plastic panels stretched across what had once been plate glass above the dealer's front porch. Her thoughts returned to the day of the thunderstorm, when Smiler and Sad-eyes had jumped through that window, changing Paula's life forever.

For me and my son, and for Aaron, it's over.

The assassin was still on the loose, but in the wake of the incredible events that had begun last night, she was willing to believe that E-Tech and the Guardians would soon put an end to the creature.

She could not remember the Colonies ever being in such an uproar. New ICN/E-Tech/Guardian announcements seemed to pour from the channels every hour, each one more staggering than the last: Nu-Lin of the Commerce League arrested, Bishop Vokir surrendering—the two of them admitting that they were a Paratwa of the royal Caste; incredible ICN political manipulations spanning hundreds of years; secret transmission facilities under the Earth's surface; renegade Paratwa, returning from the stars . . . .

She shook her head. It was almost too much to comprehend. Even the freelancers, accustomed to detailing every sort of outrage, seemed confused by the sheer magnitude of the associated stories. Some freelancers, overwhelmed by the morass of events, were using the occasion to editorialize, lobbying for their most precious dream: the alleviation of E-Tech laws prohibiting the formation of large news networks.

Paula suspected that this time the freelancers just might gain a victory. For better or worse, change was coming to the Colonies. Things would never be the same.

She followed Jerem onto their porch, slid open the screen door, and fumbled in her pocket for the old twistkey.

Jerem rubbed his hand across the railing. "I don't want to live in a pirate Colony."

And things will never be the same between me and my son.

Ignoring his latest complaint, she slipped the key into the lock and opened the door. Jerem stepped through into the hallway.

There had been that moment, early yesterday, in Aaron's hospital room, when her son had appeared ready to release his feelings, to let out all his anger and hurt and whatever other emotions churned inside him. But the moment had passed. He had withdrawn into himself again. Raw wounds continued to fester, salted by fresh indignities: Paula's marriage plans, a new life among the Costeaus.

She sighed and stepped into the house, closing the door behind her. Jerem, too, had changed over the past three weeks. He had been thrust into a world of fear, betrayal, and violence, and he had emerged hardened, like tempered steel drawn through a solar furnace. He had entered the world of the adult.

Sulking, her son ambled into the living room. He threw the suitcase on the sofa and plopped down beside it. For a moment, Paula stared at his profile, wishing she could make things better for him and fearing that she never would.

Now he must make his own choices.

She turned away, headed for the stairs. A glance down the hallway brought her to a halt. The huge oak door, leading to the gallery, stood slightly ajar.

She took a deep breath. She was certain she had locked the gallery the night of Max's killing, before she and Jerem had left for that frustrating interrogation at E-Tech headquarters.

Relax, Paula, she told herself. There was a simple explanation. E-Tech Security people, or the Guardians, had come back to examine the gallery, search for evidence. Probably they had picked the lock; later someone had forgotten to rebolt the door.

The explanation did not prevent goosebumps from breaking out on her arms and legs.

Slowly, quietly, she eased herself down the hallway, toward the door, her eyes glued to the big old brass knob, her body tensed for flight if that knob should turn.

Fifteen feet away. Ten feet. She heard Jerem moving around in the living room.

Five feet. She reached out to touch the knob. Jerem shouted.

"Hey, Mom! There's a Guardian cruiser out front!"

Quickly, with her eyes still riveted to the knob, she backed down the hallway. Jerem came out of the living room. She grabbed his wrist, turned and pulled him along with her.

"Mom!"

She ignored him, threw open the front door. The sleek cruiser sat on the edge of the road between her property and Max's. Two Guardians had gotten out of the car, one leaned against the front fender, his back to Paula. He was looking toward Max's yard. The other officer stood a few feet in front of the car, watching Paula and Jerem approach. The third Guardian remained behind the wheel.

Jerem twisted violently, forcing Paula to let go of his wrist. "Just stay with me," she warned.

The Guardian in front of the car wore a gold lieutenant's bar on his cap. He appeared to be their leader. With Jerem at her side, Paula approached him.

He looked resplendent in his snug black and gold uniform. Wavy blond hair edged out from beneath the dark cap. He wore the armpatch insignia of the Lamalan contingent. A high-powered thruster hung from his belt.

She stopped a pace away. He nodded to her. "Ma'am, we've been assigned to watch your house just in case there's any trouble. We were observing from the woods—we saw your taxi go by. We thought we'd check in, let you know that everything's all right."

Paula smiled. "Thank you." She hesitated. Outside, in the daylight, in the company of three Guardians, her fear that someone was in the gallery seemed silly, almost childish. But since they were here . . .

"Officer, I believe someone may have broken into my gallery while I was away. Could you and your men take a look?"

The Guardian who stood on the other side of the car turned to her. He was a shorter man, wearing wraparound sunglasses. His uniform fit poorly.

Paula tensed.

The first officer smiled. "Ma'am, we'd be glad to check things over for you."

The shorter man removed his sunglasses and threw them into the front seat of the cruiser. Paula's gaze was drawn toward the car, to the third officer, seated behind the wheel. He was not moving.

The first officer chuckled. "Don't worry about him, ma'am. He's dead."

For a moment, her mind refused to accept the words. A stream of mad thoughts wafted through her—she noticed a strip of the low decorative fence that Jerem had peeled off with a knife, years ago. She had spanked him for it. *I should have had the fence repaired. The house would be worth more.*

She threw her arm around Jerem and pulled him to her. Senseless thoughts dissolved; awareness leaped back to the present. Her body shook. She knew. She wanted to scream. She could not.

The tall Guardian, smiling madly, brought his hand up to his face. He sneezed.

The shorter one grinned. "My. Allergies!"

The scream came. She opened her mouth to release it. Too late. The taller one moved with blinding speed. His hand clamped across her mouth.

No! She kicked, aiming for his crotch. His crescent web ignited; her foot bounced away as if it had struck a layer of thick rubber. She lost her balance. The tall Guardian, his hand still plastered across her mouth, caught her, spun her, shoved her along the path toward the house.

She grabbed for the arm, clawed at the floppy sleeve, tried to pull his hand from her mouth. Abruptly, he let her go.

He said, "Think of your son, Ms. Marth."

She uttered a sharp cry. The shorter man had a hold of Jerem. His right arm encircled her son's neck. The arm was squeezing. Jerem's eyes bugged open as he struggled for air.

The taller one laughed. His smile grew to full intensity, burning across his cheeks, twisting his mouth, distorting the shape of his face as if he were a machine being fed power far beyond rated amperage.

His voice remained calm. "Scream, Ms. Marth, and I'll rip your son's head off."

Paula threw her hands over her mouth. *Please don't hurt him! Please don't hurt my son!*

"Please!" she begged.

"Pretty word," snapped the shorter one. He tightened his grip on Jerem's neck. Her son's legs kicked wildly.

She whispered, "Please let him go! Please don't hurt him! Please!"

"Will you be good, Ms. Marth?" asked Smiler.

Tears burned at her cheeks. She nodded her head.

Sad-eyes eased his viselike grip. Jerem sank against the tway's body, heaving as he sucked in air.

"My," said Smiler. "See how easy things go when you cooperate."

She cried, "Please! Please . . ."

"Now, Ms. Marth, no hysterics. If you listen carefully and do as I say . . ."

". . . I'll let you live," finished Sad-eyes.

She gasped. "Anything!"

The smile receded until only a faint glow of satisfaction remained. "I suggest we go inside." He held out his arm. "After you, Ms. Marth."

She stumbled up the path, fighting tears, fighting the panic. *I've got to do something! We've got to get away!*

"I'm pleased to find you home, today, Ms. Marth. Truly!" Smiler sighed with mock exasperation. "I only came here this afternoon to plant my little bugs. I really thought I'd have to wait days, even weeks, before you came back. But here you are!"

"Thrills!" said Sad-eyes. "I'm so lucky."

Mind racing, she stepped onto the porch, led them into the house, into the hallway. *I'm alive. My son's alive. I must not give in. I will not!*

Smiler closed the front door. He seemed to study the dark paneling in the hallway for a moment. Then he chuckled. "I've been watching your house from the woods for the past few hours, watching to make sure that no one had set any traps."

"Not that it would do any good."

"For as most people should know by now . . ."

"Jeek be nimble . . ."

"Jeek be quick . . ."

"In other words . . ."

"I'm hard to catch."

Smiler laughed. "Anyway, there I am, standing in the woods, when your taxi goes cruising past . . ."

"Goodness! Things sometimes have a way of working out far beyond your expectations."

Jerem looked up at Paula with an imploring look, a little-boy expression he had not risked in years. *Mommy! Do something! Make it better!*

She wanted to reach out for him and hug him and tell him it was going to be all right but she couldn't because it wasn't all right and she didn't know how to make it better.

No matter what she said or did, she knew that this monster was going to kill them.

No! I must not give in!

She clenched her fists and suddenly anger overcame her and she couldn't hold it back.

"What do you want with us?" she demanded.

The tways laughed, a horrid cackle, ebbing and flowing between them, out of control, like some endless wave ricocheting between two shore points.

Smiler said, "You're going to be the bait, Ms. Marth. You're going to help us catch a man."

Sad-eyes hissed, "A man we're desperate to meet!"

"How desperate?" asked a third voice.

Everything became a blur of motion. Smiler yanked her off the floor, tucked her under his arm, raced down the hallway, propelling her headfirst in front of him, toward the gallery, where the third voice had come from. She had a sense of incredible speed, as if the hallway had become a tunnel and she a missile, rocketing toward the open door.

She glimpsed a man moving inside the gallery and then Smiler had them through the portal, into the room. Jerem came flying in behind them, carried by the other tway.

And then the ride was over and she was on her feet again, in front of Smiler, her body cushioned against his front crescent, his web humming in her ears, his right arm wrapped tightly around her neck, fist clutching the Cohe, thin needle protruding.

Ten feet away, Sad-eyes held Jerem in a similar fashion. Both tways had drawn their thrusters.

On the opposite side of the twenty-five-foot square gallery, beside a dais displaying a miniature turret lathe, stood Gillian. Paula studied him, hoping against hope.

Tall, maroon jacket, dark pants, dark brown hair cropped short, piercing gray eyes—calm eyes—trained on the empty space between Smiler and Sad-eyes, his left elbow cocked, forearm aimed upward, hand clutching a thruster pointed at the ceiling, Cohe needle peeking from his right fist.

Gillian said, "Hello, Reemul."

Smiler's arm tightened across Paula's neck. "My! Oh, thrills! You're a clever one!"

"Oh, yes!" screeched Sad-eyes. "So clever!" The tway's head gyrated. His eyes panned across the white pine walls of the gallery, then up to the darker ceiling timbers, where the brass lanterns hung, spotlighting the exhibits.

Gillian smiled. "No traps, Jeek. No one waiting above us, no targeting robots, no bombs. No one else even knows I'm here."

Gillian thought, *Almost perfect—a plan unfolding with Ash Ock clarity, structured down to the minutest detail.*

He had known, in the Council chambers, that Codrus would react to his lie about having strong feelings about Paula Marth. He knew Reemul would be ordered to trap Gillian by using the Marths as bait. He knew the Jeek would come here.

"You're slipping, Reemul. You're becoming predictable."

The shorter tway, holding Jerem, stuck out his tongue and licked at the air.

Almost perfect. Only one slight flaw. The boy and his mother are not supposed to be here.

He said, "Let's end it, Jeek." *If I show any sign of weakness toward Jerem and Paula, Reemul will kill them.*

The taller tway recovered his composure. He broke into a fresh grin. "My. You don't want me to slice them up . . ."

". . . do you?" finished Sad-eyes.

Gillian said, "Go ahead—do it."

Smiler's arm tightened across Paula's neck. She felt the needle of his wand prick her skin, below the ear. She drew a sharp breath.

Gillian stared at Paula, at the wide-open eyes, flooded with fear, and he saw that her mouth had narrowed to a quivering line, a mere scratch in the flesh above her chin. He sensed patterns of fright, some visible in the sharp muscle etchings beneath her cheekbones, some unclear, glimpsed only through gestalt: vague intimations of terror.

He allowed his mind to drift, float into an ocean of intrinsic perceptions, seeing Reemul as a gathering of forces, tangents of danger, the locus of the storm.

And he knew that he had found the way.

He stared at Paula and she dissolved into a shower of gold. He felt his body go rigid with tension. But this time he did not fight it. He did not run. He gave his subconscious feelings full rein, allowed them to overwhelm him and suddenly the gallery mutated into an exploding maelstrom of golden light—Paula and Jerem and Reemul, the machines and the walls and the ceiling—everything flashing, streaks of golden fire coming at him, blinding him.

Paula shuddered as she watched. Gillian twisted and jerked his body from side to side as if some terrible crippling affliction had suddenly come over him. She stared at Jerem, still held in the tway's iron grip, and her gaze was drawn to the tway's face and she saw that Sad-eyes had assumed a strange faraway look. He appeared to be transfixed by Gillian's behavior.

Gillian squeezed his eyes shut, opened them, a savage blink.

But in that short space the golden lightning coalesced into the form of a woman, by his side, a shimmering blend of colors, blinking in and out of existence—a vague presence, struggling to become real. It disappeared, came back, vanished again, returned furiously, fighting the elements that conspired against its unity.

I need more! I need something more!

He stared between the two tways and shouted, "Come on, Jeek! Show me! Show me the way!"

He perceived fascination on Reemul's faces, and amusement. But there was more. Through Gillian's agitated senses—hyper-alert, scanning for details, for vague patterns—he read deeper, saw that Reemul hid behind other feelings: confusion, doubt, wonder.

Gillian raised his right arm, waved the thruster over his head. Beside him, the lightning struggled for form, for solidity. It appeared and disappeared, reappeared again; the process repeating, faster and faster, like a light switch being thrown on and off with mad abandon.

Faster. Now at the speed of a strobe, blasting the gallery with golden flashes. He whipped the thruster above him and screamed. "Come on, Jeek! Take me! Take me!"

As if he were caught up in Gillian's excitement, Reemul jerked forward, both tways panting, edging toward that infinitesimal moment of repose: the assassin's crest, when everything came together, when muscles flexed into rhythms of violence.

A scream arose within Gillian, but before he could release it, his body-image vanished and he plunged into terrifying disunity—sensation vanishing—no feelings—no torso, no arms, no legs, no sense that his body even existed. Only by an effort of will could he convince himself that he was still alive.

He sensed that disunity was part of the process and he flowed with it, rode out the terror. And then the moment passed and his body-image seemed to implode from the outside in, and he came alive again, feeling everything at once. The dialectic of unity/duality—the whelm—thundered through his consciousness, and Catharine burst forth at his side, a living essence, elfin face and carefree smile, wild brown hair thrashing in its own wind, and Gillian felt himself receding, no longer a whole consciousness but a mere fragment, reinforcing the whole.

And then the interlace formed and he came back and *he* was Empedocles of the Ash Ock.

He swung his thruster down, fired at Sad-eyes, whipped his other hand up and sent the black beam of the Cohe spiraling across the gallery, toward Smiler, toward the tway's unprotected side portal.

Reemul moved.

Paula barely had time to catch her breath. Again, she felt that sense of blurred motion, everything speeded up, too fast for her senses to register. She saw Jerem being shoved violently away from Sad-eyes and then she was up in the air and Smiler, with a strength she would not have believed him capable of, was hurling her across the chamber. She landed on her feet, stumbled, hit the floor on her knees, somersaulted, slammed upside down into the wall, her shoulders crunching against the carpet, her feet nailing the recessed panel of exhibit controls.

She lay there in the corner, stunned, pain held at bay by the sight that confronted her.

Gillian and Reemul danced across the gallery between exhibits, seemingly everywhere at once, hands flashing, arms sawing at the air, black beams cutting and twisting as if some concentrated lightning storm had entered her gallery. The din of thrusters reverberated in the confined space, sounding like a triplet of screaming infants. Smiler and Sad-eyes twisted and jerked, repelling thruster blasts, trying to move closer to Gillian, and Paula sensed what they were attempting—to get on both sides of Gillian, get him in the center.

And suddenly terror struck her. *Jerem!*

She spotted her son in the middle of the chamber, lying on the floor beside the tablesaw, on his back, perfectly still.

She swallowed her shock, forced feelings into obedience. *He's all right. He's going to be all right.*

Empedocles, hyperalert, both bodies twisting rapidly, in tandem, dodging death, studied his opponent.

He won't allow himself to be directionalized—he's too quick of mind. And I don't have a team to force him into such a defensive posture.

I don't even have a tway, not really.

Empedocles knew he was a Paratwa. He existed in two distinct locations, he saw and heard and felt through two tways. But only Gillian, only that tway and his senses, were physically real. Catharine remained a memory-shadow, a distilled concentrate recovered from the repressed consciousness of Gillian, from beyond Gillian's deepest pains.

Empedocles had been torn in half but he had never perished. The power of the interlace had always existed within the very fabric of Gillian's being, the body-image of Catharine had been imprinted within his very cells. It had merely taken the proper fulcrum to bring on the whelm—to bring Empedocles back to life.

Sad-eyes jumped up on a dais, compressed his weight, and leaped for the ceiling rafters. Smiler crouched. The tway came up on his toe, stretching out his Cohe arm.

Spinsaw!

Empedocles squatted, tumbled away from Smiler. The tway broke into a skater's spin. His Cohe beam sliced through the air like a scythe, whipping above the daises, faster and faster, until it seemed like a solid dark plate hung in the air.

Empedocles came out of his roll, ducked behind a dais. *He can't get me with spinsaw. Too many obstacles. He's trying to set me up for the other tway.*

Empedocles jerked his head up, saw Sad-eyes dropping from a rafter, bellyflopping toward the floor. As the tway fell, a thick gray mist spurted from the side portals of his web.

Acid twister!

Empedocles roared to his feet, hunching low, trying to keep his rear crescent arched up over his back to prevent the deadly organic acid from spraying him. Sad-eyes hit the floor, vaulted halfway across the chamber, landed on another dais. The tway's black beam lashed out at Empedocles, seeking entry through the weak side portals of his web.

Smiler came out of spinsaw, crouching low, firing his thruster in rapid one-second bursts, trying to keep Gillian facing him.

Empedocles tucked his arms into the crescent, leaned forward, felt the hot acid coming down all around him, sizzling as it touched his web, burning holes through the ivory carpet, through the floorboard beneath, and he did the only thing he could—he charged toward Smiler and sent his Catharine-tway toward Sad-eyes. It was pure reaction, knowing that Catharine wasn't real, knowing that she couldn't help him.

Sad-eyes leaped from the dais, landed in front of the Catharine-tway, fired his thruster, through the imaginary Catharine, at Gillian. He missed. The exploding energy blasted the modular ice cutter and sent the machine crashing to the floor.

Pure instinct. Empedocles sensed his Catharine-tway in the path of the thruster and he convulsed, moving both tways, and it was that reaction that saved him from Smiler's Cohe, from the black whip that half-circled the gallery and would have nailed Gillian through the left side portal had not Empedocles turned into the beam.

But that put his right side toward Smiler's thruster. The weapon shrieked. He took most of the blow on the edge of his front crescent, but some of the discharge spilled through his portal and he felt himself being lifted, hurled backward.

I can't win.

It was an acknowledgment of reality, a recognition that one tway, no matter what he perceived himself as, still remained one tway, and Reemul was two.

Out of control, stumbling backward, he tripped over something—Jerem—the boy lying flat on his back, eyes closed, and then he crashed into another dais, somehow managing to stay on his feet, ignoring the terrible ache in his side where the thruster's energy had been neutralized, knowing that the pain would have been almost unbearable had he not shot his midsection full of anesthetics before coming here, to relieve the soreness of his cracked ribs.

And then Reemul was coming at him from both sides and he knew it was over but he also knew that he could never acknowledge defeat and he waited, leaning against the dais for support, waiting until they were only a few feet away before jerking his thruster arm out from behind the web and firing at Sad-eyes.

The tway took the blow on the front crescent, above the ankles, and his feet flew out from under him and he hit the floor hard, screeching with rage.

And then Smiler plowed in and Empedocles felt the wind go out of him as his front and rear crescents compressed against the dais. His left arm, unprotected by the web, took the worst of the blow— his fingers jerked open and the thruster tumbled from his grasp.

Red sparks sizzled as their webs came together, but Smiler refused to be repelled and his body kept pressing against Empedocles, crushing him, pinning his left arm against the dais, and Empedocles stared into the tway's face, only inches away, separated by the sparking crescents, and he saw the open mouth and the flickering tongue and the mad grin.

Empedocles flashed his Cohe hand out from behind the web, but Smiler was ready. Reemul jerked his hips sideways and a volley of tiny projectiles shot through the air. One of them plunged into Empedocles's fisted palm.

Firedart!

He had no choice. In another second the dart would ignite and his hand would burn to a crisp. He jerked open his fist and dropped the Cohe. He twisted his thumb and forefinger and ripped the firedart from his flesh, releasing it just as it exploded, saving his hand from total incineration but barely, just barely.

His hand caught fire and he smelled burning flesh, saw bright yellow flame, and then the pain hit him and the interlace dissolved and he was Gillian again, trapped, left hand pinned against the dais by Smiler's web, right hand burning, useless.

Smiler hissed at him, bright eyes flashing with triumph, and even through the web Gillian smelled heavy orange cologne and the smell somehow took his mind away from the awful burning pain and he thought:

I have been whole once again.

And he knew the thought would be his last.

And then, as in a dream, he saw Jerem, on his back, twisting his body forward, eyes wide open, knees drawing back, the boy kicking with all his might, a foot coming through Smiler's side portal, smashing the tway's ankle.

Smiler jerked sideways—off balance for just an instant, but it was enough—and Gillian's left arm was free. He whipped it down, caught Smiler's Cohe wrist, yanked the fist upward with all his might.

The needle punctured the soft flesh under the tway's right ear. Reemul shrieked as his own hand crushed the egg, sending the black beam into his brain, out through the skull, up past the ceiling rafters.

The smile vanished—the tway's eyes became black fire, burning with their own inner light. Blood poured down the side of Smiler's face as Gillian pulled away.

Something came at Gillian from behind—the other tway. He spun, saw the Cohe whipping through the air, out of control, Sad-eyes a blur of raging madness.

Gillian ducked low, came up into the tway's belly, lifted him. Crescents flashed, repelled, and then Sad-eyes was flying through the air, over Gillian's head, smashing down on top of the dais housing the tablesaw.

Gillian scooped his thruster from the floor and took aim. Smiler, still on his feet, reached out and grabbed Gillian's wrist, tried to twist the barrel away from Sad-eyes. Gillian glimpsed a blood-soaked face and sightless eyes and he knew that some infinitesimal portion of Reemul's interlace still functioned.

And then he wrenched his arm free and smashed the butt of his thruster into the side of Smiler's head. The tway sailed backward and crashed to the floor.

Sad-eyes, on his back atop the tablesaw, howling with pain and rage, twisted sideways and brought his thruster to bear on Gillian. But suddenly his arm froze and his body seemed to lift itself from the dais and he shrieked as some new agony took hold. The tway jerked his head sideways and hissed at Paula Marth.

"Bastard!" Paula cried. She dropped her hand from the control panel and watched the tablesaw's microlasers finish carving their doily design into the tway's right hip.

Gillian took aim. He fired once, through the tway's left portal, into the side of the skull. Sad-eyes heaved. The head twisted. The neck snapped.

Reemul shuddered. Both tways convulsed together, arms and legs twitching, four sets of knuckles rapping out a grim pattern on the floor and on the side of the tablesaw—mad marionettes, dancing into death.

Quiescence.

Gillian leaned against the dais. Slowly, he allowed the gun to slip from his grasp and fall to the carpet. With effort, he flicked his tongue and deactivated the crescent web. He sat down.

He stared at his right hand. It was still smoldering. The top layer of skin had been burned away by the firedart. A dull ache seemed to be marching up and down the right side of his torso. In a little while, when his adrenalin level returned to something near normal, he knew he would be in utter agony.

But for now, it was bearable. For now, it was all right.

He watched Paula struggle to her feet and hobble across the gallery. She knelt down and wrapped her arms around Jerem. The boy clutched her and they hugged each other and cried.

Gillian smiled and thought of Catharine.

Jerem pulled away from his mother. He wiped the tears from his eyes.

"It's all right, Mom—we're gonna be all right."

Paula said, "I know . . . I know."

Jerem turned to Gillian.

"We got him, didn't we."

Gillian nodded.

We got him.

In the center of the stasis chamber, a pair of vulcanized webs, one large, the other small, hung from the support straps of a thick mounting cradle. The open webs, translucent, cushioned with a base layer of stitched organic thread, were joined at the sides; matching sealant covers lay beneath them on the cool moist floor. Hidden freezers hummed loudly. Cold sterilized air was beginning to blow into the chamber from air ducts near the ceiling.

Rome stood alone with Nick and Gillian. The two men wore simple white gowns.

"It's still not too late to change your minds," Rome offered. "We could still put you in separate capsules."

Nick grinned. He turned up the collar of his gown and chewed on the edge. "Nah, we'll go to sleep together. It's more comfy that way. Besides, who knows what the world's gonna be like when we wake up?"

"Safety in numbers," said Gillian. He rubbed his good hand across the back of his bandaged right palm. The top layers of burned flesh had been surgically removed and replaced. There was little pain but the hand still itched.

Nick said, "Yeah, putting us in the same capsule makes sense." The midget winked at Gillian. "Of course, I can only hope my partner here doesn't invite the family over to visit while we're sleeping. I mean, there's just not enough room for the four of us."

A faint smile curled Gillian's lips. Someday, Catharine—and Empedocles—would return.

Nick chuckled. "It's been a hell of a month, though, hasn't it?"

"Believe it or not," Rome said, "I'm going to miss both of you."

Gillian's thoughts turned to this morning: his farewells to Aaron and Paula, and hardest of all, to Paula's son. *Be brave*, Gillian had advised, but the boy had shed a few tears anyway.

He would miss Jerem Marth.

"Just imagine," Nick said, "how calm things are gonna be around here without us. Think about that, Rome, and you'll get over your parting pains real quick."

Rome had to laugh. "You're probably right. I'm actually looking forward to some nice simple evenings at home with Angela. We're thinking about taking a short vacation, shuttle to the L4 Colonies and see what our son is up to and on the way back, visit Lydia and her husband. Maybe bounce the grandchildren on our laps for a few days."

Nick wagged his head. "Sounds like a lotta fun."

"And when we return to Irrya, I'll shorten my work schedule and start spending a little more time at home."

He stopped. *Who am I kidding?*

Nick understood. The midget regarded him wryly. "Something tells me E-Tech's gonna be very, *very* busy over the next few years."

There was no sense in denying it.

Fifty-six years from now, the Ash Ock Paratwa would return. Fifty-six years from now, humanity would have to be ready to face that threat.

A flood of change was coming to the Colonies. And Rome knew that he had to be a part of that change, that he and the organization would have to work even harder to ensure that E-Tech was not washed away in the inevitable scramble for technological advancement.

Nick threw his arms across his chest and shivered. "Hey! It's getting cold in here!"

Rome smiled. "They've turned on the coolers—they're starting to drop the room down to stasis temperature."

"So when do we get the drugs?"

"Don't worry, everything's been timed. A tech will come in shortly with your medicine. A few more minutes, I should think."

Nick grinned. "I gotta be honest with you. I'm not all that crazy about this stasis business."

"You know you don't have to go."

"No, that's not what I mean. I'm talking about the actual going-to-sleep part. It gives me the creeps."

Rome smiled. "Our stasis drugs have undergone a few improvements since the twenty-first century."

"Cherry-flavored, by any chance?"

"Intravenous. Completely painless, no known side effects. At least Codrus didn't show any when we put him to sleep yesterday."

"That's too bad."

Rome suddenly remembered something. "By the way, E Tech just completed an internal audit. Curious anomalies have been discovered in several of our Security accounts. We seem to be missing some money. Our accounting department is perplexed. Would either of you, by any chance, know anything about this matter?"

"I cannot tell a lie. Gillian stole it."

Rome nodded. "I sort of figured that the two of you had something to do with these missing funds. I suppose we'll have to make some financial alterations, do some cross-accounting. I believe the pre-Apocalyptics used to refer to such techniques as 'fancy book-keeping.'" He had looked the phrase up in their archival dictionaries.

Nick laughed. "Yeah, that's what they used to call it."

"Oh, and Begelman called from the Shan Plateau. He says to tell you that you're the best programmer he's ever had the pleasure of working with."

Nick smiled. "I'm honored. And you tell Begelman and that team to be careful down there. Codrus may have prepared other traps. Gillian may not have found everything."

"The team is being extremely cautious. They won't even fire up the transmitter again until they're certain they completely understand the technology."

Nick turned to the door as Pasha Haddad entered. The Pasha walked in a curiously stiff gait with his head raised and his arms held rigidly at his sides.

"How do, Haddad. Come to say good-bye, huh? Tell us how you're really gonna miss us and . . ."

Nick stopped. The Pasha was frowning.

Haddad put his hands behind his back and stared up at the glass-walled control booth overlooking the chamber. He spoke solemnly.

"A short time ago, an E-Tech transport shuttle, carrying the stasis capsule containing Codrus, was waylaid by a small fleet of unidentified vessels.

"The crew of our transport was ordered to accept a boarding party from one of these vessels. Under threat of total destruction if they did not comply, our crew permitted several men to come aboard. These men removed the stasis capsule containing Codrus. Then they returned to their own vessels, leaving the capsule in space. One of their shuttle pilots maneuvered his craft until its main engines faced the capsule." Haddad paused. "They used full power. The egg containing Codrus was incinerated."

"Son-of-a-bitch!" yelled Nick. "Good for them, whoever the hell they are!"

"I believe," continued the Pasha, "that it is the first reported case of piracy in over one hundred years."

Gillian accepted the news silently. But from some deep cavity of consciousness, he felt the whisper of a thought. *Now there are only three of us left.*

Angrily, Rome turned to Nick. "You knew that Codrus's capsule was being transferred to another Colony. You leaked that information to the Costeaus, to the Alexanders."

Nick was silent for a moment. Then he shrugged. "Sorry to disappoint you, Rome, but I didn't have anything to do with this. I certainly didn't like your Council's decision to put the bastard into stasis, but I was willing to abide by it."

"Then who?" Rome demanded.

The midget stared up at the Pasha. Haddad shrugged.

"We have no real clue as to the identity of the raiders. Naturally, suspicions have fallen on the clan of Alexander, but I doubt that their involvement will ever be proved. As to who leaked the cargo and course information—I must confess that I find it highly unlikely that this perpetrator will ever be discovered."

A glimmer of understanding came to Rome. He felt stunned. He stared at Haddad. "You! You told the Alexanders!"

The Pasha met Rome's gaze. "It is best not to burden the future with our own problems."

"Amen," sighed Nick.

Rome grimaced. *So Codrus is dead. And my own Security Chief is responsible.*

Change. It was already taking forms that he could not predict, nor even imagine.

Haddad said, "I suggest that we turn the investigation of this incident over to the Guardians. Perhaps they will learn who was responsible."

Nick chuckled. "Pasha, I'm beginning to like your style."

Haddad permitted himself a faint grin.

Rome thought, *Is this the kind of lawlessness our society is heading for? Is this a hint of our future? Fifty-six years from now, when Sappho and Theophrastus and their technologically advanced hordes return from the stars, will they be met by a human culture as brutal as their own?*

No. It must not be.

He turned to the Pasha. "I want a full report on this incident. Codrus's death will warrant an investigation by the Council and probably the Guardians as well. If any real evidence is unearthed, I promise you here and now that the matter will be pursued until the parties responsible are brought to justice. Is that clear?"

"Quite clear."

A tech carrying a medical tray entered the chamber.

Nick grinned. "Gee, I guess it's time for bed."

Gillian felt himself floating, adrift in some vast inner sea, with gentle white-capped waves lapping all around him. He sensed that the waves formed a barrier, a separation of space and time, between what was real and conscious and what remained hidden or lost.

He projected a thought. *I move . . .*

From beyond the waves, Catharine answered, *. . . I am.*

I want . . .

. . . I take.

I see . . .

. . . I learn.

I grow . . .

. . . I make.

The circle of waves darkened, following him into silence.

Rome waited in the control booth until the protective seven-foot-high organic shell had fully formed around Nick and Gillian.

The stasis technician turned to him. "A successful freeze, sir."

"Good. Put it into storage. And after you're through here, destroy all the documentation. I want no official record of this freeze."

The technician's frown turned into a shrug. "Very well, sir."

Rome thought, *When Begelman returns from the Shan Plateau, I'll set him to work on a new computer program. Something with a soft perimeter, subtle enough to escape accidental detection but clear enough so that fifty-six years from now, the future director of E-Tech can figure it out.*

Gillian had said, *Safety in numbers.* Rome smiled. That seemed right.

He took one last look at the egg and then he walked out into the hallway, thinking of home and Angela.